Highlander UNBOUND

JULIA LONDON

Highlander
UNBOUND

POCKET **STAR** BOOKS

New York   London   Toronto   Sydney

An *Original* Publication of POCKET BOOKS

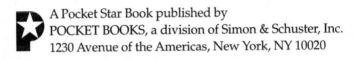 A Pocket Star Book published by
POCKET BOOKS, a division of Simon & Schuster, Inc.
1230 Avenue of the Americas, New York, NY 10020

ISBN: 0-7394-4090-X

Cover hand-lettering by David Gatti

Manufactured in the United States of America

A Special Thanks

I think that perhaps when one has been in this business a while, one tends to think about the day to day mechanics of producing a book, and perhaps loses sight of the efforts of so many people that go into producing a final product. In an effort to make sure I don't do that, I vow to take the time every now and again to think about how my dream life is *really* made possible. It's not just the writing; it's the combined effort of a lot of great people.

My special thanks to my editor, Maggie, for believing in me and showing me how to become a better writer; and my agent, Meredith, for urging me always to push the edge of the envelope. And, of course, my family, who are as enthusiastic about my career today as they were the day I sold my first book, and Louie, who keeps me grounded.

But most important, I thank the many readers out there who continue to buy my books one after the other, and write to tell me they look forward to the next. If it weren't for all of you, I'd be living under a bridge somewhere. My dogs and I thank you—we are forever indebted to your faithfulness!

Sincerely,
Julia London

Highlander
UNBOUND

Prologue

❦

NEAR ABERFOYLE,
THE CENTRAL HIGHLANDS OF SCOTLAND
1449

*I*n and around Loch Chon, they would talk for many years of how the fair Lady of Lockhart laughed like a madwoman when her husband hanged her lover—on the very eve of her date with the executioner's ax.

It was an ill wind that drifted across the Highlands in the autumn of 1449, bringing with it first the death of the obese earl of Douglas, whose heart, unable to endure the strain of his gluttony, finally gave out. In that same ill wind, his son William was swept to the title. But William, unlike his father, was fit and capable—so capable, in fact, that the mentors around the boy King James felt threatened, particularly when James, on the verge of manhood, was making a habit of refusing their sage advice. And it was in that rift between king and mentors that William Douglas did indeed see the opportunity to immortalize his power. This he did by supporting the mentor Crichton over the mentor Livingstone, which meant, that anyone aligned with Livingstone was doomed. . . .

Unfortunately, that included Anice of Lockhart, a woman as renowned for her gentle spirit as she was for her beauty, from Loch Katrine to Ballikinrain. Given in matrimony to William's cousin, Eoghann, the laird of Lockhart, along with a dowry of twenty sows, Anice soon discovered that Eoghann was neither seduced by her charm nor a kind or faithful husband, preferring a rough life of hunting and whoring. Nonetheless, Anice bore the feckless Eoghann five sons and one daughter. While Eoghann had no use for the latter, he adored his sons, and often left Anice and the daughter, Margaret, alone. Such a life of misery did the lovely Anice lead that it was little wonder she fell in love with the handsome Kenneth Livingstone.

Some would say that autumn's ill wind brought Kenneth Livingstone, a warrior and a nephew to the king's closest adviser, to the Lockhart keep. And although he was ten years her junior, one look at Anice's lovely face and Kenneth Livingstone knew the woman he would die for.

Likewise, Anice believed she deserved this chance at love; she confided as much to her lady's maid, Inghean, and pursued Kenneth's love with relish, living recklessly, engaging in her adulterous affair openly for anyone to see save Eoghann, for as was his habit, he paid her little mind.

Perhaps Anice would have enjoyed her happiness for many more years had not William become the Douglas earl. Though he could not fault Anice for straying from her marriage—he knew his cousin Eoghann to be a despicable man—he could not forgive her doing so with a Livingstone. Thus her fate was sealed—William dispatched a team of envoys to his cousin's keep to read aloud the decree of death for the adulterers.

While Eoghann did not object to William's decree that Kenneth Livingstone should hang, he did object to the same sentence for his wife, and determined that a beheading was far more appropriate for her perfidy. But he would first imprison her in the old tower so that she might observe the construction of the scaffolding from which she and her lover would meet their deaths.

As Anice's maid Inghean would later recall it for her grandchildren, Anice of Lockhart grew increasingly mad in that last fortnight, stalking about a cold chamber devoid of *even the barest of comforts, wild-eyed and clutching a small and hideous sculpture of a beastie. Inghean would never know the significance of the ornamental statue other than to understand that Anice and her lover had shared some secret jest, and Livingstone had commissioned the thing to amuse her. The ornament was ugly—cast in gold, with eyes and mouth made of rubies so that it looked to be screaming, and a tail, braided and interspersed with rubies, that wrapped around its clawed feet.*

On the eve of Kenneth's hanging, Anice called Inghean to her. She was holding in her lap something wrapped in cloth. Slowly, she peeled away the cloth to reveal an emerald the size of a goose egg. It was a gift from her mother, she said, the only thing of value she had managed to keep from Eoghann in all the years they had been married. Anice wrapped the emerald again, and speaking low and quickly, implored Inghean to help her. She pressed the wrapped emerald into Inghean's hands, then the ugly beastie, and begged that she take them to her brother, the blacksmith, and beseech him to seal the emerald in the statue's belly for safekeeping. It was, she explained tearfully, her last but most important gift to her daughter, Margaret.

Inghean could not refuse a condemned woman her request. When the deed was done, she returned to the tower, just in time to watch the crowds gather for the hanging of Kenneth Livingstone. She joined her mistress on the battlements around her tower prison and stood, terrified, as Kenneth was led onto the scaffolding. Anice, unwilling to let Eoghann see her fear, cackled like a madwoman.

Then Kenneth looked up, saw Anice standing there, and Anice grabbed Inghean's hand, her fingernails digging deep as they watched the executioner wrap the noose around Kenneth's neck. And as the executioner stepped away, Anice leaned over the battlements so far that Inghean feared she might fall, and screamed, "Fuirich do mi!"

"Wait for me!"

The executioner pulled the rope; Kenneth's fall was quick, as was the break of his neck, and he hung, limp, his suddenly lifeless eyes staring blankly at the roaring crowd gathered before him. Anice let go of Inghean's hand and fell back against the stone wall of the battlement, her body as limp as her lover's.

Later, she asked for the statue and her daughter, Margaret, who was just a girl. "Heed me, lass," she whispered when Margaret was brought to her chamber. "See this that I give ye," she said, taking the statue from Inghean, "and promise me ye'll guard it with yer very life!"

When Margaret did not answer right away, Anice shook her. "Do ye hear me, Maggie?" she insisted. "This that I give ye is more valuable than all the king's jewels. When the time comes and ye fall in love, but yer father gives ye no hope for it, then ye look in the belly of this beastie, do ye ken?"

Margaret glanced fearfully at the awful little thing and nodded.

The next morning, as her husband and her two oldest sons looked on impassively, Anice knelt before the executioner's block.

In one mean strike of the sword, Anice was sent to meet her lover.

As little Margaret grew older, the times grew more turbulent. The earl William died by the king's own hand, and suddenly the nation was plunged into a bitter clan war. Douglas warred with Douglas and with Stuart; all alliances were suddenly suspect. Indeed, the three youngest Lockhart sons took issue with their father and their two older brothers, and made their allegiance known to the Stuarts. In the midst of that bloody clan warfare, Margaret, now fifteen, fell in love with Raibert of Stirling, who pledged his allegiance to the younger Lockharts. Margaret came to Inghean to tell her that she had given the statue to Raibert for safekeeping, that they would flee to England with her brothers. She kissed Inghean good-bye and slipped out into the night.

Inghean never saw the lass again, and in fact, it would be

years before she would know that Raibert had been killed in the battle in Otterburn, and that the younger Lockharts had taken the beastie with them to England. The beastie, but not their sister, Maggie, who was left behind with a broken heart and put away in a convent by her father, where she would die a year later by her own hand.

Inghean would live for many years afterward to tell the story of the Lady of Lockhart. Yet over time her memory would fade, and she would forget the very small details. By the end of her blessedly long life, the tale of the Lady of Lockhart had come to be known as the Curse of the Lady of Lockhart, for more than one had seen the madwoman laugh at her lover's hanging, and more than one could believe she had cursed her daughter.

When Inghean at last took leave of this world, the truth of the Lady of Lockhart took leave with her. The so-called curse was separated from fact, and grew to encompass all females born to a Lockhart. The beastie became nothing more than a prized belonging that spawned centuries of clandestine border crossings between England and Scotland by more than one Lockhart wishing to possess it, a practice that would endure for hundreds of years.

By the time Scotland was at last united with her sister England, local legend had it that a daughter born to a Lockhart sire would never marry until she "looked into the belly of the beast." Family lore interpreted this curse to mean that any daughter born to them must face the Devil before she would marry, and the strength of that curse was bolstered by the strange fact that no Lockhart daughter ever married.

One

❧

A thick mist swirled around the sheepskin *ghillie brogues* that covered his feet, making it impossible to see where he was stepping. But stealth was imperative—he could see the French camp through the trees directly ahead and wondered how they had managed to track him all the way to Scotland. Obviously, they were still searching for him, still intent on killing him, just as they had been on the Continent.

Liam crouched down behind a tree, observing them. They had stopped for the night, lying about a small fire, one of them roasting some small animal, blessedly unaware of the danger that lurked just beyond the tree line. *God, but he wished he could see his men!* His Scottish compatriots were just on the other side of the French camp, waiting for him. Liam stood, tried to move again, but the thick mist prevented it, and in fact, his legs felt as if weights had been tied to them, as if he were dragging them through water.

Suddenly, to his right, a flash of color—*a French soldier!* Liam quickly reached for the dirk at his waist, but it was gone, dropped from the belt of his kilt. The soldier, returning from the call of nature, was startled to see him and fumbled for his pistol. *His dagger, where was his dagger?* There was no time to think—Liam instantly dropped to his haunches, and in one swift movement pulled the ebony-handled *sgian dubh* from its sheath at the top of his stocking and lunged before the Frenchman could cry out.

They fell to the ground, Liam landing on top and knocking the air from the man's lungs as his pistol went flying into the mist. Silently and quickly, as if the man were a beast, Liam slit his throat as he had been trained to do, rolled off him and onto his feet, crouched down with his hands held before him, waiting for the next Frenchman.

What was that? A soft whistle—the bastard Frog somehow had alerted the rest of them! *Jesus God, where were his men?* His breath coming in heavy grunts now, Liam took one step forward, felt something whisk across his ear, and unthinkingly swiped at it. Another step, and a movement to his left caught his eye. He jerked around, could not help but gasp at the sight of the two-headed troll that faced him, the same one that—*Could it be?*—had haunted his dreams when he was a wee lad.

He had no time to think; the troll started for him, swaying side to side to maintain its lumbering girth. Something was pushing at Liam's back, pushing him off balance, but he ignored it, focused only on the troll coming toward him, his hands outstretched, as if he meant to snatch him. His heart pounding, Liam gripped the bloodied *sgian dubh* and readied himself. Just as he was about to throw himself forward and tackle the troll, he felt a sharp jab to his bum, almost as if someone had wedged a boot—

Liam's eyes flew open; he saw his brother Griffin standing over him, a feather in his hand, and remembered, groggily, that the war with France was over.

"Ye were dreaming again, laddie," Griffin said matter-of-factly, and added with a lopsided smile, "I hope she was a bonny thing."

"*Ugh*," Liam groaned, and rolled over in his bed to bury his face in a pillow. "Why must ye bother me so, Grif? Can ye no' leave a man to sleep?"

"The sun is already shining on the loch, Liam. Yer mother asks after ye, and Payton Douglas has come—did ye no' promise him a lesson in swordplay?"

Damn if he hadn't. "Aye," he said, yawning, "that I did." He reluctantly pulled the pillow from his face and blinked against the sunlight pouring into the room. He was drenched in sweat again, the result of another nocturnal battle with the French. He'd be glad when his regiment deployed and he could put his dreams behind him.

"Father is due back from Aberfoyle today," Griffin said, crossing over to the bureau against the wall to examine Liam's things there, "and Mother requests your presence at the supper table." He spared Liam a glance. "She's no' happy with yer prowling about in the wee hours of the morning."

Liam simply ignored that—his family did not understand his need to keep his skills finely tuned, something that could only be accomplished by practicing various maneuvers at night as well as day. He pushed himself to his elbows, watched as Griffin picked up the hand-tooled leather ornamental sporran he had purchased from a leathersmith near Loch Ard. "I'll thank ye to put it down," he said as his brother peered inside.

With a chuckle, his brother obliged him by tossing the leather pouch back atop the bureau. He moved on to the length of plaid that Liam had draped across a chair, rubbed a corner of the fabric between his fingers, felt the weight of it. Griffin—who had never been given to the old ways—wore black pantaloons, a coat of dark brown superfine, and a pale gold waistcoat, striped in lovely shades of blue that reminded Liam of a flock of peacocks—particularly the fat overfed ones that roamed the gardens in and around the family estate, Talla Dileas.

" 'Twas hand woven by the old widow MacDuff," Liam informed him.

"Ah, of course it was, for who but the old lady MacDuff still makes them?" Griffin asked, and dropping the corner of plaid, turned his attention to Liam. He folded his arms across his chest, crossed one leg over the other, and glanced at his brother's naked chest. "Tell me, did ye learn to sleep bare-arsed in the army?"

"No," Liam said, pushing his legs over the side of the bed, "I learned to sleep bare-arsed in the ladies' boudoirs."

Griffin laughed, his grin as wide and as inviting as their sister Mared's. With a yawn, Liam studied his younger brother. He was built like Liam—tall, muscular, dark brown hair, and eyes as green as heather—but he wasn't quite as big as Liam, having more of the slender, aristocratic frame than the warrior physique for which Liam prided himself. And he was, admittedly, a very handsome man, whereas Liam was . . . well, plain.

Still laughing, Griffin moved toward the old plank wood door. "I'll tell Douglas ye'll join him yet," he said. "And I'll tell yer lady mother that ye have indeed promised to attend supper." He stooped and ducked out of the cavernous tower chamber where the lairds of Lockhart had slept for decades until one had come along and added an entire manor to it.

Liam stood up, let the sheet slip from his naked body, stretched his arms high above his head, then moved to the narrow slit of a window that overlooked the old bailey.

That was Payton Douglas he saw below, parrying his own shadow. Liam rolled his eyes—there wasn't a Scot around Loch Chon who didn't think he could be a soldier. But it took more than a wish. It took strength and cunning and courage. He would know, naturally—he had worked his way up through the ranks of the Highland Regiments over the last ten years, had achieved the vaulted status of captain, and had earned not one, but four medals of honor for heroic feats in the Peninsular Wars and at Waterloo. Yes, he knew a thing or two about soldiering, and in his estimation there weren't many men who had the character for it.

This was precisely what he intended to demonstrate to Payton Douglas.

It was no secret around Loch Chon that there was no love lost between the Douglases and the Lockharts; it was a distrust that went back centuries. Just what, exactly, had happened between them, Liam didn't know. He only knew that Payton was a Douglas. Nonetheless, he couldn't help but admire him—he was a capable man, prosperous in hard times . . . but not so admirable that Liam would give him as much as an inch.

Aye, he'd just have a look at what Douglas had beneath that fancy coat he wore. With a low chuckle of glee, Liam turned from the window, walked to where the plaid was draped, and proceeded to dress.

As he waited for Liam (what full-grown man could sleep so late in the bloody day?), Payton amused himself by fencing with his shadow on the old bailey wall. He hadn't a clue how to go about it, as he had never had the luxury of fencing lessons. But he had seen a few duels and was rather convinced it really wasn't so difficult. He thrust forward, withdrew, and thrust again, moving his way down the massive stone wall. But he quickly was bored with that and amused himself further by imagining Lockharts were attacking him from all angles. He spun around, jabbed his sword in the air, then spun around again, prepared to lunge, but with a small exclamation of surprise, he stumbled backward, knocking up against the wall and dropping his old dull sword.

"Christ Jesus, Mared, ye could startle a man clear out of his wits!" he exclaimed hotly as he tried to catch his breath.

Having appeared from nowhere, Liam's younger sister shrugged insouciantly, flipped the long tail of her braid over her shoulder, and adjusted the heavy basket she held at her hip. "Ye should look where ye point that thing."

Oh, how very helpful. Hands on hips, Payton glared down at Mared. Fat lot of good it did—she hardly seemed to notice. This one had to be the most exasperating of all the bloody Lockharts, which was in and of itself a rather remarkable accomplishment, since they were the most exasperating group of human beings he had ever known.

Mared's dark green gaze flicked to where his sword lay on the ground. "One canna help but wince when a man is foiled by a stone wall, can one?" she drawled.

Oh, *aye,* she was exasperating, maddeningly so, and Payton wished to high heaven she weren't so bloody beautiful. But in that gown of emerald that matched the deep color of her eyes, she was, in a word, bewitching. The emphasis, of course, being on *witch.* He leaned over, snatched up his sword, and proceeded to knock the dirt from the handle. "Ye've a tongue as sharp as a serpent, Mared," he said, looking up from the sword's handle, "but damn me if ye donna look as bonny as a clear summer day."

With a snort, Mared rolled her eyes. "There's no point to yer flattery, Douglas."

"Should beauty no' be admired, then?"

Mared's eyes narrowed; she reached into the large basket she held, withdrew a bramble berry, and popped it into her mouth. "Ye must take me for a featherbrain," she said, nonchalantly chewing the berry. "Ye donna admire beauty, ye admire land, that's all." She helped herself to another berry. "And ye ask after the Lockhart lands as if they were barren."

Ah-ha! So she had heard of his inquiries as to the acreage dedicated to cattle on Lockhart land, inquiries that had been made *discreetly* in Aberfoyle. How she had discovered it, he could only guess, but he'd wager a month's income that it had something to do with those green eyes of hers. "*Ach*, yer a naïve lass," he said, with a dismissive flick of his wrist. "Ye confuse a man's appreciation with yer foolish pride."

"Foolish pride?" She grunted her opinion of that sentiment and ate another berry. "And ye confuse ambition with centuries of history, Douglas."

Now it was Payton's turn to snort disdainfully, and he pointed the tip of his sword to the ground where her scuffed black leather boots peeked out beneath her gown. "Foolish and stubborn, that is what ye are, Mared Lockhart. Will ye deny, then, that the Douglas and Lockhart lands, if they were one, would prosper more than when they are apart?"

"*Diah*, ye must have lost yer mind! Why would a Lockhart *ever* join with a Douglas?"

"So that he . . . or *she*, as the unlikely case may be . . . might double the estate profits by giving wider range to the sheep. *That's* why."

Mared stilled. Blinked. "I think ye *have* lost yer bloody mind!" she exclaimed, and suddenly burst out laughing. "Honestly, Douglas, do ye truly think we'd trade our coos for *sheep?*"

Payton glowered at her. Beauty or not, she was as

thick-skulled as every Lockhart he had ever known. "*Ach,* ye're a foolish lot, ye Lockharts! Ye willna face the truth, willna admit ye are drowning in debt and that yer cattle willna bring what ye need to survive! *Sheep,* Mared! They need less land and can traverse the terrain, whereas yer bloody coos devour what grass there is by midsummer. And everyone around Loch Chon knows that without the rents from yer tenants, ye canna keep yer head above water."

Mared's eyes sparked with fury. She abruptly adjusted the basket she was holding and wagged a slender finger at him. "Ye willna speak to me thus, Douglas! And ye will *never* put yer dirty hands on Lockhart land!"

"Mared, *leannan,* let the poor bastard be!"

Mared and Payton both turned as Liam strode purposefully into the old bailey, his plaid swinging around his knees, a thick leather belt holding the pristine white shirt he had tucked into the folds. Payton could not help but smile—Liam Lockhart held fast and strong to tradition and honor, and wore his Scottish pride like a bloody badge. He truly admired his loyalty. And he envied Liam's life thus far—on more than one occasion Payton wished he had gone off to experience life as Liam had done instead of attending the college as his father had insisted.

Liam stopped several yards in front of Payton and Mared, braced himself on his sturdy legs, and withdrew his sword from its scabbard. He held it as if it weighed nothing, point down, and silently perused Payton. After a moment, he gave a sly smile to Mared. "Best remove yerself from harm, lass," he said casually. "Douglas here would like a wee lesson in swordplay. Am I right, Douglas?"

"If ye'd be of a mind," Payton answered amicably.

"*Ach,*" Mared muttered, "what foolishness." But she

did as Liam suggested, walking to a crumbling old bench along the stone wall. To Payton's dismay, she put her basket aside and sat herself down, as if she intended to watch the lesson.

"So ye desire a lesson," Liam said again, slowly lifting the tip of his sword and drawing Payton's attention away from Mared.

"Aye," he nodded. "I've heard there's none better with a saber than Liam of Lockhart."

Liam snorted, lifted his sword. " 'Tis true—I *am* the best. No man proved better." He took a step, then another, slowly circling as Payton stood patiently, letting the captain have his moment. Liam came to a halt in front of him, and touched the button of Payton's waistcoat with the tip of his sword. "Have ye ever fought a man sword to sword?"

"No."

Liam grinned. "I thought as much, or ye'd know to remove yer coat. Ye canna fight all trussed up like a Christmas goose."

Payton gave him a thin smile, thrust off his coat, and, for good measure, his waistcoat, too, tossing them onto the bench where Mared sat. She smiled wickedly, as if she hoped to see him sliced to ribbons. Payton wasn't entirely sure she wouldn't be obliged. He turned to Liam. "Let's have at it then, shall we?"

A broad, predatory smile spread across Liam's lips. *"En garde,"* he said quietly, and instantly moved one leg back, settling on it, while he held the other out from his body, bent at the knee.

Payton lifted his sword, mimicking him, but Liam groaned, rolled his eyes, and touched his sword to Payton's. "What are ye doing then, Douglas? Put yer hand on yer hip there, and lift yer sword . . . aye, that's how 'tis done. Ye'll want to sweep aside or force mine down, do ye see?" he asked, demonstrating. Payton nodded that he did, and listened intently as Liam went on to explain how to lunge in attack, recover, and lunge again, attacking head, flank, and chest. "The blade precedes the body—it should land on yer target before yer foot hits the ground. Do ye see, then?"

"Aye," Payton grunted.

They practiced lunging, legs bent, and recovering to the *en garde* position. Then Liam showed him how to parry, to defend himself in the face of attack, to crossstep, launch an attack, and cross-step again. His technique was, Payton thought, amazingly delicate for a man so large. He felt thick and awkward in comparison, not at all graceful like Liam.

"Aye, ye've got the feel for it," Liam said, nodding, after they had shadow-fenced along the old bailey wall. "So let's see how ye be in combat," he said, and startled Payton with a sudden lunge forward that left the tip of his saber resting on Payton's belt.

He glanced up at Liam, smiled crookedly. "Ye wouldna be trying to slice off me drawers, now would ye?"

Liam laughed low. "Get yer sword up, man!" he warned Payton, and thrust again, slicing cleanly through the billowing sleeve of Payton's shirt. Suddenly, they were moving, Payton retreating, lumbering backward, desperately trying to defend himself without falling. "*Ach*, did ye learn nothing? Heel to toe, heel to toe!" Liam shouted at him, but Payton unexpectedly collided hard with a wall and dropped his sword. Liam thrust the tip of his saber to Payton's neck. "*Tsk-tsk*," he said, shaking his head. "Pity, this. I have ye in death's grip."

Payton's chest was heaving. He blinked against the sun glinting off Liam's sword, thought about Mared watching him take this beating, and slowly slid down the wall to his haunches, groping for his sword as Liam calmly kept him penned. He nodded, tried to catch his breath. "I see why they say ye are the best, Lockhart."

"*Aye.*" Liam grinned. "Ye've too much in the arm; no' enough in yer wrist," he said. "And ye must remember to keep yer eye on the best angle to strike."

His sword in hand, Payton nodded, slowly pushed himself up to his feet. "No' enough in the wrist," he repeated. "Like this, then?" he asked, and before Liam could respond, Payton lunged, miraculously catching him off-guard. He lunged again, heel to toe, heel to toe, thrusting wildly at the head, chest, and flank, forcing Liam to retreat.

The two danced to the middle of the old bailey so fast that Payton couldn't even say how it had happened—but he was still in command, still directing the play. The rapid sound of steel on steel sliced through the morning air, setting his teeth on edge. Liam seemed to be back on his heels, and Payton desperately fought to keep him there, jabbing forward, again and again, until he had forced Liam up against the wall, swept his saber aside, and penned him at the throat with his arm.

But instead of being angry, Liam laughed. "Ah, so ye *did* learn a thing or two," he said, and abruptly and fluidly pushed and slipped out of Payton's hold, spun around, and knocked Payton back with the force of his saber across his chest. Payton went down with a great *thunk,* landing square on his back and with the wind knocked from his lungs. Liam was instantly on top of him, a boot on his abdomen, the tip of the saber at his throat, and his free hand held high in the air in triumph.

For a brief moment, Payton believed Liam would kill him. Until Liam threw his head back and laughed, and offered him a hand up.

And somewhere on the edge of his consciousness, Payton heard Mared exclaim in disappointment, "*Ach,* for the love of God!"

* * *

Carson Lockhart arrived at Talla Dileas from Aberfoyle late that afternoon, kissed his wife, Aila, fully on the lips, and motioned for Dudley, his longtime butler, to pour a dram of whiskey so that he might wash the dirt of the road from his throat.

Aila put aside her mending and watched her husband, quietly assessing him. She had been married to the man for thirty-eight years and could read him like a book. And judging by his dejected expression, she could see that things had not gone well in Aberfoyle. She waited until he was seated comfortably, had drunk his first whiskey and had his second in hand before she spoke. "Well, Carson. What news have ye brought us, then?"

Her husband grimaced at the question, shoved fingers through a thick shock of gray hair. " 'Tis no' good," he admitted. "They willna lend us another farthing if me very life depended on it."

That news was hardly unexpected, but they had hoped for better. The old Lockhart estate had grown increasingly hard to maintain in an era of new farming techniques and growing industry, and the family had long since overextended their welcome at the Royal Bank of Scotland. As their debts had mounted, they had come to the conclusion that they could not support so many tenants. The family had agreed they would buy out the crofters who had farmed Lockhart soil for generations—they would offer a fair price and would not, as other lairds had done, push them from their homes. Theirs was a noble intent, but that intent was quietly bankrupting the family.

Aila looked thoughtfully at the thick-paned windows that bordered a wall of what had once been the old castle's great hall. She wondered if her family would laugh at the idea she had been nurturing the last two weeks. It *was* a rather ridiculous plan, she'd be the first to admit, but in light of their dire financial situation, it seemed at least worth discussion. They had to do something soon before they lost Talla Dileas and were forced to join the thousands of Highlanders looking for work in Glasgow. The very thought made her shudder; she imagined such an event would kill Carson. She glanced at her husband, whose eyelids were sliding to half-mast, and came to her feet, moving to the great wing-backed chair on which he sat. She ran her hand over the top of his head, leaned down and kissed his forehead. "Shut yer eyes, love," she murmured, taking the whiskey glass from his hand. "We'll speak of it later."

One could hardly call it supper by their former standard of living.

It consisted of bannocks, or oat cakes, a rather spindly grouse, a bowl of bramble berries, and black bun cake. "We've no food to speak of, milady," Dudley's wife, the family cook, had complained to Aila earlier in the week. "I've naugh' but oats."

"Then we'll eat bannocks," Aila had said sharply, frustrated with their increasing poverty, and then had sent Liam into the forest to find game. The bramble berries were thanks to Mared's diligent efforts to climb to the top of Din Footh to pick them, and the black bun cake courtesy of some rotting fruit. It was fare they could expect until the first of the month when the rents came in—what paltry few were left, anyway.

When the family sat down to supper, they politely ignored the sparse menu, and sipped cautiously from a dwindling supply of wine.

Aila looked down the table, quietly admiring her children. Each of the three was educated and well traveled, something she and Carson had managed to accomplish before things got so bad.

There was Liam, big and strong, the proud soldier. He was Aila's restless child, the one who had always chafed at the lack of activity in and around Loch Chon. As a boy he had been the most trouble, getting into so many fights that his face was permanently battered. And now this jagged scar, gained at the Battle of Waterloo, new enough that it was still quite garishly red. Even now, at the age of five and thirty, having been home from the Continent only a month, Liam's restlessness rattled the old house—he had, in this short time, engaged in two fistfights, taught three men how to fence, and had dragged a protesting Griffin to hunt deep in the forest at least twice a week—to keep his soldier skills honed, he said.

Then there was Griffin, her middle child, who, like Aila's father, whom he so closely resembled, looked so handsome in all his finery and was far more interested in social events than hunting or fighting. Unlike Liam, Griffin preferred the riches of life and was ambitious toward that end, wanting a stature in society Aila feared the family would never achieve. But it was Griffin who kept them thinking, kept them looking forward—he was constantly urging his father to consider new risk-taking ventures that would make the estate more profitable. Given their present circumstances, Aila could not argue with his point of view. Carson, on the other hand, could and did. God love him, but her husband was tucked comfortably in bed with the old way of thinking and was not ready to rise up with a new day.

And then there was Mared, her darling, beautiful Mared, marked by a ridiculous ancient curse that she'd never marry until she faced the Devil himself. Mared hardly believed in such nonsense—certainly none of the family did—but many of the locals in and around Loch Chon did. They regarded her as something of a curiosity, whispered behind their hands about her. Long ago, when she was just a wee lass, Mared had abandoned any pretense of believing she could overcome the wretched curse and lived as she desired, convinced she had nothing to lose, but sadly, just as convinced she had nothing to gain.

Aila would do anything for the four people seated at her table. Anything. Even break the law, for she was certain the English would perceive her plan to be unlawful, even if it was right.

Liam happily devoured his supper, oblivious to the lack of variety, regaling them with tales of the fencing lesson he had given Payton Douglas. "He gave me quite a fight, I'll hand him that," he said. "With a bit of proper tutelage, he'd make a decent soldier, he would."

Mared snorted. "Ye speak as if he is our friend, Liam," she chided her older brother. "Have ye forgotten? He is a Douglas! And he wasna so promising as ye say."

"Ah, Mared, how coldly ye speak of our neighbor!" Griffin exclaimed laughingly. "I'd think ye'd be kinder in yer manner, since ye spend so much time traipsing past the man's house," he added, absently pushing a bit of grouse around on his plate. "Donna pretend now—ye've a soft spot in yer heart for the Douglas."

The dark rose of a blush bled into Mared's fair cheeks; she gaped at her brother. "How *dare* ye say such a vile thing, Griffin! I'd sooner cut me wrist and bleed to death before I'd find room in my heart for a Douglas!"

"Ah, come now," Carson said gruffly through a mouth full of bannock cakes. "The man's really no' so bad, is he, then?"

Appalled, Mared shifted her gaze to her father as Griffin and Liam exchanged a chuckle. "Father, ye donna know what ye say!" she exclaimed, sparing a heated glance at her brothers. "Do ye know what he said to me just today, then?"

"Aye—that his heart had winged its way to yer window, but ye wouldna let it in," Griffin said poetically, to which Liam guffawed.

Mared grasped the edge of the table and stared at her father. "He *said* if we were of a mind to save our land, we'd join the Douglas lands as one and give over the coos for sheep!"

That stopped everyone cold. Liam and Griffin leaned forward at the same time, both of them frowning at their little sister. "Ye misunderstood him, then, Mared. He'd no' say such a thing," Griffin challenged her.

"Aye, he did! He said, 'Mared, will ye deny, then, that the Douglas and Lockhart lands, if they were one, would prosper more than when they are apart?' I said, 'Ye must have lost yer mind!'"

"He said *what?*" Carson bellowed.

"That we'd all prosper if our lands were together, no' apart," she repeated, smiling with smug satisfaction at her brothers.

No one said anything for a moment, until Griffin opined, "In truth, Father, he has a valid point—"

"The bloody hell he does!" Carson shouted. "I'll be damned if a Douglas will possess one *rock* of Lockhart land!"

"I should have sliced his arse right off his backside when I had the chance!"

"Liam!" Aila interrupted.

"So Douglas wants our land, does he now?" Carson demanded. Mared nodded furiously. "And there's no' a blessed thing to be done for it, no' with the debt we carry," Carson moaned further.

" 'Tis true, Father, that we're losing income with the beeves," Griffin observed.

"I'll *no'* change the way the Lockharts have prospered for five bloody centuries, Griffin!"

"There is perhaps another course, *mo ghraid*," Aila ventured, drawing everyone's attention.

"What?" Carson demanded.

Aila lowered her wineglass and looked at the four of them. "Bear with me, then," she said. "Ye'll think I've gone daft. But I've been reading a book written by yer father's father—a family history of sorts. It tells about the tragic death of the first Lady of Lockhart. Ye will remember her, will ye no', from yer studies?"

Mared nodded eagerly; Griffin rolled his eyes, and Liam looked at her blankly.

"*Ach,* Aila, ye donna believe that Lady's curse, now, do ye?" Carson groused.

"No, Carson," she clucked. " 'Tis no' the curse that interests me. 'Tis the beastie."

"The *beastie?*" Liam scoffed. "Mother, they donna exist—"

"I *know,*" she said, politely but firmly cutting him off. "But there *did* exist a gold statue of a beastie with ruby eyes, mouth, and tail. It was given as a token of esteem to the first Lady of Lockhart by her doomed lover." That succeeded in gaining everyone's undivided attention, and Aila proceeded to tell them how the Lady of Lockhart had given the statue to her daughter, how it was stolen by the English Lockharts, then the Scottish Lockharts, and back and forth, again and again, until no one could remember any longer. "The point is," she concluded, "the beastie has been in England since the Jacobite rebellion. But it belongs to us. And 'tis worth a small fortune."

Griffin's green eyes suddenly lit with understanding. "Mother, God bless ye!" he exclaimed. "Do ye suggest what I think ye suggest, then?"

Aila smiled.

"I donna understand," Mared said, looking to Griffin.

"If the statue belongs to us, we could *sell* it. Do ye

see, Father? The gold and rubies—there'd be enough to pay our debts!"

"Aye, I see," Carson said slowly, shifting his gaze to Aila. "But how is it then, that yer dear mother supposes we get it *back?* You know what they say about the blasted beastie—'tis English, for it always slips through the fingers of the Scot who possesses him."

A fine question. And one for which Aila did not have an answer. "I've no' thought of *everything,* Carson," she said with a frown. "But I put no stock in curses and magic. The beastie is in England because the English Lockharts stole it from the Scottish Lockharts, and I rather suppose we must have someone steal it back."

"*Steal* it?" Mared squealed.

"*I'll* fetch it," Liam said instantly and matter-of-factly.

"Oh, Liam, I didna mean my children," Aila quickly interjected.

"Honestly, Mother," Liam said with an impatient shake of his head. "Ye have a fine idea indeed. And ye canna deny that I am the likely one to go. I am a *captain* in the army, eh? A *captain* in the most esteemed military regiment of the crown."

When no one seemed to understand his point, Liam groaned. "I've been *trained* for this sort of thing, have I no'? Trained to find things, and should something go wrong, I am best appointed to manage, then."

"Aye, aye, indeed ye are," Mared readily agreed. "I saw him duel today, Mother. 'Tis true—he's quite good."

"I should hope he willna have to *duel,* Mared," said Aila.

"And he's been to London—a year's training at the military college," added Griffin.

"During which time I acquainted myself with our cousin Nigel Lockhart, irritating bootlick that he is," Liam gruffly reminded them.

Aila looked down the table at Carson. His gray-green eyes were gleaming now, and he nodded. "Aye . . . they are right, love. Our Liam is perfect for it. We need only make a plan."

Liam draped one arm across the back of his chair. "I've an idea," he said, and with all confidence, over the black bun cake, he laid out his scenario—he would go to London and befriend Cousin Nigel. "Like taking candy from a bairn," Liam scoffed. He would present himself as a disenchanted, disowned Scottish Lockhart— "Shouldna be very hard to portray," quipped Griffin— and relying on the assumption that everyone enjoys a little gossip now and then, particularly the airing of dirty family linens, Liam would use that to ingratiate himself to Nigel and earn an invitation to the Lockhart house in London, where he would find the statue.

Once he discovered its location, he would simply slip into the house under the cloak of night, retrieve it with all due stealth—"I've been commended for me cleverness," Liam reminded them—and be halfway back to Scotland before the English Lockharts ever knew the blessed thing was gone.

By the time they had moved into the old great hall, the five Lockharts had argued the plan from every conceivable angle until they were convinced that their plan was not only workable, but really rather brilliant in its simplicity. If their arms had been a bit longer, they might have exhausted themselves with all the pats they gave each other on their backs.

Two

LONDON, ENGLAND

So sure of his abilities and the importance of his mission—and rather anxious to get onto something more exciting than the bucolic life around Loch Chon while he waited for word of his regiment's next destination—Liam insisted on leaving by the end of that very week. With his plaid and his dirk carefully packed in his knapsack, along with proper clothing borrowed from his father (and simply taken from Grif), and as much cash as the family could scrape together secreted away in his sporran, Liam kissed his mother and his sister, clapped Griffin on the back, and shook hands with his father as he set off to retrieve the beastie.

He arrived, via the post coach, at High Wycombe, just west of London, late on a wet and dreary afternoon, the kind that comes early in autumn to portend a particularly nasty winter. He wrapped his regimental coat around him, adjusted the heavy knapsack on his back, and walked the mile or so from the coach station to the Hotel Marlowe, where he knew there would be various ranks of military men milling about. He was not disappointed. By the end of the evening and after a few too many tankards, Liam had what he wanted—

the name of someone in London who might help him find lodging. It was a name that was even known to him—Colonel Alasdair MacDonnell of Glengarry. Liam knew all about the man's military career, having made it a point to follow as many Scots as he could. But what he didn't know was that the colonel had helped establish the Highland Society of London, a gentleman's club of sorts that catered to the old clans of Scotland. Colonel MacDonnell, they said, could be found at the club on St. James Street most afternoons.

Liam could not possibly have been happier.

Feeling particularly sprightly the next morning, Liam was the first passenger on the public cab at dawn bound for Piccadilly Circus. But as the cab drew closer to London, the driver managed to squeeze eleven people into the interior (and what seemed like another ten on the bumper seat and running board), which forced Liam up against the stained and threadbare wall of the coach. The crush of humanity included a small lad with big brown eyes who stared at the scar across Liam's left cheek the entire trip, a man with a crude crate of squawking chickens, and a baby who, having chewed something quite vile, judging by the remnants that covered his wee fingers, had the audacity to pound his chubby little hand on Liam's knee.

Unfortunately, Piccadilly Circus was little improvement. Once he was able to extricate himself from the overcrowded cab, Liam was in the middle of a street teeming with people and carriages, carts filled high with goods, various braying animals, and a veritable field of pungent horse manure. Aye, it was all coming back to him now, the many reasons he did not care for London. First, it was full of Englishmen, a lot he had never really warmed to. Second, it stunk to high heaven.

But that was neither here nor there. Liam withdrew the crude map one of the soldiers had drawn last night, determined the direction of St. James Street, and with head down, the high collar of his coat pulled up around his face, he quietly disappeared into the sea of people and animals.

He found the club on a small street directly behind St. James, just as the soldier said, and pushed open the heavy door.

An hour or so later, after a few well-crafted compliments, Liam and the anglicized Colonel MacDonnell were in a room with dark paneling and thickly padded leather chairs arranged in quiet groupings, enjoying a whiskey (for which the man wanted a *full* half crown), and reminiscing about the war. Rather, MacDonnell was reminiscing, as he liked to talk about himself. In an English accent, which really annoyed Liam.

"Ah, Waterloo . . ." He sighed after a time, and looked at something in the distance only he could see. "A bloody bad time, wasn't it? I despised sending so many men forward." He shook his head as he studied Liam. "Looks as if *you* saw your fair share of battle," he said, motioning to the scar on Liam's face. "You held a command, did you?"

No, Liam had not held a command, but had been commanded to the field many times to gain intelligence about the French and then assassinate them. "Aye," he said simply. " 'Tis hard to speak of it," he said, and hoped to high heaven MacDonnell would drop it. Fortunately, a well-fed man in blue and gold superfine came rushing in at that moment.

"Ah, what have we here, MacDonnell? A countryman?" the man all but squealed in the exact same English tone as MacDonnell had affected.

"Lockhart. Served at Waterloo," MacDonnell said proudly.

"*Captain* Lockhart," Liam reminded him.

"Lockhart," the man repeated, and fairly bounced

like a ball onto one of the leather seats. "I'm Lovat. Well, then? You've brought a plaid, have you? We have fourteen now, not counting your contribution."

He looked so terribly eager that Liam reluctantly reached for the knapsack at his feet. He had noticed the various squares of clan tartans on the wall, had hoped he would not be asked. Slowly, he opened the knapsack, pulled out his carefully folded plaid, which he would wear when the time came to complete his mission.

"*Ooh,*" Lovat drooled. "It's the entire tartan, is it?" he asked, reaching for it. But Liam could hardly stomach the thought of these two men touching his plaid and instantly jerked it from Lovat's reach. Lovat reared back, blinking like a doe. Liam held up a finger to Lovat, silently telling him to wait, then leaned forward, extracted his *sgian dubh* from the top of his boot, ignoring the wide-eyed look of Lovat as he pressed the tip against the plaid. Gritting his teeth, for this act pained him greatly, Liam dragged the tip of the dagger across the fabric, cutting a small square from one corner, which he handed to Lovat as MacDonnell looked on admiringly.

"Ah, lovely," Lovat said. "Fine quality. Your contribution to our quest to preserve clan history is greatly appreciated, Mr. Lockhart."

"Captain," Liam muttered.

Lovat smiled, folded the square, and tucked it away in his coat pocket. "How long are you in London, then?" he asked amicably.

"Indefinitely."

"Taking up residence, are you? That makes, what, a dozen or more, does it not, MacDonnell?"

"A dozen?" Liam asked.

"Displaced Scots."

Why a Scot worth his salt would be *displaced* to London was something Liam could not fathom. He'd rather sail to America than be stuffed inside the bounds of London for all eternity. "Aye, that I am," he said on a weary sigh, trying very hard to sound displaced. "And ye'd be most kind if ye could direct me to lodging," he said. "I shouldna like a large place—something very simple would do."

"Lodging?" MacDonnell echoed. "Aren't there Lockharts in London? I'm certain I've heard the name. Perhaps you should seek quarters there?"

"Ah . . . no," he said carefully. "The Lockharts of London . . . well, my father, ye see, has had a bit of a falling-out with Uncle. I think it best if I billet nearby . . . but I'm no' a rich man."

Lovat and MacDonnell looked at him as if he had just announced he had developed leprosy.

"Ye understand . . . *sheep*," he said, by way of vague explanation.

"*Aaah*," they both declared in unison, nodding their heads in sympathy.

"Have ye any knowledge of a room or two for let, then?"

Lovat's brow wrinkled as he thought about it, but MacDonnell nodded thoughtfully. "There is one place . . . but really, I couldn't recommend it in good conscience."

Lovat looked at him questioningly.

"Farnsworth," MacDonnell said with a grimace.

"Egad!" Lovat exclaimed. "I can't say as I've met a tighter Englishman. And he's rather disagreeable, all in all, don't you think? Oh, I shouldn't recommend it, really, Captain. You'd do far better to present yourself to your uncle."

"I'm afraid that's no' possible. At least no' at the moment," Liam said, and sighed in an effort to demonstrate how deep the family feud ran.

MacDonnell considered him for a moment, then

shrugged. "I suppose it's really not *so* bad as that, if you can stomach Farnsworth. He at least has the suite of rooms to let. And it's perfectly situated for town, I daresay, just there in Belgravia," he said, motioning toward the back wall. "Not the fashionable side of the square, but nonetheless . . . Really, you could do much worse, Captain, although you ought to clear it all up with your uncle."

"Yes, milord, that is me primary reason for coming to London," Liam quickly assured him.

"But still, Farnsworth is such a dour man," Lovat complained. "He's an eccentric old bird. He likes the gaming tables to be sure, but God forbid he should lay one single farthing of his own considerable funds on the table. He lets the suite and uses that income to feed his dreadful lust."

Ah . . . a pinchpenny with a nasty little habit. One who perhaps could be manipulated should the situation warrant. Liam bit back a smile—it sounded perfect. "Might I have the direction, then?" he asked pleasantly, and reached for the last of his whiskey.

Three

⤳

*L*iam found Belgrave Square easily enough, but wasn't very sure at all which side was fashionable, and as a cold wind had begun to pick up, he hoped that something fashionable would present itself sooner rather than later.

As he walked across the square, he noticed that a woman approaching him was struggling with her parasol—and as a strong gust suddenly caught it, turning the thing completely inside out, Liam glimpsed her angelic face. She saw him, too, and smiled. Liam instinctively put his head down as he had learned to do because of his battered face, and hastened his step to get around her as quickly as he could. Unfortunately, the wind came up again, snapping her parasol, and she moved directly into his path as she wrestled with it.

"Oh, dear, I do beg your pardon, sir!" she exclaimed, smiling still, laughter glimmering in her blue eyes. "And it's not doing me a bit of good in this climate, so I suppose I should put the thing away once and for all."

Surprised and pleased that she did not recoil or stare curiously at him, Liam smiled back, tipped his hat, and stepped to his right at the exact same moment she stepped to her left. Her cheeks turned an appealing shade of pink as she laughed again. "I *quite* beg your pardon, sir! I'm rather out of sorts today, aren't I?"

"Shall I?" he inquired, gesturing at the mangled parasol.

"Would you mind terribly?" she asked, handing it to him. "You're so kind."

He took the thing from her; his fingers brushed the smooth silk of her gloved fingers, which sparked a peculiar warmth beneath his collar. Liam forced the parasol right side out, pleased that he had done so without tearing it, and risked another look at the angel.

"Oh, *thank* you!" she exclaimed, smiling gratefully. "I am forever in your debt, sir," she said, holding her hand out for the parasol.

Liam could not seem to find his tongue or wrest his gaze from her smile as he handed the parasol to her. She grasped it firmly, her slender fingers grazing his rough ones once more, and stuffed it securely under her arm. "I will just step aside now and let you pass," she said with a little laugh, and still smiling, she made a show of stepping out of his way. "Thank you again, sir," she said, with a demure nod.

"Of course," Liam muttered, stealing a last glimpse of her bonny face as he passed, walking on. When he reached the end of the square, however, he turned around to look at her and that bonny smile again, but the angel had disappeared. Pity, that. Liam continued on.

He found the Farnsworth household, all right. At first glance, it looked to be a house of great means, since it dwarfed most of the houses surrounding it. The huge structure took up almost an entire face of the square, with big banks of windows, ornate stone trim, and gaslights that illuminated the huge front door and steps leading up to it.

But then the door was opened by a woman who so closely resembled Liam's auntie Gwyneth (his father's scary spinster sister, may she rest in peace) that Liam inwardly recoiled. From the gray hair peeking out from beneath the woman's cap to the pinched face to the long, skinny frame, it was like looking at a ghost from his past.

"Yes, sir?" she asked, peering at him through beady little raisin eyes.

"I beg yer pardon, mu'um, Captain Lockhart calling for Lord Farnsworth, if ye please."

She frowned, looked him up and down, glared at the knapsack on his shoulder with an unmistakable look of disapproval. "Is he expecting you, Mr. Lockhart?"

"Actually, that'd be *Captain* Lockhart. But no, I've no' met his lordship. I've come to see about the rooms for let."

Auntie Gwyneth seemed to consider that for a moment, puffing out her cheeks and peering at the square behind him. After a moment, she focused her eyes on him and asked, "Have you a card, Captain?"

A card? Bloody hell, of course he had no card! What, did she think he passed them about to the French? He delved deeply into the pocket of his regimental coat, managed to look as if he couldn't understand what he might have done with his cards, and shoved his hands into the pockets of his trousers, then his waistcoat, until Auntie Gwyneth sighed with great exasperation. "Yes, sir, please step inside and I will announce you to his lordship!"

Liam quickly did so before she could change her mind. Inside the foyer, it took a moment for his eyes to adjust to the dark, for it was not properly lit, and he began to see the accuracy of Lovat's description of the place.

"I'll be a moment," Auntie Gwyneth said, and proceeded to stomp away in what sounded like her very own pair of regimental boots.

Liam stood patiently at the door, taking in his surroundings, quickly deciding it was the most austere house he had ever seen. The walls were darkly paneled and devoid of any artwork—with the exception of a couple of portraits above the stairwell leading to the upper floors. Liam could see into what looked to be the main drawing room, and the furniture there appeared to be only nominal and efficient—one couch, one settee, and two chairs were all that graced the room. Oddly, the hearth was cold on such a gray and blustery day. In fact, the house had quite a chill to it.

Curious now, Liam took a few steps forward to have a look down the front corridors. To his right, a corridor of bare planked wood ran past several closed doors. There was a spindly console halfway down, but even it was devoid of any adornment. The wall sconces were empty, and as the floor-to-ceiling windows were covered with heavy velvet drapes, there was precious little light. To Liam's left an identical corridor stretched, but at least it was lit, and it boasted a narrow ribbon of carpeting down the center. But here again, the doors were closed, the heavy drapes drawn.

He stepped back, wondered about the musty odor that seemed to permeate everything, and thought perhaps old Farnsworth had lost his furnishings to gambling. But then, MacDonnell and Lovat said he never spent as much as a farthing of his own money on his habit. Perhaps, then, the man didn't have any money to speak of, in spite of Lovat's claims to the contrary. Liam had heard that some Englishmen had lofty titles but no income because of old entails that left them on the verge of poverty. That would at least explain the sparse furnishings.

And perhaps Farnsworth was just a cheese-paring, parsimonious bastard. He certainly wouldn't be the first miserly Englishman, nor would he be the last.

The sound of a cow clomping across a barn caught his attention, and indeed, Auntie Gwyneth appeared in the foyer once again. Nose wrinkled, she glared at his knapsack. "His lordship will see you in his study," she announced, and without further ado, she pivoted and began clomping down the corridor on Liam's left.

He quickly fell in behind her, following closely, absorbing as much as he could. Not that there was much to see. He noted that every other wall sconce in this corridor was lit, and judging by the black scars on the wall above them, the candles used in this house were the cheaper tallow, not beeswax. There was a handful of portraits, mostly small, dark, and nondescript, save the portrait of an elegant blond woman, dressed in the fashion of the last century, holding a small dog on her lap.

Auntie Gwyneth abruptly stopped in front of two very dull double doors and turned the handle of one, pushing it open just a crack. "Captain Lockhart," she announced, and stepped aside with what Liam was quite certain was a sneer.

He ignored her, pushed the door open wider, and stepped into the study, where he was immediately hit with a blast of warmth from the blazing hearth. Unlike the rest of the house, this room was well appointed, with various pieces of artwork, a thick Aubusson carpet, leather chairs, a handsome couch, and a long French-style desk that he knew from his travels was almost certainly a collector's item. Behind the desk, beneath portraits of two very stern gentlemen, sat a man with a bald crown surrounded by a ring of coiffed hair, a monocle through which he peered at Liam, and clothing that strained across his belly. His feet, Liam noticed, did not quite reach the ground. And he was scowling mightily.

"Well, then? What is it?" he demanded coldly.

So much for civility. "Lord Farnsworth," he said, bowing low. "Allow me to introduce myself, if I may. I am Captain Lockhart of the Highland Regiments of the

Royal British Army, in service to His Majesty, the king."

"A *Scot?*" Farnsworth exclaimed, pushing himself off his chair to stand on tiny little feet covered in tiny Hessian boots. "What in blazes is a *Scot* doing in my house?" he asked, as if the word actually caused him a pang of nausea.

Bloody little . . . Liam caught himself. "Me father is no' accepting of service to the English king," he said simply.

Farnsworth's eyes narrowed as he assessed Liam. "The *English* king? What are you saying, that you've been disowned?"

"One might say that I prefer London to Edinburra," he lied.

Farnsworth tottered around the desk until he was standing in front of it, and casually crossed one tiny foot over the other as he leaned against it, reminding Liam, strangely enough, of a dancing elf. "What you prefer is no business of mine, sir," Farnsworth said gruffly. "I will ask again—what are *you* doing in *my* house?"

"I was given to understand that ye might have a room for let."

Farnsworth snorted. "I might. But I wouldn't hire out rooms in my house to just anyone, now would I? Frankly, I'm not of a mind to have a Scot in my house. I had a servant once—the dirtiest and drunkest human filth I've ever seen. *You* wouldn't be kin to Angus, now would you, Captain?"

All right, now *that* wasn't very kind. Liam had the capacity and a growing desire to smash the fat little pea, but he had been in the company of men far better and far cleverer than Farnsworth to be so easily goaded. He smiled. "I rather think no', milord."

Clearly disappointed that Liam hadn't taken the bait, Farnsworth crossed his arms across his mountain of a belly and considered Liam for a long moment before he spoke. "I don't want your kind here. Be gone with you."

"I have money," Liam calmly responded.

Farnsworth snorted. "Oh you *do*, do you? And what makes you think I need your bloody money?"

"I wouldna imply such a thing, milord. I merely meant to convey that I have the cash to let the room, if ye're of a mind."

Farnsworth walked to the hearth, looked up at a gold mantel clock, his chubby hands clasped behind his back. "Highland Regiments, you said?"

"Aye."

He said nothing for a moment, then: "I expect my rents the first day of each month. I won't wait for some military pension."

"As ye wish."

"And it's not *one* room, it's two. It's hardly worth my while to let the one. Breakfast and supper only. No tea. No luncheons."

"That will do."

Farnsworth whipped around—rather quickly in spite of his girth—to glare at Liam again. "Have you a manservant? I'll not feed him if you do."

"No man. Only me."

"No valet? No driver?" he pressed.

"I come with what ye see, milord," Liam said calmly. "I am accustomed to looking after meself."

Farnsworth nodded, strolled toward Liam, studying his uniform. "A captain in the military surely must be trustworthy," he said to himself.

"I've taken a vow of honor, milord."

"Don't be coy!" Farnsworth snapped. "You've taken no such vow when it comes to women, have you? I'll not have any lewd behavior under my roof!"

That angered Liam. He could tolerate a man's condescension only up to a point, but to call his honor into question— "Milord, I am an officer in the royal military and a gentleman, and I'll no' stand for ye to besmirch me good name," he said coldly.

That actually seemed to shrink Farnsworth a little, but the man quickly puffed his chest again like a preening blue jay. "I will not provide a chambermaid. You must keep your quarters clean. A footman will bring your food to your quarters twice daily, along with linens, remove your rubbish, fill your basin, and provide you with coal. That's all, nothing more. And I'm not a gentleman's club, Captain. I don't want your company—is that understood?"

"Aye, milord."

"And I'll not have you wandering about my house. Your rooms, should I decide to offer them to you, are on the ground floor. There is no need for you to ever ascend those stairs. I am abroad quite frequently and will not be here to monitor your movements, so I must have your word on this. You will *not* go upstairs."

"Ye have me word."

Farnsworth clenched his jaw and strolled to the hearth again. "This is my home. I am doing you a rather remarkable favor," he said to the fire. "And for that, I require forty pounds a month," he said, and glanced over his shoulder at Liam.

How Liam managed to keep from choking at the usurious rate was nothing short of a miracle. For that amount, he could let an entire floor in some hotel, and the thought did cross his mind. But there were three advantages here that he could see: one, the house was centrally located; two, he could use this address to ingratiate himself to the good citizens of the *ton;* and three, he could come and go from this house with little fear of detection—by Farnsworth's own admission, he was frequently gone, which gave Liam even greater ability to maneuver.

"Very well, then," Liam said, and reached for the small leather purse in his pocket to extract the money.

"I must have two months' let up front," Farnsworth said quickly.

Liam looked up and pierced him with a look of exasperation that caused Farnsworth to flush and look to the fire again. Nevertheless, Liam walked to where he stood, handed him the eighty pounds, keenly aware that left him with just three hundred pounds. Farnsworth, who even in his boots did not reach Liam's shoulder, snatched the bills from his hand and quickly pocketed them. Without another word, he walked to a bellpull on the wall and yanked it hard. He then went to the door and stood there until Auntie Gwyneth appeared.

"Show the captain to the rooms for let," he said, and without looking at Liam again, he waddled to his desk.

The rooms he had rented for the outrageous sum of eighty pounds were devoid of any furniture save a bed and an armoire in one room, and a table and a chair in the other. Auntie Gwyneth, having shown him the lay of the ground floor, muttered something about fresh linens, and returned a few minutes later with two towels and a set of linens for the bed. Behind her was a rather sickly looking footman, who carried a basket of coal for the small brazier. The hearth was, apparently, for appearances only. The windows were cloaked in the same heavy velvet that was in the corridor, but in here the velvet was quite threadbare. For someone who lived among London's *haute ton*, Farnsworth maintained an unusual level of austerity in his home. It was worse than anything Liam's family had been forced to suffer in recent years. In fact, Talla Dileas looked rather warm and inviting compared to this place.

Grousing beneath his breath, Liam lit the brazier and unpacked his things. He hung his clothing in the armoire, laid his plaid on the bed, hid his *sgian dubh*, pistol, and an extra, smaller dagger beneath the mattress. On the table, which he dragged into the main room, he arranged his toiletries, a small polished stone he had taken from a stream that coursed the mountain of his family's estate, his war medals, and his sporran. Beneath the table he laid his boots, his *ghillie brogues*, and the belt he wore with his plaid.

It was early evening when he had finished settling in and heard the knock at his door. The same sickly young man who had brought his coal stood at the door holding a tray. "Your supper," he said blandly, and proceeded to the table, where he placed the tray, then quit the room again without so much as a look at Liam.

Friendly people, these English. Curious, Liam walked to the tray, lifted the silver dome, and instantly blanched. He slammed the dome back down, for on a cracked china plate had been a fish of some sort and a helping of steamed cabbage. Liam was quite used to living off the land and even eating what most people would consider inedible, but he had never, in his thirty-five years, been able to eat a fish with its eyes still staring up at him. He pushed the tray away from his things and decided this was as good a time as any to go out and have a look around town. Perhaps find a leg of mutton if he were lucky.

He walked to the door, closed it, and locked it from the inside. He took the key from the lock and put it in his pocket. He tried the door, and satisfied that no one could gain entrance without a key, he turned and walked to the window, threw back the drapes, and looked down. The drop to the mews below was no more than twelve feet. Shoving into his coat, Liam opened the window, stepped out on the sill, closed the window carefully behind him, and dropped to the ground.

* * *

It was well past midnight when he returned to Belgrave Square, this time with a tankard or two of stout ale under his belt to warm him. He was all but whistling—he had not expected to be quite so successful in the twenty-four hours he had been in London, but then again, he should hardly be surprised. He was excellent at what he did, if he did say so himself.

Tonight, when he had by chance wandered onto Pall Mall, he'd had a bite to eat and noticed there were a number of gentlemen's establishments there. After he'd finished his supper, he'd made his way into one, content to just look at the serving girls for a time. But as luck would have it, he'd struck up a conversation with an elderly man who was intent on telling someone his life story that very evening. Unable to divest himself of the man, Liam had let him talk.

When the man at last had finished his discourse on the plumbing problems in his house, Liam asked if he knew of the Lockharts. Not only did he know them, but he directed him to the house with the elaborate $\mathscr{L}$ engraved on the door fan.

An hour or so later, Liam stood across from the mansion with the $\mathscr{L}$ engraved on the fan above the door. It was a larger house than Farnsworth's—much nicer. And the area, which the old man had called Mayfair, seemed very prestigious. The English Lockharts had done well for themselves, Liam thought, so well that they wouldn't miss a wee beastie, now would they?

He made his way back to his rooms on Belgrave Square, entered through the front door, and groped about until he found candles and matches. With his candle finally lit, he moved forward, his boots echoing loudly on the plank floors. At the door of his room, Liam checked that the door was still locked, then opened it with his key. His plaid was exactly where he had laid it, but he would have to be more careful—one corner was carelessly bunched. Liam put the candle down, sat on the edge of the bed to remove his boots, and unthinkingly looked at the table where he had arranged his things. A breath caught in his throat—the toiletries and sporran had been switched around, and the rock from Talla Dileas was much closer to his medal of honor than he had left it.

Someone had been in his room and gone through his things!

Four

≈

Liam immediately suspected the puny footman who had brought him the fish. But as that dead thing still lay there, starting to reek, he dismissed that notion. Farnsworth, then? That didn't seem likely—as peculiar as the old bird was, he did not seem the type to concern himself with his tenant's few personal belongings. Which left Auntie Gwyneth . . . *or French operatives?*

That notion was hardly far-fetched, Liam realized—he *had* been a wanted man in France, and in fact, there had been a fairly hefty price on his head before the Battle of Waterloo. Was it possible Bonaparte sympathizers still wanted him dead? Or even the new loyalists? But how could they have tracked him here so quickly? He had sailed from Glasgow to Liverpool on a packet ship. It seemed near to impossible for them to have discovered that, since he had left Talla Dileas so quickly. In Liverpool he had boarded the first of several coaches he took precisely to avoid detection. No, it seemed highly improbable that the French could have found him so quickly—if they were even still looking for him.

So if not Farnsworth or the French, then who? *Ho, there!* He was overlooking another very viable possibility—the English Lockharts. It was far more likely that MacDonnell or Lovat had mentioned his presence to his cousins. As he recalled, Nigel had been a frequent patron of the gentlemen's clubs—or had it been the brothels? Liam paused, stared blindly at the window. Aye, but *why* would Nigel do such a thing? If he knew or cared that Liam was in London, even if he knew precisely where, he would have no cause to enter these rooms in such a manner. Would he not have called for him, like a gentleman?

Liam dragged his fingers through his hair, then shook his head. The only way to know for sure was to set a trap. What a bloody damned annoyance.

He slept badly that night, partly because he waited for the intruder and partly because the pillow Farnsworth had provided him was so thin as to be nonexistent and his pistol beneath it made for a strange lump against his skull. When weak light at last filtered in his window the next morning, he groaned and made himself rise. He was still in yesterday's clothes; his mouth tasted rank.

Liam bathed as best he could with the ice-cold water in the basin, then dressed in clean clothes. As he was tying his neckcloth, there was a knock at his door. He opened it to the footman, who entered carrying another tray, his expression stoic. He walked past Liam without a word, put it down on the table, and picked up the tray from the previous evening, wrinkling his nose. As he turned to quit the room, Liam moved toward the door, blocking his exit.

"Do ye have a name, then?" he asked, stopping the man mid-stride.

The man's eyes darted to the door, then to Liam, and he nervously cleared his throat. "Ah . . . Follifoot, sir."

"Follifoot," Liam repeated, assessing him. Honestly, Follifoot looked too weak and nervous to be the one to risk his neck entering Liam's rooms without permission.

Nonetheless, Liam took a step closer, causing Follifoot to have to bend his head backward to look up at him. "Here now, Follifoot, ye wouldna enter a man's rooms without his permission, eh?"

Follifoot's watery brown eyes widened. "*No*, sir! I would *never!*"

In truth, he looked so horrified that Liam had to believe him. Not Follifoot, then. Unthinkingly, he turned away, his mind racing ahead to other possibilities.

"Sir, I beg of you, please don't accuse me of such a thing to Lord Farnsworth!" Follifoot pleaded. "If you say such a thing, he'll toss me out on my ear!"

Liam ignored his plea for the moment. "Who might have a key to this room?" he demanded.

"I . . . I can't rightly say—the housekeeper, Miss Agatha, perhaps?" he suggested weakly.

"Perhaps," Liam said, casting a cold smile at him.

But Follifoot instantly shook his head. "Miss Agatha would not have done so, sir, if you will pardon me saying so. She's a daily—she departs promptly at five o'clock each day and doesn't return until six o'clock the following morning."

"What of his lordship, then? Was he in residence last evening?"

Follifoot winced. "Can't rightly say, sir, but I rather think not. Most nights he goes to the gaming hells in Southwark. I'd reckon he did so again."

Aye, so would Liam—the fat little pea had eighty pounds burning a hole in his pocket. He considered the fragile Follifoot, decided he was credible in a weak-willed way, and fished in his pocket and withdrew a crown. He held it up for Follifoot to see, turning it over between his fingers, then laid it on his tray. "I'll thank ye to keep our conversations to yerself, Follifoot," he said.

Follifoot nodded eagerly and sort of sidestepped around Liam, inching for the door, anxious to be gone. "W-will there be anything else, sir?"

"*Ach*, run along with ye, then," Liam said, and smiled ruefully as Follifoot awkwardly tried to escape with his tray. As he stepped through the door and reached to close it, he looked at Liam once more, and a shudder of fear passed through his eyes.

That didn't bother Liam—he was accustomed to such a reaction. After all, he was a big man, six feet and three inches in height, and years of fighting and war had rearranged his face a bit. His nose was flat, a scar ran from his brow halfway down his left cheek, and there were a variety of nicks about his face and hands. While he was hardly hideous (according to Mared), he realized that his looks, coupled with his size, often caused a body to look twice, and caused men like Follifoot to scurry as far away from him as possible.

That was just as well; he had no use for weak men. With a shrug, Liam walked to the tray Follifoot had left and lifted the silver dome. Runny eggs, a tomato, and something that resembled black mud. It was a wonder to Liam that Farnsworth could be so corpulent given the lack of culinary talent in this house. Yet as unappetizing as the meal was, Liam forced himself to eat. If there was one thing he had learned in his years of military espionage, it was to eat every chance he had, because he never knew when the next opportunity would present itself.

He cleaned the plate, set the tray outside his door, then went about setting his trap by rearranging his room and moving the table near the window, close enough that if one were hiding behind the drapes, one could surprise an intruder. On the table, he made sure all of his belongings were displayed, even adding his carefully folded plaid to the mix. Then he straightened the bedding and withdrew his pistol from beneath the mattress and stuffed it in his pocket. Satisfied that everything was in order, he walked to the window, opened it just a crack, then turned and walked to the door, quitting the room. In the corridor he made a show of locking his room. From there he clomped down the bare corridor, making sure that his boots made as much racket as possible to announce his departure for the benefit of anyone in the house who might be the culprit, or aiding one.

As he stepped outside, he shut the main door loudly behind him and bounced down to the street, whistling an old Scottish tune in spite of the rain, so that anyone observing him would think he was on his way. But instead of turning toward town, Liam turned in the direction of the narrow mews that ran alongside the house, and when he was certain no one was observing him, he slipped through the mews gate.

The mews was deserted. Little wonder—the day had all the markings of being another miserably wet one. Climbing up to the window of his rented room was difficult; the brick was quite slick what with the rain, and it took Liam several attempts to gain a foothold and hoist himself up. But in the space of ten minutes he had slipped into his room again to wait for his intruder.

As luck would have it, he did not have long to wait—it astounded him that the intruder would dare to come again so soon.

When he heard the first attempts to open the door, he silently and calmly slipped behind the heavy drapes, his pistol at his side. Whoever the intruder was, Liam was rather thoroughly flabbergasted by his clumsiness—he heard the lock click several times, even heard what sounded like a kick against the door. Such technique could get a man killed, and while he dearly hoped to avoid that possibility, he was quite prepared for the necessity.

The door at last opened with a bang, then closed quickly. Liam scarcely drew a breath as he listened to the footfall, which was, he thought with some confusion, awfully light. And he was further baffled by the pattern of the footfall, which seemed to be going in a circular motion, from wall to wall, round and round. *What in the hell was the idiot doing?* A thief or assassin worth his collar would not squander precious minutes in such a manner, would come directly to take what he must. Yet the footsteps continued in a circular motion, slowly drawing closer to the table.

Then the footfall stopped.

And the bedsprings creaked loudly beneath the weight of a person.

The improbable notion that perhaps his room was being used as a rendezvous for a tryst flashed in Liam's mind. That, naturally, would explain the light footsteps (a woman) and the dalliance about the room (a woman). But as he considered the plausibility of it, the creaking on the bed began again in earnest, starting slow, then gaining momentum. *Jesus God, how could it be?* He had heard only *one* person come into the room, and as *one* person could hardly have relations with one-self—practically speaking—that could only mean . . .

The intruder was jumping on the bed.

The realization hit him hard, and in a burst of frustration at the intruder's ineptitude, Liam suddenly pushed the drape aside and strode forward, angry to have wasted so much time on this ridiculous task.

The scream of terror that split his eardrums was almost lost in his shock at seeing a little girl fly off the bed in an astounding acrobatic move and run for the door. But Liam was much quicker than she and in three strides was at the door before her, sealing the escape by pressing his broad back against it.

The girl screamed again, and in a panic ran for the bed, then around it—twice—to the table, and at last the drapes, which she dove behind, whimpering loudly.

Bloody hell, this was not good, not good at all. Liam stood, legs apart, rubbing his chin as he listened to the child's sobs, which seemed to be growing louder, and would inevitably bring the whole damn house down around his head. "Mary Queen of *Scots!*" he bellowed. "Stop yer caterwauling!"

But the crying did not stop, and Liam marched to the window, reached behind the drape, and grabbed onto a small shoulder. He pulled the girl out from behind the drape—*Good* Lord, *what wailing!*—and forced her into a seat at the table.

Tears streamed down a small face gone quite red with the exertion. Her blond curls, having come loose from their pins in her panic, seemed to be going in all different directions. Every sob racked her little frame so violently that Liam worried she might actually harm herself. Confused, flustered, and quite uncertain what to do, he could only stand there staring down at her.

She at last looked up at him with wet but pretty pale blue eyes, and her gaze slid to his hand. All at once her face screwed into a mottled mass of features, and she screeched. Startled, Liam glanced down—he was still holding the pistol, which he immediately put down on the table. He pointed a finger at her, said sternly, "Ye donna touch it, now, or I'll bite yer fingers off, one by one—I swear I will."

Her eyes grew impossibly wide; for a moment there was silence. Then the girl opened her mouth to let loose a wail like he'd never heard.

Liam felt a moment of panic—if the rafters didn't come tumbling down, all of Belgrave Square would hear that scream and think he had murdered the child. "Stop it at once!" he demanded loudly. "I'll no' have ye screaming like a banshee!"

The girl opened her mouth again, but only a hiccup came out, and she blinked up at him, wide-eyed. "What's a banshee?"

"A *banshee!*" he said impatiently, waving his hand at her. "A spirit of sorts . . ." He looked up at the ceiling, trying to think how best to describe it. "She looks a wee bit like the trolls—" Oh for God's sake, what was he doing? Liam growled, jerked his gaze back to the girl, and pierced her with a heated gaze.

She had stopped crying now, was looking at him openly, curiously. *Ach,* but he didn't like that look. It was too . . . straightforward, too direct. This child, who-ever she was, must have been sent here by someone who meant him harm. However improbable that sounded, what else would she be doing in his rooms? But Liam had never really been around children, and he really didn't know how to go about interrogating someone so . . . so *small.*

He punched his fists to his hips, puffed his chest. "All right then, lassie, ye'll make it easier on us both if ye'll tell me who sent ye here."

The girl swiped at the tears beneath her eyes. "You sound very strange when you speak."

Liam blinked, thrown off course for a moment. "Aye! And so do you!"

"Why do you speak that way?"

Why indeed! Liam snorted. "I'll ask the questions, if ye donna mind."

"What's your name?" she asked, leaning back and putting her hands primly in her lap, as if they were about to have a nice, polite conversation. "My name is Natalie," she informed him before he could respond that his name was none of her concern.

"I donna care what they call ye—" Liam stopped, perplexed by her sudden shout of laughter.

Her nose wrinkled appealingly. "You sound *very* funny when you speak!"

Oh, no. He was not going to be fooled by charming little giggles. "Never mind *that,*" he said, and leaned over her to demonstrate that he was quite serious. *"What* are ye doing here?"

"What are *you* doing here?" she responded.

"I asked ye first."

"Where do you live?"

Liam straightened up. All right, then, it really should not be this difficult. He glared down at her, trying to think what to do. She was a *child,* damn it all to hell.

"I was born in Laria," she said blithely. "It's a kingdom just this side of Austria."

That unbalanced him momentarily as he tried to remember a place called Laria.

"But my father brought us here when I was a baby." She smiled up at Liam, her eyes as blue as a summer sky. "Where were *you* born?"

"Under a bridge."

"Is that why you have a scar?" she asked in sweet honesty.

Unconsciously, Liam touched the scar, and duly perplexed now, sank onto the corner of the bed. He gazed at the girl as she studied his features. "Be a good lass now, and tell me who sent ye here. Will ye tell me please, *leannan?"*

"Oh, my name is not Leannan. It is Natalie."

"No, no, *leannan* is our word for 'sweetheart'—never mind. Who sent ye here, then, Natalie?"

The bridge of her nose crinkled as she giggled at him. "Why, no one!"

"Where are yer parents, then?"

Her feet, encased in tiny velvet slippers, began to swing beneath the table. "Well, my father is an admiral in the Royal Navy—"

An admiral! Liam sat up, duly impressed.

"—and Mother is in Laria. Just for a visit, of course. Did it hurt very badly?"

"Eh, what?" he asked, confused.

Natalie pointed to his scar.

Silly child; Liam clucked at the very suggestion. *"No,"* he said sternly. "Where is your father, then?"

"Oh, he's at sea. He's fighting a rather nasty war with the French people."

But the war with France was over—she was confused. He thought to ask more, but the girl had slipped off her chair and walked around the table . . . to where his plaid was laid out.

Liam leapt to his feet. "Donna touch it!" he cried, and Natalie yanked her hand back as if it had been burned. Liam snatched up his plaid and quickly moved to the other side of the bed to put it out of her reach. "You shouldna touch things that donna belong to ye," he chided her. "This is very precious."

She sniffed somewhere behind him. "I'm sorry. But it's so pretty."

"Well, now, I wouldna call it pretty, but 'tis precious to me nonetheless—" The sound of her little feet inter--rupted him; he whipped around. She was almost to the door, her hand reaching for the knob.

"Wait!" Liam exclaimed. "Ye didna tell me who ye are!"

"But I did!" she exclaimed cheerfully as she opened the door. *"You* didn't tell me who *you* are," she said. "I'll come again on the morrow, and you may tell me then." And as casually as you please, she walked through the open door, leaving a gaping Liam behind.

Five

❧

*L*ittle Natalie became a frequent and uninvited guest to Liam's rooms from that point forward.

The only bright spot, as far as Liam could see, was that she could not enter his two rooms unless the door was unlatched. He had quickly discovered, the very morning of their improbable acquaintance, how she had managed to unlock the door—the latch was old and in need of repair, and she had been able to jiggle it out of place. Liam had corrected that problem with his dagger—she would not be jiggling anything else out of place.

What really disturbed him was exactly how he had missed such a fundamental thing as a loose lock, which caused him to wonder if perhaps his skills were eroding.

No longer able to enter his rooms on her own, Natalie began to make a habit of popping in with Follifoot when Liam's food was brought, or worse, taking the tray from Follifoot and delivering it herself, even though she was hardly able to carry the heavy wooden thing. On those occasions Liam would instantly take the tray from her lest she drop it, and Natalie would rush through the door behind him, intent on becoming his dinner companion, apparently of the understanding that the one not eating should be talking. And she would sit on the edge of his bed, her feet swinging, oblivious to the fact that he was paying her no mind, laughing when he

belched his opinion of the grotesque meal. And talking.
Talking.

The girl was absolutely astonishing in her ability to talk without taking as much as a breath! From the moment she managed to gain entrance to his rooms, she never stopped, going on and on about such things as her age (nine years, four months, and on her next birthday, the *two*-digit number of ten, which, according to Natalie, was quite significant); her mother (in Laria, seeking treatment for some hideous disease about which Liam did *not* want to know the details); and less frequently, her father (whose naval career was *quite* stellar, and one that left Liam suitably impressed).

The girl also talked at length about the province of Laria (wherever that was—Liam could not recall it from his studies), and her friends there, who were, from what he gathered, frequent, gift-bearing visitors to London.

When she wasn't talking, Natalie filled in all the silence with her many, *many* questions, seemingly unconcerned whether Liam answered or not. Which he didn't, as a rule. He was, and always had been, a rather private man. But none of that stopped Natalie. She managed to drag his name from him and instantly proclaimed she would name her baby Liam. She asked him about Scotland (*Miss Agatha says it is a place for heathens*); about his family (*Have you brothers and sisters? And what are their ages? And did you play together when you were children? And what was your favorite game? Do you know my favorite game? My favorite game is princess. Did you ever play princess? Do they have princesses in Scotland? Is your sister a princess?*); about his plaid (*How do you wear it? When do you wear it? Where do you wear it? May I wear it? May I touch it? May I look at it one more time, please?*).

Liam did what he could to rid himself of the girl short of bodily picking her up and tossing her out the door, and even that thought crossed his mind more than once.

As it happened each night, he would tolerate the almost insufferable chatter until he had finished his meal—on the days he could stomach the meal—then would spend a good quarter of an hour chasing her about and herding her out like a cat, wondering why the girl's governess (which she claimed not to have) never came looking for her. She was probably exhausted from all her chatter, Liam figured. And since Miss Agatha and Follifoot seemed to avoid this end of the house, he hadn't yet found a chance to inquire about the governess.

But once the door was shut on Natalie and he was certain of no other interruptions, he put together the pieces of his plan. As his first order of business, he had gone about the task of reacquainting himself with London so that when he encountered his cousin Nigel, he could put up a reasonably believable front that he had exiled himself here. Toward that end, Liam walked the entire length of Hyde Park, memorizing its various trails and gathering places. He made certain that the features of Bond Street, Piccadilly, Vauxhall, and Covent Gardens were known to him. He memorized even the various theaters, as well as their bill of plays. He studied the English habits, tried to affect the same pretentiousness in his carriage and speech. By week's end, he was quite certain he knew enough about London to carry on a rather convincing conversation with his cousin Nigel.

Having accomplished his first task, Liam had turned his attention to the second, which was to force an encounter with Nigel that would seem to his cousin to have happened by chance. It would not do to have Nigel think he had come looking for him, because then, when the beastie turned up missing, old Nigel might put two and two together. It was important for Nigel to believe *he* had discovered *him*. In order to do that Liam had to learn Nigel's habits. Then he would put phase two of his plan into motion—ingratiating himself to the English Lockharts.

On his first afternoon of scouting for Nigel, Liam grew too hungry and cold to look for him any longer, and gave up for the day, returning to his bleak little rooms. He was walking up the steps to the Farnsworth house when he happened to notice a round figure scurrying toward him on spindly little legs. He had not seen Lord Farnsworth since taking the rooms a fortnight ago, and was struck by the notion that he looked like a grotesque caricature of a dandy in his tall beaver hat as he toddled down the street.

Oblivious to Liam, Farnsworth reached the steps of the house and began hopping up, one at a time, but stopped mid-stride when he realized Liam was in front of him.

Farnsworth scowled, tipped his hat, and said brusquely, "Captain."

"I beg yer pardon, milord," Liam said as Farnsworth hopped up another step, passing him. "A word?"

Farnsworth paused, sighed loudly to the heavens. "Yes, what is it?" he demanded impatiently, turning slightly and tipping his head back to glare at Liam. "You'll not come complaining to me about the state of your rooms. I was quite clear about the arrangement—"

" 'Tis not the rooms, milord. 'Tis me caller."

"Caller?" The notion clearly startled Farnsworth; his hard, beady little eyes grew wide as crowns, then quickly narrowed. "*What* caller?"

"Miss Natalie is her name. I hoped that ye might have a word with her governess—"

"*Governess!*" he spat.

Liam blinked. "I assume she has a governess, what with her father away."

"What?" Farnsworth asked again, incredulous for a moment. But then something seemed to pass over his eyes, and he puffed his cheeks out so far and hard that Liam half expected him to levitate. Yet he remained firmly rooted by his girth, glaring at Liam, his face mottling as the moments ticked past. At last, he said through clenched teeth, "I will speak to my daughter immediately." He hopped up to the next step. "Now if you will excuse me, Captain, you are keeping me from my supper!"

He twirled about, and without looking back, hopped quickly up the steps until he was at the door, which he pounded with his walking stick. After a moment, the door swung open and Miss Agatha appeared. She took Farnsworth's hat and walking cane, and then pressed herself up against the door to give Farnsworth wide enough berth to pass. As she did so, she glanced at Liam, her eyes glazing with her refusal to recognize him, and she shut the door behind the rotund Farnsworth as if she hadn't seen him at all.

Yet Liam hardly noticed the slight, because he was literally reeling from Farnsworth's admission that Natalie was his daughter. *His* daughter! That beautiful little lass belonged to a rigid beast of a man only one step removed from ogre! There was, apparently, no accounting for nature's humor, and with a strong shake of his head, Liam continued on.

Unfortunately, Farnsworth did not speak to his daughter, because she appeared at his door a half hour later. Liam had tossed aside his hat and coat, had unbuttoned his confining waistcoat, unwrapped the stiff neckcloth he despised, and washed his face when he heard a knock on his door. Glancing at his pocket watch, Liam assumed the knock was Follifoot's, come to bring him his supper. But when he opened the door, a diminutive Miss Natalie smiled up at him.

"This is my new frock," she said, holding out the sunny yellow gown for him to see. "Do you like it very much?"

"Ah, for the love of . . ." Liam groaned, rolling his eyes. " 'Tis bonny. Now be a good lass and go to yer father, will ye?"

Natalie blinked big blue eyes. "My father? How shall I do that? He's at sea, you know."

Wise to her now, Liam frowned. "Is he indeed? Well, then, why should Lord Farnsworth claim ye as his own, eh?"

Natalie's face clouded momentarily; but then she shrugged and inched her toe across the threshold. "He's *not* my father," she insisted, and suddenly looked up again, her face brightening. "Shall I sing you the song I learned in my lessons today? *'Oh, where, oh, where is my true loooove, has he gone the way of the morning dooooove—'*"

"Will ye stop that shrieking!" Liam exclaimed, and made the mistake of turning away from the door. Natalie was instantly inside, headed for the plaid he had draped carefully across the chair.

"Now, Natalie," he warned her. "Ye're to run along and leave me be—"

"This is very pretty. Do you ever wrap it around your shoulders?" she asked, stroking the very edge of the woolen fabric.

"NO!"

"In Laria they wear things like this all the time and particularly to balls."

To *balls?* "I thought ye said ye left Laria more than two years ago," he said, grabbing her wrist and moving her hand away from the plaid.

"Oh, yes, but we visit all the time."

A light suddenly dawned in Liam; he folded his arms, gave her a stern look. *"How* many times, then?"

The girl instantly dropped her gaze to the plaid and shrugged. "I don't know, really. Dozens, I should think."

"Dozens, indeed," he drawled. "And where is yer mother, then? Flying like a bird across the sea to Laria?"

"Oh, no," Natalie quickly corrected him. "She's in her bed now. She's very sick."

"*Aaaah* . . . in her bed, is she?"

Natalie suddenly pivoted away from him and the plaid and walked to the window. "Do you think it shall rain *forever?*"

Ah, but Liam had not achieved the rank of captain in the Highland Regiments without having learned a thing or two about deception. "Out with it, then, lass. Is there something ye are no' telling me now?"

She shook her head.

"Perhaps something about yer mother?" he pressed, distantly aware that the approaching footsteps he heard through the open door would be Follifoot. Liam walked to stand beside Natalie at the window. "Perhaps yer mother is no' very sick after all, eh?"

"Oh, no, she's *quite* ill," Natalie insisted. "I mean, *sometimes* she opens her eyes, but only when my father comes home from the sea," she said, as the footfall grew closer. "And then, only for a moment or two, because she misses Father so very much she can hardly bear to lay eyes on him."

"What a tragic tale of love," Liam said with a snort. "Do ye think perhaps 'tis because yer mother really does no' exist but within that wee brain of yers?"

"She exists, truly! But because she's very sick, Father is taking her back to Laria."

"Is that so?" Liam said, his frown growing deeper. "And will she leave her young child here to fend for herself?"

Natalie's smile was thin. "Well . . . she *must*. Because even when she's not very sick, she's . . . she's *crippled*," she whispered.

"NATALIE ELIZABETH HORTENSE FARNS-WORTH!" a woman exclaimed from somewhere behind them, causing both Liam and Natalie to jump a good foot in the air and whirl about to face the door. Liam almost stumbled; Natalie shrank up against him, silent for the first time since he had had the misfortune of meeting her. As was Liam, stone-cold silent, rattled straight out of his wits. He was simply too stunned to speak. He found himself in a catatonic state of staring at perhaps the loveliest woman he had ever clapped eyes on, the angel he had seen before, that day in Belgrave Square with her parasol.

She was standing just inside the door, having come, apparently, from out-of-doors, for she was carrying a coat of sorts draped over her arm and dangling a wet bonnet from long, tapered fingers. Her hair, the color and sheen of corn silk, was bound up in the current fashion on the back of her head, but a long strand of it had worked its way loose and was drifting across her eye. Wearing a gown of white with an overskirt heavily embroidered in tiny roses, cinched high beneath her bosom, she looked exactly how he pictured the angels to be, and he swallowed hard, trying not to gape.

Not that she seemed to notice, so intent was she on removing Natalie from his rooms. "Natalie Elizabeth Hortense, come away from there straightaway! Why in heaven's name are you bothering this poor man? And however did you manage to escape poor Agatha?"

Natalie reluctantly left Liam's side and shuffled forward until she was within her mother's reach. The woman snatched her hand, yanked Natalie to her side, then looked at Liam with Natalie's wide, pale blue eyes, framed in long golden lashes.

And remarkably, those eyes looked at him without seeming to notice his battered face. *Again.* A shy smile slowly spread across her luscious lips as she took a step backward, dragging Natalie with her. *"Oh!"* she exclaimed, a light dawning. "You're . . . my good sir, I must ask your indulgence once more and beg you please forgive my daughter. She's a horrid little thing for running off and I assure you it will not happen again. I am so sorry if she has been a bother."

"No. Ah, no" was all Liam could manage to spit out, so entranced, astonished, and dammit, so very *discombobulated* was he. A million things raced through his mind, not the least of which was that this was Natalie's mother, the same mother that he was quite certain did not exist. Not only did she exist, but she existed in a way that made his mouth go bone dry and his blood race.

"*You*, my dear girl, are in quite a spot of trouble," the woman continued with an affectionate ruffle of Natalie's head. "Please offer your apologies to the gentleman for being such a pest."

"Oh, but he doesn't mind, Mother, truly," Natalie tried.

And incredibly, Liam heard himself say, "Oh, no, I donna mind. She's a bonny lass, she is."

The woman suddenly looked surprised. "Ooh, I hadn't realized you're a *Scot!* How terribly romantic!"

He was slipping—he could literally feel himself *slipping*, melting right there, seeping through the floorboards. "Aye," he managed roughly. "A Scot. From Aberfoyle."

"Aberfoyle. I shall have to find it in the atlas. I beg your forgiveness, Mr. . . . ?"

"Captain," he answered stupidly.

"Captain," she said, her smile widening a bit. "Navy?"

"The Royal Highland Regiments," he quickly corrected her.

"*Ah*," she said appreciatively. "I've read a bit about them. Brave men, they say."

Liam straightened, clasped his hands behind his back and gave her a stiff nod.

She smiled. "Well then, Captain, if you'll excuse us, we'll leave you be. Good evening," she said, and with

Natalie firmly in hand, turned and glided out of his room.

"Captain Lockhart," Liam thought to add, but she had already gone.

He stood there for several moments staring at the door, trying to collect himself, his thoughts still jumbled up by her sudden appearance—no, *existence*. Aye, her existence startled him, but it was his mind and body's fierce reaction to her that was far more startling. Not only was it ridiculously lacking in self-control, but it was frightful for a man who prided himself for his calm bearing. He was no novice when it came to women—he'd had his share of them, to be sure, from one end of the Continent to the other. But in truth, those had been base women of no distinction. Not like *her*. Not a lady. It was a rare event for him to ever be in the company of ladies, save his mother and sister, and each time he found himself in such company, he felt awkward and self-conscious. Ladies, real ladies seemed so . . . so *fragile*. And perfect. The exact opposite of him.

Yet he had certainly *seen* ladies, especially here in London, walking along in their bonnets, each one indistinguishable from the next. But this one—this one was different from the women of quality he had seen on the streets. He'd thought so the moment he had seen her that blustery afternoon, battling her parasol. There was something about her—perhaps her eyes, eyes that looked at him directly without grimacing. Or her perfect smile. A smile that reminded him of the Scottish sun when it rose each morning, all golden and warm and slowly spreading through him.

Whatever it was, it had taken him completely off-guard, had knocked him clean off his bearings, had made mush of his brain and a damned fool of his mouth. Worse, he thought as he moved to shut the door behind her, *far* worse, devastatingly worse, was the fact that if the exquisite creature who had graced his door was indeed Natalie's mother, then she must also be Farnsworth's wife.

That thought made him shudder with revulsion.

Six

With a firm grasp of Natalie's wrist, Ellen Farnsworth was marching the girl up the winding staircase when Lord Farnsworth appeared on the landing before her, his monocle squeezed tightly between folds of pasty flesh so that his dark frown looked hideously lopsided.

"There's the little chit!" he snapped. "She'll chase away my tenants if you don't do something about her!"

Natalie immediately shrank into her mother's side; Ellen put an arm around her shoulders and sighed wearily. "I'll speak with her, sir. You have my word she will not bother him again."

Farnsworth barked a nasty laugh, then leaned forward, peering at her with one enormous eye. "Your *word*, Ellen? Don't promise me anything so worthless!"

Lord God, how she despised him. A thousand retorts rattled about her head, but Ellen bit her tongue, unwilling to have a row on the stairs. She gave Natalie a reassuring squeeze. "If there's nothing else, sir, we should like to retire," she said, moving forward.

"Just see to it that she stays in her rooms!" Farnsworth said sharply, and bobbed aside so that Ellen and Natalie could pass. Ellen did not look at him; she forced Natalie along, pushing her up the stairs ahead of her until they reached the next landing, then took her daughter by the hand again, dragging her quickly along to the suite of rooms they shared. She opened the door to her sitting room, sent Natalie ahead of her, then stepped inside and leaned heavily against the closed door, squeezing her eyes shut for a moment to push back a headache that was beginning to rage.

"I'm sorry, Mother," Natalie murmured tremulously.

Ellen opened her eyes and looked at the girl. "Oh Natalie. What am I to do with you?" she asked sadly, extending her hand. Natalie instantly walked into her embrace, put her arms around her mother's waist, and buried her face in the folds of her gown. Ellen held her tightly, wondered what exactly she *was* to do with her——with both of them, really. They couldn't exist like this for the rest of their lives.

She sighed, ran her hand across the top of Natalie's head. "Darling, you know you are forbidden from entering those rooms or bothering the tenants."

"I'm very sorry, Mother, truly I am. But . . . but the captain really is rather friendly."

Ah, Natalie. This beautiful child, whom she cherished above all else, had a wretched habit of inventing tales and altering the truth, of stealing into the tenants' rooms and going through their things. Abominable behavior, but what could she expect? With no friends to speak of, the girl was desperate for companionship and Agatha, bless her, was hardly a suitable playmate.

"I promise I won't do it again," she said helpfully.

Ellen cupped the girl's chin and turned her face upward. "You must *mean* your promise, Natalie. No more visits to the tenant's rooms. Will you promise me?"

Natalie nodded solemnly.

Ellen kissed her forehead. "Go to your room, then, and write it one hundred times. 'I will not enter the tenant's rooms,' " she said, motioning toward the bedrooms. Natalie sighed, walked slowly to the door.

When she disappeared inside, Ellen walked to the pink-and-white striped silk chaise, tossed her pelisse and bonnet onto it, and moved from there to the windows, where she gazed out across the square at the dreary evening.

Her heart was still pounding.

At first, when she had seen Natalie within his rooms, her heart had seized at the sight of that enormous man with that coarse face towering over Natalie. But she had quickly understood, judging by the way he held himself, that he meant no harm, was more curious of Natalie than anything else. Little wonder, that! Laria and a crippled mother, indeed!

The captain had surprised her on another level, too, after she had recalled their encounter in the park, because he wasn't like the men Farnsworth usually let the rooms to—the previous tenants had been older and decrepit in many ways, usually up from the country for some reason or another, usually alone. The *captain* (Ellen smiled at the memory of how his chest had puffed up with the mention of his rank) was much younger, obviously vibrant and ruggedly strong . . . and a *Scot!* Another surprise, knowing how intolerant Farnsworth could be of the world at large, particularly people who were not of noble English birth. The captain must have offered cash for the let of the rooms, or else the bloody penny-pinching old hypocrite never would have let a Scot into his home.

With a perplexed shake of her head, Ellen turned away from the window and walked from the sitting room into a small adjoining dining room. She paused at the door, surveying the room with a frown. Like most rooms in the mansion, this one was marked by Farnsworth's austerity. Only one painting (a poor rendition of a fox hunt) graced the walls; the sideboard boasted only one service (tarnished silver), and no china or crystal. The table, once polished to a sheen, was dull and scratched. The chairs were in various stages of disrepair, and the silk-covered seats were worn. Not from a lack of funds; Farnsworth was wealthy. He was just a miserable old miser.

Had it not been for the crates of quality furnishings and accoutrements she had brought from the country, the rest of the suite Ellen shared with Natalie would be as barren and devoid of character as this house. Their suite was the one bright spot in it, actually. It was done in soft pastel silks and brocades; thick rugs scattered about the floors warmed the austere rooms. With the exception of any notable pieces of art, which Ellen really didn't miss, they were comfortable. Thank God for small favors, she thought to herself, for that was the only thing about this house or her life that was comfortable.

Yes, well. No point in spending yet another evening dwelling on futile hopes, sliding deeper into misery with each passing hour. Too much of her life had passed laboring from one day to the next, wishing things were different, wishing *she* were different. And she had at last reached the point where she hardly remembered or felt anything anymore—the point at which she'd just as soon be drawn and quartered than fall into the abyss again. So Ellen pressed her lips together, walked to the bellpull, and yanked hard, signaling to the bare-bones staff below that she and Natalie were ready for their evening meal.

Below them, Liam was staring at his evening meal with a mixture of disgust and awe. God only knew what the cook had intended it to be, but the kindest thing Liam could say about it was that it looked and tasted like a batch of gruel gone off. Yet it was something to tide him over until he could leave again under night's dark cloak to look for his cousin and find something decent to eat. Until then, he was a man who lived by a soldier's rules. He ate.

Afterward, while his body attempted to digest the stuff, Liam propped his feet up near the brazier to warm them, and amused himself with thoughts of Natalie's mother, summoning the image of her as she had stood in his door, angelic. Beautiful. Voluptuous. Breasts as soft and full as . . . as goose-down pillows (the most luxurious thing he could conjure). That image inevitably led to other, more provocative thoughts; he imagined her somewhere in this very house, perhaps preparing for a bath (as best he could, being terribly ignorant of how a woman actually prepared for a bath, knowing only that Mared took a ridiculous amount of time in the process). Perhaps *in* her bath. *Ah* . . . now *there* was an image that he could hold on to for quite some time.

Until it became physically uncomfortable to imagine it any longer without taking matters into his own hands, so to speak.

At which point, Liam realized he was acting like a green-horned schoolboy, and thought it time to put himself to more productive endeavors. He went to his knapsack and rummaged about until he found one of several pieces of vellum he had carried to London with him, and the pencil his mother had given him. He wrote a terse letter home to inform her that he had arrived safely in London, and that their plans were moving along smoothly. He did not say more than that, because, first, he was not much of a correspondent, and second, if the letter should somehow be confiscated, it would be perceived as nothing more than an innocent epistle home. He wrote:

Dearest Mother, greetings and salutations from
London. The weather is quite wet. The parks are large

*and green and all proceeds as planned. The buildings
are of stone, but they are blackened with the soot of
many chimneys. I do not care for the food. Devotedly, L.*

Liam studied the contents for a moment, decided
that while it lacked the poetic nature of Griffin's letters,
it was practical, innocuous, and clear. He folded the
vellum, used the single candle Farnsworth had allotted
him to seal it, and tucked it away until the morrow to
post. Having accomplished that small task, Liam
walked to the window and peered outside. Night had
fallen at last, and he was eager to get on with his task
and get out of this ugly town as soon as possible. He
crossed to the basin, washed his face, combed his hair
with his fingers, and retied his neckcloth. Then, Liam
slipped out through the window to the alley, pausing
below to look up at the lights above his rooms, wondering if she was up there.

Seven

❧

Finding Nigel proved to be easier than finding an
elephant in a crowded ballroom.

Liam had ventured out dressed in a suit of clothing
he had borrowed (loosely speaking) from Grif. He wore
a coat of dark blue superfine (too tight in the shoulders), dove-gray trousers (too tight in the legs), and a
waistcoat so foppishly embroidered that Liam feared
someone might actually mistake him for a dandy. But
then again, he reluctantly admitted to himself, he *did*
resemble the other gentlemen milling about London
(not that he *wanted* to look limp-wristed and fastidi-
ously groomed). The only detracting feature was his
hair, which was swept back and long, to his shoulders.
That was because he did not have (nor would he *ever*
have) the proper utensils to *coif* his hair, thank you,
God. But it was not so distracting that he could not
pass for a gentleman of means.

He strolled along St. James and Pall Mall, and the
gentlemen's clubs catering to a privileged clientele
there, paying careful attention to his gait (slowing it
down) and mimicking the English walking style—
leaden and indolent. While it took a bit of going about
and in and out of several clubs, Liam finally found him,
and truthfully, he couldn't have missed Nigel if he had
tried—his cousin had certainly wintered well these last
several years. The buttons of his waistcoat were under

such a strain that Liam feared, should one work its way loose, that it might put someone's eye out.

As he settled in with a Scotch whiskey, neat, Liam smiled. His plan was working beautifully. All he had to do now was put himself in Nigel's path. Then Nigel would see him, believe he had stumbled on his Scottish cousin quite by accident, and inquire as to what he was doing in London. The rest would be child's play. Unfortunately, Liam was soon to discover, getting Nigel to recognize *anyone* was a damn sight harder than finding the old goat, because jolly old Nigel had fallen so far into his bloody cups.

In the first club, Liam positioned himself just at the door so that when his cousin left, he could not help but notice Liam standing there. Indeed, no one else could help but notice—he was the subject of several curious glances as he waited.

Unfortunately, Nigel *didn't* notice Liam there, and in fact, brushed past him so carelessly that Liam was pushed into the wall.

A bit nonplussed by that, Liam had gathered his wits and followed Nigel and his companions to the next club, where they immediately sat down and engaged in a round of cards. Biding his time once again, Liam had a whiskey. Then two. Then a third, rolling his eyes in exasperation as he listened to his cousin's wheezing laughter at every bawdy joke his companions told.

When at last Nigel and his companions decided to quit the establishment, Liam once again positioned himself where Nigel might see him. His cousin came lumbering toward the door directly behind his two companions, and this time actually peered at Liam with watery, bloodshot eyes. But there was no flash of recognition, no hint of anything in residence behind those eyes, and Nigel continued on, lurching for the door.

Blast it! Sighing impatiently, Liam leaned against the

door and watched as his cousin fell out the door (his complete spill stopped only by the bodies of his companions), righted himself, slapped one poor chap on the back, and lunged for his carriage.

As he watched the carriage (listing to one side) pull away, Liam could clearly see meeting his sot of a cousin would require a different strategy. With a shake of his head, Liam headed for his rooms on Belgrave Square.

At noon the next day, Liam was starving, having opted, in spite of his military training, to forgo the dark, foul-smelling shape on his morning plate. Absolutely infuriated by the lack of food in spite of the ridiculous rent he had paid Farnsworth, and literally starving for something good to eat, Liam decided that if he was going to survive his London mission and have enough funds to return home, he was going to have to take matters into his own hands.

With a pistol in one pocket, his *sgian dubh* in his stocking, and a pillow covering attached to his belt, Liam set out, striding purposefully across town, past rows and rows of ornate town homes and into the lush green paths of Hyde Park. He walked past trees and benches and play areas where children frolicked. He joined the English on the main promenade, hardly noticing their curious looks in his direction as he strode, arms swinging, eyes straight ahead, his stomach roaring with hunger. He kept walking until he came upon a little pond he had discovered several days earlier, and a smile broke his stoic face. There they were, the four geese he had seen previously swimming languidly across the pond. *Breakfast.*

Oblivious to anything else around him, Liam slipped his pistol from his belt, waited until the geese neared the edge of the pond. Sighting the healthiest of the four, he fired. The three surviving geese immediately set off in a racket of flapping wings and honking beaks as he ran down to the pond, splashing headlong into the water before the dead goose could sink or float away. He caught it up by the neck, was inordinately pleased to see that he had managed to shoot the thing so that most of the meat was still intact. Aye, she'd make a delectable meal!

Liam turned, sloshing his way back to the edge of the pond.

Only then did he notice that several people had come running at the sound of gunshot, and now stood, gaping, as he bent down on the pond's edge and quickly began to pluck the feathers. Let them gawk. Bloody English had never gone hungry, was that it?

"I beg your pardon, sir! What do you think you are doing?"

Liam glanced up at the sound of the effeminate male voice, his gaze landing on a thin little man who peered at him through wire-rimmed spectacles. Behind him stood a woman gripping a parasol as if she intended to use it on him.

"You can't just go about killing the geese!" the man insisted.

Liam looked around. "I didna see a posting forbidding it."

The man lifted his chin. "Clearly, sir, this is *not* a hunting park, nor has it been for more than one hundred years! I daresay there's no *posting,* but I should think common sense and decency would dictate your behavior!"

"A desire for decent food dictates me behavior, sir. How can ye expect a man to live on the rubbish ye English call food?"

The man gasped his outrage; he looked at his companion, then at Liam again. "You are *poaching* sir! You leave me no choice but to summon the authorities!"

Bloody hell. He'd not be able to clean his goose without an audience, apparently. Exasperated, Liam muttered a little Scottish saying about the English under his breath, shoved the half-plucked, oozing goose into his pillow casing and stood.

The Englishman took two quick steps back as he peered up at Liam.

"I'll take me goose elsewhere, then, if it bothers ye so," he said gruffly, and slinging the bag over his shoulder, disappeared up the path, leaving an errant feather to drift between him and the gawking onlookers.

Liam marched back to Belgravia, but not without a small detour to the markets, where he purchased a head of cabbage for a half-pence. With the cabbage in one hand, the goose dangling over his shoulder, and his mouth watering with the thought of cooked bird, Liam strode through town, taking the most direct route to the Farnsworth house, directly across the middle of Belgrave Square. His stride was long and urgent, so urgent, in fact, that he almost walked right over little Natalie when she suddenly darted from behind a hedge, her bright red cape streaming behind her.

"Good afternoon, Captain!" she called brightly, skipping toward him. Her hair, he noticed, lit by the early afternoon sun as it was, looked as silken as her mother's. "Where are you going?"

Aaah, bloody rotten hell, then! Liam stopped. Closed his eyes. Sighed heavenward. God intended for him to starve, apparently—he felt near to death he was so famished, and the last thing he wanted was a conversation with a child. *This* child in particular. He lowered his head. "My destination is hardly yer concern, is it, lass?" He attempted to step around her, but Natalie moved, too, blocking his path.

"Do you know where *I* am going? To the milliner."

Liam had no idea what a milliner was, and furthermore, he hardly cared. His stomach was roiling, and he still had to dress the damn bird, no thanks to that spit of an Englishman and his tender feelings. "Splendid," he drawled. "Now if ye'd move out of me way—"

"I am going to be fitted for a new hat . . . for the Christmas pageant in Laria," she said, walking in a tight little circle before him, round and round, "and *I* will be one of the actors."

"Bloody grand, that is," he said to the little dervish. "But if ye please, *suithad!*"

Natalie paused in her circling to squint up at him. "What does *that* mean?"

"It means 'Go now and be off with ye!' " he said, gesturing impatiently for her to run along, and as he did so, he noticed two girls on the path walking toward them, a woman trailing lazily behind. They looked to be about the same age as Natalie. "Ah, there now, some children to play with ye," he said, and pointed at the girls.

But as Natalie followed his gaze up the walkway, she instantly stepped back, so that she was standing directly in front of Liam. "I . . . I don't know them," she mumbled.

The child was missing the point. His patience now gone the way of his stomach, Liam clamped a hand firmly on her shoulder. "All right then, ye little bugger, run on, then! I've a goose and a cabbage and I'm near to starving, I am!"

But Natalie didn't seem to hear him; annoyed, Liam groaned and looked up at the girls walking toward them . . . but he noticed that they were walking slowly, their hands shielding their mouths as they shared their whispers, their eyes full of laughter. It took him a moment to understand that whatever the whispering, they were laughing at Natalie. And if he had any doubt, Natalie pressed up against him, and her little hand reached up to touch his on her shoulder.

Confused, Liam looked at the girls again. They were walking and giggling in a way that seemed derisive, and worse, the woman walking behind seemed oblivious to them, examining rosebushes along the path as she was. Why anyone would laugh at a lass as bonny as Natalie, Liam could not begin to imagine, and surprisingly, it angered him. He instantly felt the indignation he had felt as a child when children would taunt Mared about that ridiculous curse. All right, then, he'd just ask the children why they were laughing, have a little chat. But as they neared, Natalie suddenly bolted, disappearing into a gap in the hedge, and the two girls burst into gleeful laughter.

Liam looked at the hedge, then the two girls, who had scurried on. He could not begin to interpret the children's actions, but he did understand one thing quite clearly—they had upset Natalie, and without thinking, he walked through the hedge after her.

Only he was larger than the gap, and it took him a moment to push through the hedge and out the other side. He just saw Natalie's red cape disappear around another hedge. *Damn it all to hell, then.* Liam strode after her, rounding the same bend as she had, but instantly and awkwardly drew up at the sight of Natalie's mother sitting on a bench, quietly reading. Natalie ran and slipped in beside her mother, then laid her head on her shoulder.

Liam froze where he stood, paralyzed by the sight of that bonny woman again, and suddenly filled with indecision. He looked down at the cabbage he held and immediately decided to turn and retreat the way that he had come with all due haste before she—

"Captain?"

Damn. With a wince, he looked up; her blue eyes instantly arrested him on the spot. *Run!* his mind screamed, but Liam stood like a deaf-mute, staring doltishly at her fair face. He shoved the cabbage under his arm, looked right, then left, but saw there was no easy, polite method of escape. His palms were sweating now, and he adjusted the bag on his shoulder, shifted the cabbage again.

"Good afternoon, sir," she said.

Jesus, Mary, and Joseph! Liam swallowed and growled, "Good day."

She smiled that bloody gorgeous smile of hers that made him feel warm and golden again, put the book aside, and stood, leaving Natalie to sit staring morosely into space. "I see Natalie found you again. I thank you for seeing her safely back to me. I confess she quite got away—I was rather absorbed in my book."

Liam put his free hand on his waist. Then dropped it. Then took the cabbage from beneath his arm and held it. "Ah. I . . . *see,*" he said with a slight nod. I *see?* What sort of ridiculous response was that? He cleared his throat and looked toward the hedge again. *Think! Think, think . . .*

"Do you walk in our little park often?" she asked, and Liam jerked his gaze to her again.

"Ah . . . no. 'Tis the path to town. For me, that is. I mean, considering where it is I go." *Ach, ye imbecile! Shut yer gullet, then!*

"Ah." She smiled, put a hand to the side of her gown and ran her palm across it. He noticed her fingers were long and delicate—

"Well. I shan't keep you from your tasks," she said, and with another quick, alluring smile, carefully resumed her seat and picked up her book.

Liam shifted the bag with the goose in it, dislodging a feather from his shoulder. He told himself to turn and walk away, but his mouth opened of its own accord. "I beg yer pardon, madam," he blurted, "but might I ask, where is Laria, then?"

"Pardon?"

Had he said it incorrectly? "Ah . . . *LAA-ree-aah,*" he said again, enunciating carefully.

Natalie's mother looked at him in surprise, then at the heavens as she shook her head, muttering something unintelligible before she turned a charming smile to him again. "I *do* beg your pardon, sir. I'm afraid my daughter has quite an imagination. Laria exists only in her mind."

Only in her . . . *Ach,* what a bloody fool he was! Strangely, he could feel a curious heat rushing up his neck. He should have known, what with the crippled mother and all that. The beauty was smiling, clearly amused by his foolishness. That was *not* an image he would have linger, so Liam took an uneasy step toward her, smiling thinly. "Then I should presume there will be no Christmas pageant, eh?"

She laughed, tossing her head back, drawing attention to the smooth curve of her neck. "A Christmas pageant? Did she say such a thing? Goodness, Natalie!" she exclaimed, smiling down at the girl. Natalie scooched further down on the bench.

Liam took another step forward. "And . . . a milliner—more fantasy, is it?"

"Oh, no, the milliner is quite real, fortunately," she said, and laughed again, a sound so low and rich that it gave Liam goose bumps (the goose notwithstanding). "The milliner fashions hats," she explained, "but we mean to only *look* at them," she added, looking sternly at Natalie for a moment. She smiled up at Liam again. "Captain . . . I beg your pardon, but have you a name, sir?"

"Lockhart. Captain Lockhart."

"How do you do, Captain Lockhart? Ellen Farnsworth."

Ellie. A lovely name for a lovelier woman. It suited

her, he thought. " 'Tis a pleasure to make yer acquaintance," he said properly, bowing low, cabbage in hand. And it was indeed a very special pleasure, he thought, straightening again to gaze at her smiling blue eyes— until he realized he was gawking, and instantly took a step backward, a wee bit flustered. God blind him, what was the matter with him? He was not the sort to be so easily unsettled! He was a Highland soldier, an assassin, a man with nerves of steel! "There ye are. I suppose I ought to be on my way."

"You've sprung a bit of a leak," she said pleasantly.

Horrified, he blinked. "I beg yer pardon, I've done *what?*"

"You seem to be leaking," she said again, nodding politely to the bag he was holding.

Liam looked down, saw it was the forgotten goose that was leaking (*not* him, thankfully!), but felt his heart nonetheless climb right to his throat. Marvelous, this was. He was a rustic bumpkin who carried his food about in a pillow casing and a cabbage in his hand! He stared at the blood dripping to the ground and wondered what a true gentleman might say in an awkward moment like this. *Righto, so I have.* Or *Bugger me, look there, will you?* Liam remembered his training—when one is in a situation from which one cannot cleanly extract oneself, one should retreat with all due haste— and took one involuntary step backward. "Well then. Good day to ye."

"Do enjoy your day, sir. It's rare to have so much sunshine this time of year," Ellie said, looking at the blue sky with a smile on her face.

"Aye," he said stupidly, and pivoted sharply, striding instantly in the opposite direction, as fast as his legs would carry him, the goose leaving a thin red trail behind him.

When he reached his rooms and shut the door firmly

behind him, he realized he had been clutching the bag so hard that his fingers had frozen in a cramp.

What in hell was the matter with him? He was acting as if he'd never seen a woman before! Disgusted, Liam stalked across the room and tossed the bird in the bag into the basin, walked to the small brazier, stirred the coals from the morning's fire, and added more. As he waited for the coals to heat, he returned to the basin, took out his dagger, and began to clean the bird, plucking her feathers in a sharp, jerking motion.

A half hour later, he had removed all his clothes but the buckskins, had eaten his cabbage, and was roasting his bird over the brazier coals. When he finished his meal, and was at last fully sated, he cleaned up best he could, dumping what was left of the bird into the bag. He wandered to the lumpy bed and fell onto it, thinking about Ellie.

He must have fallen asleep, for the next thing he knew the smell of entrails was quite strong, permeating everything in the room. Liam glanced at his pocket watch—it was late afternoon. He had slept for more than two hours! A bloody waste of time—if he wanted to find Nigel before the chap fell into his cups again, he'd best be about it!

However, the stench in the room was unbearable. Who knew when Follifoot might come around to remove the remains? Liam took the foul-smelling bag to the window. He opened the double panes, leaned over, and looked at the mews below, spotting the rubbish heap he had noticed earlier. He lifted the bag, gave it a good swing, and watched it fall, landing atop the heap. Satisfied, he began to pull inside the window, but a movement caught his eye, and he leaned out, looked to the right. There on the walk in front of the house was Farnsworth, tottering off on his little feet, wrapped in a cloak.

Gone gambling for the evening, he supposed. Behind him, Miss Agatha appeared, scurrying across the square, trotting off to a life heaven knew where before she had to return to Hades House the following morning.

Liam pulled himself back in and shut the window, staring at the dingy, cracked pane for a moment as a very dangerous and ill-advised thought played at the corner of his mind. A thought so ludicrous, so absolutely preposterous, that it was a damn disgrace to the soldier that he was. After all, he had his work cut out for him with Nigel and the English Lockharts, didn't he? Losing his focus could only compromise his mission; how many times had that been drilled into him? Single-minded, focused on a task. Isn't that what they had taught him in the military?

He shook his head, returned to the basin, and used what little water there was left in the ewer to clean up. He dressed in more of Grif's foppish clothes, combed his hair, and washed his mouth, preparing to set out for the evening.

When the familiar knock came to his door, he opened it, stepping aside so Follifoot could bring in whatever foul thing they had served up that night. As usual, Follifoot was silent as he passed by, carrying a tray laden with something that smelled remarkably like raw haggis.

Liam picked up his coat, slung it over one arm. "Be a good lad and clean up the basin, will ye?" he asked, and walked out, smiling at the shock on Follifoot's face. He proceeded down the long corridor, turned at the bottom of the winding staircase toward the door, one foot in front of the other, on his way out to find his cousin.

But the foot came down and stopped dead, immobile. Glued.

Slowly, Liam turned and peered up the winding staircase, leaning as far to one side as he could to see around the bend. Nothing. Not a sight of anything or anyone, not even a peep. His fingers drummed impatiently against his thigh. *Lunacy, sheer lunacy!* Of course now he knew why Farnsworth had forbade him from climbing those stairs. If *he* were going to leave a wife as bonny as Ellie here alone, he would not only forbid it, he'd put an iron gate across the bloody staircase. Armed guards. Hell, he'd not leave her, which just proved once again that Farnsworth was a stupid bastard.

Aye, better to leave well enough alone, he told himself, even if he *did* have a burning need to show her that he was not some rustic bumpkin, contrary to all appearances thus far. He had given Farnsworth his word. Besides, what should he care what she thought of him? She was a married woman, a mother, and English, for chrissakes, a member of the Quality and all that, the last sort of woman who should ever spark an interest in him. Actually, he had no business thinking about her at all. At *all.*

Except that he couldn't seem to get her out of his mind.

Just go, then! Disgusted with himself, Liam snapped back around, faced the door, and reminded himself that he had to find Nigel before the goat drank his weight in whiskey, or else he would lose another entire day. But the sound of Follifoot at the basin drifted down the corridor, rattling Liam in his indecision, and suddenly, in a moment of sheer insanity, he pivoted on his heel again, looked up the winding staircase, and darted stealthily upward.

Eight

❧

When Follifoot brought tea, Ellen informed him that she and Natalie would not require supper, to which Follifoot smiled sympathetically. Damn Farnsworth, but the old man was so very tight with his precious pound sterling it was a wonder he could get anyone to cook for them. *This* cook, whoever she might be, had to be the worst yet. The food was bland and nondescript, and in the most unfortunate of cases, inedible. Thank God for Agatha—the dear woman had taken pity on poor Natalie and what she called the new cook's tripe. Once or twice a week, she prepared a delicious meal for them. This evening, the smell of roasted beef wafted through the suite of rooms, causing Ellen's mouth to water.

Ellen walked to the room adjoining the sitting room, where Natalie was hard at work on a new drawing (to add to the hundreds she had already made). She paused, peeked over her daughter's shoulder, and saw that this one was like most of the others—a damsel in distress, a princess locked in a tower, awaiting the knight who would come and rescue her.

Just like the two of them.

"Agatha has roasted a beef for us. We'll dine when you've washed your hands."

Natalie frantically began to color one part of her castle, not ready to put it away just yet. "One minute more, Mother, please?"

"A minute more, then it's up to wash your face and comb your hair," Ellen agreed, and brushed her hand across the top of the girl's head. She left her daughter then, in her world of drawings and one-act plays, all of them about a lonely princess in a tower.

Ellen went to her dressing room and surveyed her gowns. It really didn't matter if she dressed for supper or not, since it was only she and Natalie, but she stubbornly refused to give in to the hopelessness of their virtual exile, and insisted on carrying on as if they were indeed out in society. She chose the blue silk her sister Eva had given her. Like all the gowns Eva gave her, it was a little snug in the bodice, but it was very pretty, and frankly, Ellen could use something to brighten her day. This was the part of the evening she hated most, dressing alone, looking at herself in the mirror, reminded that she was twenty-eight years old and shut up like an old widow.

Please, God, something had to change. Something. Anything! But what? And how? Those questions beat a steady rhythm through every thought and every dream—even now, as she let loose her hair, methodically brushed it, and wrapped it in a simple chignon, it played in her mind until she couldn't see anything but hopelessness staring back at her.

Hopeless, yes. But then she'd think of Natalie, whose stories grew more fantastic with time, and she felt a keener sense of urgency to find a way out. It mattered little for herself. She had long since passed the point of tears—they simply weren't good enough for the sort of pain she felt inside. But for Natalie, she could not, *would* not, allow them to live like this for the rest of their lives. She would not allow Natalie to end up like her, alone. Dead. No hope of happiness.

God in heaven, her impotence was choking her.

Ellen stood abruptly before she drowned in it. She

went to gather Natalie, who was still working on her drawing of the princess in the tower. After some cajoling, she finally convinced Natalie it was time for her supper, and helped the girl change her apron, wash her face, and comb her hair.

Together, they opened the door of the austere dining room and instantly heard a scratching sound.

"It's the mouse," Natalie opined.

"Wretched little thing," Ellen muttered, disgusted. The very thought of a mouse in her suite made her skin crawl. "Must be starving, too, as often as it comes round. Please set the plates, Natalie," she said, gesturing toward the sideboard where a few plates were neatly stacked. "I'm going to find him," she added, picking up a poker.

"Don't hurt him!" Natalie cried.

"I won't," Ellen lied, and walked out into the corridor. She paused, listening, and thought she heard something in the old sitting room across from their dining area, which Agatha used for her sewing. She walked into that room, looked around at the cloth strewn about and the pair of silver shears Agatha had proudly shown her one day. Ellen picked up the shears, turned them over in her hand, and wondered what they would bring on High Street.

And just as suddenly, she dropped the shears. What was she now, a thief? Disgusted, Ellen turned her back on the shears and walked out, the mouse forgotten.

When she entered the dining room, Natalie was sitting patiently at the table. "Did you find him?"

"No," Ellen said.

"Good!" Natalie exclaimed, clapping, as Ellen put the poker aside to uncover the dish Agatha had left. Roasted beef, leeks, and potatoes . . . it smelled heavenly. She dipped the ladle into the dish, put some on Natalie's plate, then her own. Ellen looked at her daughter and asked, "Would you please say grace?"

Natalie nodded, clasped her hands together and bowed her head. "Dearest God," she said softly. "Bless us our bounty and Miss Agatha for bringing it. And please find us a new place to live. Amen."

And please let me never think of stealing from Agatha again, Ellen thought. *Please, God. Amen.*

Natalie picked up her spoon, dipped the edge of it into the beef. "Did you ever know any princesses, Mother?" she asked.

"Just you, darling," Ellen said, reaching for her spoon. A muffled sound in the corridor caught her attention, and she lifted her head. The mouse again.

"I'm going to be a princess someday. Do you know the story of the princess in the tower? She lived there for ten years, and no one knew it, except her father, but he was a king and he was a very mean man."

"Mmm," Ellen said, tasting the beef, the excellent flavor spoiled only by the sound of the mouse again. She sighed wearily; Farnsworth wouldn't pay for a rat catcher unless a rat found its way to *his* door.

"And he wouldn't let her out of the tower because he didn't want anyone to marry her. But one day, she put her head out the window and looked all around, and—"

"Don't forget to eat, darling," Ellen gently reminded her, and Natalie quickly put a spoonful in her mouth.

"The princess looked all around, and she could see cows and sheep and donkeys and dogs, and . . ."

"Cats?"

"Cats!" Natalie exclaimed, and put another spoonful in her mouth as she considered that, before she finally shook her head. "No. She didn't see any cats," she said definitively. "But every day she put her head out the window to have a look around, and *one* day, she saw a man on a horse, and she waved to him, and she said, '*Good day, good daa-aaay!*' "

Another sound from the corridor, and Ellen put her spoon down, stood resolutely from her chair. "Did the man see her?" she asked as she surreptitiously picked up a poker from the hearth.

Caught up in her story and oblivious to her mother's actions, Natalie nodded eagerly as Ellen walked calmly to the corridor door. "Yes! He saw her and he thought she was the most beautiful girl he'd ever seen!"

"Ah," Ellen muttered absently, gripping the poker to give the mouse a good what-for, and abruptly threw open the door, but was so startled by the shadowy figure of a large man that she shrieked, dropping the poker with a loud clatter on the bare floor. Behind her, Natalie shrieked, too, and dropped her spoon onto her plate.

"I can explain, I can!"

What was this? The *captain?* Incredulous, Ellen put her hand over her wildly beating heart and peered out into the dim corridor to make certain it was him. "Captain Lockhart, what do you think you are about?" she demanded hotly.

"I can explain, I swear it," he said, looking very sheepish.

"Captain *Lockhart!*" Natalie squealed with delight.

"Then by all means, *do* so," Ellen snapped, ignoring her daughter. "Are you in the habit of sneaking about a ladies' suite?"

His green eyes widened with shock; Ellen couldn't be entirely certain, but she thought he even blushed.

"What? *Sneaking . . . ?* Lord God, *no,* of course no'! I am a *captain* in the Highland Regiments of the Royal Army in service to His Majesty, the king! I would never do such a thing!"

He declared it so loudly and emphatically that Ellen couldn't help but believe him. Yet there he stood. "Then *what,* pray, are you doing at the door of my dining room?"

The captain bit his lower lip, and for a moment he

reminded Ellen of a giant little boy. "In truth, I . . . I gave me word to his lordship that I'd no' come up those stairs, but I . . . I . . ." His voice trailed off, his brows dipped in confusion, and he suddenly jerked his gaze to the room behind her. "What's this smell, then?" he asked, peering over Ellen's shoulder, trying to see into the dining room.

The beef. *Of course!* The poor man had been subjected to the cook's fare, too—he likely was starving. Ellen glanced over her shoulder at the large soup tureen. "So you've sampled our haute cuisine, I take it?"

He sighed. "I'm afraid I've had the bloody misfortune, indeed." He caught himself, coloring slightly at his curse, but Ellen laughed. It *was* a bloody misfortune!

Standing there in his overcoat and looking rather abashed, the captain tried not to look at the tureen. "I beg yer pardon and yer forgiveness, madam. I didna mean to startle ye so," he said, his gaze now falling to the poker lying on the floor between them. "I didna mean to climb the stairs a'tall—"

"It's quite all right, sir. I understand completely, I assure you—I'm afraid we haven't had much luck keeping a cook in our employ," she said, stooping to retrieve the poker. "Fortunately, Miss Agatha has taken pity on my daughter and brings us a complete supper every now and again to spare us the awful rot we are served. I assume the scent of her roasted beef wafted its way down to you?"

"*Beef?*" he asked in a reverent tone.

"Mother, he must have some!" Natalie insisted, coming to Ellen's side to tug on her gown. "Please say he might!"

Ellen looked at the captain, who was now staring at the poker she held as if he wasn't quite sure what to make of it. It occurred to her that even with that rather jagged scar, he was really a handsome man, in a rough, Highland sort of way. In fact, in spite of his rather mean looks and his frank manner of speech, she had the sense that he was really a gentle giant. She rather liked this Scot, and it was no secret that Natalie certainly did.

This Scot, on the other hand, seemed to be growing more uncomfortable by the moment, and abruptly put a hand on the nape of his neck and stepped back. "I beg yer pardon, I do—"

"Please stay, Captain!" Natalie pleaded. "I drew a picture. Would you like to see my picture?" Naturally, she didn't wait for a response, but turned and ran for her picture so fast that Ellen could hardly stop her.

She smiled at the captain, silently debating whether or not she *dared* invite him in, for Farnsworth would surely toss them out in the street if he discovered the captain here. But then again, Farnsworth was gone for the evening. How would he know? Follifoot would not come up again tonight. And the captain *was* a rather intriguing fellow. But he must have sensed her debate, for he stepped back. "You mustn't mind her, of course," Ellen said quickly.

"No, no, I . . ."

"I would invite you to try some of the beef, but you look dressed to go out."

That drew a suspicious glance from the captain, but when she merely lifted a curious brow, he looked down at his clothes, as if he had no idea what he was wearing until that very moment. "*Oh*. Aye, aye . . ."

"Ah. Well, then." It was a foolish idea to begin with. Deadly, really. "Perhaps the next time Agatha—"

"But I'm no' expected for a time yet," he quickly interjected, and glanced up at her again. "The beef . . . *ach*, the truth is, the beef, it smells heavenly."

Ellen smiled broadly. Damn Farnsworth after all. "Then you simply must come in and have a plate of it."

"Oh, no, I really shouldna—are ye certain, then? I'd no' be intruding on yer family supper?"

"Of course not! It's only Natalie and me, and I think you know how *she* feels," Ellen said, laughing, and if he had any doubts, Natalie came bursting through the opposite door at that moment, her drawing clutched tightly in her hand. She rushed to stand in front of the captain and thrust the picture up to him, stopping just short of actually punching him in the nose with it.

"It's a princess," she said breathlessly.

The captain reared back, took the drawing, and squinted to carefully consider it. He nodded thoughtfully, said, "A fine princess she is, lass. None bonnier." He handed the drawing back to Natalie, who clutched it against her chest and looked up at her mother, beaming with pleasure.

It was so rare to see such a smile from Natalie that Ellen's heart tipped a little.

She gently pushed Natalie toward her chair. "Please do come in, Captain. We'd be very much honored to share our supper with you." She stood aside to give him entry. "And please do make yourself quite comfortable. But I must warn you," she said with a grimace, as he dipped his head and stepped across the threshold, "I'm afraid we've a small rodent who visits the dining room almost as frequently as we do."

"A mouse, eh?"

"I can't seem to catch the wretched creature and be rid of it," Ellen said apologetically, shutting the door behind him. "Natalie, will you make a place setting for our guest?" She gestured toward a chair directly across from where Natalie was sitting. The captain looked at it, then at Ellen, and hesitantly shrugged out of his coat.

Ellen immediately took the heavy garment and draped it across the nearest chair, then walked to the head of the table. From the corner of her eye, she watched as the captain moved woodenly toward the chair she had indicated, then sat gingerly, managing to wedge his large frame between the table and the small seat. Natalie skipped around the table to where he sat, bringing his plate and spoon, which she set directly in front of him. And then, without warning, she threw her arms around him and gave him a big hug.

"Natalie!" Ellen cried.

The captain smiled thinly, reached up, and patted her arm. "There now, lass," he said, *"Suithad."*

Much to Ellen's great surprise, Natalie let go and walked to her seat, as if she understood what the captain had said.

Baffled, she leaned across the table and ladled some beef onto his plate. "What was that you said . . . what language?" she asked as she set the plate in front of him.

"Gàidhlig . . . and a little Scots, I suppose," he said with a shrug, watching her, his hands folded tightly in his lap.

Ellen sat, put her napkin in her lap. The captain picked up the one Natalie had lain next to his plate and did the same.

"That's very interesting."

He nodded absently as he stared at her plate. Rather odd behavior, she thought, and picked up her spoon. The captain instantly picked his up. "Please," she said, nodding toward his plate, and dipped her spoon into her beef.

The captain did exactly the same, carefully took a bite of the beef, then closed his eyes, savoring it.

Natalie laughed.

The captain opened his eyes and looked at her. "Laugh if you will, wee one, but ye donna understand a man's hunger." No sooner were the words out of his mouth than he glanced at Ellen.

Ooh, he had not meant *that,* she told herself, but felt herself color nonetheless, and focused on her food. "So . . . are you in London for long, sir?"

The captain dug his spoon in the beef again and took a healthy bite of it. "Canna say, exactly."

She waited for him to say more, but he kept eating, as if he hadn't done so for days. She poured him a glass of wine and remarked, "You said you hailed from Aberfoyle. I was wondering, where is that, exactly?"

"Ah, she's north of Glasgow."

"Is it very pretty there?" Natalie asked.

The captain stopped in his devouring of the soup to consider her question. "Not as bonny as Laria, I'd wager, but a lovely hamlet all the same."

"And what did you do in Aberfoyle?" Ellen continued.

The captain blinked. *"Do?"*

"Did you have an occupation, sir? I mean, of course, before your military career?"

"No," he said, quickly shaking his head. "The family . . . me father, he's the laird. We live on the land. On the old Lockhart estate, that is, north of Aberfoyle, on the banks of Loch Chon." At Ellen's blank look, he put down his spoon. "Loch Chon. She's a wee bit north of Loch Ard." Ellen had no idea what he was saying and shook her head. "You donna know?" he asked, incredulous. *"Mi Diah,* The Trossachs is the most beautiful place on God's earth!"

"Is it really? Natalie and I have not traveled much. Perhaps you could tell us?"

The captain rolled his eyes, placed his spoon carefully next to his plate, then braced his hands against the edge of the table. For a long moment, he looked at the ceiling, as if uncertain quite where to start.

" 'Tis truly beautiful, on me life. I will no' do her justice, I know. But the hills, they bleed into Loch Chon, with trees so thick they look like the sweep of a lady's ball gown, all purple and green and gold. And the water, 'tis very clear, like crystal, yet so dark a man canna see his own arm. And the hills, with the winter snows, stand majestic above the loch." He lowered his gaze and looked at Natalie. "At Loch Chon, where me family lives, ye can smell the green and the grass when the rains come. It's fresh, then, like the world has been washed and come round to a new beginning. And then ye look up, and ye see a sky as blue as yer eyes, lass, and a night as black as India ink, with stars that sparkle like gems against it. And just when ye think it could no' be more beautiful than that, the moon, she rises like the Lady of the Loch, hangs full and ripe above yer head, just waiting to be plucked." As he spoke, he lifted his hand upward, as if the moon were indeed within his grasp.

Entranced, Natalie followed his gaze up.

But the captain lowered his hand and casually picked up his spoon. " 'Tis a bonny place, then," he said matter-of-factly, and shoved another hearty spoonful of beef into his mouth.

Neither Ellen nor Natalie spoke for a moment, until Natalie murmured sincerely, "It sounds like Laria. Pretty and green and clean . . ."

The captain suddenly looked up, turned his head toward the door.

". . . and there is lots of sunshine—much more than here in London," Natalie blithely continued as the captain suddenly came to his feet.

Ellen put her spoon down. "Captain? Is something wrong?"

He put a finger to his lips, moved quickly and gracefully for a man his size, then stopped again, his head cocked, listening.

"Actually, it never rains in Laria. Except in the spring before the flowers bloom. But that's really all," Natalie continued, staring off into space as her mind conjured up her imaginary kingdom.

The captain moved again, toward the door, then

froze. Ellen's heart seized—she imagined Farnsworth on the other side of the door and felt a jolt of panic.

"And the summers are nice and warm and the birds sing all the time and—"

The captain moved so quickly that Ellen scarcely realized what he was doing before the sound of a loud *whap* startled Natalie out of her recitation and propelled Ellen to her feet with a gasp. The captain bent over, scooped something up, then turned around, his fist closed. "Mouse," he announced, obviously pleased with himself.

Natalie shrieked, clamped her hand over her mouth in horror.

"You *stomped* the mouse to death?" Ellen exclaimed, just as horrified.

The captain looked at Natalie, then Ellen, his expression confused. "Aye," he drawled, then looked at Natalie again. "What, then? Ye wanted to *keep* it?" he asked, incredulous, and groaned loudly when Natalie began to wail.

Nine

❧

With the dead mouse quickly put out of sight in his pocket, two females gaping at him in raw disbelief, and really, being quite stuffed to the gills on goose and beef, it seemed as good a time as any to take his leave, so Liam grabbed up his overcoat.

Natalie was looking up at him as he shrugged into his coat, both hands clamped across her mouth, her eyes wide with shock, which, he thought irritably, begged the question of why exactly they should go around complaining about the *radan* if they didn't want it removed from the premises? And how did they propose he do that, if not by the boot?

"I beg yer pardon, Natalie, lass. I didna understand ye were so attached to the, er . . . mouse."

Still wide-eyed, Natalie looked at her mother, who, regrettably, looked almost as horrified. Bloody hell, then, he'd made quite a blunder, had he not? Just proved that he should never have climbed those stairs, damn fool that he was.

"I, ah . . . I should thank you," Natalie's mother said uncertainly, but she didn't sound as if she really wanted to thank him at all.

"Aye," Liam grunted as he took a giant step backward, toward the door. "I should be on me way, then."

"But . . . but you didn't finish your meal, Captain,"

she said, looking at his plate, which was, by anyone's standard, near to empty.

"I thank ye kindly for the hospitality, and in particular, the most excellent beef," he said, bowing sharply. "But I regret to say I am expected elsewhere."

Natalie's mother nodded, folded her hands in front of her. Knuckles white as snow, he noticed. "Thank you for joining us. It was quite, ah . . . lovely. And thank you for . . . well . . . you know. *That*," she said, glancing at his pocket.

But he had thought she had *wanted* it gone! "Ye've been too kind, truly ye have," he said, groping for the door behind his back and swinging it open.

"Please. Think nothing of it."

Would that he were so fortunate. Would that he could forget ever setting foot on those stairs, but something told him this little impromptu supper and his slaying of the mouse would be on his mind for quite some time to come. "Well, then, I wish ye a good evening," he said, and backed out the door, shutting it quickly in case she thought to say more. Then he turned and strode quickly to the curving staircase, feeling like a wayward school lad as he paused on the top step to listen for any sound below. When he was convinced there was none, he hurried down the faded carpet of the steps, across the landing of what seemed to be an empty first floor, and down to the main foyer. He paused there, cocking his head first to one side, then the other, listening carefully. Quiet as a kirk on Monday.

Assured that no one saw him sneaking down from the floors above, Liam straightened the lapels of his coat and strode outside, pausing to toss the mouse carcass into the shrubs that lined the front of the house before jogging down the steps to the street and square below.

He marched across the square and wandered up the few streets to Hyde Park, where several hacks were gathered, but opted for the more austere and prudent form of travel (his feet), and hied himself across Mayfair to St. James. There, he slowed to the lazier, English pace as he looked for his cousin among the dozens of men who went in and out of the gentlemen's clubs along St. James and Pall Mall.

There was no sign of Nigel as yet. Liam checked his pocket watch, saw that it was still early—he might still catch the old sot before he drank his weight in ale. With his hands clasped nonchalantly behind his back, he strolled up St. James Street like all the Englishmen, peering into different windows, trying to appear interested. But in truth his mind was on Ellie (as he had named her in his imagination). *Diah,* she was beautiful, as beautiful as any woman he'd ever seen ... or dreamed of, which actually constituted a much larger group of women. She reminded him of the French actress he had once seen in Rouen. That woman had long blond hair, skin as fair as a new bairn's, eyes as blue as a robin's egg. He'd only seen her for a moment as she crossed the cobblestones in the company of a high-ranking British officer, but she had glanced over her shoulder and smiled, and for many nights after that, Liam had dreamed that she smiled at him.

He had thought there was no one bonnier. Until he'd seen Ellie, of course, with her smile as bright as a thousand stars, her skin as smooth and rich as butter cream, and her eyes as crystal blue as an early morning sky. Unfortunately, each time he looked at her, his brain shriveled up to a bean and he lost the ability to use his tongue. It was one of those rare moments in life he wished he had a wee bit of Griffin in him. Grif knew how to charm a lady—not he. No, he'd never been a ladies' man, had never been in the company of ladies long enough to know what to *do*. Aye, but he was a *soldier*, a man who made his living in the pursuit and destruction of the enemy, spending days and weeks in trenches and camps. He was not some parlor Paddy who had spent years on the settee learning how to make ladies laugh.

Then perhaps, he sternly reminded himself, he'd do best to stay *out* of the parlor to begin with instead of lurking about and practically inviting himself in for supper.

Liam turned and crossed the street, strolled down the walk past Brook's and White's, looking at the gentlemen who came out of the clubs in twos and threes, trying very hard not to scowl. Englishmen, really! While he'd known several good, courageous Englishmen in the course of his military career, and could honestly avow to admiring a handful of them, it seemed that in London they were all a bunch of fops, dandies, and coxcombs. There wasn't a one of them who hadn't curled his hair or cinched his waist or padded his shoulder. It wasn't right, to Liam's way of thinking, went against the grain and the natural way of things. Men should be men and leave the cosmetics to women.

He paused at the corner of St. James and Pall Mall, propping himself against the corner of one building, and observed a group of young men sauntering across the street, laughing with one another. A carriage careened around the corner and sent the young men scrambling in different directions. It hardly surprised Liam to discover that the reckless carriage transported his cousin—the body of the vehicle surged toward the walkway, and out tumbled his rotund cousin, followed by a new pair of male companions.

One of the young men, who had come very close to being splattered on the street by his cousin's reckless driving, said something that caught Nigel's attention.

He pirouetted on his heel, pitched toward the upstart, his finger wagging, and responded with something that caused the young men to laugh uproariously. As they regrouped and walked away, more than one turned his head to have a look at Nigel and laugh again.

Nigel attempted to straighten his waistcoat, but one hand wouldn't function properly, so he quit trying and pivoted around and let one of his companions push him in the direction of the door of the Darden Gentleman's Club.

"*Ach,* ye blasted sot," Liam muttered underneath his breath. "Ye leave me no option, do ye?" With his jaw clamped tightly shut, Liam pushed away from the building and marched to Darden's.

The inside of the club looked like most the others he had visited—dark paneling, thick leather chairs around small tables, the golden glow of wall sconces, the cloudy drift of smoke that burned his eyes. Liam walked deeper into the club, shrugging out of his coat. A man appeared on his right, offering to take it. "No, I'll keep it," he said, jerking it back from the man's helpful hand. One never knew when one might have to make a hasty exit.

He paid the required fee for gracing this club—a bloody two pounds, he noted with disdain—and the man pointed him toward the common room. Liam walked across the thick carpet toward a small table in the center of the room. It was hot as blazes in here, with twin hearths on opposite walls stoked to infernos. Thin-blooded bastards, the English Quality. With a humph, Liam dropped into a thickly padded leather seat and tossed his coat onto the chair next to him. When the footman arrived, he asked, "Have ye good Scotch whiskey?"

"We have whiskey, sir. I could not say if it was Scotch or Irish."

That rankled—Irish whiskey could hardly be

counted in the same class as Scotch whiskey! "A dram of what ye have, then," he said, and wondered if the footman always looked that pinched or if he was merely sneering at his scarred face.

Never mind that. He had a look around; the tables in the common area were all but full, and in addition he could see four doors leading to other areas. Private rooms, no doubt. Probably where Nigel was now with his sycophants, filling their gullets with port. The footman brought him a dram of inferior whiskey, and Liam sipped carefully, as this quest to put himself in front of Nigel was costing him a pretty pence, and he would do well to make his whiskey last. Which made him wonder, rather impatiently, how exactly he might acquaint himself with the private rooms.

But as good fortune would have it, jolly old Nigel came bursting out of one door a moment later, laughing so uproariously that several of the club patrons swiveled in his direction to see what he was about. "Keep your cards on the table, Maxwell. I'll just be a moment," Nigel called loudly to his companion, then proceeded to bang his way through the tables toward the front of the club. There he spoke to the man who had let Liam in, talking loudly about something to do with the fire. When the man seemed to promise to take care of whatever it was that had upset his cousin, Nigel turned, obviously prepared to teeter-totter back to his private room. Not one to miss an opportunity, Liam threw the rest of his whiskey down his throat at the same time he came to his feet and grabbed his coat, slinging it over his arm.

He stepped in front of Nigel as his cousin reached the last table between him and the private room. "Pardon, sir," he said, looking Nigel directly in the eye.

"Yes, yes, of course," Nigel muttered, trying to bob around Liam without so much as a glance.

Jesus, Mary, and Joseph. Liam suppressed a sigh of irritation and said, in a voice of incredulity worthy of the theater, *"Mo creach,* could it *be?* Cousin Nigel?"

"What? What's that?" a startled Nigel asked, raising his bleary gaze to Liam's face, squinting. "Pardon?"

All right, then, how hard would he make this? "Nigel, old chap! Do ye no' remember me, then?"

"Remember you? I daresay I don't, sir. I—" He stopped, peered closely at Liam, then reared back, hands on belly. *"Liam?* Cousin *Liam?"* he exclaimed. "By jove, it *is* you!" he exclaimed, still peering, as if he couldn't believe his eyes. "How long has it been? Ten years?"

"No' as long as that. Seven?"

"Seven! *Seven* . . . bloody saints! Well, *you've* changed a bit, haven't you? A bit gray around the gills, what?" Nigel observed, then, his gaze traveling the full length of Liam. "A bit thicker, too, I'd say!"

Coming from someone who had gained at least two stone and had added the distinction of *sot* to his mantle since last they'd met, Liam didn't think his cousin's observations were terribly amusing. "A wee bit of gray, I suppose," Liam admitted. "Ah, but ye look the same, Nigel!"

Nigel grinned, smoothing his soiled waistcoat. "I suppose I've done rather well, all in all. Well, then, Lockhart—do tell what brings you to London after all these years? The last we saw you, you had purchased a commission into the navy, wasn't it?"

"Army. Highland Regiments."

"Aaah," said Nigel, nodding slowly.

The goat had no idea what Liam meant by that. "Just back from the war against Bonaparte," he added helpfully.

"Oh." Nigel's eyes grew round. *"Ooh,"* he said again. "Back to London, really? I thought your people were in Scotland."

Aye, thank God. Liam glanced ruefully at his cousin and tried hard to affect a sad mien. "I'm afraid we've had a bit of a falling out," he said quietly.

"A *what?*" Nigel all but shouted, not understanding.

Liam clenched his jaw, leaned forward, and said again, "A falling *out.* I'm rather at odds with me family."

"The Scots?" Nigel asked, confused.

"Aye, the Scots." God blind him, what a blockhead! "Father in particular. He's of the old way of thinking. Doesna believe in the Royal Army, if ye take me meaning."

Nigel blinked, swayed backward, then forward again. Suddenly, his eyes widened. "Ooh, I *seeeeee,*" he said low, nodding enthusiastically. He suddenly clamped a hand on Liam's arm. "There now, cousin, you simply must come join me and my companions."

Victory. "Ah, I wouldna think to intrude—"

"No intrusion! The more the merrier!" Nigel paused to stifle a hiccup, then asked, "You enjoy a good card game, don't you?"

"Aye, of—"

"Of course you do! Come along, then—you must tell me all about my Scottish cousins," Nigel blithely continued, pushing Liam in the direction of his private room. "Ah, yes, the *Scottish* Lockharts. How frightfully *quaint.* What, there were four or five of them, weren't there?" he asked, as if referring to a herd of livestock.

"Five in all," Liam bit out as he turned and accompanied Nigel to the private room.

Nigel stepped through the door first, unremarked by his two companions, who were engaged in a heated argument over a card. "Look here, Maxwell! Uckerby!" Nigel boomed, drawing Liam forward. "Look who has come to join us! My Scottish cousin Lockhart!" That succeeded in gaining the two men's attention, and they turned identical bloodshot gazes to Liam.

"My Scottish cousin Lockhart!" Nigel said again, then laughed and clapped Liam so soundly on the back that he nearly lost his breath. "He's from *Scotland.*"

In spite of the fact that he was forced to endure the company of Lockhart, Maxwell, and Uckerby for the rest of the evening, and worse, well into the early-morning hours, Liam felt good about his progress with Nigel. They had not spoken again of his defection from the Scottish Lockharts, but Nigel did invite Liam to join him again the next evening at the exclusive White's, where Nigel held a membership. "There's better gaming there, you know," he informed him. Liam certainly hoped so.

The next afternoon, in between thoughts of Ellie, Liam penned another letter home.

Dearest Mother, Cousin Nigel sends his regards.

he wrote, then paused to study the letter and found it lacking somewhat. He therefore added:

I ate quite a good goose yesterday. Fondly, L.

He sealed the letter, took it to the post, then walked to Hyde Park.

He had determined, in the bright light of morning, that his stomping on a mouse in the dining room and in the course of a delightful supper had been rather inelegant. It was, upon reflection, something he was quite certain his mother would have objected to and a deed for which she might have perhaps tossed him out on his arse. Which meant, naturally, that he must apologize to Ellie. And he could hardly make an apology empty-handed, could he? He needed something to soften his transgression, such as flowers. Big and beautiful flowers. Hence his trek to Hyde Park, where he

remembered there were several gardens full of bloom-
ing roses.

Indeed, there were several gardens, and Liam
perused them all, finally deciding that the small garden
near Park Lane had the best specimens. So he circled
round until he reached that garden again, stepped over
the rock border separating the roses from the pedes-
trian thoroughfare, and carefully moved to the middle
of the patch to closely study the various bushes. After a
quarter hour of hemming and hawing, he settled on the
bloodred roses in the very middle of the garden, and
pulling his dagger from his boot, he made several cut-
tings, exclaiming sharply with every prick of a thorn.

When he at last had what seemed to him a suitable
bouquet to accompany his apology, he slipped the dagger back into his boot and turned toward the thoroughfare. A frown instantly washed over his face as he
glared at the various onlookers who gaped at him in
surprise and dismay. Barmy English! What, were these
the only roses in all of Britain, then? Would the entire
populace of London begrudge him a measly dozen of
them? Liam carefully inched his way through the
thorny bushes to the edge of the garden, stepped over
the rock border, and straightened his clothing. With a
scowl for the lot of them, he set off, his homemade bouquet in hand, feeling rather cheerful for the first time
since he had arrived in London.

Ten

❧

*H*aving passed another interminable day with a walk in the square and a call on her sister Eva, Ellen took the eardrops her sister had given her *(they are really too vulgar for polite society . . . but* you *can wear them)* to High Street, where she sold them for a paltry three pounds. Cheap, the shopkeeper had called them.

Ellen returned to Belgrave Square late that afternoon, and met Agatha in the dark foyer just as she was leaving.

"Natalie's napping. And *he's* gone for the evening," she said, meaning Farnsworth, which was always welcome news. "And oh, yes, mu'um, I brought a cake," Agatha added as she draped a cloak around her bony shoulders. "It was all I could manage today."

Dear, dear Agatha. How the poor woman managed to endure Farnsworth was beyond Ellen's ability to comprehend, much less try to provide for her and Natalie. "How thoughtful of you, Agatha. A cake is just the perfect thing. Thank you," she said, and reached for Agatha's hand, squeezing it tightly. "I don't know what we'd do without you."

That set the woman's mouth in a frown. She tied the cloak tightly at her throat in sharp jerking movements, then turned toward the door to take her leave. But she paused, frowned at Ellen one last time for the day. "I'm sorry, mu'um, but I can't help worry about the two of you, if you don't mind me saying. It ain't right."

No, it wasn't right. It bordered on criminal, actually, but what could she do? Ellen forced a smile. "Please, you mustn't worry. We are quite all right—it's truly not so bad."

Agatha snorted her true opinion of that, but seemed unwilling to say more, and glanced at the door. "Well, then, I'll take my leave until the morrow," she said, and tightening her cloak about her, she walked to the door, muttering to herself.

Ellen watched until she had closed the door behind her, then felt that horrid loss of liberty she always felt when the door of the old mansion closed. Agatha was right, of course—this wasn't right, not right at all to be banished to the second floor of this wretched house, to live out her days between those rooms, Belgrave Square, and Eva's house. It was unconscionable, yet she was trapped—Farnsworth held all the cards. He doled out money sparingly, and in her case, not without a certain amount of begging. He lived so austerely that there was nothing in the house of any value that she could sell to earn her freedom. And Eva, dear God. She loved her sister in some way, but Eva was permanently cowed by Farnsworth, permanently angry with Ellen, and was fearful of giving her as much as a quid. Her sister eased her conscience by helping Ellen in other ways—by giving her hand-me-down clothing.

Beyond Eva, Ellen had no real contacts other than her dearest childhood friend, Judith. But Judith lived in King's Lynn, which might as well have been across the North Sea. Their friendship existed in letters only— Ellen hadn't seen Judith in fifteen years, and worse, she had never had the courage to tell her the complete truth about Natalie.

No, there was no easy way out of her predicament, a fact Ellen had finally accepted when her mother had died more than two years ago. Up until then she had held on to the hope that someone—*Daniel*—would save them. Now she knew no one would save them but herself, and given her lack of resources and abilities, she was doomed to live this empty, dark existence until she found a way to free Natalie from it.

There was no question of that—she *would* find a way, or die trying.

Wearily, Ellen turned from the door and made her way to the second floor, where Natalie was hard at work setting up a tea service on her little table. Ellen discarded her pelisse and bonnet and moved woodenly into her bedroom. At her bed, she dropped to her knees, shoved her hand between the mattresses, and withdrew the thin cigar box she had stolen from Farnsworth's study a year ago. She flipped open the lid and gathered up the pound sterling and the coins she had saved. Most of it had come from selling her mother's jewelry, trinkets here and there. Or Eva's gifts, when possible. She added the three pounds she had received from the shopkeeper and looked at the contents of the box. Given that she'd accumulated the money over two years, it was frighteningly little. At this pace, she'd be six feet away from her grave before she'd save enough to send Natalie away.

Ellen closed the box, shoved it back between the mattresses, and pushed herself to her feet. She walked to the windows of her room overlooking Belgrave Square, saw the clouds gathering on the horizon, behind which the sun was starting to slide. She was sick to death of fretting, of floating just beneath the surface, seeing life as some watery image beyond her grasp.

She preferred to think of something warmer; and interestingly, for the third or fourth time that day, she wondered, with a smile slowly spreading her lips, what the captain was doing.

Now *there* was a man who was very different from

the rest of his tedious sex. Quite amusing, really, and quite a fun diversion from the usual monotony of her life. All in all, she found him rather wildly charming. Just thinking of him stomping on the mouse made her chuckle. Not that she approved of his method for ridding the house of the pest, certainly not, but one couldn't help but admire a man who took life by the bollocks and met it head-on. Ellen rather suspected the captain was not a man given to convention in anything and did exactly as he pleased, the world be damned if they didn't care for it. She particularly admired that, since her own life had completely buckled under the pressure of bloody convention.

The captain's sudden appearance was, much to her considerable surprise, like a shock of light in her gloomy little world.

Feeling a little lighter, Ellen turned away from the window, yanked on the bellpull, signaling for an early evening tea.

She busied herself with another boring and not entirely forthcoming letter to Judith *(we're quite fine, the weather is tolerable)* while she waited for the tea. She had not quite finished when she heard Follifoot's muffled knock on the sitting room door, followed by Natalie's cheerful voice. She completed the letter, glanced at the clock—six o'clock. Farnsworth would be gone now. She repaired to her vanity to freshen up.

She emerged from her room a quarter hour later, and was surprised to hear Natalie talking. "Now you take a sip, like this," she heard her daughter say, and thought certainly she had captured the weak-willed Follifoot, and quickened her pace to free the poor man.

It was not Follifoot, however.

Actually, it was Liam, who was feeling rather huge and awkward at present, perched precariously atop one of Natalie's wee chairs at her wee table such as he was, his knees almost to his chin. In one hand he held the roses, which, he was alarmed to see, appeared to be wilting. In the other he held a wee teacup between thumb and middle finger, the thing dwarfed by his man's hand. Yet he followed Natalie's careful instructions, lifting the tiny thing to his lips and tossing the imaginary contents back as he would a dram of whiskey.

"Captain?"

Her voice stunned him; he had not heard her coming. He instantly jerked his gaze up, saw her there in the doorway, a long tail of silken hair falling over her shoulder, and her pretty blue eyes widened in alarm. Liam came out of his chair so quickly that Natalie had to grab the little table and her teapot to keep them from toppling over, and his miniature chair went flying backward. The captain looked at the chair, then at Ellie, and realized he was still holding the flowers and the teacup.

"I, ah . . . Good evening, then." He gave her a quick bob of his head and shoved the teacup at Natalie, who dutifully took it and put it aside.

"We're having tea," she cheerfully informed her mother. "Follifoot brought it."

"Yes, I see," Ellie said, still looking at Liam with an expression that appeared both perplexed and pleased that he had come again—at least that was what he *hoped* her expression meant. He could feel his skin growing warm under her careful scrutiny, and anxiously shifted his weight from one leg to the other. "I . . . I suppose ye might wonder what brings me round, then, eh?" he blurted uncertainly, not mentioning that he'd slipped into her rooms while Follifoot had been setting down the tea service.

"I must say I am a bit surprised," she said, gliding further into the room in a gown of pale green that made her skin glow. "Nonetheless . . . we're happy to have you call again, sir. We quite enjoyed our supper, didn't we, Natalie?"

"I thought the supper was very good, but I didn't like him killing the mouse, really," the lass admitted.

"*Mo creach,*" Liam muttered. "I didna mean to hurt ye, lass," he said with much exasperation, to which Natalie shrugged insouciantly as she arranged a stuffed bear on the chair that had been opposite him.

Liam forced himself to look at Ellie again and figured there was no going back now. He might as well have his say and be done with it, let the chips fall where they may. "Very well, then. I've come again to apologize, if ye'll allow it. I couldna sleep knowing I'd unhinged ye so, and I'm dreadfully sorry for it."

Her eyes widened with surprise, and she flashed him a warm, perfect smile. "Oh, *Captain!*" she exclaimed laughingly. "You must not fret over such a trifle! It certainly did not unhinge us, and I, for one, am grateful for your assistance."

At least she didn't despise him. Good. *Bloody* good. All right then . . . Liam shifted his weight again, dropped his gaze to the carpet, wished to the Lord above that he had, just once, learned a bit of charm from Grif, and wondered what he would say *now.*

"I beg your pardon, but . . . are those flowers for us?"

Liam jerked his gaze up to Ellie; she nodded at the roses, and he looked at them in his hand, having completely forgotten they were there. "*Ach!*" he exclaimed, annoyed with his awkwardness. "Of course they are!" he said gruffly, and thrust his arm forward.

Ellie walked to where he stood, smiling. He offered the bouquet again, only more gently this time, and as she took them from his hand, her fingers brushed his, and he felt a jolt directly to his groin, strong and pure. So strong, in fact, that he inadvertently yanked his hand back as if he'd been singed. He couldn't help

noticing the flush in Ellie's porcelain skin, and wondered if it was possible that *she* had felt it, too.

Whatever she might have felt was abruptly hidden
behind the bouquet, which she quickly brought to her
face, inhaling deeply. "They are beautiful," she murmured softly. "Where ever did you find them so late in
the season?"

"Hyde Park."

Ellie glanced at him from the corner of her eye,
slowly lifting her head. "Hyde Park?"

"Aye."

Her brow crinkled; she looked again at the bouquet,
holding it up so she could see the jagged ends where he
had cut the flowers with his knife. She glanced at him
again, and Liam smiled hopefully. Ellie's face suddenly
broke into a wreath of smiles; she laughed gaily, the
sound of it musical. "You *cut* them from the bushes in
Hyde Park? How delightful!"

Before he could admit to it, she twirled around,
marched for the sideboard, and stuffed the roses into a
ewer of water, arranging them just so. "They're simply
gorgeous, Captain, none more beautiful."

Gazing at her now, those were his thoughts exactly.
None more beautiful.

"What a delightful treat!"

Now Liam was smiling, feeling a bit prideful that he
had done so well. "*Ach,* ye probably receive fancier
flowers than this. But it was the least I could do, seeing
as how I killed yer mouse."

Ellie turned to face him again, still smiling, and
brought the flowers over, placing them in the center of
the tea service.

"I was glad to be rid of that mouse," she continued.
"And now you've gone and brightened my evening
with these lovely flowers. Of course you'll take tea,
won't you?"

Aye, he wanted to take tea, wanted to very much. But he also understood that it was untoward to be lurking around a married woman as he was. "I've imposed on yer hospitality too much as it is."

"I insist," Ellie said pertly. "Natalie, come, will you?" she asked, reaching for her daughter's hand. Natalie came to stand beside her mother. "If you will excuse me for just a moment, sir, I shall put Natalie to the useful task of drawing you a picture."

"Oh, *yes!*" Natalie cried. With a sidelong look that Liam could not quite read, Ellie turned away, leading a skipping Natalie through the door.

He stood there, silently debating. The soldier in him knew this to be very dangerous ground. But the man in him was held captive, unable to walk out that door. The man in him was, as a matter of fact, seizing him fully, holding common sense and decency prisoner, and allowing the baser Liam to crawl out and assume command.

Carefully, reluctantly, guiltily, Liam sat on the edge of the upholstered armchair and looked around the room. It was much more cheerful than any part of the house he had yet seen—there was furniture, and decent furniture at that, and little knickknack clutter that signaled females were living within these walls. He rather liked it. It reminded him of his mother's sitting room, except that it wasn't nearly quite so cold.

Ellie reappeared a moment later, moving gracefully but purposefully across the room, to a sideboard near the window. She picked up a cake of some sort, which she placed on a small table between them.

"I'm afraid the tea is a little weak, but I promise the cake will be quite delectable," she said cheerfully.

Liam nodded, feeling all at sixes and sevens, uncertain as to what the protocol was in taking tea, yet another social custom at which he was completely inept. He fidgeted with his neckcloth, pushed his hands through his hair and off his brow, and finally folded his hands in his lap and sat stiffly, staring at her.

Ellie glanced at his hands, then smiled up at him. "How long have you been in London, might I ask?"

"A fortnight."

She nodded, seemed to want him to say more, but he was entirely unclear what else he might possibly add to that response. She asked, "Have you come on business, I suppose?"

A rather delicate issue, that one. "In a manner of speaking. I've come on a family matter."

"Ah," she said.

Liam said nothing. He slid his hands to his knees, braced them there, and tried not to stare at her, yet he couldn't help taking all of her features in, from the smart little nose to the point of her chin, the perfectly sculpted ears, the—

"*Ahem.*" She touched the back of her head, drawing his attention away from her neck. "Well, then, Captain, perhaps you will say how long you *do* intend to stay in London?"

Liam shrugged, said, "No' long, if I can help it."

"Oh." Her hand fell to her lap, and she lowered her gaze, and while he couldn't be very certain, he had the distinct feeling that the answer disappointed her. She leaned over, dropped the silver tea ball in his cup. "Ah . . . one sugar or two?"

"Four."

Her hand stilled a moment, but she picked up the teapot, proceeded to pour the water, and carefully dropped the first sugar cube. As Liam watched her long, tapered fingers, he found himself consumed with envy of Farnsworth, ridiculously so, and in a less-than-lucid moment, he surged forward, propped his arms on his knees. Startled, Ellie reared back, another cube of sugar held captive over his teacup as she warily watched him.

Liam reached for the cup, took it away from her. He did not, however, drink the tea, and realized, after a moment, that his mouth was moving ahead of his bean brain. "I beg yer pardon if I should speak out of turn, but I confess I feel a wee bit out of sorts, I do. I've thought about it—little else, really—and I canna help wonder why yer husband does no' sit with ye in the evenings? How is it that he should leave a woman as . . . as *bonny* as yerself alone?"

She seemed stunned by his question, and well she should be. It was none of his affair, none at all, and there he went, behaving like a rustic again. But now that he had said it, he was desperate for the answer, and inched forward as she reared further back. "Call me a bloody bastard if ye will, for 'tis certainly naugh' to me, is it? Yet I swear on me honor, I'd no' leave a wife as beautiful as ye with the likes of me in the house, I swear I wouldna."

Ellie lifted a hand to her neck. He had upset her terribly, hadn't he? *Mary Queen of Scots,* what a stupid—

"It is I who should beg *your* pardon, sir, for you are mistaken. I have no husband here."

That did not register on any part of his brain. He tried to make sense of it, tried to see how—*"What?"* he choked, then shook his head and frowned. *"Ach,* I'd no' claim him were he mine, I donna doubt it, but why would ye call yerself Farnsworth, then?"

"Farnsworth?" she echoed incredulously. "You thought Farnsworth . . ." Her burst of laughter startled Liam badly; he juggled the little teacup and hastily set it down, looking at her in utter confusion as she laughed until her eyes were swimming with tears. "By the saints, Captain, I've not laughed so hard in ages!" she managed to get out between gales of laughter. "Farnsworth

is not my *husband!* He is my *father!"* she cried, and was overcome with another fit of laughter she could not quell.

In truth, Liam's first inclination was elation and relief that someone as loathsome as Farnsworth wasn't touching her. That quickly gave way to bewilderment, for it seemed entirely impossible that someone as hideously ill-favored as that man could sire someone as beautiful as Ellie. And if he wasn't her husband, then who was? *The admiral.* Of course! Well, then, he'd misunderstood! She was married to the admiral . . . which did not exactly relieve him in any way. If anything, it made him feel even more anxious.

"Captain, your tea," Ellie reminded him, and Liam glanced at the teacup he had set on the edge of the table.

"I beg yer pardon, I must apologize," he said, reaching for the cup of tea. "I'm no' generally such a jolly busybody. I beg ye forgive me indiscretion, madam."

But Ellie was glowing with her smile, and reached across the table, still holding the sugar, and flicked her wrist at him. "Please, Captain, shan't we be friends?" she asked, dropping the last sugar cube in his tea.

Friends. Aye, he liked the sound of that, given that he had no other, more appealing option. "I'd like that very much, I would."

"Then I'd like it if you would call me by my Christian name, Ellen."

Liam unthinkingly shook his head.

"No?"

"I shall call ye Ellie. I had that in me mind the first time ye said yer name, and I'm afraid ye'll always be Ellie to me."

Her long lashes fluttered pleasingly; she picked up a plate of tea biscuits. "No one has called me Ellie since I was a girl."

"I donna mean to offend ye—"

"And you don't."

He smiled. "Naturally, ye must call me Liam if we are to be friends, eh?"

Her glorious smile returned. "*Liam!* How lovely! It suits you, I think."

He'd prefer not to think of his name as lovely, but to hell with it—if it made her smile, then God blind him, it was a lovely name. He glanced at the plate of tea biscuits. "So, then, if ye donna mind me asking, is yer husband at sea?"

"At sea?" she asked, puzzled.

"The admiral," Liam clarified.

Ellie's brows dipped into a confused vee. "The *admiral?*" she echoed, and seemed so mystified that Liam instantly suspected he had been duped again by the little demon Natalie. *Confound that child!* He frowned into his teacup. Was there no end to the tales she had told him? Had the imp uttered one bloody word of truth? "Yer daughter has quite an imagination, does she no'?"

A light of understanding dawned on Ellie's face. "I see," she said simply. "I confess I don't quite know what to do with her." She extended the plate of tea biscuits to Liam; he took a handful. "In spite of Natalie's wishes to the contrary, the truth is . . . I am not married."

A widow! Liam had munched two tea biscuits before the implication of *that* sunk into his brain, and it intrigued him terribly. Actually, he felt dangerously on the verge of bursting into song. He popped two more biscuits into his mouth, considering Ellie—a young, beautiful widow. No doubt she was the object of more than one gentleman's fantasies; he could just crowd his in next to theirs, he supposed, but really, she was far too good for the likes of some foppish Englishman. In fact, he thought, gazing at her expressive eyes, the high curve of her cheekbone, the purse of her full lips, she was really too good for *any* man. Save him.

"I beg your pardon. Perhaps I have said too much," she said demurely.

"No' at all," he quickly assured her.

"Are you married, Captain?"

"No."

"No one waiting for you at home?"

"For *me?*"

She nodded.

Liam laughed, looked again at the tea biscuits. Ellie extended the plate, and he took another handful, and realized that he felt safe with her. "No. I've been in the king's service at one place or another too long, I think." Aye, and who would have him? He was a soldier, and an ugly one at that.

"Ah," she said, nodding. "Then perhaps you've come to London to find a wife?"

He all but choked on his biscuits. "God, *no!*" he sputtered. "Ye donna understand, then, Ellie. Our family is at odds with our English cousins," he began, and amazingly, in spite of all his military training to the contrary, he talked. Not that he spilled the whole sordid story, preferring to leave some of it out, such as how destitute they were, but at least that the English Lockharts had something that belonged to the Scottish Lockharts, and how he had come to see if he might get it back. Naturally, he did not reveal that he intended to steal it. Or that it was worth a fortune.

Ellie did not ask too many questions, which he found rather refreshing, given that his sister Mared was an interrogator worthy of the Inquisition. Better still, she smiled a lot, seemed interested, made the appropriate responses in all the right places.

When he realized he was actually monopolizing the conversation, he was mortified, and stopped himself. He asked about her. "And where do ye hail from, then?"

"London," she said simply. "This is our ancestral home."

Didn't say much for her ancestors, unfortunately. "And the lass's father. Where did he hail from?"

She colored slightly, averted her gaze for a moment. "Ah . . . Cambridge."

"And yer mother, is she here, too?"

"Quite dead, more than two years now."

"Terribly sorry."

She acknowledged him with a modest nod of her head. "It's just me and Natalie now." She shifted, unknowingly revealing the shape of her bosom.

Diah! All right then—he had to go, and go *now*, because he was, inexplicably, and for perhaps the first time in his life, quite smitten. *Smitten!* Which meant that he could not trust himself. At least, he didn't *think* he could, for the last time he had been so horrifyingly smitten, he had been all of twelve years old, and he had indeed been terribly untrustworthy around the object of his great esteem. Well, that young Highland lad was alive and kicking in his groin at the moment.

"Well, then! Thank ye kindly!" he said abruptly, coming to his feet.

Ellie looked perplexed, but preceded him to the door, her long tail of hair dancing above her hips. Liam was so entranced by the swing of her curvaceous bum that he nearly trampled over her when she suddenly stopped and turned about. He did not realize they were at the door, that she had opened it, even, was actually aware of nothing but the sweet scent of lavender that suddenly filled his senses. And as Ellie stepped up against the wall to let him pass, he discovered that he was, indeed, *quite* untrustworthy, a bloody rake, really. An animal instinct had consumed him, something far beyond his capacity to control, and he unthinkingly leaned forward, following her scent, so that his chin was just at her temple.

Ellie didn't move, just froze there, trapped. Liam closed his eyes, slowly bent his head, taking in the heady, feminine scent of her perfume, his lips grazing her hair, then turning just slightly so that his lips whispered across the creamy skin of her cheek.

Instead of screaming, as he half expected, she released her breath in one long sigh, looked up at him through thick golden lashes, the blue in her eyes shimmering like raindrops. Her cheeks were softly pink, and he was overcome with an intense, hard longing. He took her hand in his, caressed her palm with his finger. *"Duin an doras,"* he whispered hoarsely, feverishly. *"Fuirichidh mise."*

Close the door. I'll stay.

Ellie flushed dark, her lashes fluttered shut. "I . . . I don't know what you say," she murmured.

Liam dropped her hand, gently laid his at the base of her bare neck. Her skin was soft and warm against his callused palm, and he whispered in her ear, *"I know."* He moved his head; his lips whisked across hers, shimmering like a whisper of silk.

He breathed her in once more, made himself remove his hand from her heated flesh.

Ellie drew a long, ragged breath as she gazed up at his mouth. "M-my father," she whispered, "leaves every evening at five o'clock promptly, after the daily servants leave." She lifted her gaze then, and looked him boldly in the eye. "After they are gone, there is no one here but Follifoot and a scullery maid."

Desire coursed through him hot and molten; Liam grasped her hand, lifted it to his mouth, and pressed his lips against her palm, lingering there, battling between the desire to stay and the very real need to go. At last, as common sense battled to the forefront of his brain, he let go and stepped around her. "Sweet dreams, lass," he said, and walked out the door, down the hall, his mind swimming with the image of her, his groin pounding with desire for her.

Eleven

How long she might have stood there, melted hard against the door, Ellen really didn't know—not only was she incapable of movement, her head had filled with cotton. The only sensation that assured her she was still very much alive was the burn of her skin where his lips had touched her. Lightly, her fingers fluttered against her cheek as she recalled his breath, a salve to the delicious sting of his lips. She retraced the path of his fingers, her hand fluttering to her collarbone, where his huge hand had engulfed her throat and shoulder, the pressure of it so unbearably light.

God in heaven, she hadn't felt so on fire since . . . since Daniel.

Daniel, damn him. She hadn't thought of him in so long, perhaps as long as forever now. Time passed so monotonously here that minutes bled into days and then months and years without her noticing them. But she had, finally, put him out of her mind, packed him into some neat, tiny parcel and buried him away in a lifetime's worth of memories. The bitter sting had subsided, and on those rare occasions a flash of color or the scent of a man's cologne jarred her memory, the whole affair seemed like something from a dream.

Certainly there had been no one since Daniel, certainly no one who made her skin burn with a mere touch, no one—no moment to remind her that she was a woman, a living, breathing woman. *Until now,* until this very moment, and God help her, she was alarmed by the powerful reaction of all her senses to the Scottish captain.

Ellie . . . he had called her Ellie! Her beloved grandfather had called her that; it had been that kind old man's pet name for her. Yet he had never said it quite like it sounded on Liam's lips. The way *he* said it made her light-headed. Dizzy.

Ellen pushed away from the door, drifted toward the couch, smiling, and melted into a chair, burrowing deep into the cushions, hugging herself as she thought of the bold man who had just left her sitting room. There was something about him, something that, in concert with his hard exterior, made him extraordinarily appealing in such an unconventional way. He was raw flesh and bone, no pretense about him, purely masculine and unapologetic for it. And he made her laugh—Lord, how he made her laugh! Laugh like she hadn't done in ages.

Ellen remained in that dreamy state of wonder until Natalie came bouncing into the room. "Oh, did the captain leave? I haven't finished my picture!" She fell onto her knees next to her mother, her expression curious. "Why are you smiling, Mother?"

"Am I smiling?" she asked airily, feeling it sink even deeper into her soul. "I suppose it's because I had a very pleasant chat with the captain."

"I rather like him," Natalie said, fidgeting with the hem of Ellen's gown. "He's rather snuggly, don't you think?"

"Snuggly?" Ellen laughed, brushing a strand of hair from Natalie's eye. "What do you mean?"

"Oh, I don't know . . . he's the sort that I'd like to hug, like a bear. Do you?"

Oh, yes. Yes, she most certainly fancied a hug. "Perhaps," Ellen confessed.

Natalie put her head on her mother's knee. "But he speaks very strangely."

"That's because he's from another part of the world."

"What do you suppose it's like there, where he lives? Do you suppose they have fairy princesses?"

"I rather think they do," Ellen said dreamily, reminded of the Scotland he had described.

"I think I should like to visit one day. Perhaps he will invite us," Natalie said hopefully, and abruptly sat up, her eye on the cake Agatha had left.

Funny, Ellen thought as she moved to cut her daughter a piece of cake, but she rather thought she'd like to visit there one day, too, and cheerfully indulged Natalie's discourse on princesses and castles, allowing her own mind to fill with visions of Scotland and her chest with the raging desire to feel his touch again.

Across town, at White's, Nigel was all smiles and well on his way to his usual state of inebriation. But he was also deeply involved in a game of whist, paired with the hapless Uckerby, who, judging by the look of it, was probably the reason why Nigel had lost an astounding two hundred pounds. He therefore had little desire to chat up the past with Liam. In fact, the more Nigel lost, the more he drank and the less enthusiastic he was about the prospect of a bit of prattle with his long-lost Scottish cousin.

Therefore, Liam accomplished little that night, other then drinking too much himself, and privately lamenting the fact that he might instead have been carrying on a very pleasant conversation with Ellie, as opposed to watching a large man blubber in his cups with every losing hand. By the time Liam made it back to Belgrave Square, he had quite a head on him. Yet he had managed to secure an invitation to join Nigel for a partridge shoot the following day, an event at which a lot of bloody fops would, apparently, take out their guns and shoot at birds to fill the endless time on their hands. Liam was beginning to appreciate that this mission was destined to take more time than he could have ever anticipated.

In his rooms, he divested himself of the stiff clothing as quickly as possible, and in his shirttails, he penned another letter home:

Dearest Mother, London smells quite awfully.
It shall take a wee bit longer to clean it all up. Kindest
regards and so forth. Yours faithfully, L.

Liam sealed it with a drop of candle wax and the slap of his fist. Then he stood, swaying only slightly (a marked improvement), and shrugged out of his shirt. His nose instantly wrinkled—his clothing was beginning to smell, he noted, and he thought he'd rather have to do something about that. He draped the offending garment over a chair, peeled off his trousers and his drawers. Naked, he walked across the room and fell onto the lumpy bed, legs splayed and arms wide. The last vision in his mind before he drifted off into a whiskey-induced sleep was of Ellie, standing against the door of her suite of rooms, looking like a bloody angel. *Leannan.*

He was up before dawn the next morning, a little bleary-eyed, but no worse for the wear. Stuffing his knapsack full of clothing, he walked outside to Belgrave Square and a darling little bird pond there. The water was ice cold, and it was still very dark, so that he could just make out the shirts and trousers he was washing. He realized, of course, that it might have been a bit more prudent of him to wash the garments in the hip bath Follifoot drug to his room on occasion, but he calculated that by the time Follifoot had made the required number of trips with his buckets to fill the damn thing, it would be done and over if he simply availed himself of the square's pond.

And it was a fact that by the time the sun had come up and the denizens of London began to make their way out-of-doors, Liam was in his rooms again, his clothing strewn about on every conceivable surface to dry.

He was shaving when Follifoot arrived with his breakfast.

The hapless footman's watery eyes bulged with surprise as he glanced around the room and saw the freshly laundered clothing lying about.

"Close yer gob, Follifoot, ere the fireflies roost within," Liam warned him as he scraped his whiskers with a dull blade.

Follifoot closed his gaping mouth, set the tray down. Whatever he had brought, the odor was so pungent that Liam wrinkled his nose and grimaced at the footman over his shoulder. "What is it, then?"

"Couldn't rightly say, sir. Something rather brown-looking."

"Brings to mind a barnyard!"

Follifoot shrugged. As much as Liam didn't want to waste precious coins on food, he gestured impatiently at the tray. "I'll no' have it. Take it to someone with the balls to eat it, then," he said, and hoped he might find something to put in his stomach between here and Wintershire, where he was to meet Nigel at precisely ten o'clock.

With a sigh, Follifoot picked up the tray, and went out with one last look at the laundered clothing.

In Wintershire, Liam found Nigel straightaway, standing atop a small hill, holding his gun like a newborn bairn in the crook of his arm. "Ah, Cousin Liam! So you came round after all!" he crowed.

Actually, it was more surprising that Nigel should find his way out of his house before noon. "Aye," Liam said gruffly, and noticed that Nigel was peering at his shirt, which he had opted to wear without the confining waistcoat.

"I didn't think to ask if you had proper attire," Nigel said, more to himself than to Liam. "Ah, well. There's nothing to be done for it now, is there?" He laughed as Liam looked down at his clothing, perplexed. "Have you a gun? I took the liberty of bringing one of my father's better guns," he said, and bent over, digging in a canvas bag at his feet, withdrew a long-nosed gaming pistol, and handed it to Liam. "Thought you'd like to have a go with it."

By the look of it, the thing had been scavenged from the last century and was useless for small game—it would blow a partridge to the four corners of the earth. Nevertheless, Liam smiled his thanks, and asked, "Do ye like the hunt, then?"

Nigel laughed, rocked up to the tips of his toes as he jauntily braced his gun against his shoulder. "Can't say, really. I've not made it a pastime." He rocked back down to his heels.

Undoubtedly, because there wasn't enough port involved in hunting for Nigel's liking.

"Well, then. We're to meet Uckerby—he's the chap with the license, naturally, as his father is the earl. And Hingston. That makes four, of course. We're shooting against another foursome . . ." He paused, put a finger to the side of his nose as he thought about that. "Can't rightly recall who . . . Givens, I think. And Henley. Browning and Farnsworth—"

"Farnsworth?" Liam asked, surprised.

"Yes, of course. He wouldn't miss a gaming opportunity, would he? I rather imagine this outing is double the pleasure for him, then, eh?" Nigel laughed roundly, but at Liam's stoic expression, he sobered. "You see what I mean, don't you? Gaming in the sense of laying a wager or two on the outcome? And then of course we're *shooting* game, so in a word, that is gaming, too . . ." Nigel's voice trailed off; he looked sulky for a moment, but quickly brightened again. "Shall we have a go of it, then?" he suggested cheerfully, motioning for Liam to follow.

The game, as Uckerby described it, consisted of two rules—each team put a wager for what they expected to bag, and at the end of the hunt, the gamesmen would count the game shot by each team, and one would be declared the winner. Much to Liam's chagrin, he was forced to put up thirty pounds for the dubious pleasure of joining a hunt with an ancient gun. Their team was led by Uckerby, who gave them strict instructions to bring back four partridges a man, for he had seen Givens hunt, and he couldn't shoot the top off a mountain, Browning was far too timid, and Farnsworth too blind to do them much good. Uckerby used these facts, along with something having to do with the whist game last night, to determine the required number of partridges per man, which, as it happened, was the bag limit in the park.

"Very well, then, tallyho and all that," Nigel said brightly, and turned to Liam. "Let's shoot together, shall we?"

If he had been in London for any other reason, *anything*—Liam sighed, tipped his hat to Nigel. "Will ye lead the way, then, cousin?"

"Yes, yes, of course! Pip-pip!" he said jauntily, and they were off.

Their first hour was an unmitigated disaster. Nigel shot at precisely four flying objects, of which only one was a partridge, and even that he managed to miss. When he pressed Liam to shoot at one partridge perched on a rock, the damn gun locked and almost blew off Liam's hand. But he had hunted game all his life, and he was not of a mind to be humiliated in front of this group of popinjays because of the ineptitude of his cousin. With a few pebbles and a slingshot hastily made from a stick and one of his stockings, Liam managed to bring down two partridges.

That feat impressed Nigel mightily. So much so that he had to take a bit of a rest. They were sitting on a large rock when Liam saw two men across the clearing, and recognized one as being Farnsworth. If Farnsworth recognized Liam, he gave no sign of it, and he and his companion tottered on into the woods.

"Farnsworth, ridiculous creature," Nigel grumbled as he examined his gun. "A tighter man you've not met, I'd wager, the bloody miser. And the way he treats his daughter . . . *tsk-tsk.*" Nigel shook his head.

Now he had Liam's undivided, rapt attention. "His daughter? And how is it that he treats her?"

Squinting into the distance, Nigel sighed. "Oh, dear, how should I say it? Won't allow her to go out into society, that sort of thing. Not that I think he should, really, given all that went on. Have you seen her?"

"In passing," Liam lied, then couldn't resist. "Pretty lass, is she no'?"

"Pretty? I hadn't noticed, really. But she deserves to be out, I should think. My dear sister Barbara says that the whole of her clothing comes from her sister Eva. Shameful!" Nigel paused, looked curiously at Liam. "You've not met Barbara, have you? Lovely girl, truly. She's come out last Season, you know. My father hosted a very large ball in honor of the event. *Four hundred* in attendance." He nodded proudly.

"Hmm," Liam said, shifting his gaze to the sun, his mind still racing around the tidbit Nigel had offered about Ellie.

"It was quite the event, really. Champagne and dancing . . ." He sighed dreamily. "The invitations were *quite* coveted."

Liam looked away so Nigel wouldn't see him roll his eyes with impatience. "Aye, then, cousin, we'd best be about our shoot," he tried.

But Nigel hadn't quite finished. "We had the floors polished with beeswax, you know," he said, and leaned toward Liam to whisper, "Just like Prinny. And of course, Father laid in *six hundred* candles. *Beeswax*, not tallow."

"Ah," Liam said, and calmly contemplated gouging out his eyeballs as a feasible alternative to Nigel's blathering.

But then Nigel suddenly gasped and sat up; he turned a very bright grin to Liam. "Why, *yes*, of course! You must come to our ball, Liam—say you will!" he said excitedly.

"What?" he sputtered, caught off-guard. "A *ball?"*

"Of *course* a ball! I was just about to say that Father thought the first ball such a frightfully grand success that he is determined to host another. The invitations have all been sent round for this very fortnight! Yes, of course you'll come, and I shall make you a proper introduction to my sister Barbara!"

Oh, no. No-no-no, he'd be far gone from London by then. And even if he weren't, wild horses could not drag him to some glittery, pompous ball! "How kind ye are, Nigel—"

"And I can't imagine Father would mind, really, but perhaps it would be best if you came round and paid a call, you know, just in case there is some objection— you *did* say something about scandal, didn't you?"

"Did I?"

"I'm certain you did—something about your father and a difference of opinion and all that."

"Ah," Liam said, feeling suddenly very chipper. "A difference, aye. My father . . ." he paused, looked meaningfully in the distance, and sadly shook his head. "I shouldna speak ill of him."

"Of course not! I perfectly understand. I suppose each and every one of us has a row with our fathers now and again."

"In all fairness, 'twas more than a row," Liam said. "The good Lockhart name is at issue—*ach,* there I go, speaking ill."

"*Liam!* We're cousins!" Nigel exclaimed, slapping an arm around his shoulders and squeezing hard. "Has he done something wrong? Spied, perhaps? There were quite a lot of them wandering about during the war, you know," he suggested helpfully.

"Oh, no, he'd no' spy."

"Wouldn't he?" Nigel asked, clearly disappointed.

" 'Tis that our loyalties differ . . . there are loyalists, and there are . . . well . . ."

Nigel brightened. "Rebellion, do you think?"

Liam resisted the urge to snort at that ridiculous suggestion, managed instead to shrug noncommittally. "We're cousins, Nigel. I'd no' taint yer good name, which is why I really shouldna bother yer father—"

"Nonsense! He won't be bothered in the least! Just come round to meet him, will you?"

Liam looked at Nigel with the most innocent look he could muster. "Do ye really think I should, then?"

"Naturally! You'll want to pay your respects, I should think, what with this unfortunate rift with your father over *our* good name, cousin—and you'll certainly want to meet your uncle and give him *your* side of the story, should things turn . . . well, you know. Frightfully *scandalous,*" he said with all authority. "You know how people talk."

"I see yer point."

"Really? Well, then, if it's all the same to you, shall you come around Sunday afternoon? Five o'clock? Say, for tea?"

Liam had to struggle to keep the smile from his face. Finally, the opportunity had presented itself. Everything was beginning to fall into place.

"Well, then? Will you?" Nigel asked eagerly.

"Thank ye kindly. I shall look forward to it, I will."

Nigel reared back, clapped his chubby hands together. "*Splendid!* Now, shall we find your partridges? I've got two by my count, which means I need two more, and *you*, of course, need four. Goodness! We'd best be at it!" Nigel said, coming to his feet, and instantly lumbering off in the direction of the tree line.

Mi Diah, Liam thought, and with a long, tortured sigh, followed his cousin into the woods.

Twelve

*E*llen made Natalie stay in Belgrave Square much longer than was customary for them—the sun was shining brightly, an unusually warm day for autumn. It was so very pleasant it was easier to relive the memory of his touch, and Ellen wanted to recall the exquisite sensation, hold on to it as long as her mind would allow her. There was something about her father's house that deadened it, that wouldn't allow her to capture the feeling and remember what it was like to feel alive again.

She would have been content to stay in the square all day, but Natalie grew bored of it, and at last, Ellen took her daughter by the hand and strolled up Park Street to have a look at the mansions there, resolute in her determination to relish every moment of this glorious and rare autumn day, and more reluctant than ever to return to the dark and wretched halls of her father's house.

They found themselves at the entrance to Hyde Park, where London's elite strolled about and sought amusement. To watch the procession of *haute ton* ladies in expensive walking gowns and showy bonnets, and gentlemen in embroidered waistcoats atop meticulously groomed horses was thrilling, and a pastime that inevitably made Natalie long to belong. But she and Natalie would never be a part of this society again, and it seemed unfair to give Natalie any hope that she would, so Ellen typically avoided it.

It was days like this, Ellen thought, as they entered the park, that she was so thankful Natalie was still too young to understand why they were outcasts. Inevitably, the day would come when she would ask the questions Ellen dreaded, the questions for which she really had no good answer. And really, as time passed, she could only know for certain that she had once fallen in love, fallen hard and long, and had given her all to it, and then . . . *now.* Now there were just the two of them, living in the wreckage of her carelessness, virtual prisoners of a father who would neither forgive nor forget.

Natalie would eventually ask, but today was not that day, and Ellen smiled at her daughter, who was fairly floating along the ground. "Are we going on a walkabout, Mother?"

"I think we shall."

"*Ooh,* how splendid!" she cried, and slipped from her mother's grasp, skipping ahead, her bonnet askew, eagerly trying to take in all the sights around her. Ellen hurried to catch up with her, feeling remarkably light of step herself for the first time in a long time.

They walked at a leisurely pace, taking in the lovely gowns and bonnets of the ladies who strolled along the promenade. Dashing gentlemen rode by on horseback, and couples laughed with one another as they rolled through in impossibly clean and highly ornamented curricles and broughams. They were so taken by the sights that it was some time before Ellen realized how far they had walked. They had come to a small clearing near a pond where the sunlight washed over the grass, and three geese glided serenely from shore to shore to rest beneath the boughs of willow trees. Nearby, atop an incline, children played, squealing with laughter. Natalie looked at them wistfully, and Ellen, wanting so for her daughter to have playmates, put her hand in the small of her daughter's back. "Go and play," she said, and smiled at the buoyancy in her daughter's step as she ran toward the children, slowing only when she neared them, approaching more cautiously.

Ellen took a seat on a bench in the clearing, turned her face up to the delicious warmth of the sun, and closed her eyes, eagerly letting her mind return to Liam, to the feel of his callused hand on her skin, the heat of his lips in her hair. He had left her a mess, her insides simmering with need, her imagination racing. The entire day had seemed all upside down somehow, and when she closed her eyes, she could only see Liam. She closed her eyes quite often, actually, so that she could gaze at that rugged face, every crevice, every scar, every speck of color in his green eyes, then wish fervidly for the sensation of his touch and the burn that went so deep inside her.

It was in the depth of that wish that she felt the warmth leave her face; a shadow had crossed the sun, and she opened her eyes. She gasped at the shadow (Liam!), thought for a moment that it was her imagination until she lifted her hand to shield her eyes and could see him. "Wh— How did you find me?" she stammered.

" 'Tis ye that found me, Ellie," he corrected her, moving so that the sun was not in her eyes.

That was when Ellen noticed his attire—what was left of it, anyway. It looked as if he had rolled down a hillside—his shoulder-length, wavy hair was in wild disarray, and what looked to be a twig of some sort was protruding from one tress. He had slung his coat over his shoulder, and his cambric shirt, terribly wrinkled and muddied, was hanging loose to mid-thigh. His buckskins were stained at the knees, and on the tip of his forefinger, he held a neckcloth, sopping wet.

"What . . . have you met with an accident?" she asked, alarmed.

Liam laughed at that, a deep, warm laugh, and suddenly went down on his haunches before her. "In a manner of speaking, ye might say as much, aye." He laughed again. "The accident is me cousin, Nigel. He invited me for a shoot, and we had a wee problem."

"Involving mud, I take it?"

"That, and various other," he said, his green eyes dancing with amusement. "I did a bit of laundering here."

"Here?" she asked, confused.

"Aye," he said, motioning to the pond. "Ye've stumbled upon me pond, Ellie."

She looked at the pond, then at Liam again. His pond? He had laundered his neckcloth in the *pond*? The very notion was so absurd and so very resourceful that she burst into laughter. "Oh, my, Captain Lockhart, why on earth did you not leave it for Follifoot?"

"Follifoot?" Liam chuckled and shook his head. "I'm afraid yer father didna include the good services of Follifoot in the rent."

"Do you mean to say that you are laundering *all* your clothes in this pond?" she asked, appalled.

"*Ach*, 'tis no' like that," he said, sounding a little indignant. "I use the bath for me drawers."

Ellen blinked.

Liam smiled, as if it were perfectly natural to launder one's drawers in one's bath.

She eyed his wrinkled shirt more closely. "I *see*. And by the look of it, you've done quite a bit of laundering recently," she added, smiling up at him.

Liam looked down, but whatever he might have responded was lost as they were both startled by the cry, "You're *beastly!*"

Ellen's heart filled with panic; she jerked her gaze to

where the children were playing. Natalie was standing on the edge of their circle, facing a boy and a girl, her bonnet gone. Ellen came to her feet at once, watched in horror as the girl pushed Natalie down. A mother—no, a governess—was running toward the children from the opposite direction, and Ellen realized she was running, too.

She reached Natalie at the same time the other woman did, and grabbed Natalie by the shoulders to lift her to her feet.

"Goodness, what are you about, Miss Lucy?" the woman exclaimed as she grabbed the other little girl.

"She's *wretched!*" the girl wailed. "She tells horrid lies and she's *cruel!*"

"Cruel!" Ellen exclaimed, looking in disbelief at Natalie.

The woman shook the girl. "I hardly care if she's a devil, Miss Lucy! Proper young ladies do not go about pushing other young ladies down!"

"But Miss Potts, she said her father would kill his lordship!" the boy insisted.

Ellen gasped, looked down at Natalie, who had yet to look up. "Did you say such a terrible thing?" she demanded.

Natalie nodded sheepishly.

"*Mary Queen of Scots,*" Liam muttered next to her.

"She's *beastly!*" Lucy wailed again.

"But you wouldn't allow me to play!" Natalie objected suddenly and strongly.

"That's because you said you were a princess, and your father was a king—"

"I only wanted to play!" she tearfully insisted.

"Still, you shouldn't walk about telling lies," the boy said haughtily. "God will smite you for it."

"She really shouldn't," Miss Potts said to Ellen. "She's upset the children."

"I believe *your* children have upset my daughter," Ellen shot back.

"I don't *want* to play with *you!*" Lucy said petulantly, crossing her arms over her chest. "You wear horrid frocks and tell horrid stories!"

"*Ach*, what a vile tongue ye have there, lassie! Do ye know what we do with naughty children at Loch Chon?" Liam demanded.

That certainly silenced everyone; the two children and their Miss Potts gaped up at Liam, dumbfounded.

"We eat them and put their eyes in our pudding."

Miss Potts gasped in horror; little Lucy backed up into her skirts and the boy darted behind her, staring fearfully at Liam.

"How *dare* you, sir!" Miss Potts hissed.

"Yer children are unruly," he responded calmly, and Ellen wanted to kiss him, then and there.

From the look of it, Miss Potts wanted to kill him. She glared at Ellen, then at Liam as she gathered her two charges close to her. "I'll be certain his lordship hears of this!" she said sternly.

"And ye'd do well to loosen that corset a wee bit, lass," Liam offered helpfully, to which Miss Potts gasped again, pulling her charges away and up the hill.

Ellen waited until they were out of earshot, then stared down at Natalie so harshly that the girl openly cringed. "Laria, is it? You've decided to let everyone in on your little kingdom, have you?" she demanded angrily.

Natalie shrugged, looked at her dress. "There's nothing wrong with my frock!" she said petulantly.

Ellen looked heavenward for a moment, trying to regain her composure. Of course there was nothing wrong with Natalie's frock, other than it was permanently stained along the hem and it was old, passed down from Eva. That was, however, beside the point, and she grabbed Natalie's hand. "It's time we returned home," she added, and abashed, glanced at Liam. "I am terribly sorry, Liam. We are not generally so . . . so—"

"Quite all right. I'd see ye home, I would, but I've something I must do," he said, looking terribly unsettled by the whole thing.

Ellen could hardly blame him—she was mortified that Natalie had behaved so badly in front of him, even more mortified that she couldn't seem to befriend other children. She bade him a hasty good day and pulled Natalie along with her to escape his gaze as quickly as she could.

Neither she nor Natalie spoke as they made the long trek across Hyde Park, and there was no point in it as far as Ellen could see. She could hardly begin to count the times she had talked to her daughter, had warned her, had *begged* her not to slip from reality, to stay grounded in London. But Natalie was getting older, and Ellen could feel her slipping from her grasp, and she felt especially desperate now that her daughter was wrapping her strange little world like a cloak around her, taking it with her wherever she went.

At home again, Ellen sent Natalie to her room as punishment for her little brawl, and watched the girl walk, head down, to that space that was her own private prison. Honestly, sometimes when Ellen looked at her daughter she saw a *real* princess. A mother, a wife, a lady of stature. But lately she looked at Natalie and saw only a little girl lost, with no hope of a future, no hope of ever escaping these dank, confining walls.

Oh, her father ensured that all their most basic needs were met—they had food and clothing (not exactly *haute couture*, but clothing nonetheless). They had a roof over their heads, Agatha and Follifoot to tend to them. What Farnsworth had taken from them was, of course, their spirits, which had been exactly his intent—all for her ancient sin of having fallen in love. Ellen couldn't care less if he took the spirit from her, if he beat her down and trampled what was left of her pride. But she couldn't bear to see him take it from Natalie. Natalie was innocent.

Lord God, she had to do something, had to think of an escape, a plan, before Natalie was lost forever.

Ellen glanced at her writing desk. There, tucked beneath a book, was a letter she had started to her dear friend Judith many weeks ago. A letter in which she asked if she and Natalie might call for a fortnight. She had the funds for the public coach; they could reach Judith tomorrow if she so desired. Yet she had never sent the letter because one question continued to trouble her: Where would they go after the fortnight? How would they live? What would they do?

Ellen fell onto the couch of her sitting room, stared at the cold hearth, her mind swirling around every conceivable idea toward that end.

Downstairs, Liam had returned from Hyde Park, having cleaned his gun and dressed the two partridges he had convinced Nigel to let him keep. Those he carried in a leather satchel he had purchased with his dwindling funds. The satchel was, however, something he considered a necessity, as it was apparent to him he would be forced to find his own food if he wanted to eat.

And now, standing there, staring at the clothing strewn carelessly about the room, he noticed with a wince (since Ellie had noticed) that Griffin's clothing was indeed quite mussed, even if he had done his level best to clean it. His mind was instantly decided—he walked across the room, put the partridges aside, and yanked on the bellpull.

When Follifoot appeared a quarter hour later, Liam smiled. "Ah, Follifoot, yer looking well indeed," he said with enthusiasm. "Ye look like a man who'd feel up to fetching a few buckets of hot water, eh?"

Follifoot's expression crumbled; he glanced at the clothing strewn everywhere.

"I know what ye'd be thinking," Liam said. "And ye'd be right. I did indeed launder the clothing. But I didna clean meself," he said, and chuckled cheerfully when Follifoot's shoulders sagged with his moan.

Two hours later, Ellen had bathed and changed into a gown of gold crepe that fell in soft folds over a long chemise of cream. It was one of her favorite gowns, one she had reserved for months for a special occasion . . . but hope was springing less and less eternal.

She sighed, looked at the passable lamb stew Follifoot had carried up. Natalie had left it untouched, had cried herself to sleep after Ellen had scolded her for what had happened in the park. She was still asleep, her arms curled tightly around a lumpy pillow, a frown on her soft, pretty face. Ellen quietly pulled the door to her room to and returned to the sitting room, feeling terribly restless. The house was quiet and empty now; she was alone with her dreams of escape.

She glanced at the window, noticed in the late evening sky that clouds had formed, hanging ripe overhead, and felt in her bones the rain returning.

The knock at the door startled her. She had not thought he'd come after what had happened and came quickly to her feet, rushed to the oval mirror above the settee to check her reflection. She smoothed her hair, pinched her pale cheeks, and shook the fabric of her gown to make it fall correctly over the chemise. And as she muttered to her heart to stop beating so painfully in her chest, she opened the door.

She saw only the ruggedly handsome man with leaf-green eyes and that prideful look—all that she had yearned for today. He was here, come to her door . . . to her arms, she hoped. Except . . . *except* . . . She couldn't help noticing, that her proud Highland soldier was wearing . . . was *wearing* . . . (What exactly was it?) . . . a *frock.*

At least it *looked* like a frock of some sort, except not a frock, exactly. A skirt of some type. A plaid, woolen thing, belted at his waist, topped with a small leather bag, above which he wore a pristine white shirt and a dark coat. Even more alarming was the shoes he wore, laced up over stockings, all the way up to his knees. His *bare* knees. His startlingly *appealing* bare knees.

"*Féileadh beag.* A kilt," he said, by way of explanation. "The Highland regiments wear them."

Ellen blinked and looked at his legs again.

Liam looked at her curiously. "Ye see the medal on me chest, do ye no'?"

She dragged her gaze from his legs to the medal on his chest. Medals, actually. Four, to be exact. "Ah! Military medals. I——I . . . I've never seen a kilt. Quite . . . fetching," she said uncertainly.

"*Ach,* yer blushing now," he said, smiling. "Have ye no' seen a man's legs, Miss Farnsworth?"

Her blush seated deeper. "I, ah . . . *ahem*—"

"Have I come at a bad time, then?"

"N-*no*! No!"

"Because I brought ye a fine supper, I did. I thought perhaps ye could use it."

"Really?" she asked, ridiculously pleased.

"Aye, really. Would ye like it?"

"Yes! Yes of course!" she said, stepping aside and gesturing for him to come in.

Liam strode purposefully across the threshold, his plaid swinging carelessly around his knees. "Do ye like partridge, then?" he asked, taking a small leather satchel from his shoulder.

"Partridge?"

"Partridge. A fat little bird," he said, reaching into the satchel. He withdrew a handful of raw meat, held it up for Ellen's inspection. "Caught just today."

She gaped at the bird flesh. "It's been dressed," she said aloud.

"Of course it has, lass! The pond is good for more than laundering!" He smiled. Ellen had a sudden and vivid image of him cleaning the fowl along the banks of that pond. First his neckcloth, then the bird—

"Ellie," he said, clucking his tongue. "Ye look as if ye expect to eat it thus," he said. "Of *course* I'll cook it for ye."

"*Cook* it? And how exactly will you do that?" she asked, confused.

"Ye've a fire, do ye no'?"

Ellen looked at the fire, then at Liam. "Do you mean to suggest that you are going to cook that bird over that fire?" she asked, incredulous.

"Aye, of course."

"But . . . but with *what*, if you don't mind my asking?"

He winked, leaned over, and withdrew a long dagger from his stocking, pierced the meat he was holding. "If ye donna mind me saying, Ellie, ye could stand to be a wee bit more ingenious, like yer Natalie."

Ingenious like Natalie? And as if she hadn't been astounded enough, he walked over to the fire, went down on his haunches, thrust the bird into the fire, all the while whistling a cheerful little tune.

Thirteen

❧

The smell of roasted partridge was enough for Ellie to overcome any misgivings she had, apparently—and Liam was pleased that the partridge did indeed smell divine. After a moment of looking rather shocked, Ellie pulled an ottoman over to where he was crouched in front of the fire, sat on the edge of it, leaving enough room for him (or rather, that was how he eagerly interpreted the move). They sat, side by side on the ottoman, his knee tantalizingly close to hers, taking turns roasting the fat little bird.

"You've apparently done this before," she said, as she attempted to turn the partridge and drip the fat away from the fire as he had shown her.

"I canna count the times. One learns to feed oneself in war, I suppose."

"I can scarcely imagine it," she said thoughtfully. "The public accounts of the war were quite subdued, really. I believe they must have omitted the offensive details."

Because the details were simply too horrid to write about, he'd wager. " 'Tis just as well ye never know, Ellie," he said. "A lady has no reason to hear such ugly things as goes on in war." And he sincerely meant that, hoped she'd never hear the truth.

"Really?"

"Still haunts me dreams." That, and trolls, the nasty buggers.

Ellie seemed to consider that for a moment, then blurted. "But don't you ever want to talk about it? Sometimes I feel positively full to bursting with . . . with things about life, and I'm quite desperate to just say it and have it out. Don't you ever feel the same?"

That surprised him. As far as he knew, ladies weren't supposed to be bursting with troubles. Liam glanced at her from the corner of his eye and wondered if it were possible that life could be so hard and complicated for her as it was for him. "I canna say so," he said when she looked to him for an answer. "Most of it I'd rather no' hear meself, much less trouble anyone else with it. I do just as well to forget."

"Truly?" she asked him earnestly. "I mean, can you *truly* forget?"

"Truly," he lied, and lifted the partridge off the fire to have a look. "Just a wee bit more."

She seemed to accept his answer—or at least his inability to talk about what had happened in the war—and stared wistfully into the fire.

They sat in companionable silence for a time, watching the bird roast. But there were so many thoughts going round in Liam's head, so many things he wanted to know about the woman sitting next to him, what the thing was filling her to the point of bursting that she wanted out of her. Whatever it was, he was acutely aware that he wanted to remove it, replace it, fill the void completely with himself. He leaned forward to better position the partridge, smiled at Ellie, and silently acknowledged that he was quietly going mad. Mad with desire, with thoughts completely new and foreign to him.

The companionable silence seemed suddenly deafening, and when he could no longer endure it, he blurted, "What is it, then, that is wrong with yer daughter, if ye'll pardon me asking?"

The question startled Ellie; her back instantly stiffened. "I gather you mean her tales," she said tightly. "I don't suppose she can help it, really—her imagination, that is. And honestly, it's not as if she has something with which to occupy her time. I teach her the best I can, but I'm hardly a governess. I urge her to read, I urge her to—"

Liam put his hand on her arm to stop her. Ellie flinched; she looked down at his hand. "I didna mean to upset ye, Ellie. I would never."

"You did not upset me," she insisted, but clearly he had.

"Donna misunderstand me now," he said gently, letting his hand slide slowly down her arm to her hand. "Yer Natalie, she's a bonny thing. I've come to feel quite an affection for the wee banshee."

That brought a soft smile to Ellie's face and she sighed, bowed her head, and looked into the fire. "She *is* a bonny thing, Liam. She's my precious darling," she said quietly. "I wish you could know how very beautiful she is. But we've been practically put on the shelf up here, and it seems that her stories have started to become more real to her than not. I worry for her."

"What is it ye mean, 'on the shelf'?"

Ellie shrugged. "Our situation— Oh dear, the bird is burning."

He had been so engrossed in her that he had forgotten the partridge. He grabbed the stick, took the bird from the fire, and lay it on the leather satchel. "God blind me," he muttered beneath his breath as he turned over the bird, pausing to suck on one burned finger, then another. He peeled back a layer of blackened skin, pausing again to wave his burning fingers in the air, but the meat was tender and succulent and he grinned broadly. "*Ah*, look at her now! A fine meal we've got, Ellie! Where is the little one, then?"

"Sleeping," Ellie said, returning his grin. "My heaven, how delicious it all smells! Wait! I've got just the thing for it," she said, and stood, hurrying into one of the adjoining rooms as Liam speared a second partridge and affixed it over the flames. Ellie returned a few moments later with a quilt under one arm and carrying a bottle of wine. She smiled at Liam as she glided into the room. "The quilt was my mother's," she said, "and the wine is from Agatha, bless her. I thought we might dine as if we were alfresco."

Liam didn't know what *alfresco* meant, exactly, but when Ellie moved the ottoman and spread the quilt before the hearth, he instantly nodded his approval, for it seemed he was better acquainted with alfresco than fancy tables. Ellie fetched two chipped china plates, two crystal tumblers for the wine, two linen napkins, and a bowl of water, which she placed off to one side. "For your fingers," she informed him, although Liam wasn't entirely certain what he was to do with his fingers and the bowl.

When the second bird was roasted, they sat facing each other on the quilt, Ellie with her legs tucked to one side, Liam cross-legged, a layer of woolen plaid the only thing between her and the part of him that most wanted to touch her. It was wildly decadent, this picnic near the fire, and Liam couldn't imagine his mother engaged in such an activity (although Mared brought to mind a wholly different thought). It seemed terribly inappropriate, somehow, for a woman of noble standing to be sitting here on the floor with the likes of him, eating partridge with her fingers and sucking the juices from them in a way that made it near to impossible to think of anything else but her, much less eating. That was why, he supposed, he found the whole thing so frighteningly seductive. He had never wanted a woman so badly in his life.

Which was why he asked about her mother again. It was his one weak attempt to subdue the desire raging through him, for talk of anyone's mother generally did it for him.

"She died in Cornwall," Ellie said matter-of-factly.

He instantly mumbled his condolences, which she quietly acknowledged before tearing off another bite of partridge. "I miss her terribly sometimes," she said, after chasing the bite down with a sip of wine. "Natalie and I were much happier there, I can assure you . . . although I don't think Mother was very happy at all. She preferred London, naturally."

"Ye lived with the wee princess in Cornwall, then?" he asked absently, stuffing the last of his partridge into his mouth, trying very hard not to look at the tantalizing bit of her flesh above the décolletage of her gown.

"Natalie was born in Cornwall." A shadow glanced Ellie's features; she paused, looked up, tried, he thought, to smile. "And what about your family? Have you a father? A mother?"

Liam laughed as he picked up his wineglass. "Naturally. A mother and a father. A brother and a sister, too."

"All in Scotland?"

"Aye, of *course!* Where else do ye think they'd be?"

"Scotland, of *course*," Ellie said, playfully mimicking his gruff tone. "They must miss you. I meant to inquire, how have you found London?"

How had he found London? A blight, a dirty stinking . . . "Lovely," he said. "Almost as lovely as ye are, Ellie."

Her smile deepened and she flushed an appealing shade of pink. Demurely, she glanced at her hands. "Then I suppose your family matter is coming along as you had hoped?"

"No' as I'd hoped, exactly. Cousin Nigel is a difficult man to come to know, he is," Liam said, not wanting to think of Nigel at the moment, not wanting to think of anything but her.

"Oh?"

"Do ye know him, then? Nigel Lockhart, of Mayfair."

Ellie thought, her brow furrowed prettily, but shook her head. "I am acquainted with the Lockhart name, but I'm afraid I've not been introduced to your cousin."

Liam was glad for it. "*Ach,* Nigel," he said with an impatient roll of his eyes. "I met him for the first time many years past, when I was at the military college. I remembered him straightaway when I saw him—but it has taken Nigel a wee bit longer to recall *me.*" He glanced at Ellie, smiled wryly. "The lad is rather fond of his ale, he is."

"But of course he has recalled you now, has he not?"

"Aye. Recalled me so favorably that he's asked to introduce me to his father. I'm to take tea on Sunday."

"How nice for you! Then you may ask for your things to be returned," she said, obviously recalling their previous conversation. The conversation in which Liam had, less than truthfully, admitted to wanting something from his cousin.

He shrugged halfheartedly. "I'm no' the sort for tea, truth be told. In fact, I hardly know how to go about it. There wasna a lot of call for it in the war, and truthfully, I need more than a spot of tea to do what I must."

Ellie seemed confused. "But what do you mean? I thought you had come to ask after some family property. Surely you could broach it at tea? After all, conversation is really what a tea is all about. One sips, one talks. I should think it the perfect opportunity for you."

"No' exactly," Liam muttered.

One fair brow rose in question.

Liam shifted uncomfortably. *Never trust a stranger.*

Never trust anyone but yourself. Never let them see the truth so they can't hurt you with it. Diah, but he wanted to tell her—the man in him wanted to trust her, wanted to tell her everything, but his instincts, honed by years of war and espionage, warned him against it. Screamed at him, more accurately.

Ellie smiled at his silence. A smile that, *heaven help him!* could melt the most hardened of defenses. Had Ellie been on the other side during the war, he would have sold all of bloody Britain for the favor of that smile. "Aye, they've something I want," he said flatly. "Something that belongs to me family, and something they may no' even know they have, in truth. And I've come to fetch it back."

"What is it?"

"A beastie."

"A *beastie?*"

"An ornamental one, no' a real one, of course," he said in all earnestness. "A gold beastie with ruby eyes and a ruby mouth and a ruby tail—"

Whatever he thought, he did not expect Ellie to laugh so . . . so *easily.*

"What, then?" he demanded. "What is it ye find so amusing in that?"

"Do you mean to say that you have come all this way to ask for a statue of a *beastie?*"

"Aye!" he insisted indignantly, folding his arms across his wrinkled shirt. She laughed again, beaming at him. "Seems a frightfully long way to come when you might have simply written and *asked* them to return it."

" 'Tis more complicated than that, Ellie," he said gruffly. " 'Tis a valuable statue and no' something they'd likely give up freely." And without conscious thought, Liam spilled the whole story to her. Told her of the family troubles, of the lore surrounding the solid gold beastie, that it was worth several thousand pounds, that it belonged to them. When he had finished, he felt rather exhausted and light of bearing. " 'Tis a matter that must be handled delicately, then."

"*Oh*," she said, sober now, having listened intently to his tale. "Then it sounds as if your tea is quite important."

"Aye, that it is. The family is counting on me."

"They must be terribly proud of you, to put so much faith in their brave and handsome soldier," she said solemnly.

Liam snorted. "Ye've had too much of the wine, then, if ye find me handsome."

She laughed; her blue gaze fell to his scar, and beneath her casual perusal Liam felt his skin go hot, thought perhaps the wine had fermented too long, because the way she was looking at him was actually making him a little dizzy. Without warning, she leaned across the quilt toward him to have a closer look, and he instinctively, unthinkingly, moved to cover the ugly scar with his hand.

Ellie startled him by catching his hand with her own, her long, delicate fingers closing tightly around his. "*No*," she murmured, and pushed his hand aside, then touched his scar. The soft glance of her fingertips against his face sent a white-hot bolt of lightning through his body. His blood was suddenly churning; he felt as if he were drowning somehow, being pulled beneath the surface by the mere touch of her fingers. She traced the length of the scar, from his forehead to the middle of his cheek where it ended, then back again, her fingers flowing over him like the water over the rocks in the streams that fed Loch Chon. It seemed minutes, if not hours, before she shifted her gaze from his face to his eyes. "Did it hurt terribly?"

"No," he said hoarsely. "No' as much as this."

Ellie's gaze roamed his battered face. "Do I hurt you, Liam?" she murmured. He nodded. "But how can I hurt you?"

"Because I want ye, Ellie," he confessed in a gruff whisper. "I want ye like I've never wanted for anything, and it aches in me bones."

She didn't say anything, just traced a line from the scar to his lips, letting her fingers rest against them.

I've no' hurt as much as this, he thought, and impulsively grasped her hand, kissed her palm, his lips lingering there, wanting so much more but at the same time fearing anything more as he had never feared anything in his life.

But then Ellie withdrew her hand and laid it tenderly against his rough cheek, and Liam lost all power of reason. He reached for her, seized her, really, and pulled her hard to him, across the quilt, without thought to the partridge or the wine. His lips landed blindly on her forehead, then her cheek, sliding recklessly to her lips. He tasted the wine she had drunk, the faint hint of roasted bird. He felt the succulent surface of her lips, ripe and full of promise, and held fast there, frozen by the exquisite feel of her in his arms.

It was Ellie who moved first, Ellie whose fair lips parted slightly—*so slightly*—and she whispered, *"Do you want me, Liam?"* before dipping her tongue between his lips to touch him. And then Liam was falling, drifting down to the bottom of the sea in which she had pushed him.

Somehow he managed to lay her down beside him, the vague thought that he might never have such a chance as this again sounding in his brain. His lips moved across hers, lips that were incredibly soft, feeling and tasting them, inch by extraordinary inch. Then he tasted the inside of her mouth, reveled in the feel of her teeth, her tongue, and the sweet, smooth flesh of her mouth. One hand fell to the slender column of her neck, drifted down to the silk of her bosom, his knuckles grazing her skin, his hand cupping the soft weight of her breast.

Heedless of anything but the strong, magnetic allure with which she held him captive, he grabbed a fistful of her silken hair, which had somehow come tumbling down from its carefully constructed coif. He felt miles and miles of corn silk as the sweet scent of lavender filled his senses. Her body, so enticingly pressed against his, was firm, a testament to her youth and good health, yet at the same time, she was so amazingly soft, so astoundingly plush, her breasts, supple and ripe, practically spilling from her gown. He touched his lips to her neck, the pure satin of her skin, and shuddered when Ellie whispered in his ear, *"I want you too . . ."*

Pure male instincts took hold of him—he was without reason or thought, filled with a prurient sense of longing as her hand, her small, perfect hand, slid to the nape of his neck, her fingers entwining in his hair, then down his arm, squeezing it, her fingers softly kneading the flesh, moving to his rib cage, his back. Liam kissed her wildly, deeply, his heart and mind raging to be inside her . . . and he was, he realized, through the fog that had shrouded his mind and all common sense, just moments away from *being* inside of her. But then the sound of . . . of *what?* . . . filtered into his consciousness.

Liam forced himself to stop; Ellie, precious Ellie, heard it too, and she fell away from him, the heat of her body fading from his as her breath came in long, deep draws and her gaze fixed on the door. There it was again, that *sound*. Slowly, unsteadily, Ellie came to her feet, repairing her bodice and shaking the wrinkles from her gown as she stared at the door.

It came again—someone was climbing the stairs.

Liam rose silently, listened to the unmistakable footfall of Farnsworth, his little feet betraying his girth.

"My *father*," Ellie whispered frantically. Her eyes were wide with fright—the blood had drained from her face and she lifted her hand to her throat, terrified. She feared the little pea hen of a man, which angered Liam, irrationally so. Yet whatever the bastard had done to her, it would have to wait. He calmly swept his arm around Ellie's waist and pulled her into him, kissing her hard and passionately, letting her know all the desire that would remain within him. But she pushed against his chest, and he cupped her chin, kissed her softly, tenderly one last time. "Donna fear," he said, and hearing the footsteps again on the last stretch of stairs, walked away from her, toward the window. He lifted the heavy frame, looked down at the alley below. Not a particularly congenial exit, but there was nothing that could be done for it. "Close it after me, Ellie," he said, and with one last smile for her, he disappeared through the window.

Fourteen

❧

*H*er heart racing badly, Ellen closed the window behind Liam *(What did he do, jump?)* as she heard her father's footsteps on the stairs. He never came to this floor unless he had something to complain about, and if he found Liam in her suite—well, that was something Ellen really didn't want to contemplate.

Frantic, she rushed to hide the wine and the glasses, threw the carcasses of the bird onto the fire and shoved Liam's forgotten leather satchel under the sofa, along with the quilt and dirty plates. She was foolhardy— *reckless!* What of Natalie? Had she no more regard for her daughter's well-being than this? Of course she did, yet she could feel the well of resentment bubbling up. She was almost nine and twenty years. She shouldn't be forced to steal about like some wayward schoolgirl!

The pounding at her door caused her to jump with a soft shriek. She stood for a moment, fighting for composure. With one last wild look around, she kicked a corner of the quilt beneath the sofa and strode to the door, taking a deep, steadying breath as she pulled it open.

Her father was standing there, looking his usual hateful self.

"Good evening, Father."

He glared at her with his little eyes narrowed in suspicion, as he was wont to do. "What in blazes is going on here?" he spat.

The color drained from her face. *Follifoot*. He must have seen Liam, must have mentioned—

"I am not in the habit of seeking your audience, Ellen! If I desire to speak with you, I demand you come when I say!"

That confused her—she certainly had not received word that he wanted her. "Come when you say? I—"

"I left *explicit* instructions for you to come to my study at precisely seven o'clock! It is now well past eight o'clock!"

"You sent for me? But I—"

"You will not keep me waiting like some jilted lover!" he said acidly.

Ellen felt her blood run cold. "Father, I was not made aware that you had sent for me. Of course I would have come had I known."

Farnsworth was not listening—he was peering past her into the room Liam had just vacated. "What in the devil are you about?" he demanded again, pushing past her, waddling into the room.

Her heart in her throat, Ellen watched him clasp his hands behind his back and stroll to the middle of the room, glancing about as he fished his monocle out of his pocket. He peered very closely at the furnishings.

Ellen panicked. She followed her father, stood in front of the sofa lest a corner of the quilt somehow be seen.

"Where's the girl?" Farnsworth asked, whipping around so suddenly that Ellen reared back.

"Asleep, sir."

"Asleep, is she?" he snarled suspiciously. "Perhaps I'll just have a look!"

"By all means. She's just through there," Ellen said, pointing to the appropriate door.

But Farnsworth did not bother to look where she pointed; he was too busy peering suspiciously at her. "What's that *smell*?" he demanded.

Liam. Oh God, like a dog on the hunt, he had smelled him. Ellen swallowed. "P-pardon?"

"*Smells,* I said! Rather like greasy meat."

The partridge—

"Just where would you get your hands on poor quality meat?" he pondered.

How odd that this remark, of all those he had made to her in the last two years, should ignite such resentment, but it enraged Ellen. Her very own father held her in slightly better stead than a prisoner, fed them nothing short of swill, and then had the audacity to ask her where she might have found *meat?* She could feel the color bleeding hot into her face again. "If I am in the possession of such meat, sir, it has come from your very own kitchen."

"Don't be smart with me!"

"I am hardly being smart. I am merely stating a fact."

Farnsworth's eyes widened at her cheek. "I'll not abide your impertinence, Ellen!" he snapped, then made a show of strolling to the window to gaze out into the night. Ellen watched him rise up on his toes, then settle down again. Her irritation was mounting—*impertinence?* When he deigned to acknowledge her and Natalie at all, he treated them like lowly servants. She had endured it, had thought she was shielding Natalie from the worst, but at the moment she was hardly in the mood to humor him with her acquiescence. She was, lest he had forgotten, his *daughter,* for God's sake! No matter what she had done, she deserved better from him.

It was at that precise moment that her sense of reason and consideration flew out of her head. "Pray tell, *Father,* to what do I owe this extraordinary visit?" she asked, her voice barely civil.

"Determined to earn my wrath, are you? If you had come below when I said—"

"I obviously did not get the note, for surely I would have come to you rather than have you climb the stairs to my suite."

"Oh, *really?*" he drawled, pivoting and walking toward her again. "And why should I *not* come to your suite if I like? This *is* my house, is it not?"

"A fact you have made abundantly clear and on more than one occasion."

"I can only surmise that you are perhaps trying to *hide* something," he said, baiting her.

He was successful. Years of regret and repugnance evaporated all of her patience. "*Hide* something?" she snapped, clearly surprising him. "What could I possibly *hide*, Father? I have no funds other than the paltry few crowns you'll allow me, I have no social connections, I have *nothing!* I have only Natalie! Tell me, please; exactly *what* do you think I could possibly be hiding?"

Farnsworth's monocle fell from its superior perch with her outburst and he blinked rapidly. "*What?*" he asked in stunned breathlessness. "What did you say?"

Ellen had done it; she folded her arms across her middle, waited for the bitter rancor she knew would come.

"How *dare* you speak to me thus!" he cried, obliging her. "I have every *right* to disown you for what you did! And you would have the gall to complain to *me?*"

"Dear *God!* It was ten years ago, Father! One summer, one mistake, ten *years* ago!"

"Do not think to lecture me on the timing or enormity of your foolishness! Your actions brought a blight to this family and I shall not forgive it! Do you think I enjoy harboring a whore and her bastard child in my house? If I could toss you aside like so much rubbish, I would do so!"

He might as well have slapped her. She felt as if she

were nineteen all over again, feeling the seed of his
hatred take root, wanting to shield her unborn child
from his vitriol. It had been a futile desire—his hatred
had grown inside her, poisoned Natalie. Ellen despised
her father, and honestly, she could not remember a time
when he had been either loving or particularly paternal. He had, she realized after long nights of introspec-
tion, hated her long before she'd met Daniel and her
nightmare had begun.

But she was not the same nineteen-year-old debutante now, and somehow she found her voice. "You've
made it perfectly clear that you do not want us, sir,"
she said, the calm tone of her voice surprising even her.
"You may trust me, we both know it and feel it
deeply . . . but that has been your wish all along, has it
not? To make us feel your hatred? Rest assured, if I had
the means, I would not so much as darken your door.
But as I have no means, and no hope of gaining them, I
have nowhere to go with my daughter. I can only con-
clude you rather enjoy keeping us prisoner here."

"*Ha!*" he spat at her. "Don't be absurd, Ellen! If your
mother hadn't died when she did, you'd not be in
London. I would have left you in Cornwall to *rot!* But
she *did* die, and I had no choice but to bring you here,
did I? I will never forgive you, and I will not allow you
to besmirch my name or Eva's reputation any more
than you already have! For if there is one thing in
which I am entirely confident, it is once a whore, *always*
a whore!"

She was numb now, so numb that his brutal words
had no effect on her, and she smiled thinly at his
attempt to hurt her. "You have nothing to fear, Father.
You have isolated us from the world so very well that
there is no possible way to dishonor you. After all, it
takes two."

Farnsworth gasped, but Ellen had already turned

away, was walking blindly toward the door, wishing (God forgive her) that her father was dead. Just gone. Or someone entirely different than the bitter little man that he was.

She reached the door, put her hand on the knob, and turned to face him. "What was it you wanted?" she asked coldly.

His face had mottled with anger; he moved quickly toward her, seeming as anxious to be gone as she was for him to leave. "I intend to be gone a fortnight come Sunday morning. Agatha will be here in my stead to keep an eye on you," he said coldly. "Heed me, Ellen, if you *are* hiding anything, I will discover it. And if you think I will not exact appropriate punishment, you would do well to think again. Do I make myself exceedingly clear?"

"Exceedingly," she said acidly.

He stopped directly in front of her, stood eye to eye. He leaned forward, so that his face was inches from hers, and Ellen fought to keep from recoiling at the stench of his breath. "There is one more thing, girl. Do *not* cross me! And keep that bastard of yours away from my tenant! If you cannot conduct yourself appropriately and see to it that the girl does likewise, there will be hell to pay. You have my word on that."

Ellen turned her head, heard his grunt of disgust as he walked through the door, and closed it with a loud bang behind him. Her chest heaving, she waited until she could hear him on the stairs. Only then did relief flood her; she leaned against the door, the weight of his hatred forcing her to her knees, the familiar tears of frustration spilling onto her cheeks.

She had to find a way out, using whatever means necessary. She had no other option.

And as she sat there, huddled, an idea slowly came to her. It was absurd, ridiculous . . . but it was better than nothing, she supposed, and after several moments, she slowly pulled herself up. With a hand on her belly to push down the sudden nausea, she walked to the secretary, uncovered the letter she had written to Judith. Hardly sparing it a glance (she had read it so many times, she knew it by heart), she sat down, took a breath, and dipped her pen in ink.

Ellen sent Natalie down to Liam the next afternoon with a mission: Bring back his wrinkled clothing. She had borrowed the clothing iron from Agatha with an excuse of having rumpled her gold silk (*I'll press it for you, milady. Just leave it be,* Agatha had insisted), and after much discussion, she had returned to her rooms with the clothing iron, triumphant.

When Natalie came upstairs with Liam's wrinkled clothing, she heated the iron as Agatha had shown her and attempted to press a waistcoat. Unfortunately, she had heated the thing too thoroughly and burned a hole straight through the linen fabric. She could cross chambermaid off her list of potential occupations, then. A little frantic, she had gone up to the unused third floor of the mansion, to the rooms in the very northern corner that held trunks and boxes full of family belongings.

In the third trunk she found the men's clothing she had seen once before. She began to sort through the items, and in one pocket of a pair of trousers she found a calling card: LORD RICHARD FARNSWORTH. Her father's brother had died of a fever just three years ago. Uncle Richard had been a surprisingly affable man, quite the opposite of her father both in mien and appearance. He was much larger than Farnsworth— tall, dapper, and known as one of the great London dandies of his time. Ellen continued sorting through the old clothing, and while she found only a few formal clothes, and some riding and walkabout clothes, too, she found one delicately embroidered waistcoat, the color of lichen moss.

The color of Liam's eyes.

That afternoon at precisely five minutes after five o'clock, Ellen walked to the window and saw her father toddling off to his usual evening of gaming. She returned to her task, finished the last pair of Liam's trousers (without any burns, thank you), and neatly folded them, adding them to the stack of freshly pressed clothing she had managed to complete without incident. She then repaired to her dressing room and selected a white gown adorned with tiny silk rosebuds across the bodice and down the train. Eva had expensive, albeit overly modest taste, but the gown was very nice, really. She was fastening the last of her mother's necklaces, the one with red glass beads she could not bring herself to part with, when she heard Natalie's voice.

"You really eat a frightful lot of cabbage, you know."

Ellen fastened the necklace, took one last look at her hair.

"Aye, lass, I eat cabbage, no' hasty pudding. I shouldna like a prince to come and rescue me, would I now?"

That made no sense whatsoever and gave Ellen pause.

"Well, he won't rescue *you*, because you're not a princess. You're a captain. But he'll come for my mother if you don't."

Ellen did not need to hear more. She dashed toward the main room before Natalie could say anything else to humiliate her. She stopped at the door; her gaze met Liam's, and a flush of warmth ran through her. This Scot had truly captured her fancy, hadn't he? She marveled at it, smiling broadly. "I'm so glad you've come, Liam!"

Standing in the middle of the room, holding a large bouquet of pilfered flowers, he frowned and tried to smooth as many of the wrinkles from his trousers as he could, but having no luck with them at all, seemed to resign himself to their existence. "I donna know what to say to something so kindly put, in truth. Other than there is naugh' that could keep me away," he blurted.

Her flush turned even warmer; still smiling, she walked toward him, nodded at the flowers. "Shall I presume they are for us?"

Just like he had the first time, Liam looked curiously at the flowers, almost as if he were surprised to be holding them. "Aye, they are. I took them from yer neighbor's garden so as not to ruffle any feathers in the park. Yer fellow countrymen seem rather tenderhearted about it."

"They're beautiful. Why don't you put them in water, Natalie?" she suggested, to which the girl happily agreed, and they watched her skip across the room and disappear into the adjoining room.

"Ye're all I can keep in me head, Ellie," Liam said, drawing her attention back to him. He was looking at her strangely, as if he weren't quite certain who he was seeing, and slowly shook his head in bewilderment. "*Ach,* I see that smile, and I think to meself, could she be smiling at ye, lad, with yer broken face and rustic ways? And then I see that, aye, she does indeed smile at me, and I feel me heart melt a wee bit more."

"*Ooh,* Liam . . ."

"Aye, ye're a bonny thing, Ellie Farnsworth, and I'm right glad to have known ye, I am." He fished in the pocket of his dreadfully wrinkled trousers, withdrawing something that he held tightly in his fist. "I've something for ye, *leannan.*" He opened his fist, revealing a smooth pebble in the palm of his hand. "I know it doesna seem to be much; 'tis a stone from the stream that runs across Talla Dileas—home, that is—and I carry it with me always," he said, tapping a fist to his heart.

She moved closer; the stone, small in his bearlike hand, was polished smooth, variegated, with streaks of earth brown and autumn gold running through it. It was beautiful, and it conjured up the description of his home he had given her over beef stew that night.

"It means much to me," he said, with a slight shrug of his shoulders, and gestured for her to open her hand, then laid it in her palm. Ellen turned it over, felt the smooth sides with her forefinger, and wondered about a man who would carry a small stone. So loyal, so true. *So different from Daniel . . .*

"Ye donna look pleased," he said, his voice belying his disappointment. " 'Tis a silly pebble, I know, but—"

"Oh, no, Liam, you are wrong. I am *very* pleased—but I don't feel deserving." She smiled gratefully. "I think it is the most beautiful gift I have ever received, and I shall treasure it always."

Liam nodded, looked at his feet, and Ellen saw the giant little boy she had seen in him the first time he had called. "Bloody hell, then, I'm becoming as barmy as the English," he said disgustedly.

Ellen laughed, withdrew a linen from her pocket and carefully folded the stone in it, then slipped it into her pocket again. "We think alike, sir, for I have something for you, too," she said.

"Mother, won't you tell him the surprise?" Natalie said, coming through the door with a vase full of flowers.

"I was on the verge of admitting that there has been something of an accident," Ellen said, exchanging a giggle with Natalie, and at Liam's curious look said, "I'm afraid, sir, that your waistcoat met with a terrible demise."

Liam winced unabashedly. "*Ach,* now, do no' tell me such a thing! Grif will have me very head, he will!"

"Can I fetch the surprise, Mother, please?"

"Yes," she said, laughing as Natalie skipped to the other side of the room, picked up a package wrapped in brown paper and raced back to hold it proudly before Liam.

"Go on. Take it," Ellen urged Liam.

He frowned. "I'll warn ye now, I'm a soldier. I donna like surprises by nature."

Natalie giggled.

Liam grunted his disapproval, but took the package from her and tore at the string that bound it. *"Mary Queen of Scots,"* he breathed harshly as he withdrew the waistcoat.

"Don't you like it very much?" Natalie asked excitedly.

"Like it?" He turned it over. *"Ahem . . .* of course I like it!" he said, as if that were a ridiculous question. "But 'tis far too extravagant for the likes of me," he said, and held it out to Ellen between two fingers. "Ye shouldna waste yer good coin."

"Oh no, we didn't purchase it," Ellen said happily. "We *found* it. It belonged to my late uncle. I think it should fit you perfectly. Hold it up, will you?"

"I'm certain it will do—"

"Liam. Hold it *up,* please."

With another grimace, he did as she asked. "Perfect!" she exclaimed as Natalie clapped cheerfully, and they laughed again at Liam's look of pure chagrin.

The clothing decided, whether he liked it or not, Liam stayed for the remainder of the evening, long after Ellen had put Natalie to bed. They talked like two old friends, each reliving stories from childhood, talking about their lives until now. Each carefully skirting the darker things that they would keep to themselves for the time being.

Ellen asked more about the beastie. It was supposedly made of solid gold, he said, with ruby eyes, a ruby mouth and tail. Stood perhaps as much as a foot high. He told her the story of its many trips between England and Scotland, the legends surrounding it, and he admitted more fully the animosity that ran between the two branches of the Lockharts because of it. Together they speculated where the Lockharts might have put something so old, with Ellen theorizing it would be the main drawing room, where they would want to display their treasures to impress callers. But Liam shook his head. " 'Tis no' a pretty thing," he said. "Most would find it hideous, if the descriptions of it are accurate."

"What do you think it is worth?" she asked.

Liam shrugged. "Solid gold, rubies . . . We believe it is worth several thousand pounds."

Several thousand pounds . . .

He seemed reluctant to say more, and their talk turned to tea, with Ellen explaining the protocol. On her fourth try, Liam exclaimed with great exasperation, "What a lot of bother for something as tasteless as tea!"

She could hardly disagree.

As the evening faded to night, Liam gathered Ellen in his arms and kissed her deeply, his desire unapologetically evident. He was not alone—Ellen felt her body come alive with his touch, as if he had breathed life into a dying thing. She wanted to feel him, feel his body on her, his body inside of her. That very thought brought a rash of heat to her face; she felt ashamed, as if desiring the touch of another human being was wrong somehow. She didn't want to think of it at all, really, because in the circle of his arms, Ellen felt herself falling all over again, only harder than she had ever fallen before, and she thought the world was finally crumbling beneath her feet.

It was a magnificent fall from grace.

Fifteen

❧

*O*n Sunday, Liam arrived at the Lockhart mansion at precisely four o'clock, wearing the foppish, repulsively embroidered waistcoat Ellie had given him, and was shown to a very large salon by a very stiff butler who asked him to kindly wait for Nigel. Not surprisingly, Nigel was a little late in rising from his afternoon nap.

That was all well and good, really, because Liam was taken aback by the opulence of the drawing room and needed a few moments to regain his composure. The Scottish Lockharts were losing ground every day, but the *English* Lockharts were apparently living quite high on the hog. From the rich mahogany floor-to-ceiling wood mantel to the leather wing-backed chairs and overstuffed divan, thick Aubusson carpet, and heavy brocade drapes, there was nothing that did not seem steeped in money. Mountains of it.

Liam stalked from one end of the salon to the other (even larger than the old great hall in Talla Dileas!), taking in all the belongings. The walls, consoles, and shelving were chock full of fancy ornaments, china figurines, and sculptures made of precious metals. On the walls hung large paintings in gilded frames. There were, as best he could identify, Persian, Chinese, French, and Italian trinkets and art scattered about. But not a beastie among them.

While Liam was brewing to a full head of steam,

Nigel did at last deign to appear with his father in tow, from whom, Liam could see instantly, Nigel had inherited his robust figure and lack of common sense.

After introductions were made and the ladies' apologies given, the gentlemen had assumed their seats, and the old man asked of Liam, "A Lockhart, are you?" to which Liam grunted an affirmative reply. "Scots, too? I wasn't aware of any Scottish Lockharts, was I, Nigel?"

"Eh, what?" Nigel asked. "Well, it's really so far north and rather remote, isn't it? That makes them rather distant cousins after all. I shouldn't think that we'd know necessarily, sir."

"Distant cousin? How odd . . . I always thought that meant the *degree* of removal, not necessarily the *distance*," Lord Lockhart pondered.

Mary Queen of Scots, Liam thought irritably, wishing it did indeed mean distance, and swallowing his tea, said pleasantly, "Perhaps, then, ye donna recall the family history?"

"Ooh, is there one? A family history, that is?" Nigel the Dolt asked, holding his teacup aloft so the good butler might put a spot of whiskey into it.

"Surely ye've heard the tale of the first Lockharts, eh?"

"Do you mean our ancestors?" Lord Lockhart asked helpfully.

God blind him! "Aye. Our ancestors," Liam responded, and proceeded to tell them how the split of the Lockharts had come about after the earl of Douglas had died, being careful to omit any references to the sorry lot of cowards *their* side of the family had proved to be.

"Quite interesting and all that, but what have the Lockharts to do with this Douglas chap?" Nigel asked, adopting an identical perplexed look to the one his father wore.

Family history was not, apparently, high on the

English Lockharts' agenda. Then again, who needed history when one had so many resources and a priceless beastie to boot? Liam devoured another cucumber sandwich and tried a different tack. "Right ye are, Cousin Nigel. There's no' much to say about the Douglases—or the Lockharts, for that matter. Just that they were a lot of Highlanders and old loyalists to the clans."

"To *clams?*" the elder Lockhart demanded. "What sort of person is loyal to a *clam?*"

"Not *clam*, milord. *Clan*," Liam clarified, and proceeded to paint a false picture of the Scottish Lockharts (who became, the more he talked, a group of backward cave dwellers who spoke their own guttural language, adhered to their own animal standards, and basically ate tree root and grunted quite a lot). His purpose being, of course, to separate himself from them so the rift between father and son might be believed. And he managed to do it with something of a straight face, and frankly, had the two English Lockharts *quite* enraptured. They sat on the edges of their seats, gasping at all the appropriate moments and shaking their heads in silent sympathy for a man so hopelessly different from his family. "Ye can see me dilemma, then," he said hopefully, after confirming for Lord Lockhart that his father was indeed a rustic madman.

Holding their teacups in identical, effeminate fashion, Lord Lockhart and Nigel stared wide-eyed at him. "Well of *course* we can see!" Nigel said, nodding furiously. "In truth, Cousin Liam, you mustn't go back there!" he added with a shudder.

"Ah, I couldna do so. Me father, well . . . he's got himself a bit involved in . . . *Ach,* best no' to speak of it."

As if they were one person, Nigel and his father both surged forward. "You may speak freely with us, sir," the old Lockhart assured him. "We are family, after all."

Not if he had anything to do with it. "Aye, indeed,

milord . . . but it's rather difficult to speak of, what with the . . . well, *consequences* and all."

"*Consequences?*" Nigel squealed.

"Rather dire," Liam added with a shrug, then muttered behind his teacup, "Perhaps unlawful."

"Oh, dear. It must be something quite . . . wretched?"

"Quite. I canna condone it, what with being a soldier in the king's army, that is," he said helplessly as the butler moved woodenly to the old man's side and leaned over his shoulder.

"I beg your pardon, my lord," the butler whispered rather loudly, "but Lady Lockhart is leaving for her fortnight in the country and is waiting for you in the family drawing room."

Lord Lockhart frowned and waved a hand at the man. "Can't she just go on, then?" he asked irritably.

The butler was not deterred. "She's rather insistent, my lord."

"Yes, yes," Lord Lockhart said, putting his teacup aside. "Can't keep the dear waiting," he added with a roll of his eyes to Liam and Nigel, and pushed his girth to standing. "Well, then. We simply must finish our visit another day. Will you come again, Cousin Liam? We're quite anxious to have the whole story."

"It would be an honor."

"And naturally you'll be attending our annual ball, Wednesday next, as our special guest, will you not?"

The very word *ball* sent shivers of fear down his spine. "Ah, milord, I canna—"

"Of *course* you can! Don't be ridiculous! I should be quite offended if you refuse, for we're *family*," he said, balancing his ample girth on a spindly little cane. "You *must* come. We'll show you about to all our friends. I won't take no for an answer."

Bloody hell. "Thank you," Liam said, rising. He towered

over his uncle, who put a liver-spotted hand to Liam's chest and patted him like an old dog. "Never fear—we'll clean you up and turn you out, you'll see," he said as he started out the door. "They'll never know you're a Scot once we're through with you, will they, Nigel?"

"No sir! All right, then? Pip-pip," Nigel said, waddling after his father.

"Pip-pip," Liam echoed, and waited until they had quit the room behind the butler to slap his teacup down on the service tray and toss aside his napkin. "Bloody barmy English," he muttered as he marched from the room to have a quick look around before the butler could find him.

While Liam was sneaking about the ground floor of the Lockhart mansion, Ellen was staring across a table at her sister Eva as she embroidered linen kerchiefs with the family initials, wondering how two people born of the same parents could be so very different.

For the first part of her visit, Eva had, in a near monotone, attempted to regale Ellen with an account of their meal just last evening. She had begun by recounting the menu (*braised lamb with rosemary and potatoes, although she did not care for the potatoes*), the wine (*a rather disagreeable vintage, although she really couldn't recall which vintage it was, precisely*), and the exact time they had sat for the evening meal (*always at eight o'clock, but for Willard's late meeting, which put them back a full quarter past*). Then she had begun to explain how she came to be embroidering the linen napkins with initials (*Willard thought them rather plain, all in all*).

Ellen stitched an *E* on her kerchief, thought of the flowers in her dressing room stolen from Lord Parnham's prized garden, and instantly put her hand in the pocket of her gown, felt the polished stone there, and suppressed a quiet smile.

When Eva finished reciting the evening meal, she reminded Ellen that she had two gowns to pass along to her. "From two Seasons past, I believe, so I should think no one will take any notice," she assured Ellen.

"Of course not," Ellen responded automatically, knowing full well that no one would take notice of her in anything she wore. It was almost as if she existed like a ghost, where she could see everyone around her, but no one could see her.

"I've also a little frock for Natalie," she continued blandly, "that belonged to the daughter of my house-keeper. But really, I'm so cross with the girl that I shouldn't give it to her a'tall," she said with a sniff.

"Indeed? And why is that?" Ellen asked calmly, expecting a host of minor social violations, the sort Eva typically liked to catalog for her.

"Because she's telling awful stories to Frederick! They're keeping him awake at night," she said petulantly. "Her conduct and imagination are *very* unseemly. You should *do* something."

Do? And what exactly would Eva suggest? What was *unseemly* in this family was that she had nowhere to take Natalie but to this stodgy old house. That, to Ellen, was a far greater crime than a child's bizarre storytelling. Nonetheless, she could not ignore the fact that Natalie's expanding imagination had moved beyond the point of making excuses for it. She shoved her unfinished kerchief into her reticule. "Let's fetch the gowns, shall we?" she suggested tightly.

Eva was more than happy to send her on her way.

As she and Natalie walked home later that afternoon, Ellen decided that in the last fortnight or so Natalie's tales had become bolder and more fantastic. And on those occasions when she tried to talk to her about it, the girl was dutifully contrite, but would return to her fantasy the very next day. Her daughter's malady, whatever it was, was not something Ellen knew how to address. Yet it was a growing concern, and she felt instinctively and certainly that if she didn't get Natalie away from here and into some semblance of a life, it would only get worse.

She looked down at Natalie walking next to her, trailing her hand along anything she could touch, oblivious to her mother's concern. "Darling, have you been telling stories to Frederick?" she asked.

Natalie glanced at her from the corner of her eye and hesitantly shook her head.

"Should I presume, then, that you didn't say anything that might have frightened him?"

Natalie did not look at Ellen, but kept her eyes on her feet.

They continued walking in silence.

It was moments like this Ellen felt so very alone. No one but she knew the troubles clouding Natalie's mind; no one knew the two of them even existed, really. They were living like lepers in a city teeming with life, and her daughter was wasting away in a little fantasy world Ellen could no longer control or even enter.

It was time to go. Ellen could feel it in her very marrow.

She was so lost in thought that she almost collided head-on with Liam on the walkway near the Farnsworth house. He caught her arm as she walked past, and Ellen shrieked with alarm.

"Did ye no' see me, then?" he said, instantly letting go of her arm as she whirled around to face him. "I thought surely ye did, Ellie, for I was standing directly before ye."

She caught her breath; he looked different—dressed in black superfine, dark brown trousers, and the embroidered waistcoat she had given him. The shirt he wore—one she had pressed—looked as pristine as any she had seen, and the neckcloth . . . well now *that* was an interesting knot. All in all, he looked stunningly handsome. How strange, therefore, that she should prefer the *other* Liam. The soldier Liam. The Liam who stomped mice and roasted partridges at the hearth.

"*Mi Diah,* donna say ye've forgotten me already!" he exclaimed with a nervous laugh.

"I know who you are," Natalie offered hopefully.

Liam smiled, cupped her chin. "Of that I am as sure as that the sun will rise."

"Pardon, but I didn't see you standing there," Ellen said. "I'm not accustomed to ... well ..." She didn't say more, but looked meaningfully at his clothes.

Liam instantly looked down and groaned. "*Ach,* I feared it would be so! I've become a bloody coxcomb, have I no'?"

That was so absurd, Ellen couldn't help but laugh. "I am quite confident, sir, that you will *never* be a coxcomb. Were you just leaving?"

"Just returning. I've had the pleasure of meeting me Uncle Lockhart," he said, and gestured for her to proceed down the walk. He fell in beside her, hands clasped behind his back, looking like a typical London gentleman.

"And how did you find him? Is he well?"

Liam looked at her from the corner of his eye and smiled wryly. "Well enough, I suppose. But it is a fact that the English Lockharts are cut from a different cloth than their Scottish cousins."

Ellen refrained from remarking that that was perhaps the world's greatest understatement, and asked about the tea.

"Bitter stuff," he said. "And ye didna mention the whiskey," he added. Before Ellen could ask what he meant, Liam confided, "And I didna see the beastie."

"No?"

He shook his head, frowning. "I'm afraid I must go

back," he said, sounding as if he were marching off to Hades. They reached the steps leading up to the house; Liam cupped her elbow as they started upward. "The old man, he's invited me . . . *demanded,* really . . ." His voice trailed off, his expression changed, and for a moment, he looked almost ill.

"Demanded . . . supper?"

"No. No' as easy as that." Liam rolled his eyes and sighed heavily. "A *ball,*" he said, looking now as if he were in physical pain.

"A ball, a ball!" Natalie cried, clapping her hands as Liam opened the front door for them. "May we go, Mother?"

"Of course not, darling. One must be invited to attend."

"Oh," she said, her face falling. "It would be *so* lovely."

"No, lass, 'tis no' lovely at all," he said miserably. " 'Tis a bloody disaster."

"A disaster?" Ellen laughed. "Why ever would you say such a thing? Natalie is right—a ball in Mayfair is all the rage, you know."

"A *ball* in Mayfair is no' something for a soldier."

"Oh, Liam, soldiers attend balls all the time! Surely you know that a young lady's heart will beat wildly at the sight of a man in uniform."

Liam came to a dead halt in the foyer, peered down at her with forest eyes so deep that they stirred the pit of her belly. "I donna *want* young ladies' hearts to beat wildly," he said emphatically. "And I canna dance."

"Of course you can."

"No! I've two left feet if I've one!"

"Miss Farnsworth, will you be taking supper this evening?"

They all turned startled gazes to Agatha, who had come into the foyer without being heard. And there she stood, her arms folded tightly, her eyes narrowed with suspicion as she glared at Liam.

"Personally, I wouldna advise it," Liam said cheerfully, to which Agatha's scowl deepened.

"Yes, Agatha," Ellen added, ignoring Liam's wisdom. "At the usual time, please."

"Very well," she said coldly, still eyeing Liam, and held out her hand to Natalie. "Come then, miss, it is time for your bath."

Natalie walked to Agatha, slipped her hand into hers, and as Ellen watched them climb the steps, she was struck again by how sad it was for someone as small as Natalie to be so troubled.

"What is it, then?" Liam asked her softly, his gaze following hers to Natalie's retreating figure. "Ye seem suddenly downcast."

"Nothing, really," she murmured, and attempted to smile. "It's just that she's growing up so fast. But as for *you*, sir, we shall simply have to teach you to dance. It's quite simple, really."

"Oh no," he said, backing up. "I'll no' be so dandy as that—"

"You'll never find the beastie if you don't attend this ball, isn't that so? And if you attend you must at least *appear* to be socializing, mustn't you? And if you are going to at least *appear* to be social, then it stands to reason that you must dance. Am I quite right?"

"*Aye*," Liam said, and groaned again, looking as truly miserable as anyone Ellen had ever seen.

And true to his word, having reluctantly agreed to dancing lessons, Liam snuck up the two flights of stairs after Follifoot brought the obligatory and positively vile serving of what he claimed was lamb for his supper. Liam had attempted to eat it but at last gave in to his stomach's wailing for him to stop.

He left the offal on the table, took a piece of vellum from his knapsack, and penned another letter home.

Dearest Mother, the weather has turned foul, the small game is wretchedly undernourished, and it appears as if I shall be forced to dance at my cousin's ball. Yours faithfully, L.

He sealed the letter and then dressed in Highland fashion as was his preference. He quit the room, moving quietly down the long corridor in his *ghillie brogues*, and quickly climbed the stairs to Ellie.

She was waiting for him, looking angelic once again in a gown of pale blue silk. As she had been previously, she seemed a bit taken aback by his *féileadh beag*, which gave him, oddly enough, a sense of enormous pleasure. Natalie was dressed, too, he noticed, and she gleefully rushed forward to tell him she would also learn to dance. Indeed, Ellie had pushed aside the sofa and made an area where she could teach both her daughter and her father's tenant the latest ballroom dances.

Against Liam's better judgment, Ellie lined him up head to elbow with Natalie, and taught (or rather *attempted* to teach) the two of them the steps of the quadrille, the minuet, and lastly, the waltz. Liam grudgingly admitted that little Nattie was by far the better dancer. For him, the movements seemed ridiculously without purpose and put him at sixes and sevens to the point he couldn't remember which foot to put where or when.

When they practiced the more complicated quadrille, however, even Natalie was beginning to lose her natural grace, and after the two of them collided more than once, they could not help dissolving into a fierce fit of laughter. Neither could Ellie, her cheeks glowing with her enthusiasm, and Liam thought she had never looked lovelier.

When it came time to put Natalie to bed, the girl didn't protest, no doubt exhausted from his attempts to lead her around the dance floor.

Ellie returned a few moments later with a soft smile on her face, and Liam was struck with the notion of how lovely it would be to see that smile each and every day.

"She's asleep," she said, reaching for his hand. "Come on, then. I've something to show you."

Liam slipped his hand into hers and followed. Ellie walked to the door, opened it, and proceeded out onto the corridor. Liam woke up then and tried to pull her back. "Ellie, what are ye doing? Do ye think to bring yer father's ire down around ye, then?"

"It's all right," she said, gently pulling him along. "He's gone a fortnight."

A fortnight. That was perhaps the best news Liam had heard in quite sometime, and in his near euphoria, he stumbled behind her. But when they reached the stairs, she started up. "Ellie!" he whispered, alarmed and stealing a glance over his shoulder. "What of Follifoot?"

"Asleep," she whispered. "There are only two others in this house besides myself and Natalie. Agatha's gone home. Follifoot sleeps like the dead each night, thanks to his whiskey, and the scullery girl sleeps below. It's just you and me awake and moving about, Liam. So would you care to come along or would you prefer to retreat to your rooms?" And then she smiled, a wickedly seductive smile.

They could hang him for all he cared.

Liam grabbed Ellie's waist with one hand, and with the other pushed her quickly up the stairs.

Sixteen

❧

The third floor of Farnsworth's house smelled musty, the result of having been closed off for several years. A fine layer of dust coated the wainscoting; cobwebs hung thick in the corners. Naturally, it was as austere as the rest of the house—Ellen knew as much, as the discovery had been a delight, and she had eagerly gone through the rooms, methodically looking for something of value she might sell. And while she discovered a veritable treasure trove of Farnsworth family things, years of living that had been boxed and stuffed away, there had been nothing of real value.

Such typically was her luck.

There was, however, something of value for Liam, and she led him to a room at the end of the corridor, opened the door, and drew him inside. "Stand just here," she said, and groped around for a candelabra she had left on a previous visit. After a few moments, the room was filled with the eerie, triumvirate light of three small candles.

"What is this place?" Liam asked, walking deeper into the room and looking at the trunks and crates scattered about.

"I'm not entirely certain," she confessed, following him, the candelabra held high. "A graveyard of sorts."

On one end of the room were several paintings and portraits, covered with stained canvas cloths. A smattering of furniture—chairs with torn seats, a settee with a broken leg that sat miserably lopsided. On the other end of the room were more paintings and an armoire with broken kitchenware that looked as if someone had thought to mend them at one time. A single threadbare rug lay in the middle of the room, and beneath the dormer windows was a row of sea trunks.

"Why did ye bring me here?" Liam asked, looking closely at the settee. "Would ye have me repair it?"

"No, of course not!" Ellen laughed. "I brought you here because I rather thought you'd need something to wear to the ball. Assuming, of course, you don't intend to wear your skirt."

" 'Tis no' a skirt, Ellie. 'Tis a *kilt*."

"I beg your pardon," she said, nodding her head in acknowledgment of his tender feelings on the subject. "Do you intend to wear your *kilt* to the Lockhart ball?"

"*Nooo*," he drawled, "but I've clothing enough."

"I'm certain you do, sir, but I'd be rather surprised if you had formal evening clothes in your wardrobe."

"I beg yer pardon?"

"An evening coat. With tails," she said, her hands sketching them in the air. "And an appropriate waist-coat and neckcloth. And shoes—"

"*Ach*, I'm no' a Christmas goose! I will do just as well in me own clothes."

"But you'll at least have a look, won't you?" she asked sweetly, already walking to the trunks along the wall. She lifted their lids so that he might have a look inside. After a bit of hesitation, Liam moved cautiously to stand beside her, peering over her shoulder into the trunks and piles of men's clothing.

"Yer uncle, eh?" he remarked at last.

"And others before him."

He sighed, scratched his head, muttered something in his native tongue beneath his breath. "All right, let's have a quick look about, then."

Inordinately pleased, Ellen put the candelabra aside on an old console, and together they dug through the three trunks, laughing at some of the fashions of the past, but finding two coats with tails, a white waistcoat with silver embroidery, and a neckcloth of silver. "Oh, *my*," Ellen said admiringly as she held the neckcloth to the waistcoat. "How grand you will look, Liam!"

"I'd no' call it grand, exactly," he muttered.

"Come now, Captain. It's the way of the Quality."

"Aye, and 'tis the way of the Quality to dance about willy-nilly. I'll make a bloody fool of meself, I will. I can only pray I donna fall flat on my arse," he groused.

"You've nothing to fear!" Ellen said, laughing at his expression of misery. "You did splendidly in our lessons." She suddenly stood, extended her hand to him. "Come then, let's rehearse again, shall we?"

"No, I—"

"I won't let you fall."

He groaned again, peered up at Ellen and her hand. "I have yer promise no' to laugh," he said, grudgingly gaining his feet and putting aside the clothes they had found.

"You have no such promise from me, sir," she said, laughing, and taking his hand firmly in hers, dragged him to the middle of the old rug. She pivoted about, determined there was enough room, and faced him. Holding her skirt, she curtsied deeply before him. "Will you do me the honor, sir?"

"Aye. I said I would."

Still bent in a deep curtsy, she peeked up at him through her lashes. "Yes, I realize that you did. But now you should offer your hand to help me up."

He immediately stuck out his paw of a hand and pulled her, a little roughly, to her feet. And stood there, woodenly holding her hand, staring into her eyes.

"If you'd like, you might kiss the back of a lady's hand," she said softly.

His gaze unwavering, he brought her hand to his mouth and touched his lips to her knuckles, his eyes never leaving hers. A rush of heat swept over her; she felt strangely unsteady in her skin.

Liam slowly lifted his head. "Now supposing that the lady has agreed to dance with the likes of me," he murmured, still holding her hand, "which dance has she chosen?"

"The waltz," Ellen said, a little breathlessly. "Do you remember?"

"Oh, *aye*, I do."

His gaze steady on hers, he slowly pulled her to him until she was standing close enough that he could put his hand on her waist, his palm covering almost all of her rib cage. Liam was staring at her, his gaze boring right through her, seeping down into her very depths, and Ellen felt strangely exposed, as if he could actually see who she had been, who she had become, what the future held for her.

Her skin flushed dark and hot; she looked away, unable to endure the intensity of his gaze, in spite of wanting to feel the burn of it.

"What is it then, lass? Have ye forgotten the waltz?" he asked softly.

"Ah . . . no, I just—"

"If I recall properly, it goes something like this," he said, and began to move, slowly and deliberately, his eyes never leaving her face. "*One*, two, three, *one*, two, three," he murmured, moving her cautiously but fluidly from side to side. "Ye are the teacher, Ellie. Ye must tell me how I do."

How did he do? She could scarcely speak at the moment, her heart and body feeling the flow of silent music through them, her mind returning to days long since lost to her, days in which she would dance and laugh and feel a man's arms around her. How long had it been? Years, certainly. Decades, centuries. A lifetime since she had known a man's touch, since she had felt immortal.

Liam began to hum, moving her across the room, his steps growing more fluid, the rhythm of his body a natural grace. "Tell me, Ellie," he said, his voice husky. "Tell me how I do."

She realized she was staring at his neckcloth and glanced up at the man who had kissed her so passionately, saw the pink scar in the shadows of his face, the intense green eyes, the strong jaw, and thought him the most handsome of men, a prince.

"Well?" he murmured.

"Astonishingly well."

"That's right kind of ye," he said, and suddenly pulled her tightly into his body, twirling her around. Ellen felt her skirts swirl away from her body, a sensation as natural as it was ancient, one that snapped something in her—a need, a desire, she didn't really know—but Ellen closed her eyes and let her head drop back, unwilling to stop her fall into the bliss of carefree dancing.

They danced to his low hum, Liam an expert now, twirling her this way and that, letting her float along with him, making her skirts swirl wide and full around their legs. It was glorious, magical, transporting her back to a happier time. His arm snaked behind her back; he drew her even closer into his body, so that she could feel the hardness of his torso and thighs, the sheer masculinity beneath his native clothing. Her body hungered for him to hold her, to crush her between his arms.

He must have read her very thoughts; without warning, he suddenly touched her exposed neck with his lips, brushing the hollow of her throat, the curve to her chin, and around to the soft spot just below the ear.

She was dancing in a dream. This felt exactly like so many dreams—intoxicating, dizzying—and Ellen, dancing in her dream, lifted her head, put her hands on either side of his head and drew him to her. The only difference between this moment and her dreams was that he was not Daniel.

He was Liam.

And Liam said not a word when she kissed him, just lifted her from where she stood, walking with her in his arms as her lips found his ear, her tongue the length of his scar. He moved to the broken settee and let go his grip of her, letting her slide the length of his body to the floor. She could feel his hardness beneath the kilt, the rigid length and width of it, pressed against her groin. *It had been so long, so very long . . .* Her body was quivering—the caress of a single finger felt like a thousand little fires on her skin. Every touch of his lips drenched her in an ethereal silkiness.

"God forgive me, Ellie," he whispered into her neck. "But I want to take ye now, make love to ye. I would show ye how mad with desire ye've made me, how I adore ye."

"*Yes,*" she whispered, feeling almost delirious now. "*Yes, yes, make love to me, Liam . . .*"

He made an animal-like sound deep in his throat as he swept her up and into his arms and laid her on the crooked settee, coming over her and balancing himself with one leg on the floor. Slowly, carefully, reverently, he began to kiss her, leaving no patch of skin untouched. His hand caressed her, his rough fingers sliding over her neck, down the curve of her shoulder to the swell of her bosom above the bodice of her gown. With his knuckles he drew a line from one breast to the other, into the crevice between them, and he sucked in his breath, his hand stilling there.

Ellen closed her eyes and allowed herself to fall headlong into desire. *"Please don't stop,"* she whispered, neither alarmed nor caring of her wantonness, driven by an overwhelming passion to a point where propriety no longer mattered. She just wanted to feel him, to touch him, to have his hands and mouth wander over her body, which had been dead for so many long years. She gripped Liam's head and drew him up to kiss him, filling him with her breath and her tongue. He clasped her tightly to him, pulling her onto his lap, and kissed her so wickedly that she was quickly burning inside, a burn that roared white hot between her legs. As if to answer her raging passion, Liam pressed his erection against her, let her feel what she evoked in him as he dragged his mouth to her breasts.

Somehow he managed to unfasten her bodice so that he could lift her breasts from the fabric, sucking them, devouring them until her nipples were jutting out, begging for more. With his hands and his mouth, he performed a torturous dance on her, bringing her to a point just short of begging. "Let me see ye, lass," he whispered raggedly. "Let me see all yer beauty," he urged her as he began to disrobe her.

Without conscious thought, Ellen helped him, until she was standing before him. He openly admired her naked body, gazing for what seemed several long minutes, his eyes drifting from the top of her head, to her breasts, swollen from his attentions, to the hollow of her stomach and the tuft of blond hair at the apex of her thighs.

"Mi Diah," he breathed. "There are moments when I look at ye, and I see a bit of yer lovely skin, and I swear I can taste it in me mouth. I can *smell* it. Ye are beautiful, Ellie, just as I knew ye'd be."

Oh *hell*, now she was melting, spilling into a puddle. And as she watched, Liam solemnly removed his shirt and leather belt, the strange shoes, and then let the plaid drop, holding it with one finger as he stood, legs braced apart, so that she could see him, too.

Ellen gasped softly, her eyes widening with wonder. He was all man, big and bold and hard. In the candlelight, shadows of sinewy muscles rippled across his stomach. His arms were Herculean, as big as her thigh, and his legs, taut and lean, all muscle. Narrow, strong hips, and in a patch of dark hair, his member, proud, erect . . . and enormously engorged.

Liam grinned proudly. "Ye see how much I want ye, *leannan?*"

"Yes."

Still smiling that terribly wicked smile, Liam turned away for a moment, laid the plaid across the rug, then took her hand in his and pulled her into his embrace once more, crushing her to him so hard that it felt as if her bones were melding into his. And then she felt as if she were suddenly drifting, landing softly on the plaid beneath him, the warmth of his body seeping into hers. Around them, pale candlelight danced across the walls, reminding Ellen of how this exquisite moment had begun.

Liam kissed her again while his hands wandered the length of her, feeling her arms, her legs, then floating, feather light, to her waist, stomach. The sensation of his callused skin on her body was like lightning—she felt each caress down to the very depth of her. Spurred by his languid exploration of her body, she reached for him, cupping his testicles in her palm as he drew a tortured breath, feeling the girth and weight of them in the palm of her hand, sliding slowly to the velvety tip and back.

She sighed, reveling in the feel of a man.

Liam gasped quietly into her ear; his breathing was becoming more ragged with each stroke she made of the smooth skin covering the marble shaft. He was so thick, so long, so hot, and without thinking, she was gripping him harder, stroking him faster. When his breath came in short spurts, he grabbed her wrist and pulled her hand away from him. "I'll no' have it thus," he rasped, and still gripping her wrist, he put her hand above her head. Ellen lifted the other arm, entwined her hands and smiled deeply as Liam began another, deeper exploration of her body with his mouth.

Slowly, he made his way down her arm, his mouth moving from her underarm to the crook of her elbow, the inside of her wrist, and her palm. With his lips and tongue he traced a path down her side to her hip, nipping the skin there, then moved on to the top of her thigh, her knee. Ellen drew one leg up, but it quickly fell away from her body, and Liam moved like a cat into the valley between her legs, his body long and sleek and absurdly graceful. He paused to first breathe her in, his gentle breath tormenting her.

His catlike movements had destroyed any semblance of self-control; Ellen grabbed at the leg of a chair behind her head and gripped it tightly, trying to steady herself as Liam's tongue slipped between the folds of her sex. "*Aaah*," he sighed into her body, and Ellen was suddenly writhing, lifting her hips to meet him. But Liam caught her hips, held her still so that he could lave her at his leisure, tasting and nipping as he desired. His onslaught was slow and steady, unmindful of her bucking, and when Ellen thought she would simply die of his attentions, his lips closed around the bud of lust that pulsed with years of pent-up desire.

He drew it between his teeth, sucked it, and Ellen cried out as she felt herself explode into tiny shards of flesh and bone, raining down on Liam. She moved wildly, trying to escape the consummate pleasure; it was too great, too intense, too perfect. Still, Liam was not through with her, and he was too strong for her to resist. Effortlessly, he held her steady in his hands and continued to nip and suck that tiny bud until Ellen felt tears of pure carnal pleasure on her face.

Physically drained and emotionally exhausted, she whimpered under his gentle assault, but Liam would not stop, just kept devouring her as if she were some sort of delicacy, until Ellen felt the pressure begin to build in her again, building to a stupendous end that would leave nothing of her.

Of a sudden, Liam lifted his head and came over her, kissed her roughly, passionately, leaving the taste of her own body on her lips as his thigh parted her legs. Stroking her hair, he lowered his body to hers and pressed the tip of his erection against her damp heat.

"I've never desired a woman as I desire ye, Ellie. Ye've made me feel alive, *so* alive!" Gently, he slipped the tip of his erection inside her. Ellen's body seized—years of celibacy had left her body stiff and unyielding, but Liam rested there, patiently giving her body time to accept him. Ellen touched his forehead with her fingers, then his lips, marveled at how this man had come into her life and let her live again. She lifted up on her elbows and softly touched her lips to his to assure herself that he was real, that *this* was real. "Make love to me, Liam," she murmured.

"*M'annsachd,*" he murmured, and slid inside, opening her body to him, moving with fluid grace, withdrawing to the tip, then thrusting again and watching her eyes with each stroke. "Come to me again," he whispered hoarsely. "Feel me inside ye, Ellie, and come to me again." His strokes moved faster; he clamped his jaw, still watching her, his body straining to hold back. Ellen lifted her hips so that he could better reach the very core of her, heard his encouragement, heard his shallow breathing as he came close to his own climax.

And just as she found her release again on a cry, he

pressed his lips to her ear, muttered, *"Tha gràdh agam ort,"* and threw back his head, bearing his teeth, letting loose a guttural growl of pleasure as he spilled hot and wet inside her. With a final shudder, he collapsed to his side, one arm draped across her bare middle, his breath coming in uneven pants.

They lay there for some time, panting, entwined in one another's arms, until the silence and the room's chill began to descend on them. Liam pulled the plaid around them for warmth, tucked Ellen's head on his shoulder, and closed his eyes. Ellen watched him, twirling a finger in the wave of his hair. She hadn't felt so much a woman in more than ten years now. Liam had unleashed the old Ellen inside her, the one who had been full of life, carefree, and willing to give her heart up to love. The same Ellen who had been crushed by love's betrayal and disappointment, who believed she'd never see the sun again in her lifetime.

After a moment, Liam lifted his hand, brushed the hair from her eyes, and kissed the tip of her nose. *"Leannan,"* he whispered, then kissed her lips tenderly and rolled onto his back, staring up at the light flickering against the molded ceiling tiles.

Ellen moved onto her stomach to gaze at him, feeling an incredible mix of elation and sadness all at once.

Liam opened one eye and smiled. "Ye certainly know how to dance, lass."

She smiled.

He lifted a strand of her hair between his fingers, brushed his thumb across it, feeling it. "I've no right to say it, but I wish we might have known one another before . . . before our paths were chosen for us."

So did she. She smiled ruefully, but remained silent, for there were no words that could describe how badly she wished it were so. Unfortunately, the past was what it was, and she could do nothing to change it.

They lay that way, smiling at one another, until the chill was too much to be borne, and finally, reluctantly, they dressed, gathered their things, and proceeded, hand in hand, down the dark corridor, feeling their way to the stairs.

When they reached the landing of Ellen's suite, Liam gathered her up, kissed her like a man gone round the bend with love, then left her. She stood there, listening to his almost silent footsteps as they hurried down the stairs, refusing to listen to the niggling voice in the back of her head, the one that had worried one night not too long ago that a single kiss shared would produce a million consequences. And now the consequences were raining down on the most vulnerable part of her—her heart.

Her big, empty heart, which was just waiting to be filled again.

Seventeen

※

*I*t was, without even the smallest doubt, Liam thought, the worst thing that could have possibly happened to him. Never had he felt more defenseless or physically and emotionally vulnerable, yet there he was, returning again and again to the very place he should have avoided, as often as time and circumstance would allow, while he bided his time until the Lockhart ball.

Liam was first and foremost a soldier, a man married to the notion of service to his king while others stayed home and sired children. And it was a fact that he had not and never would have, in a thousand or perhaps a million years, believed himself capable of falling in love.

Yet that was precisely what he had gone and done, falling like a rock down the side of Ben Nevis, gathering dangerous velocity as he hurtled toward a certain crash into the pit of love. Ill-advised? Yes. Ridiculously lacking in self-control? Yes. Possible to abandon? Not even in hell. How could a man deny himself such bliss as this? How could a man possibly stay away from a woman such as Ellie, even knowing that he must eventually complete his mission and return to Scotland?

He *would* return to Scotland—that was inarguable. There was his career to think of, first. He had signed on to the Gordon regiment, and would be off to the Continent and points abroad within a matter of months, if not weeks. Second, there was his family to think of. Without the bloody, blasted beastie, they would certainly lose Talla Dileas. They were depending on him, and he would not let them down. And then there was Ellie—sweet, beautiful Ellie. An Englishwoman, the daughter of a noble. As gentle and fragile and exquisite as the roses he took from Hyde Park—precisely the sort of woman who was bred to be anything *but* a soldier's woman.

No, no, it was inconceivable to think anything should ever come of this unprecedented feeling of devotion, of this extraordinary feeling of tenderness toward another human being. It was, Liam at last decided, something he should avoid thinking of altogether for the time being, which was precisely what he was trying to do. With Farnsworth away and Miss Agatha only mildly suspicious, and Follifoot suitably silenced with a generous banknote, Ellen and Liam spent as much time together as possible in the course of the next few days, thinking nothing of consequence, nothing but the glittery feeling between them.

They met in Hyde Park each morning, walked among the privileged of London like an old married couple with Natalie scampering around them. They talked of nothing, really, and yet everything. They laughed privately with one another at the antics of the Quality around them, admired horses and dogs, and remarked on the more colorful of walking costumes.

Each night Liam would wait until he knew Agatha had retired to her own bed somewhere far away, and then would steal up the stairs with whatever fowl or game he had managed to catch that day. As Natalie played with her dolls or drew her pictures, he and Ellie would roast it while the cook's offering sat untouched in the corridor. Over the course of supper, while the lass prattled on about her Laria, Liam and Ellen stole glimpses and smiles from one another and tried desperately to respond to the girl.

It went without saying that Liam's favorite moment came when Natalie was put to bed and he and Ellie were alone (not that he was such a bloody dog as to think of *that* constantly, which he did not . . . not *constantly* anyway). He very much enjoyed Ellie's company, and in quiet moments of reflection he fancied the two of them had been fashioned by God's hand for one another, their temperaments perfectly suited. In addition to that terribly important fact, Liam was tearfully thankful to discover that his Ellie had quite a lustful and varied appetite that pleased him enormously.

It also astounded him. Granted, he had never been with a lady before. But he had heard some English officers speak of marital relations, and had privately wondered how a man was to exist if his wife was as prudish and *sodden* as he had heard the officers bemoan. It seemed to him that a man might as well give over to his very own hand rather than expend so much energy on a lifeless lump of flesh as some English women appeared to be. And it was Liam's long and avid opinion that a man needed to release the lusty demons within him in order to maintain a certain level of discipline required for soldiering, a fact *all* Highlanders knew to be true. So he considered it his great fortune indeed to have found a woman who seemed to need that primal release as much as he did. Whatever his imagination could produce, Ellie was game to try, and better yet, had some rather provocative suggestions of her own.

Their lovemaking was the stuff of dreams, unconventional, free-spirited, and always tender. That was because he loved Ellie, adored her with every fiber of his being, and he wanted to take as many memories of her as his heart could hold.

He truly believed Ellie wanted the same, but there were moments when he would catch her looking pensively into the fire or staring blankly out the window, and in those precious few moments, he wondered what she was thinking, wondered absently if he really knew her at all. It was the soldier in him, he supposed, the part of him relentlessly conditioned to trust no one and suspect everyone. For the first time in his life, he despised that untrusting part of him, did not want to question her motives. But there it was, that small seed of fear that, unchecked, could spread like wildfire.

Yet the desire to be with her was even more powerful, and in those moments he thought he should stop coming to her suite altogether, that he should spare her any pain from his ultimate departure—he never proved strong enough. He despised that about himself, despised that he should be so smitten and so weak. Ah, but then Ellie would smile and light that fire in his heart, and he'd forget everything he had ever known, including his common sense.

It was in that state of blissful, magical repose on the eve of the Lockhart ball, and the need to know every inch of her, every thought, that Liam asked Ellie what had happened to her. He had been thinking of their dance and the way she looked, how gracefully she went about, expertly falling into his rhythm, and he could imagine her dancing through thousands of fancy balls. He had even asked her to attend with him, but she had laughed, shaking her head.

"Why no'?" he had asked.

"I can't leave Natalie alone, and besides, I was not invited. It would be terribly gauche."

That was when Liam had realized that she never went anywhere or did anything, really. Until now, he had supposed that was because she was a widow, but even that thought led to the more inevitable question of

what had happened to her, and perhaps more important, to Natalie's father.

"Who?" she asked, sitting naked on the edge of his
bed in his sparse rooms (their change of venue something she had suggested), his plaid barely covering her
thighs, the heat of their lovemaking still warming them
both.

"Him," Liam said, one arm behind his head, the
plaid also draping his groin. "Natalie's father."

Ellie flashed him a smile over her shoulder. "Ah . . .
so you would know my story, would you, Captain
Lockhart?" She twisted on the bed and faced him.
"Should I tell you?"

"Please."

"And why should I? Will it change anything?"

"No. Never," he said emphatically, and reached out
to stroke the smooth skin of her arm. "There is naugh'
that could ever change the way I feel about ye, Ellie."

She smiled and folded her arms beneath her bosom.
"You're very certain of it, are you? Perhaps you should
wait before you avow it so strongly, sir. Mine is not a
happy tale."

"I had gathered. But neither can it be so bad, Ellie."

She smiled enigmatically and traced the tiny path of
hair that led from his stomach to his groin. "Actually,
it's rather *lurid*," she whispered, and suddenly moved
to straddle him, letting his plaid fall to the floor as she
braced herself above him, letting her hair form a silken
curtain around them. "Are you *certain* you want to
know?"

"If I could, *mo ghraid*, I'd climb inside that wee head
of yers and wander about until I knew everything
about ye, I would."

Ellie laughed, collapsed on his chest, and sighed, her
breath warm across his nipple. "All right," she said at
last. "I'll tell you. But I warn you, you may not view me

so favorably when I am done." With that, she pushed herself up, leaned over Liam and the side of the bed, and picked up his plaid from the floor, wrapping it tightly around her shoulders. With her flaxen hair wildly mussed from their enthusiastic lovemaking, her skin still softly glowing, she settled beside him.

"The story of Ellen Frances Farnsworth begins in the summer of her eighteenth year . . . when I was one of the more favored debutantes in London," she said simply, without pride. "During the Season that year, I was invited to so many routs and balls and supper parties that I could scarcely keep up with them all. My mother helped me, but she often said that if an invitation to an event was worth having, I was the first to have it." She laughed sheepishly. "It was true that I was quite popular. I was something of a free spirit, really, enjoying the attentions of all gentlemen, and none in particular. I loved life and parties and pretty things."

Liam nodded, pushed himself up so that he was leaning against the bare wall behind him, already fascinated by the image of this youthful Ellie, dancing her way from ball to ball, laughing, smiling, and tearing young men's hearts to pieces.

"My cousins—I never really knew them, actually, for they never came to town during the Season. Some sort of falling-out with my father, if I recall correctly," she added with an inadvertent roll of her eyes. "But that year my cousins Malcolm and Lettie came to town along with their particular friend—" Ellie coughed, cleared her throat. "Um . . . with their friend, Mr. Daniel Goodman. From Cambridge."

Her voice was a bit unsteady; she looked away from Liam to the brazier and the embers there. "Mr. Goodman was . . . frighteningly charming. He was the son of an academician, and he had been educated abroad, and he was fun-loving and, oh, such a terribly good dancer," she said wistfully. "Everyone thought him particularly handsome, and all the girls were wild for him. I confess that the moment Mr. Goodman was introduced to me, there was an instant attraction between us."

Liam thought that was as it should be, if the man had half a brain . . . but hearing it from Ellie's lips was nonetheless unsettling.

"We began to see quite a lot of each other—we were always invited to the same supper parties, always taking as many dances as we could. I suppose I fell quite alarmingly in love with him, and I thought he was in love with me."

Now Liam simply despised handsome Daniel Goodman, would just as soon wring his neck than hear his name again, and mentally kicked himself for having asked the question in the first place. Worse, he heard a ring of familiarity that bothered him—*I fell quite alarmingly in love with him, and I thought he was in love with me . . .*

"In fact, we were so in love that we began to think of ways to meet at the Season's events and sneak away so that we might be alone," she continued, her voice gone flat now. "Daniel was very clever and a rather persuasive man. And . . . and I loved him desperately. I loved him like I had never loved anyone or anything in my young life. So, then, one thing led to another, and well . . . you can think what you will, but we became lovers."

She said it so softly that he had to strain to hear her correctly. Instant and intense jealousy swept through Liam. Of course he knew Ellie had been with a man before him, but in his naïveté, he had somehow assumed it to be perfunctory. Not passionate. *Not love.*

Ellie did not seem to notice the sudden tension in him; she was looking at her hands now, a habit, he had come to learn, that meant she was perplexed or uncertain. "I was so stupid, Liam, so frightfully naïve. I thought the sun rose and the moon set by him. I counted every hour until I could be with him again. I felt my entire body light up when he walked into the room, and I thought I should be with him always. Of course I did, or I would never have risked so . . . so *much . . .*" She paused then, looked away for a moment.

"Did he hurt ye? Did the bloody bastard—"

"Liam," she whispered softly, and without looking at him put her hand on his, silencing him. "My parents were very much against him. Father didn't think he was suitably credentialed to marry me, and thought even less of his income. My mother, well . . . I don't think she ever found him particularly genuine. I thought she was just going along with my father, but looking back now, I know that she must have seen what I couldn't." With a regretful shake of her head, she continued, "But I refused to stop seeing him. Then, one day, my parents announced that we were away, all of us, me and Eva, too, to the country, to visit friends for a week or so. My mother said it was time that Mr. Goodman and I had a bit of a respite from one another.

"But her plan didn't work in the least. I scarcely ate, I scarcely thought of anything but Daniel, and I sat in my room and watched the hands of the clock move, almost minute by minute, counting them down until I could return to my true love. Oh, I put on a good front so that my parents would not suspect I was pining so— I joined in all the lawn games, and the board games, and I danced after supper, and I played the pianoforte and sang cheerful songs. I did all the things a carefree debutante was supposed to do, so that finally, after a week, my parents determined it was quite all right to return to London."

Ellie looked up to the bare ceiling, her eyes focused

on some distant recollection. "When we arrived in London, I was the first to reach our door, and I sought out our butler, who assured me a handful of letters had been put on my bed, awaiting my return. I rushed to my room, found the letters, and there it was—the letter from Daniel I had been seeking. I pulled it open, tearing a corner in my haste, only . . ." She paused; Liam could see the sheen of tears in her eyes. "Only it was not the love letter I had been expecting. Quite the contrary, actually. It was a letter telling me that Daniel had gone away indefinitely, as his father had fallen ill in Belgium. There was no mention of love, of quietly dying until he could lay eyes on me again. Nothing. Just 'I've gone away indefinitely.' "

It was a poignant story to be sure, but it confused Liam. "But . . . but what of Nattie?"

Tears suddenly sprang from her blue eyes. Ellie was crying now, tears running silently down her face that she unthinkingly swiped with his plaid. "Oh, Natalie, my darling, dearest child! How can I begin to say it all?" she cried. "I did not know I was with child until perhaps a fortnight after I returned to London. I tried desperately to find Daniel, but he'd left no direction. My cousin Malcolm did not know where he had gone, said only that he had left in the night. My cousin Lettie had returned home, and no one in all of London seemed to have any knowledge of him! I wrote letter after to letter to Cambridge, hoping one would reach him somehow."

"Do ye mean to tell me, then," Liam asked low, his heart suddenly heavy, "that the man doesna know of his own bairn?"

Ellie shook her head no. "I never saw him again. To this day, I have no idea what became of him."

Goddamned Englishman! Now Liam was incensed— of course he had known Natalie did not know her father, not really, but he had naturally assumed the poor man had died. Never in his wildest dreams had he thought that Ellie had engaged in some illicit love affair and borne a child out of wedlock. And miraculously, while he found that news somewhat disconcerting, it did not change his opinion of Ellie. It did, however, produce a desire in him to kill one bloody English coward.

Fury and pain propelled Liam up off the bed, and he began pacing, oblivious to his nakedness. "Bloody bastard, he is. A coward. I'd slice off the man's balls if I had half a chance—"

"Liam!"

"What sort of man would leave a woman as bonny as ye, Ellie, after he'd compromised ye so completely? What bloody bastard would take yer virginity and run away when there's a chance of having planted his seed in ye?"

Ellie said nothing, just bowed her head, avoiding his hard gaze.

Instantly contrite, Liam moved to his knees before her. "Ah, Ellie, I speak harshly, I know, but I swear on the grave of William Wallace, I'd kill a man for such cowardice—"

"You mustn't blame him, Liam!" she exclaimed through her tears. "There were *two* of us just like there are two of us here! I was a willing participant and it was *my* foolishness that has brought me here to live like a prisoner in my father's house!"

"Ye're no' a prisoner!" he scoffed.

Ellie laughed sardonically and pushed him away. "Look around you—surely you've noticed! I've no acquaintances, save my sister. I've no engagements! Farnsworth has never forgiven me and he never will!"

Yes, of course he had noticed, but he had not understood why. How devastating—she had loved him, loved him enough to have trusted him. *Jesu!* the very thought sent a knife through Liam's gut, and with a groan he pressed his forehead against her knee.

Ellie's fingers curled in his hair. "My father *hates* me, Liam. By the point I realized I had been jilted, it was the height of the Season, and my parents, blissfully unaware of my condition, had begun to shop for potential suitors to marry me. Of course, I had to tell them the truth about my plight. Farnsworth was furious—he disowned me then and there, said I was no longer his daughter. My mother was devastated. She was so ashamed she could scarcely look at me. After a wretched two days of arguing, my parents determined that the scandal would be too great for us to bear in London, particularly as popular as I was, so my father sent my mother and me to Cornwall. I protested quite strongly—I didn't want Mother to be punished, too— but he was quite adamant that he'd not risk my whoring about again. My parents never slept in the same house again. I lived with my mother in Cornwall, where Natalie was born, and there we remained until Mother died. Eva remained in London, but Farnsworth had lost what little heart for fathering he'd had, and he married her off to the first potential suitor that came along. I daresay she's never forgiven me either."

"If he hates ye as ye say, then why are ye here?"

"I don't know! When Mother died, Farnsworth sent for me. I hoped that perhaps time had softened his opinion of me, but if anything, his opinion had worsened. He abhors me, Liam, and the only reason he keeps me at all is because of his fear of scandal. He would rather have me under his own roof then chance I should"—she looked up at Liam through wet lashes, bit her lower lip—"that I should dishonor him," she whispered. "And Natalie, my poor innocent child . . . well, you've seen what's become of her."

It seemed impossible to absorb it all; it shocked Liam, but left him sympathetic at the same time, for had not the very same thing happened to him of late? Nonetheless . . . "Ye're a grown woman, Ellie. Why do ye no' leave?"

She laughed derisively. "One day I will. My father gives me precious little to live on, and I have no income of my own. But I scrimp every pence I can, and when I have sufficient funds, I will go someplace where Natalie can live without the shadow of my actions hanging over her head. I *swear* it."

Ah God, if only he had the means, he'd give her the sun and the moon and the stars . . . but he was only a soldier, and his pitiful stipend was already devoured by his family. Liam could do nothing but gather Ellie in his arms and hold her.

They fell asleep that way, drifting off with their private thoughts.

Sometime before dawn, Liam awoke to find himself alone.

Eighteen

❧

Reliving her story had exhausted Ellen. After years of the whole ugly tale corroding in her heart, the sheer effort to say it all aloud had taken a toll. After slipping from a sleeping Liam's loose embrace, she had come upstairs, wearing just a chemise, and had fallen onto the old counterpane on her own bed. She was almost immediately in a deep sleep, her mind refusing to belabor her past another moment. It was a dreamless sleep, and it wasn't until Natalie was shaking her that Ellen could even drag herself up from the depth of it— groggy, she forced her eyes open.

"Mother, you're still abed!" Natalie complained.

"I'm sorry. I wasn't feeling well," she said truthfully, and pushed herself up to her elbows, eyeing her young daughter. Natalie's frock, she noticed, was all askew. "Turn round," she muttered through a yawn.

"Won't you feel better now? Captain Lockhart said to come and fetch you, for he's to take us on a picnic today," she said as Ellen fumbled to rebutton her dress so that it hung properly. "And he said he'd teach me how to fish!"

"Did he?" Ellen asked, smiling.

"He said the fish aren't as big as they are in Scotland, and that they'd likely all float to the top and take all the sport from it, but all in all, we'd have a jolly good time of it. But that first we'd walk through Vauxhall Gardens."

Ellen's smile deepened. "Vauxhall Gardens . . . I haven't been there in years," she said, patting Natalie's shoulder. "All right, then, run along and find your boots. I'll not have you fishing in those slippers."

Natalie made a sound of elation and ran to the door.

"Mind that you stay in your room! I'll come fetch you when I'm ready!" Ellen called after her.

"I'm going to fish!" Natalie responded with great enthusiasm, and skipped out of the room so quickly Ellen wasn't certain if she had heard her or not.

She sighed, stood up from the bed and stretched her arms high overhead, almost regretting that she had betrayed Natalie by revealing the truth about her paternity to Liam. Yet she instinctively believed that if there was anyone she could trust with Natalie's secret, it was him. Ellen wandered over to the window and pulled open the heavy drapes, feeling the instant warmth on her skin as sun spilled into the room. That was the way with Liam, wasn't it? Every day filled with sunshine, every day warm and bright and happy.

And as she padded to her dressing room, she thought that he was indeed an honorable man, a gentleman. The sort of man who could hear the truth and not instantly label her a whore. Nonetheless, she had feared deep inside that he would be daunted, disgusted by her lustfulness, and find her behavior so wanton as to *believe* her to be a whore.

That was a risk Ellen had taken quite willingly—she had needed (for reasons she truly did not understand so much as know innately) to be honest with him, both physically and emotionally, even if it meant losing him. She didn't understand it, but there was nothing to be done for it now, and he had, in all truthfulness, seemed more sympathetic than appalled. And he had invited them to Vauxhall Gardens. She could think of nothing better than a stroll in the sunshine to clear those old cobwebs from her heart.

Liam was waiting for them in Belgrave Square; Natalie rushed forward to show him the scuffed boots she would wear for fishing, over which Liam fawned appropriately. He looked up as Ellen approached, his winsome grin deepened, and his dark green eyes danced with pleasure. "Ah, lass, what a vision ye are. Ye'd charm the collar right off a priest, ye would."

As a matter of fact, she *had* donned her best walking gown—albeit last Season's fashion—a golden brown brocade with dark maroon trim and a pelisse that matched exactly.

Liam extended his right arm to Ellen and his left to Natalie, who colored deeply before shyly slipping her hand through the crook of his arm. "*Ach*, there's no' a luckier man alive," he said jauntily, and indeed, he looked quite proud of them, Ellen thought. Not ashamed. *Proud.*

They walked to Vauxhall Gardens, strolling deep into its bounds. The day was brilliant and blue, with just enough of a nip in the air to add color to the faces of the many people strolling about the gardens and supper rooms. Natalie dashed ahead, only to scamper back to make sure Liam and Ellen were coming, then dashed ahead again.

As they neared the middle of the gardens, Natalie came running to them, her eyes glistening with excitement. "Come see, come see!" she cried, grabbing Liam's hand. In the middle of the expansive gardens, a man in a green coat had erected a scarecrow of sorts, wearing the red jacket of the military on which a crude heart was drawn, a pair of torn and dirty trousers, with feet and hands of straw and sporting a pumpkin for a head, complete with a smiling face. In addition to the man with the patched green coat, four gentlemen were standing about, examining the scarecrow, and a small crowd had begun to form around them. The man in the green coat gestured to the scarecrow, explaining something to the four gentlemen, then suddenly ran to the scarecrow, whirled about, and walked thirty paces away, into the crowd. Everyone moved aside save the four gentlemen, who moved to position themselves in the place Greencoat had marked.

"What are they about?" Ellen asked curiously, taking several steps toward the group.

"A game of odds," Liam said as he watched Greencoat withdraw a dagger from his waist and hold it aloft for the growing crowd to see. One of the gentlemen said something that made the crowd laugh.

"May we watch?" Natalie asked excitedly as Greencoat whisked off his hat and began to pass it around. Several gentlemen in the crowd tossed money into the hat.

"Ah, the winner divides the spoils with the man in the green coat," Liam informed them, and with his hand on Ellen's back, moved her and Natalie closer to the contest.

The first gentleman positioned himself directly in front of the scarecrow and took the dagger from the man. With a great heave, he flung the dagger toward the stuffed redcoat, but he let go too late, and the dagger speared the ground only a few feet in front of him. The small crowd broke into laughter as Greencoat scrambled to retrieve the dagger.

"They are too great a distance from the target," Liam said. "There's not a man among them who could spear even a palace wall from that distance."

He was right; the next contestant sent the dagger fly-ing, but it landed wide of the scarecrow, spearing noth-ing but leaves and dirt. Another man tried; his attempt landed well short of the tree. The small crowd was growing; Greencoat called for more gentlemen to play, and an ale vendor wandered close by, passing cups to several in the crowd.

Greencoat took the proceeds of the first round from his hat, then passed it again. Another gentleman had his turn, and with great theatrics, he flung the dagger with ferocious strength; it sailed very long of the stuffed redcoat. The crowd laughed as a friend stepped up and clapped the gentleman on the back.

Greencoat retrieved the dagger, looked once again to the crowd. "Come, now, who else will try?" he called, and caught sight of Liam, towering above most. "You there, sir! You look as if you could spear our foe!"

The crowd turned to look at Liam.

He grinned down at Ellen. "Aye, of course I could," he called back, grinning. "I'd surely give it a go had I the promise of proper recompense for me troubles."

Greencoat jingled the hat, grinning. "Half for you, half for me, sir," he said. "There's thirty pounds in here if there's one."

"That's a princely sum," Liam said. "But 'tis no' enough."

The crowd was beginning to enjoy the exchange, and moved so that there was a clear path between Greencoat and Liam. Ellen instinctively pulled her bon-net forward to hide her face.

"Why, sir, what more could you ask?" Greencoat shouted. "The prize is fair!"

"Aye, 'tis a fair prize but no' the fairest prize, eh? It would seem to me a lady's kiss would be just reward for such a feat."

A happy, enthusiastic cry went up from the crowd;

mortified, Ellen shrunk back. "Liam!" she hissed. "What are you *doing?*"

"I'm attempting to win yer heart, *leannan*."

Greencoat made a show of a thumping heart, earning a laugh from the crowd. "What say you, miss?" he called to her.

"Say *yes*, Mother!" Natalie squealed with delight, and several in the crowd began to call their encouragement, too.

Ellen peeked up from under the rim of her bonnet and looked at Liam. He flashed a beguiling smile that simply rocked her, and feeling rather playful, feeling *alive*, she lifted her head, pushed her bonnet away from her face, put a finger to her mouth, and tapped it against her lips as she playfully considered his offer. "And if you do not succeed, sir? What shall by *my* recompense?" she asked to the delight of the crowd.

Liam's green eyes grew brighter; he threw back his head and laughed with the crowd. "A fair question. If I miss the redcoat's heart, I shall give ye a medal of honor, one from the king, bestowed on me during the war."

That was met with thunderous approval from the crowd that Ellen could hardly deny; with a laugh, she put out her hand to Liam. "We have a bargain, sir. Upon my word, if you should put the dagger in the heart of that redcoat, I shall give you a kiss."

The crowd excitedly urged Liam forward.

As did Ellen. She looked down at Natalie; her blue eyes were shining with excitement. They were having fun. *Fun!* She hadn't felt so free and joyous in years, and on a whim Ellen walked forward, took the dagger from a grinning Greencoat, and flushed with excitement, turned and presented it to Liam with a deep curtsy.

The crowd bellowed their approval; Liam grinned and took it from her. "Stand aside, lass, and see how a

Scot wins his maiden's hand," he said, and took his
position in front of the redcoat. He pointed the dagger
at the scarecrow, then slowly drew his arm back. In one
fluid movement, he flung the dagger.

He hit the redcoat perfectly in the crude little heart
drawn on its chest.

The crowd went wild and immediately took up the
call for Liam's prize. *A kiss, a kiss,* they chanted, Natalie
the loudest of them all.

Liam turned to Ellen with a triumphant grin.

"I . . . I did not believe you could . . ." Ellen stammered as she took a step backward.

"I know," Liam said, and before she could move
again, he grabbed her wrist, pulled her into his
embrace, bent her over backward, and bestowed an
outrageously bold kiss for a victorious man. Around
them, the crowd screamed with delight, cheering and
applauding. After what seemed forever, Liam yanked
her back up and let her go, his grin, impossibly, even
more triumphant. Stunned by the kiss, Ellen stumbled
backward and brought her hand to her mouth as more
gentlemen sought Greencoat for the chance to impress
their ladies.

"Ellen?"

Ellen whirled around at the sound of the familiar
voice. Her sister, Eva, along with her husband, Willard,
and their son, Frederick, were all gaping at her in
stunned disbelief. *"Eva,"* she said, her panic irritatingly
evident in her voice, her heart pounding.

"What are you *doing?*" Eva hissed loudly, eyeing
Liam as he accepted fifteen pounds from Greencoat.

"We, ah . . . well, we came out for a picnic," she said,
frantic at how her imperious younger sister, and her
even more imperious husband, Willard, were staring at
Liam, horrified.

"And exactly who is *we?*"

"Well, obviously, Natalie and myself. And Captain Lockhart."

"I beg your pardon, are we *acquainted* with Captain Lockhart?" Eva asked, folding her arms tightly across her stomach as Willard stood by, his face pinched with his obvious disapproval.

"I donna believe I've had the pleasure of making *yer* acquaintance, madam," Liam said, standing behind Natalie, his big hands protectively on her shoulders.

Eva's mouth dropped open. "A *Scot?*"

"Aye, a Scot."

Her mouth still agape, Eva looked at Ellen. "I certainly have *not* had the pleasure of making the captain's acquaintance!"

Fabulous. Bloody fabulous. Eva would act the superior, judgmental part of Farnsworth while he was away. Bristling, Ellen dug her fingernails into her palms in an effort to maintain her composure. "Eva, may I introduce to you Captain Lockhart. Captain Lockhart, may I present Lord and Lady Diffley. My sister."

"Milord, milady, how do ye do, then?" Liam asked, bowing over Natalie's head.

"And where have you had the chance to meet?" Eva demanded of Ellen, ignoring Liam's greeting.

When exactly was it that she had become accountable to her sister? "Captain Lockhart has let rooms from Father."

Eva gasped; her jaw dropped, impossibly, even lower. "He is Father's *tenant?*"

"Aye, that I am," Liam said in a voice gone cold.

Still, Eva ignored him, could only look at Ellen with outright contempt. "Do you have any idea what you are *doing?*" she hissed. "Have you lost your mind?"

"I don't know what you mean—"

"Don't you!" Eva snapped, and glanced at Willard, who was observing the whole scene with his lips pressed together, looking thoroughly disgusted. Eva forced her mouth closed, propriety suffocating everything else, and took a careful step backward, away from Ellen. "Very well, then," she said stiffly, slicing a look across Liam. "A pleasure, sir," she allowed very curtly, then shifted her gaze to Ellen. "Ellen? I suppose we shall speak of this at another time."

"Oh, I'm certain we shall," Ellen said coldly, and lifted her chin as her sister took her husband's arm and turned him away, as if to shield him from some gruesome scene, and walked on, pausing only once to shout at Frederick, who was sticking his tongue out at Natalie.

"If ye'll pardon me saying, Ellie, I think yer sister has pulled her iron drawers a wee bit too high."

That was putting it mildly. As she watched Eva's retreating figure, Ellen knew instantly and instinctively that this was the most disastrous thing that might have happened to her. On that bright, sun-splashed autumn afternoon, Ellen Farnsworth knew that her actions had just given her a mere week to find a way out of this mess for her and Natalie, for when Father returned from God knew where he had gone, Eva would certainly tell him what she had seen, and Ellen had not the slightest doubt that he would turn her and Natalie out.

How she managed to make it back to Belgrave Square without collapsing under the weight of that knowledge was nothing short of a miracle, really. Her sudden melancholy was made worse by Natalie's disappointment at having to give up the promise of fishing, even though Liam tried to persuade her that they would go another time.

Fortunately, he did not argue with Ellen's desire to go home. But he kept looking at her as if he expected her to *do* something. What she wanted to do was tell him that her sister was one of the most high-handed, superior, mealymouthed ladies that paraded about in a ridiculous bonnet, and Eva's, as she recalled, had been quite preposterous, really, what with all the feathers and silly little flowers stuck everywhere. But to conduct herself as if Ellen had committed a capital offense, when all she had done was enjoy a little sport? And exactly who had appointed Eva her conscience? No, she wasn't going to be cowed by her sister's highhanded ways. She had tasted life again, and she wasn't willing to give it up, not for Eva, not for anyone. She had done nothing wrong. *Nothing.*

Dear Liam, but there was nothing he could say to bring a smile to her face. When they reached Belgrave Square, he reluctantly retired to his rooms to ready for the Lockhart ball that evening.

"Good luck," Ellen wished him, but in truth she was too angry and resentful of Eva to think. Yet she wasn't so angry that she didn't notice the look of bewilderment on Liam's face as she and Natalie climbed the stairs.

And indeed, had he the luxury of time, Liam would have followed her and persevered until he understood what had happened at Vauxhall. But at the moment, unfortunately, he had a more important matter to attend to—specifically, a bloody-arsed ball.

His preparation—without Ellie's help but with Follifoot's bumbling hands—was excruciating. But when he at last departed for the event—with a wee approving smile from Follifoot—he was anxious to have it over and done as quickly as possible.

So anxious was he that he gave into the appeal of the faster hack chaise, cringing a bit when he gave up the crown.

He arrived at the Lockhart mansion, his tattered invitation in his pocket, and handed the invitation to the penguin manning the front door as he had seen others do, then waited patiently to be given leave to enter. He did not, therefore, see Nigel wobbling forward on his right until the man nearly toppled right into him. *"Cousin Liam!"* he shouted happily, and clapped him hard on the shoulder. *Diah,* Nigel was already so far into his cups that they'd likely have to send a man in to extract him. "You *must* come, you must come and meet my sister, *Baaaahbara,"* he drawled.

Oh, *aye,* he could scarcely wait to meet yet another overly privileged Lockhart, and sensing as much, Nigel clamped a possessive hand on his arm and began to drag him through the throng of guests, of which there had to be three hundred, if not more. They were so tightly packed into the Lockhart mansion that Liam could envision the entire house expanding and contracting with their collective breath.

The women, at least, brightened the surroundings considerably. They were dressed in varying shades of white and cream and gold, their bodices and hems intricately embroidered, and for many, a wisp of the sheerest silk covered their bosoms. Pearls, feathers, and sparkling little fluffery and ribbons adorned their hair, which was, almost to a woman, dressed in little ringlets about their heads. Delicate little slippers covered their small feet (this, he noticed, after the unfortunate incident of stepping on one as Nigel dragged him through), and he instantly feared dancing with any woman wearing *those* shoes, for he was quite certain he'd destroy them.

The men were dressed as he was—long tails, white waistcoats, and neckcloths trimmed so tightly that more than one looked as if his head might very well burst right off his shoulders. Nonetheless, Liam was exceedingly glad Ellie had insisted he take these old clothes, even if they were unbearably tight. At least he *looked* as if he belonged.

After bumping into not one, but two, doors, Nigel at last navigated his way into a room Liam had seen before. The furniture had been pushed up against the walls, and the room filled with long tables at which several people sat, eating what looked to be cake, sipping a reddish-brown-looking drink, and all laughing quite gaily.

"Would ye like a bit of prog before the whiskey?" Nigel asked Liam. Having no idea what *prog* meant, but having dwelled long enough at Farnsworth's to fear any English cook, Liam quickly shook his head. Nigel shrugged indifferently. "Just as well, really. Leaves little room for the good stuff, eh?" he asked with a wink, and nudged Liam none too gently in the ribs. "Come on, then, let's have a look for my sister. She's quite keen to meet you," he said, lurching forward.

They waded through the crowd; Liam was at least a head taller than most, so that he could see quite clearly as Nigel pushed and shoved toward the opposite end of the room, which was why, then, he was able to see Barbara Lockhart long before Nigel spotted her. And there was no question which of the ladies was his cousin Barbara—the poor lass had the exceedingly dreadful misfortune of resembling her brother exactly, down to the measurement of her waistline and the bulbous nose.

"Babs! Babs, darling!" Nigel called over the din.

Barbara instantly turned toward the sound of his voice and grinned broadly.

Nigel, panting from the exertion of having parted the crowd, reached into his pocket and withdrew a kerchief that he dabbed across his forehead. "I've the distinct pleasure of introducing you to our long-lost Scottish cousin, Liam," he wheezed.

Cousin Barbara instantly dipped (to the extent she

could do so) into a curtsy, and extended her gloved hand, over which was one very large glittering ring. Swallowing back a tedious sigh, Liam took the hand, bent over it with as much flourish as he could muster without making himself ill. "Cousin Barbara, 'tis a pleasure indeed to make yer acquaintance."

Cousin Barbara managed to lift herself from her curtsy and flutter her lashes. "*Ooooh*, Cousin *Liam!*" she exclaimed, and as he let go of her hand, she instantly snapped open her fan and began to wave it at her face with quite a fervor. "What a pleasure to at last make your acquaintance! My brother's good opinion of you is well known in spite of all that nasty family business, and truly, he's not done you *justice*."

"Has he no'?"

She giggled, slanting her gaze at Nigel. "Oh Nigel, you poor dear, I am certain you are quite parched, aren't you? Run along, then, for I'd be *delighted* to show our cousin Liam about," she said, and before Liam could move, she had slipped her pudgy hand into the crook of his arm. "Nigel's told me *all*," she whispered, looking surreptitiously over her shoulder to see if anyone eavesdropped. "Horrid people, your family. But I daresay he was quite inaccurate about *you*."

"Pardon?"

Cousin Barbara slapped Liam's arm with her fan so hard that it actually stung. "Silly boy! You're *much* more handsome than he described to me!"

How alarming, but he could actually feel himself color.

Cousin Barbara laughed. "*Oooh*, and you're a *shy* one!" she squealed, and Liam wished the floor would open up and swallow him whole.

But, alas, Cousin Barbara fancied herself his irrefutable escort, and dragged him from one room to the next, making his introduction to various ladies.

Most of their lovely faces went by in a blur, most of them looking appalled by his scar, save one very pretty auburn-haired woman with thickly lashed golden brown eyes. Wearing an astounding red gown, Miss Addison was the only one who seemed, all and all, rather perturbed by Barbara's machinations. "Really, Miss Lockhart, your cousin looks positively exhausted what with all the introductions you insist on making," she said matter-of-factly as she openly eyed Liam.

Cousin Barbara swelled up, just like a peacock. "Thank you for your kind concern, Miss Addison," she seethed, "but I *assure* you, my cousin is *quite* atwitter with all the acquaintances he's had the good fortune to make this evening."

Atwitter? He had never, not once in his life, been *atwitter* about a bloody thing. And he had never wanted to strangle a woman until this very moment.

To make matters worse, Miss Addison had the audacity to smirk at his discomfort. "I commend you, Captain Lockhart. You've a rather grand way of looking all atwitter,"

"Do I, then? I didna mean to."

"Why, how very exotic of you. A *Scot*," she observed, before slinking off to join another group of women. It was time, Liam realized with some consternation, to extract himself from his cousin's attention before he became the laughingstock of the entire ball, and he was just about to do so when the first strains of string music drifted into the room.

"Oh, how very *splendid!*" Cousin Barbara trilled. "I shall have the pleasure of the first dance with my dear cousin *Liam*," she exclaimed loudly for all to hear, and immediately began pulling him in the direction of the ballroom.

This ball, it seemed, was destined to be the venue for

the complete personal humiliation of Liam Carson Lockhart.

Or so he thought. But as it turned out, he quite unexpectedly impressed the hell out of himself.

The first dance was a quadrille, which he despised with all his heart, and was certain would end with him on his arse in the middle of that beeswax-polished dance floor beneath dozens of shimmering candles suspended above them, which would cast light on hundreds of bobbing English heads tittering all about him. If that happened, he'd simply have to draw his pistol and kill the lot of them, and he really didn't relish the thought of that.

But miraculously, as he bowed in front of Barbara, his feet began to move, and before he even knew what was happening, he was turning and dipping and passing behind the ladies like a bloody rooster. Even more astounding, Cousin Barbara begged to be led to a chair at the conclusion of the lengthy dance, exclaiming loudly about the heat and her poor aching feet. Liam was more than happy to plant her there, and even went so far as to fetch her some punch with the hope she might even put down roots. And when he was certain she would not grab him by the tails, he begged his leave and managed to escape . . . but ran smack into Miss Addison, who eyed him suspiciously as he attempted to pass.

"No doubt you meant to inquire if my dance card was full," she said pointedly.

Liam couldn't help himself; he sighed. It wasn't as if there weren't two dozen roosters all lined up along the dance floor, was it? Why him? "So ye want to stand up, do ye?" he asked.

That less-than-enthusiastic invitation caused her to raise an imperious brow, but she nonetheless held out her gloved hand and drawled, *"Yes.* I do."

He escorted her onto the dance floor, winced when a minuet was begun. He managed to guide her through the first movements—no easy feat, that, as Miss Addison watched him carefully—which meant that Liam watched *her* carefully as he attempted to discern what she was about. That in turn meant that he had less opportunity to think of his damned feet, and made more than one clumsy mistake.

"You don't dance much, do you, sir?" she purred as they dipped.

"No," he said, putting his hand on her back and forcing her to turn.

"I'm always rather suspicious of men who don't dance," she said, as she gracefully twirled away and back again. "It leads me to believe they've been living under some wretched rock if they've no more regard for society than that."

"Is that so?" he responded politely. "As for me, I am always suspicious of women who talk too much. Empty prattle, empty head."

Miss Addison smiled a little at that. "How positively charming," she said, and twirled away from him, then dipped back to him. "How did you acquire the scar?" she asked as Liam took her hand to promenade.

"Under me wretched rock."

Miss Addison laughed, a pleasantly full laugh, and at the end of the dance, Liam was satisfied she was merely a woman who was as bored as he was with all the glittery pomp and circumstance, and was only seeking amusement, nothing more. She needed, he thought, a taste of life. *Real* life, not salon life.

After escorting Miss Addison back to the pack of ladies, Liam managed two waltzes and another quadrille before he was able to extricate himself from a group of debutantes and the ballroom altogether.

The corridor was teeming with small groups, couples, and still another set of ladies stealing shy glances at various gentlemen. As he moved through the crowd, more than one guest paused to look at him as he passed, assessing him, peering at his scar. He clasped his hands behind his back as he had seen the English do and strolled insouciantly down the corridor to the staircase. He knew below were the rooms set up for dining, cards, and the manly pursuit of whiskey and cigars, for Barbara had dragged him through each in her zest to display him to the other ladies. He had noted then, unhappily, that the beastie was not among the many objects on display.

That left the upper floors. How exactly he might make his way up without being noticed posed a bit of a problem. It was impossible to ascend the staircase without being seen. Wouldn't someone stop him? Question him? That left the outdoors. All he required was a trellis, a tree, or even a hedgerow would do the trick. He was pondering that when someone touched his arm, and he turned slightly; it was Miss Addison peering up at him with a knowing little smile. Beside her stood two ladies who had been previously introduced to him, but whose names he had, of course, forgotten.

"Why Captain Lockhart, you seem positively perplexed."

"Do I, now?"

"We were just to the ladies' retiring room."

"Ah." He nodded, wishing to hell she'd go on about her retiring and leave him be.

But Miss Addison smiled boldly at him. "Perhaps *you* are in need of a retiring room, sir? I should be happy to point the way."

Her companions gasped at her boldness, but Liam rather liked it. He was always one to appreciate those who spoke their mind, and moreover, he rather liked the idea of her pointing him to a retiring room.

Preferably, one on the floor above. "That'd be right kind of ye, lass," he said, and grinned right back when the ladies tittered at Miss Addison.

She arched that fine dark brow again. "Well then, you may follow us. I believe the gentlemen are in the room just adjacent to ours," she said, and lifting her skirts, began a smooth, authoritative ascent. Her companions were instantly behind her, stealing shy looks at Liam over their shoulders, which were accompanied by titters, giggles, and a bit of whispering.

Mo creach, women!

He unabashedly followed them up, noted the door to which Miss Addison carefully nodded, and returned her smile when she slipped into the ladies' retiring room. Waiting a moment until he was certain they were indisposed, Liam moved silently and quickly down the corridor, opening each door he passed, glancing inside. But the rooms were dark—he could make nothing out—and when he reached the far end of the corridor, he paused again, ascertaining that he was alone for the moment, and slipped inside the end room.

Shutting the door quietly behind him, he paused in the dark, his hands on his hips. It would be a quarter of an hour at most before Cousin Barbara or Miss Addison would notice him missing. Not much time to search several darkened rooms. Instantly, he groped about the door for a candle, which he found on a small table just a foot or so away, along with matches. He managed to light the thing, and holding it high, had a look around. He was in a sitting room of some sort; a writing table and a smattering of soft chairs adorned the room. Paintings, ornate fixtures, and elaborate frieze moldings on the ceiling made him growl. The English Lockharts had more money than they needed, obviously, judging by the way each room was overly appointed for show. He quickly searched among the many trinkets, but there was no evidence of a beastie. There was, however, a door leading to the adjoining room.

He pressed his ear against the door, heard nothing, and very slowly, very carefully, opened it onto yet another sitting room. The English thought quite a lot of sitting, apparently. This one appeared more masculine in its decor. Holding the candle ahead of him, he moved slowly, walking the length of one wall, then the next. Nothing. As he neared the door that led to the main corridor, he could hear several voices engaged in conversation, and holding his breath, he stood there until he was certain the voices had passed. That was when he noticed the armoire. He had not seen furniture like it in any other room. He walked to it, jiggled the handle. Locked, damn it.

Cursing under his breath, he squatted, reached under his trouser leg, and withdrew his *sgian dubh* from his stocking. Then, setting the candle aside, and still on his haunches, he reached up and picked the lock. One of the doors sprang free so quickly that it startled him, and he grabbed the candle as he surged to his feet and staggered back, still holding the dagger.

He saw it.

Liam lifted the candle, saw its hideous face staring out at him—*the beastie*. It was the goddamned beastie, all right, sitting among various other dubious works of art, glaring at him. It was just as hideous as he had heard tell: Its ruby-red eyes were too big for the thing's face; its yawning mouth glittered with a larger ruby and gold fangs; and the claws, crossed on the beastie's chest, seemed to be honed to a deadly point of gold.

"I suppose you've found something quite interesting, by the look of it."

Miraculously, Liam held on to both dagger and candle at the sound of the woman's voice, and calmly slipped the dagger into his pocket before shifting his gaze to Miss Addison. "Aye, that I did," he said, and smiled.

Nineteen

❧

*I*n the hack on the way back to Belgrave Square, Liam had to congratulate himself on his quick thinking and unflappable abilities. That wasn't to say he didn't experience a moment of panic when he saw Miss Addison standing there, knowing she had slipped in through the door he had left open between the two rooms—that alone was a careless, inexcusable blunder. But he had recovered quite nicely, if he did remark it himself, and in fact left the poor woman so discombobulated, he was certain she would never remember the door to the armoire was open.

He had worried about that a bit, actually, as he never had a chance to close the cabinet, being so intent on ushering her out of the room. Ah, well. Little harm done, surely. When the family discovered the armoire open, there would be more than three hundred suspects, if indeed they ever believed the latch was unlocked by someone other than a parlor maid. And as there was nothing missing—not this time, at least—they'd likely forget the whole thing had occurred. Therefore, when and if they *did* discover the beastie missing—which Liam rather doubted, since it was locked away—the chances were very slim that Miss Addison would recall with any reliability that she had seen the armoire open with him in the room.

Actually, after the kiss he had bestowed on her, he

was quite certain she'd remember nothing else. Not that he was particularly adept at kissing, for he really didn't fancy himself so. But the element of surprise coupled with the rather illicit nature of stealing a kiss from a woman one has just met, in a dark room, in a mansion full of London's most important society members, had left them both a little breathless. Miss Addison's earlier cynical bravado had quickly melted away into moon-eyed gaping, and to keep her in that dreamy state, Liam had marched her into the ballroom, had engaged her in a rather long waltz, and had whispered little things in her ear, such as, *Yer eyes are as dark as black opals,* and his personal favorite, *Yer skin is as creamy as mother's milk.* He wasn't quite sure what that meant, but it sounded rather poetic, if he did say so himself. Certainly Miss Addison seemed to think it quite a compliment and he reckoned she'd forget the armoire ever existed if she remembered it at all.

Escaping the Lockhart house altogether had been another ordeal, but fortunately, Nigel and his chums had decided they should have a look around the gentlemen's clubs after they grew weary of dancing, and Liam had eagerly tagged along on their tails, leaving Cousin Barbara and Miss Addison smiling after him from opposite ends of the room. Once outside, he disappeared into the alley mews and stole around the house until he was standing directly beneath the last room. As he looked up at the window in the pale moonlight, he grinned happily. There it was, a trellis, attached to the brick wall beneath the ladies' sitting room he had first entered. It was as if a higher authority had built him a ladder for this very purpose, and he did indeed send up a word of thanks.

When the hack arrived at Belgrave Square, Liam was in exceedingly good spirits, and he leaped to the ground, tossed a coin up to the driver, and with a jaunty tip of his hat sauntered inside.

The Farnsworth house was, as usual, cold, dark, and as quiet as a mausoleum, a stark contrast to the gaiety of the Lockhart mansion. Liam made his way to his rooms, shucking out of the absurdly tight suit of clothing and donning a pair of buckskins, over which his shirttails hung. He then took one of his last few pieces of vellum and wrote:

> *Dearest Mother, I have attended my uncle's ball, which was far too crowded for good health, but that is the way of things here. My eyes are ruby red from the smoke of many cheroots and I eagerly await my return home to the cool Highland air to soothe them. Fondly, L.*

Humming an old Gaelic tune, he sealed the letter, put it aside for posting first thing in the morning, then looked at his pocket watch. It was two o'clock in the morning—but he was too restless, too anxious to sleep. The end of his mission was drawing near, and it excited him. The accomplishment of one successful mission meant there would soon be another, and he was ready for it, as he had wasted too much time in London. All he needed now was an opportune time to enter the house and steal the blasted beastie. Simple.

Except that it wasn't simple at all. Stealing the beastie inevitably meant there was Ellie to consider, and Liam felt his good spirits slipping.

God blind him, what was he to do about Ellie?

He loved her; there was no question of it. When he was with her, she made him feel as if he had reached for the sun and now held it in his very hand. He had never felt so light, so happy—every thought of her brought a smile to his face.

Aye, he loved her, heart and soul . . . but it was quite

another thing to think he could take her with him. What, did he think she would pack her many trunks and follow him to God knew where his military career would lead him? And what of war? Where exactly did he stow her away during times of war? Talla Dileas? Worse, even if he could come to terms with the thought of leaving this sort of love behind (really, what choice did he have?), he could hardly leave her like this, could he? He despised Farnsworth. How could he leave her to years of his cruelty? *Jesus God,* if only he had a bit of money! Unfortunately, his entire military pension, tiny bit that it was, went to help pay the upkeep of Talla Dileas and was sorely needed in that regard—he could not spite his family's needs in favor of Ellie. Perhaps he could send her his pension when the beastie was sold. *Ah!* There it was—yet it still was not enough to actually *free* her.

A dilemma, to be sure. But he had time to think on it—at the moment, he was rather chomping at the bit to tell Ellie that he had found it.

Ellie was asleep, of course. Liam stood at the foot of her bed with his arms crossed over his chest, admiring her, watching the gentle rise and fall of her chest in sleep. Her hair, long and bound at her nape, draped her shoulders in glimmering strands of white and gold. Her lips were dark and succulent even in the dim moonlight and her expression soft, as if she enjoyed a tranquil dream. He hoped, for her sake, that she dreamed of fields of gold, with flowers and butterflies and bright sunshine and gentle, warm breezes.

After a moment, he touched her slender foot. Ellie did not move. He walked to the side of the bed, reached down to stroke her cheek with his bare knuckle; that caused her to mumble and roll to her side. Carefully, he lowered himself to the edge of the bed, put his hand on the sleeve of her nightshift. *"Ellie,"* he whispered.

Nothing.

He shook her lightly. "Ellie, lass. Wake now, *leannan."*

Her eyes fluttered open; she affixed her gaze on him, blinking several times as if she didn't believe what she was seeing. *"Liam?"* she asked sleepily.

"Aye." He leaned over and touched her warm cheek with his lips.

"But what are you doing here? You should be at the ball. You should be dancing," she sighed, and her eyes were fluttering shut again.

Liam smiled, stretched out until he was lying beside her, face-to-face, and stroked her hair. "I danced. Ye would have been so proud, Ellie! But I couldna wait 'til the morrow to tell ye."

"Tell me what?" she yawned.

"I found the beastie," he whispered.

Her eyes flew open so suddenly that Liam all but rolled off the bed; she came up on her elbow, wide-eyed now, staring down at him. "You *found* it?" she whispered loudly, then looked toward the door, saw that it was ajar. With the grace and agility of a cat, she scampered over him, grabbed her dressing gown, and shoved her arms into it as she hurried to the door. Peering into the adjoining room, she carefully closed it, then flew back across the room and landed on the foot of her bed.

Liam pushed himself against the headboard, folded his arms behind his head, crossed his feet at the ankles, and grinned broadly at her.

"Well?" she exclaimed excitedly, slapping at his shoes. "You will not *dare* leave me in suspense! Where did you find it?"

"In a sitting room on the second floor."

"Just like that? Sitting out, was it?"

"Ah, no. In an armoire."

"An *armoire*," she said, nodding thoughtfully. "And then what?"

"Then what?"

"Liam! How did it look?"

He clucked his tongue. "Uglier than ye can imagine. I've no' seen anything so ugly, on me honor," he assured her.

"Yes, but the rubies?"

"All there."

"Big enough to bring the value?"

"Aye. More than we hoped, I'd wager."

"Small enough to carry?"

"Aye, of course."

Ellie suddenly came to her feet and began pacing the carpet by her bed. "Then the only thing left to do now is to figure out how to get it, isn't that so? I mean, now that you know where it is—"

Liam laughed at her earnestness. "Ellie, *leannan*, ye're no' to worry yer pretty head about it. I know what must be done."

"But how will you get in?" she asked, tapping a finger against her lips, deep in thought as she peered at him.

"A trellis. It's just below the window to the room adjacent to it. 'Tis in the mews, so no one could see a body climb up in the middle of the night."

"But what of the window?"

"What of it?"

"If it's locked from the inside—"

"Too high. More trouble than no' to lock it up and unlock it all over again."

Ellie nodded, her brow furrowing so delightfully that Liam had to bite his tongue to keep from laughing.

"Donna fret about the armoire. I popped the lock as easy as a child's toy box."

"How?"

He waved a hand toward his boot. "*Sgian dubh* . . . a small dagger. Just slipped the tip into the lock, and there it was, she opened. 'Tis an old lock, it is."

Ellie nodded, glanced away for a moment, then turned her gaze to him once more with an expression so dark that it sent a shiver down his spine. "What are ye thinking, then?" he asked softly.

She shrugged, looked at her feet. "That you'll be gone when you have it," she whispered.

Liam held out his hand to her.

Silently, she crawled up on the bed until she was lying beside him. Neither of them said a word, just looked at each other while an ocean of grief pooled between them, pushing them apart. At last, Ellie bent her head and kissed his neck, then his lips. She kissed him so fully and tenderly that he felt himself falling deep into her enchantment, his body vibrating with it. He was lost in her, lost in himself, so lost that when she bit his lower lip—hard—it startled him badly.

Liam instantly grabbed her shoulders and jerked her away from him. But instead of looking contrite, Ellie smiled wickedly, touched the spot where she had bit him, then held up her finger so that he could see the tiny bit of blood she had drawn. "You should punish me," she murmured.

Those words rifled through his entire body, igniting him. He shoved her onto her back, straddling her as he pinned her hands above her head, while his body held her beneath him. "What is it ye said, lass?" he demanded as he leaned over her, breathing her in.

Ellie smiled that wickedly seductive smile again. "I said, Captain, you should *punish* me."

Ach, he'd punish her, he would. With a throaty chuckle, he suddenly moved off her, yanking her as he went, pulling her across his lap, facedown. "It's punishment ye want, is that it?" he breathed as he casually pushed her dressing gown aside and slipped his hand beneath her nightgown.

"*Yes,*" she said, with a low, seductive laugh, moving on his lap to accommodate his roaming hand as it slipped in between her thighs.

"If ye want to be punished," he murmured as he casually explored her bottom, "ye must ask me nicely."

Ellie sighed, lifted her hips in response to his prob-ing fingers, and whispered huskily, "Punish me—" She gasped as he grabbed her bare hip and squeezed it roughly. "*Please* punish me," she continued, her breath growing ragged. "Make me sorry for having bit you," she rasped.

Liam's body came alive, and he moved beneath her, so that she could feel just how alive he was. Ellie shifted, rubbing against him, lifting her hips higher, silently asking for more until Liam could bear it no more. Suddenly he pushed her forward, off his lap, fumbling with his trousers as she pulled her nightgown up to her waist, exposing her bare bottom to him, pink from his handling. With his trousers half on, Liam mounted her from behind, thrusting deep into her damp heat as he whispered in her ear, "I shall punish ye lass. I shall punish ye until ye beg for mercy."

Ellie arched into him, lifted her head, and whispered, "*Deeper.*"

Twenty

✿

$\mathcal{E}$llie had succeeded in introducing Liam to a new sensual world; their lovemaking that night was electrifying, and left him fully sated, exhausted and feeling disturbingly warm and a little fuzzy, as if he were walking about in something of a lush fog or wallowing about in a vat of figgy pudding. . . . All right, that was definitely *not* something Liam was accustomed to feeling, and frankly, he was having a difficult time adjusting to the idea that he rather liked feeling so terribly unfocused. But dammit it all to hell, he *liked* being in love! And it didn't help that this latest, tantalizing nocturnal experience with Ellie came back to him over and over again, bringing a smile to his face.

Yet not nearly as bright or as deeply felt as the one he wore each time he saw Ellie, his beautiful, luscious Ellie.

As fortune would have it, he saw quite a lot of her after the ball. Nigel, predictably, was indisposed for two days afterward. Liam might have called on him, but the thought of encountering Cousin Barbara was more than he could endure, and besides, Nigel's taking to his bed gave Liam the opportunity to spend as much time with Ellie as he could. They walked in Hyde Park together, took tea, strolled among the shops that lined Bond Street, and even ventured again to Vauxhall Gardens, where he bought Ellie and Nat each a gillyflower corsage with his dwindling funds. It hardly concerned him, as he was certain he would be leaving London soon, now that he had found the beastie.

As to that—his inevitable departure—he and Ellie avoided the subject entirely, choosing, apparently, to leave that discussion to another, more pressing time. On those occasions Ellie tried to talk about it, usually having something to do with the nabbing of the beastie (about which she seemed rather nervous), he humored her, steering the conversation clear of such unpleasant reminders. He did not want to face the uncertain future. He wanted only to think about carefree things. He wanted only to love her while he could. He had been shown a glimpse of heaven, complete with angels, and he wasn't ready to plummet back to Earth.

So they spent their time speaking of light topics, such as the many books Ellie had read in her solitude. Liam rather imagined she and his mother could have been fast friends, as they both seemed to have voracious appetites for reading. She repeated gossip (albeit woefully dated gossip) about various people he had met and talked at length about slippers and gowns and horses and paintings and other such inconsequential things.

Liam returned the favor, teaching Ellie a bit about Scottish history, which he had not previously realized he knew quite so much about. He would have astounded and pleased his family with his recitation of events, his description of Talla Dileas and Loch Chon, and the people who lived there. He talked about Payton Douglas and his suspicion of the man's regard for his sister, Mared. He told her about Griffin and his desire to be part of the set that moved in and around Mayfair. He spoke fondly of his parents, and of his dogs, and of his horses, and naturally, the hairy cattle that grazed there.

When they weren't conversing, or playing with Nattie, or preparing edible food, they were making love. It was, to Liam's way of thinking, a fascinating, almost irrational dreamlike experience. It was tender and loving, certainly, for he loved Ellie. But it was also dangerously, precariously exciting. And it was never enough.

He had, he realized one day as he watched Ellie and Natalie walking along the path in front of him, fallen so hard into this abyss of love that he was privately fearful he might not ever recover. Every wee thing about her made him want to be with her more; every time he thought of being without her, he felt a growing sense of desperation. His was a violent conflict of emotions— part of him wished he had never found the damned beastie. Yet another part of him hoped he got his hands on it quickly, and the sooner the better, as it was best to end this now and carry on. But he was, all in all, quite unwilling to dwell on the negative, was perhaps even fearful of facing the inevitable, and he refused to let himself think in those few days, tamping everything down, down, down. He would only allow himself this glimpse of heaven and angels.

But all of that ended one afternoon not three days later when Liam ran into Nigel, who, having recovered from the overindulgence of his father's ball, was back at his usual haunts along Pall Mall, and had engaged Liam in a card game, during which he casually mentioned his impending departure from London.

Liam glanced up as he dealt cards for a game. "Leaving?"

"Yes, yes, toodle-pip, off to Bath for a day or two while Mummy's away. You know, take the waters and all that."

No, he didn't know—no one in Loch Chon ever "took" waters that he was aware. "And how long, exactly, does one take waters?"

Nigel snorted his laughter. "Cousin Liam, how very *quaint* you are. Surely you don't *really* think . . . Oh, dear, I suppose there are *some* gentlemen who go to Bath for the purpose of taking the waters there, for I understand they are quite healing, actually, but really, *most* of us go for a change of scenery."

" 'Tis rather pretty, then, is it?"

Nigel looked at him as if he were an idiot. "*Scenery,* Cousin Liam," he said, sketching an hourglass with his hands. "*Knockers.* You know, those sweet little buds of feminine flesh that make our wee willies dance with delight?"

Certainly Liam had sat around many campfires and shared in more than one discussion about the female anatomy, but he couldn't have been more shocked if his very own mother had uttered those words. *Wee willies!* Before he could regain his composure, Nigel was waving an effeminate hand at him. "Not to worry, old chap. But you should really think of coming with us," he said, arranging his cards precisely so in his hand. "We'll not be abroad more than a day or two. Uckerby's driving, and he's got a rather grand carriage, so it should be a rather comfortable journey."

"Ah, but how will Uncle ever manage without ye, Nigel?" Liam asked idly.

"Goodness to mercy, Liam, Father is coming, too, naturally!" Nigel exclaimed.

Now Nigel had Liam's undivided attention—he could hardly believe his good fortune. If the old man was gone, that left . . . "Aye, but ye'd not leave yer sister alone, would ye, Nigel?"

"Who, Barbara?" he asked, then suddenly flashed a sly smile. "Have you a particular *interest,* Cousin Liam?" he all but squealed, but saved Liam the problem of answering by announcing, "Barbara is quite capable of staying behind."

Damn.

"But she does not like to be alone, and will therefore be quite comfortable at Auntie's house."

Liam could not believe his ears or his apparent dumb luck—the Lockhart mansion would be empty and he could seize that wretched beastie in a matter of days! He laid his cards, let Nigel beat him, then as his cousin picked up the cards and began to shuffle them, he asked, "When is it ye leave, then?"

"Oh, this afternoon at four o'clock. Uckerby is of a mind to picnic near Ascot."

Today?

"You'll come then, will you?"

"*Ach*, what rotten misfortune," Liam said, quickly recovering from his surprise. "I've a rather important appointment on the morrow. Bank." He grimaced accordingly.

"Ah." Nigel matched that grimace with one of his own. "Exceedingly unpleasant business, I should think, what with your miserly father and all. Must keep *that* appointment, I suppose!" Liam nodded. "It would be insupportable to miss it?" he tried again.

"Of course."

"Oh, very well!" Nigel exclaimed petulantly. "We're to Bath often enough—we might perhaps invite you again," he said, and focused on the cards in his hand.

Liam lost two more hands, after which he glanced at his pocket watch. "Is it so late, then? Almost two o'clock," he said, and Nigel instantly came to attention.

"*Two!* Oh, dear, I must be away—Uckerby has the foulest temper when he's kept the least bit waiting." He thrust up out of his chair, and teetering on his bird legs, stuck a hand out to Liam. "Wish you well, all that," he said, and eagerly shook Liam's hand. "We'll come calling in a day or two, mark me. Pip-pip!" And with that he toddled out the door.

"Good-bye, then, Cousin Nigel," Liam muttered under his breath.

He waited a quarter of an hour after Nigel left, then walked the short distance to the Lockhart mansion, strolling past like a gent on a walkabout, surreptitiously noting the various features, reviewing his options for reaching the trellis and mentally reviewing the lay of the rooms once more. He then walked the most direct but least observable routes to and from Belgrave Square to assure himself that he knew where he was going, particularly since he would make his trek in the dead of night. And as he walked back to the Farnsworth house to wait for night, he forced himself to keep from thinking of Ellie, to keep his thoughts focused on the task at hand, repeating over and over in his heart and mind that he would get the beastie first, *just get the blasted thing.* Then, and only then, would he think what to do. He had a forty-eight-hour window before Nigel and his father would return. Forty-eight hours to determine the course of the rest of his life.

From her bench in the square, where Natalie sat beside her drawing, Ellen noticed that these last few days of warm autumn sun they had enjoyed would be short-lived—she could see the clouds on the horizon, could feel the sharp chill in the air that seemed to creep into her spine. She drew her cloak more tightly about her and saw Liam striding across the square, head down, his expression quite serious. It was a much different expression than she had grown accustomed to, and instantly curious, she nudged her daughter. "Natalie, darling, catch Captain Lockhart, will you, and ask him to come and sit with us for a moment."

Natalie looked up from her drawing, saw Liam. "He looks rather cross," she said as she slipped off the bench and went running after him. Ellen watched as Natalie caught up to him, grabbing his coat. He jerked around, obviously surprised. He looked down at Natalie, then instantly looked up, to where Ellen was sitting.

Even at that distance, she could tell by the tension in his shoulders, the dark expression that shadowed his features. She knew. *She knew.* Her heart plummeted; her hands and face went cold, and she realized, as Liam strode toward her, Natalie running alongside, that she was shaking. It had come after all, this defining moment, the one instance in her twenty-eight years that would shape the rest of her life to come. Why, oh, *why* had she fallen in love again? How had she allowed it to happen? She knew the consequences of love, knew the consequences of that very first kiss, knew that only sorrow could come of it. In these last few days, her love for Liam felt so endless that his departure could only be horrid.

Somehow she managed to find her feet as Liam reached her. He came to an abrupt halt directly before her, his eyes roaming her face. After a moment, he said roughly, "There ye are, Ellie, looking as bonny as ever." He sounded, oddly, almost angry.

Nonetheless, Ellen forced a smile to her face. "How very kind you are to me, Liam. You look to be in quite a hurry!"

"Do I?"

She put a hand over her eyes, pretending to shield them from the fading sun. "Is . . . is something amiss?" *Say no, say no, say—*

"The Lockharts . . . they are to Bath," he said simply, and looked at Natalie, who had resumed her drawing.

Ellen's instincts, then, had been deadly accurate, and her heart climbed to her throat. "Indeed! All of them?" she forced herself to exclaim.

"Cousin Barbara will stay with an aunt. But Uncle, Nigel . . ."

"But this is splendid news!" she said as his voice trailed off.

Liam frowned at her then. "Ellie, I—"

"We must have cake to celebrate," she interrupted him, before he could say words that would destroy her. "Agatha brought us a cake! Will you take tea with us, sir?"

"Oh, yes, please let's have cake!" Natalie innocently chimed in.

Liam's eyes went dark with some emotion she could not fathom. "Cake," he echoed.

"*Rum* cake," she clarified, to which Natalie exclaimed with a squeal of delight that she adored rum cake. Ellie held out her hand to her. "Gather your things, darling, we're off for tea and a bit of cake. Aren't we, Captain?" Natalie sprang to her feet, gathered her paper and pencils to her chest, and fell in beside her mother. Ellen began walking, her limbs numb, silently willing herself to put one foot in front of the other. She had given Liam no choice; he followed her on a walk that loomed in front of her as the longest of her life.

But what could she do? Her father would be home in two days. Liam likely would be gone, and she could already feel the void he would leave in their lives, a void that was already beginning to squeeze the breath from her. It was almost more than she could bear, suffocating in its misery, but she was determined not to let him see it, not to let him know how much this hurt.

When they reached the house, Liam excused himself, but came to her suite a half hour later, the same as always, bearing a small gift, a button from his regimental coat for Natalie. They took tea as they always did, enjoying Agatha's cake. But the tension was palpable, and unable to endure it, Ellen finally took Natalie to her room, then returned to broach the subject of the beastie. "You'll go tonight, won't you?" she asked as she entered the room.

Liam came instantly to his feet the moment the words were out of her mouth, pacing. "He rather surprised me, he did, with his announcement," he confessed. "I'd no' thought the opportunity would come so *quickly.*"

"It's a godsend," Ellen murmured.

"But . . ." He paused, looking helplessly at her.

"But you must do what you came here to do, Liam," she said, walking to the window. "There's little point, if any, in debating it."

"Aye," he sighed, and shoved a hand through his hair. "There's no point. I've me entire family to think of, Ellie. They are counting on me, they are."

"Yes, of course."

"But . . . it leaves unanswered questions between us, that I know, and I intend to address them, I do. But I canna do so, no' now, no' tonight. I . . . I must get the beastie, and until I have it safely in hand, I donna have the answers. That is, I mean to say . . . the two of us, 'twas no' meant to happen, I think, but now that it has, I . . . I *must* think on it."

Not meant to happen . . . Of course not. Ellen smiled and touched his face. "I'm not asking for answers. I *understand.* I only pray that you will understand, too."

He looked at her curiously. "Of course I understand," he said emphatically, pulling her into his embrace. "Ye have no' said it, but I know ye love me, Ellie. I can *feel* it through to me very bones," he murmured against the top of her head.

She said nothing, just let him hold her, knowing that it would be the last time he held her like this.

He left soon afterward—there were several things he needed to do that evening in preparation for his task. Ellen wanted to help him, but he refused it, saying if something went awry, he wouldn't have her implicated, not even remotely.

So Ellen made her own preparations, what few there were left to do. And when the clock struck midnight—a scant two hours before Liam would make his move—she made sure Natalie was sleeping, descended the staircase wearing a long pelisse, carrying sturdy walking shoes in her hand. Using her fingertips against the wall to guide her, she moved silently down the corridor toward his rooms, her heart growing heavier with each step, breaking under the weight of it all. *It was ending too soon!*

Drawing a deep, fortifying breath, she rapped lightly on the door, heard the creak of the bedsprings, and calmly pushed it open, peeking around the frame. Dressed in his kilt, Liam was lying on his side. A single candle burned on the table, casting a soft, murky light across the room. *"Ellie,"* he whispered as she slipped through the door. "I hoped ye'd come."

She stepped inside, closed the door softly behind her, and leaned against it, looking at him. Lord God, she *did* love him, even though she'd convinced herself, after so many painful months of waiting for Daniel to return to her, that she'd never love again. Ah, but what irony. *Look at you now, Ellie. Look at you, desperately in love with him.* And look what would become of them. Her lot in life, it seemed, was to love deeply just to lose it.

"Come here, lass," he said, rising to sit on the edge of the bed.

Ellen leaned down, laid her shoes by the door, then straightened again and began to slowly unbutton her pelisse, letting it fall open to reveal the gown she had discovered in the trunks on the top floor. Liam watched her, his eyes drifting from her face to her body as the pelisse fell open, his fingers curling around the edge of the bed. *"Mo creach,* what have ye got there?"

She smiled wantonly, knowing the effect of the bathing gown she had discovered. It was a paper-thin, almost transparent gown from years gone by that a modest woman would have once worn to bathe in. She shrugged out of the pelisse and let it fall to the floor.

His eyes on her body, Liam rose to his feet. "What a treasure ye bring me, *leannan*," he said admiringly. He began to walk toward her, the kilt swinging around his knees, his gaze feasting on her. "I swear to heaven, there was never a woman more beautiful than ye are. Never."

That heartfelt sentiment trickled down her spine like a tear, yet Ellen remained silent as he came forward and reached for her. When his hand touched her waist, she laughed low, put a hand to his chest and pushed away from the door, forcing Liam backward.

His lips curled seductively; he laughed with her as he caught her wrist. "What is this, then? Would ye entice me so then deny me?"

She pushed him, forcefully, and Liam stumbled backward a step or two. "Do you deserve to touch me, sir?" she asked playfully, lifting her chin.

"I donna know if I deserve it," he said, "but I crave it like water. Ye should no' play with a man who desires to touch ye as much as I do."

Ellen tossed her head, strutted away from him, aware that he could see her naked body through the flimsy material. He made a guttural, appreciative sound as she neared the table, where she saw his things so carefully laid out—the sporran, the daggers. The war medals. She turned around, leaned against the table and cupped her breast with her hand. "Do you want to touch this?" she murmured huskily.

His legs braced apart, Liam clenched his hands in a fist. "Aye."

She smiled, flicked her finger against her nipple. "Do you want to kiss it?"

Liam growled, took a step forward, but Ellen quickly moved, putting the table between them. Bracing himself against the table with his hand, Liam leaned across, chuckling. "I warned ye no' to play games with an aroused man, lass," he said sportingly, but there was a sting of truth in his voice. "If ye play with fire, ye may be burned."

Ellen leaned across the table, so that her gown was gaping open and he could see her breasts. "Perhaps. But if you want to *touch* fire, you must be prepared to hold it in your hand."

Liam instantly made a move to his right; Ellen jumped to her left, just beyond his reach, and laughed low. His smile faded. "Come now, Ellie. Ye've had yer fun."

"Have I?" she asked, laughing again as she ran across the floor to a window. She stood in front of the heavy drapes, pulled back with a thick-roped cord. "Shall I open the window so everyone sees how you chase me to ravage me?"

"Ye've no idea how close I am to doing just that," he said, walking toward her.

Ellen darted to the next window, pulled the heavy cord that held the drape, and let it fall. She tossed the cord on the bed, kicked the drape out in front of Liam and ran to the brazier. His eyes never left her; he followed her, moving slowly, cautiously, a strange light playing in his eyes. "Ye'll pay for yer foolishness," he warned her. "I'll no' be gentle."

"I do not believe I asked you to be gentle, sir . . . *if* you catch me."

That caused him to lunge for her, but Ellie managed to slip him again, running to the empty hearth, laughing breathlessly.

"Why would ye torment me thus?" he asked, just as breathlessly. "Ye desire yer punishment, eh?"

Ellen dragged her palms up her belly to her breasts, kneading them. Liam stared at her with dark, hungry eyes, and a wave of desire arched down her back, landing hot in her groin. She licked her lips, let her eyes wander his body, the broad chest, the narrow waist. The tent of his kilt.

"Ye see what ye do to me, then," he said low.

Lifting her gaze, she purposefully laughed at him. "I *enjoy* tormenting you thus."

Liam shrugged out of his shirt and let it drop. "Then by all means, come here and torment me, *leannan.*"

Ellen shook her head; Liam suddenly strode forward, and with a shriek of laughter, she made a mad dash for the bed, letting him catch her this time. He fell with her onto the bed. Ellen started to struggle, but he caught her arm in his hand and held her with an iron grip; with his legs, he locked her legs. Then, with his free hand, he unbuckled his belt.

"*Oooh*, do you intend to tie me up?" she asked with breathless anticipation. Liam's eyes widened for a moment, but he responded by straddling her, jerking her arm to the bedpost and wrapping the belt around it. "I'll be your prisoner of love," she murmured, "but it's too tight."

"I tied it loosely, *mo ghraid.*" He leaned over and kissed her as his hand sought her breast.

Ellen squirmed beneath him. "It's too *tight*, Liam."

He groaned, lifted his head, and looked up at the belt. "It canna be—"

"Here, I'll show you. Slip your hand in with mine. Come on, then, put your hand with mine."

Liam smiled as if he suspected this was more play, and slipped his hand into the loop of his belt with hers. "There ye see, then? Quite loose."

"Silly, wretched man!" she said, pausing to let the tip of her tongue run across his shoulder. "You've no idea how to play properly! Shall I show you how to take your prisoner and relieve your lust? "

Liam closed his eyes with a moan, and Ellen tugged free of the belt and moved from beneath him, pushing him down as she straddled him. She lifted the bathing gown, pressed her warm, moist flesh to his groin, partially bared now that he had removed his belt and his kilt was falling away. He sighed with ecstasy; Ellen laughed and looked up at his arm hanging loosely from the bedpost. "Oh no, this will not do," she said, and reached for the drapery cord she had tossed onto the bed. She pushed his belt away and wrapped the drapery cord around his wrist and the bedpost, tying the complicated lover's knot he had taught her one lazy afternoon when they had played with his neckcloth— the same knot she had practiced over and over in the privacy of her room. His eyes fluttered open; he smiled up at her. "Now that ye have me captive, what would ye do?"

Ellen slid down, let her mouth trail from one nipple to the other, then rose again to press her sex against his hardness. "I don't have you captive yet."

"*Ach*, lass," he groaned impatiently. "I'm captive, I'm captive, then! Ye torture me!"

"That," she whispered, "is precisely what I intend to do." She came up off the bed, untied the bathing gown at her neck and let it fall away from her body. Naked, she walked to the second window, where she untied the cord from the drape, then draped it around her neck like a boa scarf, strutting back to him. He had lifted himself up, so that his back was to the headboard, and he watched her with due anticipation, practically licking his lips.

Ellen climbed on top of him again, resumed the rubbing of her sex against his, and taking his other hand in hers, she lifted it to the second bedpost. "Shall I tell you what I intend to do with you?" she whispered. "I will tie you up. Then, I will taste every inch of you—"

He bucked helplessly beneath her.

"—and nibble away at you like cake," she continued.

"If ye go to such lengths, I must insist that ye torture me completely," he jested. Ellen smiled down at Liam; his expression was that of a man thoroughly enjoying carnal pleasure—a devilish, boyish look. Tears were suddenly burning at the back of her throat; she quickly looked away and wrapped the cord around his wrist and bedpost, tied the second lover's knot. *So many knots, Ellie, because lovers are never meant to part,* he had told her.

Beneath her, Liam chuckled. "Ye donna have to fear an escape, lass. I'll no' go before ye've done what ye will to me."

Ellen ignored him, studying the bindings. He could not possibly pull free of it. She looked at the other hand. It, too, was secure.

"Come on, then, ye've tied them so tight I canna feel me hands."

Her heart was pounding now, so hard that it felt as if it might actually break free of her chest. She couldn't seem to catch her breath. She braced her hands against Liam's chest, bent over, and kissed him gently on the lips.

"*Ummm . . .*"

She lifted off his body and onto the floor, and pulled the kilt from beneath him letting it fall to the floor. Liam opened his eyes, turned his head to look at her, his expression still one of a man anticipating a rousing, lustful bout of sex. "What are ye about, *leannan?* Come here."

She couldn't speak, could not find her voice, as she hurried to where he had dropped his shirt. She thrust first one arm, then the other, into it.

"All right, then, what is this?" he asked, his voice having lost some of the warmth.

Don't talk, not yet.

"Ellie! What are ye about?" he demanded, realizing quickly that it was no longer a game.

Avoiding his gaze, she looked around the room, saw his buckskins draped across a chair. She ran to them and put them on, but they were impossibly big. Wild with fright now, she looked around, saw the belt she had tossed aside, and picked it up.

"What in God's name are ye about?" he demanded gruffly. *"Untie me, Ellie!"*

Her fingers trembling, she managed to thread the belt partially through the belt loops. She needed a coat to hide her figure. *Why hadn't she thought of a coat?*

"Goddamn it, Ellie! Untie me!" he demanded more loudly, bucking forcibly against the bed, straining against the ropes around his wrists. "I'll skin ye alive, I swear to God I shall if ye donna untie me at once!"

His kilt. There it was on the floor. Just below the bed where he lay captive, seething with fury. Ellen risked a glimpse of him; his face had turned to cold stone, his eyes full of murderous rage. He knew what she was doing, and a dagger of terror impaled her. *She couldn't do this. She couldn't do this!*

"I donna know what ye think ye will do, but if ye think I will remain bound like a fucking hog, ye are wrong."

"I have to," she said, surprised by the strength in her voice, and moved slowly toward the kilt, watching him carefully. He looked like a beast now, one intent on his prey. His chest was rising and falling with each furious breath as he glared at her. Slowly, she went down on her haunches and reached in front of her, grabbing a corner of the kilt. Liam tried to lunge off the bed then, and with a screech, Ellen went falling backward onto her bum, dragging the plaid with her.

Knowing full well that he was captive, Liam fell back against the bed, his teeth bared now. "Ye foolish *chit!*" he spat at her. "Do ye think ye can climb a trellis? Open a window? Pick a lock? Do ye think ye willna be caught? And what do ye think Farnsworth will do to ye when they find ye stealing into a man's house! Listen to me, Ellie! Come on, then, we'll do this together—"

No! She had anticipated this. "I have to do this, Liam. I have no other option. And I am so very sorry for it, you'll never know how *truly* sorry I am," she cried, and before she dissolved into a torrent of tears, she ran to the door and slipped out into the corridor, grabbing her shoes just as she closed the door, wincing as he bellowed her name. She prayed that Follifoot had drunk the whiskey she'd stolen from her father's study and given him, and would not hear Liam's cries in his rooms at the far end of the house.

Twenty-one

~❧~

Astonishingly, it was not as hard as she had feared.

Not that it was precisely easy, either, but Ellen had been so fearful as she ran along the streets to Mayfair, dipping into alleys and behind trees to avoid being seen—fearful that she wouldn't be able to do it, that she wouldn't have the strength or the courage necessary to do it.

But she *did*.

She found the Lockhart mansion easily enough and was pleased that there were no lights, except for two on the lower floors, well in the back. The trellis was exactly as Liam had said it was, like a ladder provided expressly for this purpose. She knew a moment of panic standing there, realizing she had not thought of how she might bring the beastie down, but thought that as she had come this far, she would simply have to figure that out when the time came. First things first— she had to climb that trellis.

Fortunately, her foot was small enough to fit in the latticework, and she was relieved to discover that all the time spent climbing her grandfather's trees as a girl stood her in good stead. But her strength was not what it had once been. The muscles in her arms began to burn halfway up; she didn't think she could pull herself up even another inch. Toward the top, her arms were shaking; but she managed to grip the window ledge and pull herself up so that her bum was resting on the ledge. And just as Liam had hypothesized, the window was not locked. In fact, someone had left it ajar. Miraculously, Ellen was inside the Lockhart mansion in less than ten minutes.

She stood in the drawing room, panting heavily; fearful that someone would hear her trying to catch her breath, and strained to hear any noise that would indicate she had been discovered. There was nothing but silence, golden silence. Not even the sound of a ticking clock. She glanced around, let her eyesight adjust to the darkness, seeing, finally, the door that led to the adjoining room. Just to be safe, she removed her shoes and left them beneath the window, then wrapped Liam's plaid tightly around her shoulders as she walked to the door. She pressed her ear against it, listened intently for several moments, but hearing nothing, tried the knob. It turned easily; the door creaked only a little as she pushed it open.

The adjoining room was darker and colder than the first.

Cautiously, Ellen stepped across the threshold; the darkness, she quickly realized, was due to the drapes having been drawn shut. Without even a hint of moonlight, she could see nothing and was forced to grope along the wainscot, inching her toes forward, feeling for anything that might impede her progress, until she at last reached a window. When she pulled back the drape, weak moonlight filtered in, hardly enough to see, blast it, but at least enough to make out the various shapes of furnishings. Worse, there was no drapery cord that she could find feeling about the wall. But there was a chair nearby, and Ellen pushed that up against the wall, wound the drapes around it and hoped they wouldn't slide free.

Satisfied that it would have to do, she looked around

and saw the murky shape of the gentleman's armoire Liam had told her about. *Almost there, almost done. Almost free.*

She scurried across the carpet, dodging an ottoman a mere moment before she would have crashed into it. Her breath was coming in short gulps now, her heart beating wildly in her chest as she tried the latch. *Locked!* God, oh, God, she had forgotten his dagger! Ellen felt her heart plummet—she couldn't do this, of *course* she couldn't do this! She'd been a fool to ever think she might! How could she come all this way only to be locked out? *There are no second chances, Ellen! None! If you do not succeed, you will never have another opportunity!*

She whirled about, trying to make out other shapes, looking for anything that might help her. Seeing a table nearby, she darted forward, ran her hands lightly over it, trying to find something, *anything,* to pick the lock.

Nothing.

Tears began to well in her throat, the bitter taste of her defeat choking her. Gulping, she fought back the river that threatened to flow, knowing that even the slightest sound might bring the house down on her. She tried to remain calm, to *think,* and turned and looked at the armoire again, hating it, hating the Lockharts for locking up their foolish treasures—

Wait a moment. Farnsworth had a similar piece of furniture, on top of which he kept the key. Ellen moved quickly to the armoire and stood on tiptoe, just barely able to reach the top. With the tips of her fingers, she skirted the edge, felt something . . . *it was the key!* Ecstatic, Ellen attempted to retrieve it, but knocked it from the top of the armoire. Instantly, she was on her knees, running her hands over the carpet, desperately searching the dark, and in a final moment of sheer desperation, she found it. Quickly, for she was panicking now, she scrambled to her feet, fumbled with the lock, and managed to open it.

The door sprang open; even in the weak moonlight, she could see the gold glow of the horrid little beastie.

Honestly, Liam had not done well in describing it, for *that* was the most hideously grotesque little thing she had ever seen. No wonder the Lockharts kept it locked away; they didn't want to frighten old women and small children with it. Perhaps even more curious, she thought wildly as she lifted the heavy ornament from the cabinet, was that someone, at some time, had commissioned its creation to begin with.

It was heavy—quite heavy, actually—and she put it aside for a moment, locked the armoire, then threw the key beneath the cabinet to delay the discovery of the beastie's disappearance. She gathered the beastie up, hurried back to the adjoining room by feeling her way along the wall, knocking the drape free of the chair. In the adjoining room she hastily donned her shoes, all the while fretting exactly how she would carry the heavy ornament down the trellis. She wasn't strong enough to descend holding it. She leaned out the window and looked down. There was a bit of grass below, just a patch, really. Quickly, afraid to think too much, she wrapped the beastie in the plaid, then leaned out the window, carefully held it away from the house, and let it drop. The thing landed with a resounding *thud* she was quite certain had been heard across all of London. She instantly retreated from the window and with her back to the wall, strained to hear any sound of someone coming, either down the corridor or out the front door.

Minutes passed. When she was convinced there was no sound, that she had not been detected, she crept away from the wall and looked out the window again. The plaid bundle lay where it had landed, on the grassy patch just below. Ellen swung one leg out, got hold of the trellis, then the other, and slipped through the open window. Since she was not strong enough to pull herself up to the window latch and hold on to the ledge, she was forced to leave the window open as she began her descent.

She let herself drop the last several feet; it felt as if a thousand needles had been jabbed into her feet and legs when she landed. But safely on the ground again, with her heart pounding in her ears, Ellen picked the thing up, tried to repair the rather large divot it had made, but at last gave up on it in favor of fleeing for her life. She unwrapped part of the plaid to put around her shoulders, and holding the beastie in the last patch of the cloth, started home, dread burgeoning with each step she took.

At four in the morning, after she had packed the beastie (wrapped securely in the plaid, of course) in one of two bags she would carry and had changed into traveling clothes, Ellen at last descended the stairs and crept to Liam's room to return his clothes.

Her breath escaped her altogether as she came to the door, and her heart, pounding in her ears again, seemed as loud as church bells. She imagined the worst of scenarios—that he had escaped or was loose and waiting for her. Certainly she harbored no illusions that he would show her mercy if he had managed to free himself. But she had no time to ponder it; the coach would leave at five, and she still had to rouse Natalie.

She pushed the door open a crack and peeked inside.

Liam was where she had left him, his arms trussed to the bed, naked save for a sheet that covered one leg. There was a decided chill in the room, and she worried for a moment that he might be cold. But one look at Liam's face and she forgot any concern she had.

Although he was, mercifully, rather calm, he wore an expression much like she imagined a powerful, angry beast might wear, one who was patiently awaiting the moment he would kill his prey and devour it. He smirked at her as she slipped inside the open door, clinging to his clothes to keep from trembling.

"Ye did it, then, eh?"

Her voice failed her; she could only nod. The deep sound of his derisive chuckle unnerved her, and she quickly moved to the table where she laid his folded clothes.

Liam glanced at the clothing with an expression that almost seemed amused. "The kilt—where is it?"

Too close, too close! Ellen stumbled backward, turned, and walked to the brazier to stir the coals. "I, ah . . . I need it," she said hoarsely.

"First the beastie, and now me *féileadh beag. Tsk-tsk*, Ellie," he said. "And look at ye now, all sweetness and light, stirring me coals."

His voice was so cold and hard that Ellen shivered. What was she doing? There was nothing left to say. She stood and walked to the door.

"Wait—are ye no' forgetting something? Surely ye donna intend to leave me bound forever?"

She faltered at the door, feeling suddenly and intensely uncertain, not wanting to leave him bound, but feeling sure that she must.

"Canna look at me, is that it?" he drawled behind her. "Yer betrayal has made a coward of ye, Ellie."

She looked heavenward, swallowed hard before turning to have one last look at the man she loved with all her heart. "I . . . I *had* to do it, Liam," she said with regret.

"Oh, did ye, indeed?" he asked snidely. "Bloody stupid—I would have helped ye, Ellie, if ye had only asked!"

Exhausted, nervous, and feeling incredibly sad about this turn of events, Ellen was dangerously close to shattering. "And how would you have helped me, Liam?" she cried, the tears falling now. "Even the very shirt off your back would not be enough!" *Dear Lord, how pathetically desperate she sounded!* Shaking, she swiped at the tears on her face. "You couldn't have helped me," she said sadly. "You've been quite clear about your situation. God in heaven, I would have given anything had it not come to this, Liam, I swear it, but I have Natalie to think of! You see what is happening to her, how she is slipping into fantasy! You know what will become of her if we are forced to stay here! I . . . I had *no other choice.*"

"That's where ye're wrong, Ellie. Ye had another choice and ye still do. I'll help ye, even though ye've betrayed me. Just untie me—"

"No!" she cried, tears blinding her. "Follifoot will come in the morning," she added in a voice barely above a whisper.

"Have pity, will ye? I'm as bare-arsed as a bairn!"

She shook her head, took a kerchief from her sleeve and swiped at her tears. "I'm so very sorry! But I have to go, Liam."

"I loved ye, Ellie. I loved ye as I've never loved another. How could ye do this to me, then?" he asked, his voice having lost some of its bitter edge.

"Please!" she pleaded with him. "Please try and understand! I love you, Liam, I swear to God that I do—you *know* that I do! You shall never know the depth of my sorrow. But I must think of Natalie, and we both know you would never give me the beastie, for you need it as badly as I do. I'm *sorry,* Liam! I'm so sorry!" she cried. "But I must go now!"

"Ellie! Donna go! Untie me!"

"I *can't!*"

"I'll find ye—ye know that I will! Run as far as ye like, but I'll spend me life searching for ye, and I willna stop until I have what rightfully belongs to me and mine. Do ye hear me, lass?"

She couldn't look at him.

"I'll follow ye to the ends of the earth. I'll hunt ye like a bloody dog," he spat bitterly, and she could feel the raw loathing emanating from him.

"Good-bye, Liam," she whispered, and slipped out the door, pulling it to.

Outside, she braced herself—only this time Liam didn't shout at her to come back and untie him, did not so much as call her name. And Ellen had the horribly cold feeling that his silence was far more deadly than anything he might have said.

Follifoot's morning knock on the door earned him a gruff *"Aye!"* He pushed through the door as he always did, and walked to the table. But when he saw the pile of clothing there, he looked to the bed. In his shock he dropped the tray, sending brown liquid streaming everywhere.

"Ach, for heaven's sake, Follifoot! Look what ye've done to me boots, then! God blind me, stop behaving so gobsmacked and untie me, will ye?" Liam demanded.

Follifoot blinked; the captain attempted to lunge at him. *"Untie me. NOW!"* he roared, and Follifoot rushed to his side, fumbling with the tight cords as the captain continued to grumble under his breath. When he managed to untie the cords that bound him, Follifoot stumbled backward as the naked giant came to his feet. He paused, rubbed his wrists for a moment, then stretched his back before walking calmly to the armoire, vigorously rubbing his bum. "Feels tighter than a noose," he said calmly to the open cabinet as he withdrew a pair of trousers.

He turned, shoved one foot into them, then the other. "Have water brought up, will ye, Follifoot? I'd like a bath 'ere I stow all this away and take me leave."

"L-leaving sir?" Follifoot stuttered.

"Aye, that I am." The captain caught sight of something and he paused, walked to it, and peered down. It was a kerchief as far as Follifot could see, with what looked like a small *ℰ* neatly embroidered on it. The captain leaned over, picked it up, and held it tightly in his hand. "Aye, I'll take me leave today, Follifoot, so get on with it, man. I've a wee birdie to find so that I might wring its bloody neck!" he said, and sounded, at least to Follifoot, rather cheerful about it.

Twenty-two

~~

*H*er confidence, buoyed by the nabbing of the beastie, was effectively dashed before they had even crossed Belgrave Square. At four o'clock in the morning, with a cross nine-year-old complaining of the weight of the bag she carried and two very heavy portmanteaux cutting into Ellen's hands, she was in no mood to discover the public coaches were not running at the time or price advertised. The journey to King's Lynn, where Judith, her husband, and two children lived, cost three pounds more than Ellen had anticipated. For a woman with precious few resources at her disposal, the difference seemed like a king's ransom.

Furthermore, the coach that would carry them to King's Lynn was due to leave at five o'clock, but did not pull out of the public station until almost ten past six. By that time, Ellen was in danger of being violently ill, as she was less and less able to endure the fear of being discovered.

Natalie was not in a humor to visit an old friend, as Ellen explained they were doing, particularly if it required such an early rising. She complained that her bum hurt from sitting on the hard wooden bench, that the air smelled terribly, that the man sitting across from them was taking up more than his fair share of foot space, that she was hungry—had Ellen thought to bring anything to eat? It wasn't until Ellen snapped at her to silence herself immediately that the girl slid down on the bench and began to sulk. *Let her,* Ellen thought irritably. It wasn't as if she found this journey particularly comfortable or carefree, for God's sake. She was scared out of her wits, quite uncertain what would become of them, and hoping that they didn't end up murdered or in a poorhouse. She was doing this for Natalie's sake, even if Natalie didn't know it, and the least the child could do was not fuss so very much!

By the time they arrived at King's Lynn late that afternoon, mother and daughter were hardly speaking to one another. But when they emerged from the coach and drew clean air into their lungs again, Ellen forced herself to smile and buck up for Natalie's sake. She straightened her daughter's clothing, tried her best to wash the smudge of Agatha's cake from her cheek. *Dear Agatha, she'll fret so!* Yet Ellen wouldn't allow herself to think of Agatha now, or any of the myriad consequences of what she had done or more important, Liam . . . although she could hardly keep from it, alternating between guilt and fear and an emptiness inside her that seemed to grow deeper with each passing mile. No, she couldn't think of that now.

At King's Lynn, having ascertained the direction to Peasedown Park, Ellen picked up one portmanteau, then the second, nodded at Natalie to do the same, and smiled brightly. "Lovely day for a walk, isn't it?" she remarked, and began marching in the direction the clerk had indicated.

The afternoon was coming to a rather chilly end by the time Ellen and Natalie, both exhausted and covered with the dust of the road (and Ellen's hems soaked through, the result of their taking a more direct route through a meadow), came to a halt on the edge of the long, circular drive. They stood there in silence, awed by the massive eighteenth-century Georgian mansion. Of course Judith had described her home in her letters, and certainly Ellen had gathered it was quite large, but she had not imagined *this.*

"It looks like a castle," Natalie opined. "I rather think a princess lived here once."

"Hmm, perhaps."

"Do you suppose Captain Lockhart will come and find us here?"

A pang of regret in her chest, Ellen shook her head. "No, he won't come here, darling."

"Are we going to stay?"

"For a time."

"I'm very hungry, Mother."

"Well then! I should think it time to announce our arrival to Judith!" she said with forced gaiety, and put her hand out to Natalie, free since they had abandoned their luggage at an old thatched hut they'd passed, and together, they walked the last few yards to what Ellen hoped would be their salvation.

There were thirteen steps leading up to the massive oak door that marked the entry to Peasedown Park (this, courtesy of Natalie, who counted the steps aloud). They took a moment to ensure their clothing was as presentable as possible, given the circumstances, and just as Ellen reached for the knocker, the door was swung open. A man wearing the usual costume of a butler stepped out onto the landing with them and bowed deeply. "Madam? How may I be of service?"

"*Ahem.* My good sir, please tell Lady Peasedown that her old friend, Miss Ellen Farnsworth, and her daughter, Miss Natalie, have come to call. I dispatched a letter informing her of our visit a fortnight ago, but as it happens, I have come much sooner than I anticipated."

"Do you mean to say, madam, that Lady Peasedown is not, then, expecting you?"

The flutter of panic started in her belly; horrible images flashed through her mind, not the least of which was she and Natalie sleeping in that wretched cottage up the road. "Oh, no, not at all! She is expecting us, certainly . . . just not *today*," she attempted to clarify.

"Very good," he said again, bowing low. "Would you please step inside?"

Although Natalie was looking at her with an expression of trepidation that matched the feeling Ellen had in her gut, Ellen ushered her inside, behind the butler, afraid to be left on the stoop.

"If you will be so good as to wait here, I shall return forthwith," he said, and with a click of his heels went striding off down the long corridor that stretched before them, leaving Ellen and Natalie to gape at the most magnificent house Ellen had ever seen. She held her breath in awe; the floors were marble, the candelabras gilded and sporting dozens of beeswax candles. The walls, covered with a silk of blue and gold, matched the intricate hand painting on the wainscot. The doors that lined the corridor were framed in Greek arches; above each were scenes sculpted from mythology, as best she could guess. In between the many doors was a variety of consoles sporting hothouse flowers in large vases, a collection of life-size portraits, and a smattering of armor.

"Mother, it *is* a castle!" Natalie whispered excitedly, squeezing Ellen's hand. "It's just exactly like Laria!"

"*Ellen!*"

The sound of Judith's voice was like music to Ellen's ears; the lilt in her old friend's voice was just as cheerful as it had been so many years ago when they had been inseparable. It was a sound, in fact, that very nearly drove Ellen to her knees, so overcome with relief was she. But she managed to keep from sprawling on the floor, instead whirling about toward the sound of

Judith's voice. There she was, with the butler close on her heels, rushing toward her, looking so young and lovely and *happy*.

"Oh my stars, you've finally come!" she cried as she rushed forward and wrapped Ellen in a strong embrace. "I've *so* longed to see you! And when I missed you the last two times I was in London, I was frightfully worried I'd never see you again!"

Ellen had, of course, been in London when Judith had come, but had been too embarrassed for her friend to see the truth about her life.

"Oh, Ellen, you're still so beautiful, aren't you!"

Ellen laughed. "Darling Judith, how kind you are! *You* are the beauty among us, and you've always been so."

Judith gave her a playful wave of her hand and looked down at Natalie. "Oh *my*, this *can't* be little Natalie!" she exclaimed.

"Yes, mu'um, I am," Natalie said in all seriousness. "We've come early."

Judith laughed gaily as she leaned down to hug Natalie and kiss her cheek. "Look at you, darling, just as lovely as your mother."

"Oh, Judith, really!" Ellen exclaimed. "I look a fright, and really, for that I must apologize—"

"Nonsense! Where are your things? You'll want to change out of your traveling clothes, and— Goodness, Filbert! Is there water on the lawn?" she exclaimed, eyeing Ellen's hem.

"Quite my own doing," Ellen instantly assured her. "Natalie and I walked."

Judith looked up, obviously confused. *"Walked?"*

"Yes," Ellen admitted reluctantly, knowing how odd it must seem. "From King's Lynn. We . . . we, ah, couldn't carry our luggage so far," she said nervously, forcing a little laugh. "So we, um, left our bags in the abandoned cottage up the road."

"Oh, *no!*" Judith cried. "That won't do at *all!* Filbert!" she cried, whirling about to the butler. "See to it that their things are fetched at once! And have baths drawn for both of them! And, oh dear, find Clara, will you, and send her up to me. Ellen, you look a bit smaller than me, but I think we should find something to suit you. As for *you,*" she said, tweaking Natalie's nose, "I've a daughter just your age. Her name is Sarah, and she'll have something you can wear until your things are brought. Come on, then, you two! We've much to do before supper!" Judith said brightly, and linking arms with Ellen and Natalie on either side, escorted them down that elaborate corridor toward the grand staircase spiraling up to the rooms above.

Exhausted and on edge, Ellen spent the rest of the day waiting for the other shoe to drop. When she wasn't feeling the horrible, relentless guilt for having betrayed Liam, or the more painful sting of missing him, she was fretting about her next move and waiting for someone, anyone, to discover what she had done.

And now, dressed in an expensive gown of lavender silk, with little orchids attached to the empire waist and along the hem, she waited. She hadn't worn anything that fine since the summer of her demise—it was so lovely that she vaguely expected someone to rush into the dining room at any moment to demand that she relinquish it at once. But no one came; instead, she and Natalie feasted on beef so tender that it melted in their mouths. Still she waited for disaster, and later, in the family drawing room where they sipped little thimbles of wine, she waited. She remained on edge, certain Natalie would do something in her play to upset the Peasedown children, but bless her darling daughter, she did no such thing, and skipped out the door in her borrowed green frock when the governess came to take the children to bed. Yet Ellen continued to wait—this was too good to be true, almost inconceivable for a woman who, with no prior experience in criminal behavior, had tied a man up and stolen his treasure with relative ease.

Yet here she was, sitting in a room large enough to be a ballroom, on a settee that Judith had proudly told her had once been at Versailles, beneath a ceiling adorned with frieze cherubs and doves, carpets so thick one actually had the sensation of walking on grass, and real fires crackling in twin hearths. Judith and her husband, Richard, asked nothing about her unusual journey. They just seemed genuinely concerned that she was comfortable.

She was not comfortable, however, and in fact, was afraid to sleep, so sure that Liam would snatch her in her dream. Then again, she was afraid *not* to sleep, for that was, unfortunately, the only way she could see him again. But sleep eluded her; her heart and mind were filled with anxiety. Had the beastie been discovered missing? Did her father know she was gone? Did Eva? Had Eva told their father about Vauxhall Gardens? And what of Liam? Where was Liam?

The next day, Ellen was feeling terribly out of sorts from the lack of sleep and building anxiety, and it was in the midst of her trying to think clearly that Judith finally broached the subject of her unexpected call to Peasedown Park. They were strolling the grounds together when Judith twined her hand with Ellen's and asked, "You'll stay at least a fortnight, won't you?"

Yes! Yes, a fortnight, a month, a lifetime! "Oh Judith, I should not want to impose—"

"Silly thing! It's no imposition! I am so delighted to finally have you all to myself. Your devotion to your father is admirable, darling, but how long have we been writing and promising one another we'd one day be together again?"

Ellen laughed. "Years, I should think."

"Yes, *years*. Ten of them, to be precise."

Yes, ten years. Natalie was almost ten now.

They walked on for a few minutes more before Judith exclaimed with much exasperation, "Oh, for heaven's sake, Ellen! I *know*."

Panic assailed her—how could Judith *know*? *No one* knew save Liam! How could she have been found out so quickly?

"We've been the best of friends since we were little girls. Did you think I'd not suspect? Or that I'd not hear the gossip?"

"Wh-what?"

Judith rolled her eyes. "Ellen, darling, I *know*. But it doesn't change my opinion of you, not in the least. However it happened, I am certain you were not at fault, and certainly no one can blame poor Natalie—"

"*Natalie!*" Ellen exclaimed, horrified.

"Yes, Natalie!" Judith said, drawing them both to a halt. "I know her situation plainly. Richard knows, too, but he's not the least concerned. Of course we would *never* tell Sarah and Charles such a wretched thing, you understand."

Ah-ha! Now it dawned on her—Judith was speaking of Natalie's illegitimate birth, not her theft of the beastie. *Not her betrayal of Liam.* "*Oooh*," she said on a long sigh.

With a kind pat to her hand, Judith resumed their walking. "As I said, it makes not the least bit of difference to me. I've known for quite some time, actually."

"Have you?" Ellen asked weakly, so relieved that Judith didn't know what she had just recently done to be appallingly unconcerned that her dear friend knew the truth about Natalie.

"Well of course! I mean, there you were, the darling of all the balls, and suddenly you're whisked away to

Cornwall! And that awful Millicent Hayfield—you remember her?"

"Of course. She debuted the same Season I came out."

"Well, a few years ago, I was in London, and I happened upon her at a tea. She was agog with her *news*, as she called it. Horrid woman, terribly disagreeable, wasn't she? She delighted in telling me what everyone else suspected about you—that there was no husband in Cornwall, nor any tragic and untimely death of the mysterious man. That you had born a child—well, no point in repeating such vile rumors. I certainly would have liked to have pushed her to the ground and done something awful to her gown, but I pretended not to mind at all! And do you know that was precisely the thing to do, for Miss Hayfield was *quite* perturbed that I had not the least reaction!"

"Oh. That's . . . thank you, Judith," Ellen said weakly, uncertain what to say.

"But I would be less than completely honest if I said I weren't a bit cross with you all these years," she added with a sniff.

"I'm sorry, Judith, but surely you can understand my reluctance to admit the truth. I would simply perish if you thought ill of Natalie."

"I would *never* think ill of Natalie, darling. After all, it was hardly *her* doing that brought her into this world. No, dear, I was miffed at *you*. I would never speak of something so indelicate, but I was quite miffed that you were . . . well . . . less than circumspect. Do you understand?"

Oh, yes, quite clearly, so clearly, in fact, that Ellen was at a loss as to what to say. How was it that so many people were angered by her actions, that so many had come to believe they had a right to be angry? Did they not understand that she had been punished dearly and for the rest of her life?

Judith smiled, squeezed her hand affectionately. "But never mind, Ellen," she said in a congenial whisper. "What's done is done, of course, and there's not a thing we can do to change it. I've quite put it behind me!" she said cheerfully, as if it was somehow very magnanimous of her to put Ellen's past behind her. As if *she* had somehow been injured. "You *will* stay at least a fortnight, will you? Stay as long as you can! Your father won't mind to be parted from you, will he? He shall manage on his own?"

Somehow Ellen managed to somberly assure Judith that he would indeed do quite well without her, and in fact, had encouraged her to be away for as long as she needed. Which reminded her of the question most burning in her head and making it ache—just how long *did* she need? Or more precisely, where in God's name was she going to go from here?

The Peasedown governess, Penny Peckinpaugh, did not particularly like children, and furthermore, did not particularly like the Peasedown children. But being governess was her lot in life, and Penny dreamed of being a grand lady herself one day, so she endured the little monsters in her charge. However, the addition of the third child, Miss Natalie, had her contemplating a request to review her wages. The girl was a liar, constantly telling stories and becoming quite cross when the other children didn't believe her silly tales of kingdoms and princesses.

On this particular day, the cold north wind had ceased to blow, and Penny had ushered all the little beasts down to a small lake that was popular among the locals for picnicking. She had ordered a basket for the children (and a flagon of wine for herself) and had told them to go off and play. As they scampered off, she admired a man strolling along the edge of the lake. He was a big man, well over six feet, with dark wavy hair that hung to his shoulders. Within the confines of his greatcoat, which looked to be of the military of some sort, he cut quite a powerful figure. Even more important, from where Penny was sitting, he looked to be rather handsome in an unconventional way.

She came up on her knees, was adjusting her bonnet when Miss Natalie came skipping toward her. This was not the time for the child's ridiculous stories, and she instantly told her to run on and leave her be.

"Oh, I wasn't coming to speak to you," Natalie informed her gravely. "I was off to say hello to my friend, Captain Lockhart."

"Who?" Penny asked, gaining her feet, her eyes on the stranger.

"Captain Lockhart. He's come to rescue my mother."

Dear Lord, not *that* again. "What nonsense!" she said sharply, with a harsh look for the girl. "Shall I convey to your mother what ridiculous lies you are telling?"

The girl looked crushed. "But it's not a story!" she insisted, and with her lower lip trembling, she suddenly ran off, toward the man.

And much to Penny's surprise, the man leaned down, picked her up as she came rushing into his arms, and held her high as he twirled her around before setting her down again. Her mouth agape, Penny watched as he went down on his haunches, spoke to the little wench for what seemed like several long minutes, then suddenly stood, leaned down to kiss the girl's cheek, and went on his way.

Miss Natalie came running back to a stunned Penny.

"What is *this?*" she cried at the girl, horrified. "Are you in the habit of accosting strangers?"

"But he's *not* a stranger! He is my friend, Captain Lockhart!" she insisted again.

"If he's such a dear friend of yours, why hasn't he

presented himself to your mother?" Penny demanded, folding her arms across her middle and glaring down at the girl.

"Oh, he will," she assured her, nodding eagerly. "But he said it will be a surprise." And with that, the girl was off again, leaving a bewildered Penny Peckinpaugh to wonder if there was even one ounce of truth to her story.

Twenty-three

❧

$\mathcal{F}$inding Ellie was remarkably easy; one would think she'd have taken more care to cover her tracks.

Follifoot, for all his timidity, was really rather resourceful when given a ten-pound note. Though that had depleted Liam's funds to a contemptibly paltry thirty pounds, it seemed just the thing to spur Follifoot into eagerly confessing that as he had been collecting the post for several years, he had, quite by chance, naturally, noticed that Miss Farnsworth often received letters from a Lady Peasedown of Peasedown Park, near King's Lynn.

"King's Lynn?" Liam asked. "And where might that be?"

"North, sir. One might say in the midst of Cambridge, Norwich, and Peterborough."

Liam blinked.

"Rather near the sea," Follifoot added helpfully.

The *sea*. Of course! The lass had planned a rather grand escape with her treasure, hadn't she? Nonetheless, Liam peppered Follifoot with enough questions to assure himself that there were no other friends or relatives (just as Ellie had told him) until he was convinced there was really no other place she might have gone, save her sister Eva's. But that possibility he immediately discounted—it would be far too easy for him to track her there, and besides, from what he had observed that afternoon at

Vauxhall, her sister was none too fond of his Ellie—perhaps because his darling angel had trussed up her young sister way back when and had stolen a frock or a piece of jewelry. He certainly wouldn't put it past her.

He packed up his things, stuffed the kerchief with the delicate *&* in his pocket, and cursed her beneath his breath for having taken his plaid, too, the loss of which, to his way of thinking, was a grave insult on top of an obvious injury.

Liam arrived at King's Lynn a day after Ellie. This he knew courtesy of the clerk at the transferring station, who laughed when Liam asked him for directions to Peasedown, mentioning the sudden parade of visitors. As a point of fact, however, after asking several pointed questions as he loomed menacingly over the man, Liam learned that the parade actually consisted of only *two* other visitors—a woman and a young girl, who had walked to Peasedown just a day previous to his arrival.

Lovely. Liam could almost smell the scent of lavender bathwater in the air. He flashed a cold smile, thanked the clerk for his help, then asked where he might find an affordable inn, one that could be had for a few shillings. He was not intent on seeing Ellie straightaway, oh, no. He'd give the lass time to settle in and be comfortable in her new surroundings. Then he would surprise her as she had surprised him.

At the down-at-the-heels inn the clerk directed him to, Liam put his things aside, took out his last sheet of vellum, and dashed off a letter:

Dearest Mother, I pray this finds you well. As for me— quite cross, for London had me all in knots.
I am now unbound and destined for home. I've just one spot of trouble to address, but I shall string it all up straightaway, on my word. Might I impose on you to

ask the Douglas to be so kind and give over a lamb?
English food is rotten gruel and I am craving stew. L.

After sleeping astonishingly well that night, Liam was up at dawn, walking the long road east.

He was, like most travelers, taken aback by the considerable size of Peasedown Park. It was grand, to be sure, and he could imagine Ellie there, could even imagine her mistress of such a grand place. Upon further reflection, he decided the enormous size of the house and grounds were to his advantage, as he could quietly observe the little thief from a variety of vantage points in the wooded area that surrounded the main house.

And he did exactly that over the next few days, noting with some irritation that Ellie seemed quite at home and *completely* unrepentant. Fortunately, the weather was cool but bearable, and the thief was often out-of-doors, looking as if she were on some bloody holiday, strolling about the grounds with her friend, or reading a book beneath the arbor, or even more outrageously, participating in a game of lawn bowling, over which she grew quite enthusiastic, jumping and whirling about with each bowl.

Unrepentant was she? Before he was through with her, she'd be begging for mercy.

Safely hidden in the woods, Liam watched Ellie and the Peasedowns, and he became increasingly annoyed. He wondered just how long she intended to stay so comfortably quartered here? Had she disposed of the beastie yet? Did she suspect he had followed her or thought herself so very clever as to have eluded him completely? Did she think of him at *all*? Had she ever loved him as she had said, or had it been a ruse from the moment he had opened his fat gob and told her about the beastie? Was it possible that he, a trained soldier, a decorated officer of the British Army, could be so bloody gormless when it came to matters of the heart?

Gormless hardly began to describe his shortcoming—he was a goddamn fool, he was, for having, in the course of these few days, allowed his fury to subside a bit. A *wee* bit. Liam realized, much to his horror, that in thinking about Ellie and what she had done to him, he had, rather grudgingly, admitted that it had been a rather clever ploy. Bravo and all that, for he could not have thought of a better contrivance had his sorry life depended on it. Not that he was forgiving her betrayal by any means—never! *God*, no! He still bristled mightily at the recollection, still wanted to get his hands on her and teach her a lesson for playing with fire. But there was, regrettably, a part of him that understood her desperation, understood how she might have felt trapped by her predicament. Given what he knew about Natalie (the lass *was* awfully peculiar), he could, in a way, understand why Ellie had done what she did.

And perhaps, just perhaps, if he were a contemplative man—which he was *not*—but if he were, he might have realized that what bothered him most about the ordeal was that *he* had not given Ellie any cause for hope, and she had therefore felt forced into doing what she did. But everything had happened so *fast!* He might have worked his way through the maze of unfamiliar emotions and startlingly new feelings and cold hard facts, eventually he would have, and he *would* have found a way to care for her, even from afar.

Aye, but it was pure fancy now, wasn't it? She'd ruined any chance of it, and he'd done enough damned pining. At present he was far more interested in getting his hands on the beastie, for if there was one thing he *could* not do, and *would* not do, it was to go home empty-handed, without that damned statue.

If only he didn't miss her so terribly. If only he could go for a single moment of the day without thinking of her. If only he could stop recalling the feel of her lips against his, or her bloody brilliant smile. If only he could ignore the throbbing ache in his chest every time he thought of her, or the thing that lay like a lump of coal in the pit of his belly every time he saw her. *Damn her.*

It was so painful that he tried not to watch Ellie at all, tried to focus on Natalie, but he discovered that his feelings for the child, while wholly different, were just as strong as they were for her wretched, thieving mother. Nattie seemed happy enough—what child wouldn't on such a grand estate? Yet Liam couldn't help noticing that when she and the other children played outside, she played alone while the two Peasedown children were amused by their governess.

When he at last found the opportunity to approach Natalie one crisp morning, she was not in the least surprised to see him, but, rather oddly, seemed to expect him. "Have you come to rescue us?" she asked immediately, breathlessly.

Laria again. "Ah, Nattie, lass . . . we must be careful, eh? Wouldn't want the king's soldiers to find us and all that," he blathered.

She looked very disappointed, and he quickly pressed on, eliciting her help. "As it happens, yer mother took something belonging to me—"

"Your skirt?" she asked brightly.

Liam sighed wearily. " 'Tis no' a skirt, 'tis a—never mind. Aye, she took the kilt and a . . . a trinket of sorts. Do ye think ye could find it, lass? Do ye think we might make a game of it?"

"Yes!" she said eagerly, "I'll ask her!"

"No, no, ye mustn't do that," he said instantly, and put a finger to his lips, shaking his head.

"But why?"

"Why? Because . . . because it would ruin the surprise, it would!"

Natalie brightened. *"Oooh,* I adore surprises!"

Aye, but not *this* sort of surprise. Nonetheless, Liam succeeded in convincing Natalie to keep his presence a secret until he could surprise her lovely, perfidious mother. He did not, of course, tell her that he intended to catch the thief off-guard and bounce her right on to her pretty little arse. Or that when the circumstances were right, he'd bind her mother up much as she had done him, find the beastie *and* his kilt, then leave her every bit as aroused as *she* had left *him,* the evil, wicked temptress.

"But *when* shall we surprise her?" Natalie asked each day that he saw her, growing increasingly impatient.

"Soon, lass. Very soon," was all he could say, for he wasn't entirely certain how he would gain entry into the house. "Did ye find the trinket, then?"

"No," she would say petulantly, tiring of their little game.

"Where did ye look, then? The drawing room?"

"They have thousands of drawing rooms!" she would protest, her arms flailing wide to demonstrate just how many rooms there were in that mammoth house.

"Then ye must try yer mother's sitting room, and her bedroom. Have ye looked under her bed?"

"All right," Natalie would say wearily, and with Liam's urging she'd turn and march back to the mansion to have another look.

And then, one glorious day, Natalie said yes, she had found the plaid, wrapped around something and hidden behind a hatbox in her mother's dressing room. He cuffed her chin, smiled proudly at his accomplice. "See there? I *knew* ye could do it, lass!"

"*Now* will you rescue us?" she demanded.

He paused, caught himself, struggled with an answer. At last he smiled. "I'll see what I can do," he said, and thank the saints, that seemed to satisfy Nattie for the time being.

Lord Peasedown was a true country gentleman, as defined by his habits as he was his title. Every morning at eleven o'clock he took his curricle to town, and while his horses munched on oats in the municipal stables, he munched on luncheon at the gentlemen's club in the old part of town. Then he would repair to the common room to sip brandy, smoke a cheroot, and casually peruse the daily news dispatch from London.

One afternoon, he was pleased to be introduced to a Scotsman by Captain Pemberton, a local celebrity for his role in the Battle of Waterloo, for which he had received much acclaim. The Scotsman, also a captain, was purportedly a celebrated war hero himself (at least he was wearing several medals), and as not many visitors came to King's Lynn, Peasedown found the man rather engaging, all in all. And he liked the lilt of his Scottish brogue.

When Captain Pemberton pardoned himself to converse with another gentleman, Peasedown remarked (lest he lose this rare audience), "There was quite a lot of praise for the Highland Regiments during the war."

"Ah, 'tis kind of ye to say. But the men from King's Lynn were the better soldiers. Learned quite a lot from them, I did."

Peasedown knew this to be quite true, as he was very well acquainted with several of their fathers, and he sat a little higher in his winged-back leather chair. "I believe I can say, without equivocation, that our boys are unusually clever as a whole, and rather vigorous athletes, owing chiefly to the excellent weather here."

"Very important attributes for a soldier to have. And the weather here is indeed right bonny."

Smiling, Peasedown put down his paper. "Just passing through, then, sir? Or do you now call King's Lynn home?"

"Aye, just passing through on me way home. I've been to call on cousins in London."

"Indeed? I am to London quite often," Peasedown said, offering a cheroot to the Scot and taking one for himself.

"Then perhaps ye are acquainted with the Lockharts of Mayfair," the captain said as Peasedown lit his cheroot.

He brightened immediately. "The Lockharts!" he exclaimed. "I had the distinct pleasure of attending college with Drake!" he offered, omitting the small detail that he had not actually *known* Drake, just attended the same college at the same time.

"Did ye, now!" the captain exclaimed, just as happily. "Unfortunately, I've no' had the pleasure of gaining introduction to Cousin Drake, as we seem to be in London's Mayfair at odd times. But I should like to think that Cousin Nigel and I are quite good chums."

Peasedown beamed, delighted to know the Scotsman had just come from Mayfair, as he rather fancied himself a man-about-town, too, even though he really very rarely got to London anymore. Nonetheless, he felt the need to impress on his new friend that he *could* if he so desired. "We're often visited by our many friends from London. Mayfair in particular."

"Indeed?"

"Why, we've a visitor just now! Not from Mayfair, but Belgravia. Miss Farnsworth, the daughter of Viscount Farnsworth. He's rather prominent among the *ton*."

"Miss Farnsworth? Surely ye jest with me, sir! I'm

well acquainted with Miss Farnsworth! Quite pretty, is she no', and so very agreeable!"

As Peasedown had not expected him to actually *know* Ellen, this bit of news tossed him for a small loop. "Well . . . ah, yes, she is quite lovely," he mumbled. "You've made her acquaintance, you said?"

"Many times. Betwixt ye and me, sir, I had made it a *point* to make her acquaintance," the captain said with a subtle wink.

"Ah!"

"Rather keeps to herself, unfortunately."

"Well. I should think her going out into society is somewhat limited. She's a mother and one can only imagine what all that entails. And she's not really a debutante—a little old for that, I suppose."

"Pity, really, for a kinder person I've no' met. And so very *thoughtful.*" The captain looked away, sighed longingly, and Peasedown was instantly struck with the notion that he was rather smitten with Ellen. A bright idea took hold—granted, he usually left the matchmaking to Judith, but he *did* rather like Ellen, and thought that but for one unfortunate summer, she might have married an earl or such. It seemed to him rather sweet if Ellen were to find happiness; after all, Judith had assured him she had paid for her atrocious lack of judgment all those years ago.

On a whim, Peasedown set his cheroot aside. "If she's a particular favorite, then you *must* come and pay a call to our Miss Farnsworth. She's with us a fortnight or more, and I am quite certain she'd be delighted to receive an old friend!"

The Scotsman grinned and leaned forward, so close that Peasedown noticed a violent little twinkle in his green eyes. *"That,* sir, would delight *me* to no end, it would."

* * *

As Liam intended to depart King's Lynn soon, Pease-down figured there was no time like the present to renew the acquaintance between him and Ellie, and it wasn't long thereafter that Liam found himself in the main salon at Peasedown Park, standing at the hearth, one arm propped on the mantel as he sipped a very fine brandy and took in the opulent surroundings while Peasedown droned on about the fishing industry in and around King's Lynn. As frightfully boring as the man was prov-ing to be, Liam relished every moment of his speech, for every moment brought him closer to confronting his lit-tle larcenist. The anticipation of it was all aglow in his gut; he felt downright cheerful for the first time in days.

And he could not have been happier when a door flew open, and Peasedown was instantly on his feet with a hearty *"Here they are!"* as a woman with auburn hair and a bright smile came sailing toward her husband. And strolling languidly behind her, the unsuspecting thief who had stolen his beastie and his heart, her head down, fidgeting with her sleeve. It perturbed him greatly to see that she was even more beautiful than he had ever seen her, dressed in a beautiful gown of sea green and gold, her hair swept up in a lovely, fashionable style, walking into the room as if she had lived there a thousand years.

But then Lady Peasedown stopped and asked, "Why, Richard! Who have you brought to us?" Donning a charming smile, Ellie looked up—and froze, that lovely smile fading instantly.

Nearly bursting with satisfaction, Liam nodded politely. Ellie gaped at him, her expression one of con-fusion, and—oh, how delightful—cold hard fear.

"Darling, look at my great fortune! I had the oppor-tunity to be introduced to a dear friend of our Ellen—Captain Lockhart! They were rather well acquainted in London."

"They *were?*" Lady Peasedown exclaimed, happily stealing a quizzical glance at Ellie.

"Perhaps Miss Farnsworth does not recall our friendship quite as favorably as I do," Liam said, pushing away from the mantel and striding forward to Lady Peasedown. "I merely hope to be counted among her many friends."

Lady Peasedown's smile returned with his deprecation; she cast a sly grin at Ellie. "Why, darling, how very *cunning* of you, neglecting to mention Captain Lockhart!" She twirled away from Ellie and marched forward, hand extended. "Welcome, Captain Lockhart. A friend of Ellen's is most welcome in our home."

"Thank ye," he said, bowing low over her hand. "And a great pleasure it is to make yer acquaintance, Lady Peasedown," he said, then straightened, letting his gaze shift to Ellie, where it landed, hard.

The blood had drained from her face; she held her hands clasped tightly before her, pressed against her stomach, and she looked so aghast that Liam wanted to laugh with perverted pleasure. He strolled forward and held out his palm to receive her hand. "Miss Farnsworth. We meet again."

She glanced at his hand, then lifted her gaze to his, flinching openly at what she saw there.

"I beg yer pardon, Miss Farnsworth. I did indeed think we had forged a fast friendship. Could I have been mistaken, then?"

"No!" she said sharply, her gaze slanting to Lady Peasedown for a fraction of a moment before returning to Liam.

Oh, *aye*, he had her now—just as he had anticipated, she would not give herself away, nor would she give him any opening to accuse her. He arched an amused brow and smiled wolfishly. "Then, might I hope that—"

"Yes, yes, of *course* we are friends, Captain Lockhart,"

she said, almost irritably, surprising him. "I am simply surprised to see you, naturally."

"*Naturally,*" he drawled. "I canna begin to say how happy I am to make *yer* acquaintance again," he said, bowing over her hand, letting his lips linger there for a moment.

Ellie snatched her hand back, stole a glance at the Peasedowns, who, standing side by side, wore identical, ridiculously proud grins. "I beg your pardon, sir . . . it's just that . . . well, after our last parting, I really thought I'd not see you again."

"Did ye no' indeed? I had rather counted on it."

Ellie's eyes narrowed a bit; she forced a smile, stepped around him and moved to the hearth, fanning herself. "It's quite warm, isn't it?"

"Are you warm, dear? Richard, she's warm," Lady Peasedown said as she perched herself carefully on a loveseat and arranged her skirts to their most attractive vantage. "Do sit, Captain, and please, tell us all about how you came to meet our Ellen."

"Oh, Judith!" Ellie instantly interjected with a nervous laugh. "What a perfectly boring subject!"

"Ah, quite the contrary—nothing would please me more, Lady Peasedown," Liam said, and flipping his coat, he sat directly across from his hostess. He flashed an indolent grin at Ellie. "Where do ye suggest I begin, then?" he asked, rejoicing in the expression of pure, unmitigated terror that passed over her lovely face. " 'Tis really rather amusing, is it no', Miss Farnsworth? We were introduced by Natalie—"

"Inadvertently, really," Ellie quickly interjected. "In the, ah, square. Quite by accident."

"Accident?" Liam asked, feigning confusion. "Why, Miss Farnsworth! Yer modesty is no' becoming! Ye did indeed conspire to do it!" he said with a laugh of great amusement.

Her pretty eyes widened with shock, then narrowed menacingly. "I beg your pardon, Captain Lockhart, but I did *not* conspire to do any such thing!"

"*Ach*, it hardly matters," he said flippantly, turning his attention to Lady Peasedown. "We met by chance in the square, but our next encounter was a cozy supper party—"

"*Oh!*" Ellie interrupted with a loud bark of laughter. "Captain Farnsworth, what a way with words you have!"

"How so?"

"Why, you make it sound so intimate, when there were at least a dozen others present!"

"*Were* there? I donna seem to recall more than one or two at most. But then again, I was quite occupied with one guest in particular," he said, smiling at her.

"How very sweet!" Lady Peasedown swooned. "Who was your host?"

"Host?" Ellie echoed, her eyes all but bulging from their sockets.

"Lady Mackenzie. Are ye acquainted with her?"

"No," Lady Peasedown said, her face scrunching with careful thought. "I'm certain I am not."

Of course not—Lady MacKenzie never left the Highlands, on top of which, she had died last year. "A Scot, of course."

"*Ah*," Lady Peasedown said, nodding, turning a frown to Ellie. "You never mentioned it, Ellen!" she exclaimed.

"Didn't I?" She laughed nervously, fidgeted with her hair. "It really wasn't so very special as all that," she said, folding her arms beneath her bosom. "I rather suppose I forgot all about it, really," she added, and turned away from his pointed gaze.

"How sad that is for us both, Miss Farnsworth, for I willna forget it all me life."

Ellie colored; Lady Peasedown smiled happily. "How

very happy we are to have you here, Captain Lockhart! You simply must stay for supper and tell us more! I confess, Ellen's been rather sparing with her letters, and it would be a lovely treat to hear all about London and Ellen."

"Judith, I—"

"Ye are too kind, Lady Peasedown. I'd be terribly delighted, I would," Liam said, cutting off the little traitor before she could squirm out of supper and all that he had planned for her.

"Splendid!" said Lord Peasedown, beaming proudly at Lady Peasedown. "I just *knew* this would be frightfully fun!"

"I'll just pop in and tell Cook we've one more," Lady Peasedown said. "Richard? Shall we have a look at the wines and choose a special one for our guest?"

"Marvelous idea!"

The two Peasedowns stood and smiled at Liam and Ellie. "Mind you keep him suitably occupied until we return, Ellen," Lady Peasedown said in motherly fashion, and taking her husband's arm, she turned her smile to Liam. "What a positively *wonderful* stroke of coincidence, sir!"

"Aye . . . I couldna have asked for a greater opportunity had I been looking the good Lord in the eye!" Liam exclaimed as he followed them to the door.

"We'll return shortly!" Lady Peasedown all but sang, and walked out the door on her husband's arm.

Liam smiled coldly at their backs, shut the door politely behind them, then whirled, racing for the door at the opposite end of the room and reaching it just before Ellie, throwing his back against it and thereby effectively closing off her escape.

Twenty-four

She was going to die, right there in the main salon, either by his hand or the sudden failure of her own, wildly beating heart.

With nothing but a divan between them to protect her, she stared, mortified, trying to comprehend how he could come to be here, in this house, at this moment. Of all the things she had imagined and feared, she had never believed he could find her here or could have trumped her so completely and unexpectedly. Her mind raced around how he might have tracked her, and more astounding, how he could have *possibly* made Richard's acquaintance.

"Be still," he said gruffly, "or ye'll only make it worse, although it's right hard to fathom how much worse ye could possibly make it."

Fear gripped her. "Have you lost your *mind?*" she demanded insanely, inching her way down the back of the divan, away from him.

"Have *I?*" he answered incredulously, then threw back his head and laughed so bitterly that her fear soared uncontrollably. She darted from behind the divan to the loveseat Judith had vacated, but Liam was too strong and too quick; he was there at the same moment, lashing out with his arm, trying to grab her.

"Dear *God*, Liam, what do you think you are doing here?" she blurted in a panic as she reared back, avoiding his grasp. "This isn't a battlefield! You can't come in here and claim me like some spoil!"

"Ah, Ellie," he said, moving carefully on the other side of the loveseat, smoothly matching every move she made, "did ye *honestly* think ye'd escape me?"

The question made her suddenly and irrationally furious with him for having found her, because honestly, she *had* thought she'd escaped him. "*How* did you find me?" she demanded hotly.

Liam merely chuckled as he leaned over and gripped the back of the loveseat. "Do ye think ye are as clever as all that? Ye had nowhere to go now, did ye, lass? And who's been delivering the post to ye day after day?"

Follifoot! He had betrayed her—

Liam suddenly moved the loveseat a few inches; with a shriek, Ellen whirled and ran blindly to the opposite end of the room, granted a reprieve only by the heaviness of the loveseat that still blocked Liam's way. With a growl, he pushed it aside and started toward her—but the door suddenly opened, and both of them froze, mid-stride.

Filbert stepped in, looked curiously at her, then Liam. "Miss Farnsworth?"

"Yes, Filbert?" she asked, an absurd smile pasted on her face in spite of the breathlessness in her voice.

"Is . . . is everything in order?"

"Well of *course!*" she said gaily. "I was just about to show Captain Lockhart the, ah . . . the lovely, ah . . ." She blinked, trying to focus on the things in front of her.

"Vase," Liam politely provided for her. "Quite a lovely piece of art, is it no'?"

"Oh, *indeed,*" she said, smoothing her hair, chuckling a little hysterically. "I believe Judith said it was fifteenth century."

"Ah. Good century, that," Liam said, watching her closely while at the same time they both watched Filbert.

Filbert continued on to the sideboard, examined the various bottles there. Satisfied that all was in order, he turned, seemed startled that they were staring at him. "Is there anything you require, madam?"

Yes! A gun. A rope. A dagger or heavy candlestick would do! "Ah . . . no. No thank you, Filbert. I think we are quite comfortable." She glanced over her shoulder to see exactly where Liam had gone and was startled by his nearness; he had moved furtively and silently to stand directly behind her. "Are you comfortable, sir?" she asked, frowning, taking one step, then another, away from him.

"*Quite,*" he said, his dark green gaze ferocious in its intensity.

Filbert nodded and began walking toward the door.

"Filbert, wait!" Ellen cried, and instantly darted to his side. "Umm, there is *one* thing," she said, stealing a glance over her shoulder at Liam. "The tea biscuits Judith likes so very well? Perhaps we might have a few. You could bring them straightaway, could you not? No, no, wait . . . *I'll* fetch them. You've enough to do—"

"I beg your pardon, miss," Filbert said, looked past Ellen and nodded at the plate of tea biscuits on the sideboard.

"Stale!" Ellen cried, smiling deliriously at the butler's slightly perturbed expression.

Nonplussed, Filbert said, "I shall bring some—"

"*I'll* go!"

"Pardon, Miss Farnsworth," he said sternly, "but *I* shall bring *fresh* biscuits straightaway." He bowed, glanced at Liam again, then stepped out the door.

The instant the door swung to, Ellen was running again, this time to the hearth, where she grabbed up the iron poker and whirled around, brandishing it like a sword.

Right behind her, Liam laughed as if he were playing a child's game. Laughed so hard, actually, that it was a wonder he didn't topple right over on his bum. *That* infuriated her.

"*Mi Diah!* Ellie, ye canna escape me again—ye know it! Come now, I'll make it easier on us both. Just hand over the bloody beastie, and I'll let ye be, I will."

She could tell by the glint in his eye that she would not be so easily dismissed. "*Liar!* You must take me for a great fool, Liam! Do you think I believe that if I give you the beastie, you'll just quietly step into the night and go away?"

"No' without me supper, no," he said, grinning wickedly.

"You don't intend to dine with us!" she said harshly.

"What, *mo ghraid,* are ye fearful I'll give ye away? Tell yer friends that their illustrious guest is, in reality, a conniving little *thief?*"

Actually, that was precisely what she feared.

"Oh, no—I'll stay for supper, I will. And after that delightful repast, I'll have the beastie."

"That's all?" she asked incredulously. "That's all you want?"

"Ah, *leannan* is it no' as plain as the nose on yer face? I want the goddamn beastie, naturally. But I also want yer pretty arse on one of these fancy platters."

Ellen gasped; Liam started forward, and she raised the poker, prepared to strike.

"*Suithad!*" he growled.

Whatever that might have meant, Ellen raised the poker higher—then instantly dropped it at the sound of the door opening on the far end of the room.

Liam straightened casually, his burning gaze still on her.

"What are you two *doing?*" Judith trilled from the other end of the room.

"Stirring the fire!" Ellen said on a nervous laugh. "It's rather cold."

"Oh . . . I thought you said you were warm, dear!"

"Did you?" Ellen asked cheerfully, thrusting the poker at Liam as she started toward Judith.

Liam chuckled beneath his breath and moved to the hearth to stir the coals as Ellen sailed around him, to Judith's side, and quickly linked her arm through her friend's. Judith smiled, patted her hand, and whispered, "Your color is quite high."

Fabulous. And she was about to be quite ill, thank you.

Richard, following Judith, was all smiles himself. "What *marvelous* coincidence, Captain Lockhart! Cook informs me we are having excellent Scotch beef this evening, roasted to perfection."

"Ah, but the good fortune is all mine, sir. New friends, a dear acquaintance, and an excellent meal. The angels are smiling on me, to be sure," he said, clasping his hands behind his back and looking like some soft country gentleman.

Ellen rolled her eyes.

"And might I add that I look forward to our supper, for Miss Farnsworth has always been an excellent conversationalist," he said.

"Oh yes, she is *indeed*," Judith eagerly agreed.

"Very clever, too. And quite witty with her words."

Judith laughed, and as Liam turned away to hear something Richard was saying, she squeezed Ellen's hand. "You are so very *fortunate*, darling, to have such a brave and *agreeable* gentleman so very smitten with you, and it's quite obvious that he is. Oh, this is *very* exciting!" she whispered, and shivered, as if the whole notion of a love match gave her goose bumps.

Ellen forced a smile and extracted her hand from Judith's grip. *"Exciting,"* she muttered, "hardly begins to describe it."

Supper, much to Liam's added delight, was actually delectable, owing chiefly to the most excellent Scotch beef Peasedown had managed to purchase. Equally delectable was Ellie, who acted as if she were sitting on a pin cushion throughout the course of the meal. When she wasn't squirming in her seat or feigning interest in something one of the Peasedowns said, she was staring daggers at him.

And looking quite beautiful as she did so.

Nevertheless, her haughty attitude was beyond comprehension. Obviously, in the land of Laria, or wherever her little head was residing, it was perfectly natural for *her* to go around binding people up and stealing their belongings, but appalling for *him* to come and take his belongings back. The longer the supper wore on (and it wore on *quite* long, no thanks to Peasedown, who was, apparently, quite fond of telling long, twisted tales about absolutely *nothing*), the more incensed Liam became. She had her nerve, this mad, barmy little English chit, to treat *him* as if he were some kind of thief! In fact, he was so incensed by the time the last course of plum cake was served that he inserted himself into the middle of Lady Peasedown's discourse about a silly little problem the parish was having with missing hens.

"Hens," Ellie repeated, as if she hadn't heard Lady Peasedown clearly, her long fingers fidgeting with the stem of her crystal wineglass.

"Hens! Quite shocking, isn't it? It's rather well established, really—hens from as far away as the parish church all the way down to the river on the other side of King's Lynn have all up and disappeared! Who would do such a vile thing, do you suppose?"

"Mrs. Radley," Lord Peasedown said instantly, flicking something from the tablecloth. "I saw her in town not two days past carrying about a basket of eggs for the church wards."

"Oh, Richard!" Judith exclaimed with much exasperation. "Mrs. Radley is quite ancient, and she's been known for her prized hens for *years* now. You can be sure to find her every Thursday morning delivering eggs to the needy! I rather suppose she has all *her* hens under lock and key!"

"She might be ancient, darling, but I think it rather odd that *she* is the only one in the entire shire who hasn't lost a hen!"

"Well, if it *is* Mrs. Radley," Judith argued, "then her age must be taken into account. Elderly people can be rather batty, you know, all at sixes and sevens, not knowing quite who they are or what they are about," she added with an authoritative sniff, leaning to one side so the footman could remove her plate.

"If indeed the work of a *demented* old woman," Liam interjected amicably, looking at Ellie, "would ye dismiss her actions altogether, then?"

"Of course not!" Judith said instantly. "Thievery of any kind is insupportable."

"But what if ye had a dear demented friend do the same—"

"Which I would not, for *my* friends are neither thieves nor demented," Judith quickly assured him.

"As far as ye know. But say one was to fall on a wee bit of bad luck and were to take something that didn't belong to her—or him—and just the one time, mind ye. Would ye still condemn her—er, him?"

"Certainly! As I said, thievery of any kind is insupportable," she said emphatically.

"But Judith, surely you remember the tale of Robin Hood," Ellie interjected, her blue eyes twinkling like ice as she glared at Liam. "What if this supposed friend stole from the rich to give to the poor? Is that not commendable on some level?"

"Oh . . . well, I'm not certain *what* I would make of that, if something were taken for a good cause . . ."

"Judith, darling, please do not leave our guests with the impression that it is quite to your liking to have someone steal from *us* to give to the less fortunate. If there are those among us who go lacking, I, for one, should like to *give* charitably rather than have it *taken* from me without my consent."

"Oh *yes*, dear," Judith hastily agreed. "I should certainly and earnestly agree with *that*."

"So there is no circumstance, then, that you might see it is the *right* thing to do?" Ellie tried again. "Or perhaps less reprehensible?"

"Are there degrees of reprehension, Miss Farnsworth?" Liam asked.

"Apparently!"

"I should think there is only reprehension," Judith said, oblivious to the debate raging between her guests. "And to answer your question, Ellen, no, I could not see my way into thinking it the right thing to do, most assuredly not."

"But suppose it was something simple—a *flower*. A bouquet of flowers picked from your neighbor's prized garden—without his knowledge, of course—and given to someone's particular favorite? Surely that is innocent enough to avoid your complete censure." She sat back, folded her arms across her middle, and cocked a triumphant brow for Liam's benefit.

Judith seemed terribly confused, but finally shook her head. "No, I should think even something as small and insignificant as *that* would be insupportable. Don't you agree, dear?" she asked hopefully of Richard.

"Of course, darling. If one is inclined to take something that doesn't belong to one, be it a single rose or a precious jewel, it is still quite criminal and therefore wholly insupportable. Port, Captain Lockhart?"

"Aye, thank ye," Liam said, thoroughly enjoying himself now. "I canna argue with yer reasoned thinking, milord," he said as Filbert poured the port for him. "But I believe there are certain circumstances, perhaps quite rare, that the taking of something without permission is warranted."

"Indeed? When would that be, sir?"

"If, for example, something belonged to ye by right and was taken by a close acquaintance, and the acquaintance wouldna return it—"

"Ridiculous," Ellie muttered.

"I should think in *that* circumstance one might consider thievery a legitimate course of action."

"A *legitimate* course of action? Do not the courts exist for that very thing, Captain Lockhart? To resolve disputes among differing parties, even cousins?" Ellie asked, straightening in her chair.

"Aye, indeed they do, Miss Farnsworth," Liam conceded with a deferential dip of his head to conceal his smirk. "If one could rely on the English courts to function properly . . . and if one could rely on his acquaintances to *leave things where they be.*"

Lord Peasedown laughed at that, lifted his port glass to Liam's in mock salute. "Hear, hear, Captain Lockhart."

"Oh yes, hear, hear, what brilliance, sir," Ellie said with another roll of her eyes.

"Spoken like a true scholar of the British judiciary indeed!" Peasedown continued. "I've quite a few opinions of it myself, actually. Perhaps you might indulge me and join me on a shoot tomorrow—we could discuss it further without boring the ladies."

He received a smile from Judith and a withering look from Ellie for his thoughtfulness.

"I've one more day ere I return to Scotland," Liam said thoughtfully, stealing a glimpse of Ellie, who was, naturally, glaring heatedly at him. "Aye, a splendid suggestion. That would be *grand*, milord."

Ellie lifted her napkin and made a noise that sounded something like a snort.

"Then you *must* come for supper again on the morrow, Captain Lockhart!" Lady Peasedown exclaimed. "This has been such jolly fun, hasn't it? By my word, we'll keep you quite entertained until your departure. Won't we, Ellen?"

Ellie gave her such a look that Liam all but choked on his port.

But Lady Peasedown seemed quite oblivious to it; she put her linen aside and stood, smoothing her gown. "Ellen, dear, I think it is time we retired to the drawing room and let the gentlemen have their smoke, shall we?"

"Please," she said coldly. Her gaze skimmed over Liam, but he swore he saw the dangerous little gleam in her eye as the footman came around behind her, pulling out her chair. She rose, like a mist on the lake, as beautiful in a snit as she was in normal countenance, and walked on, preceding her hostess, sailing out of the dining room without a good evening, good day, or a lusty go to hell.

Lady Peasedown, still oblivious, paused to kiss her husband's cheek. "Don't be long," she said sweetly, then flashed a warm smile at Liam.

Poor Lady Peasedown, Liam thought as he returned her gracious smile, all her good intentions at making a match were as good as gone to hell in a handbasket.

Later, in the main salon, the evening became unbearably interminable. Ellen began to fear that Liam would never leave, and that Judith, in a burst of enthusiastic matchmaking, would convince him to stay and inhabit the suite of rooms directly next to hers for the rest of their natural lives, and the four of them might possibly live happily ever after.

But that was not the worst of it. The worst of it was—alarmingly so—that her heart had skipped a beat at the first sight of him, had twirled a bit with his sardonic smile, and her spirit had soared through that drawing room with longing and the intense need to be held. How very ironic that she should still want to seek comfort in his arms and feel his strength surround her after what she had done. How very deplorable that she would never know his touch again.

Except, perhaps, to feel his hands around her neck squeezing the very life from her, which is exactly the way he was looking at her now.

No matter how much she longed for him, *had* longed for him, the cold hard truth was that he did not long for anything but to strangle the life from her. She could see as much in the hard glint of his eyes. It was painful to see, for deep affection had once shone in those beautiful green eyes, affection that had been thoroughly eliminated thanks to her betrayal. She hated herself for it.

Add that to the guilt she carried, and she was made quite miserable. Guilt, guilt, *guilt* that consumed her. She had never thought herself capable of harming another person, certainly not by betraying one, and certainly not after *she* had been so cruelly betrayed many years ago. She sorely regretted and despised the discovery that she was, apparently, that sort of person indeed, and worse, now that she had come this far— now that she had tasted freedom beyond her father's reach, had even reveled in it—she was the sort of person who was unwilling to give up her one hope for everlasting freedom, no matter how wrongly achieved it was. Yes, she was the sort of person who was rigidly unwilling to send Natalie back to their little patch of hell, and would hang on to this freedom with every-thing in her power. Which meant, unfortunately, that she must protect that god-awful beastie with her very life.

The least he could do, she thought morosely, was stop *staring* at her. Every time she looked up from the fretting of what to do, she caught him staring at her, studying her, that awful smile of contempt on his face. And she hated the look in his eyes, hated that she couldn't quite read what it was, that she didn't fully understand it as she had just days ago. It made her positively demented in her anger—she wondered what *he* would have done had he been in her shoes? Undoubtedly ask politely, *may I have the beastie, please?* Honestly, what moral high ground! And now he had come and ruined everything! It infuri-ated her, almost as much as her own bloody irrational thoughts about it. Was she insane? *Quite* possibly! And to hell with her, but she didn't give a bloody damn!

When Liam at last stood and bade them all a good night, and Richard insisted he take the curricle so that he might return promptly at eleven o'clock for their little shoot, Ellen could scarcely stand still, so anxious was she to rush upstairs and assure herself that he had not, by some miracle or magic trick, snatched the beastie back.

They all accompanied him to the front entry, walk-ing languidly down the long corridor, Judith smiling at her, Liam eyeing her carefully, and Richard still talking about a particular dog he intended to bring along tomorrow, as if anyone could possibly care. They stood as Filbert handed Liam his hat, gloves, and regimental coat (still missing the button he had given to Natalie, which the poor girl carried, closely guarded, in her lit-tle reticule).

He casually shrugged into the coat, then donned his gloves, shook Richard's hand—*Looking quite forward to our shoot, I am,* bowed over Judith's hand—*I couldna possibly be more charmed, Lady Peasedown, ye've made me feel so welcome, ye have*—then turning to Ellen as Judith and Richard beamed like proud parents.

He held out his hand; Ellen reluctantly put her hand in his gloved one. His fingers closed around her hand, squeezing it painfully, so painfully that she could feel it buckling her knees. Somehow she managed to keep standing, keep smiling. Albeit a very *thin* smile.

"Ye canna imagine how happy it leaves me to make yer acquaintance again, Miss Farnsworth. As I said, heaven's angels have taken a particular fancy to me."

"I should not go so far as that," she retorted coolly, and tried not to wince at the pressure on her hand.

"Aye, no doubt ye're quite right, for if heaven's angels *truly* fancied me, they'd no' have let ye escape in the first place, eh?"

"*Ooh,*" Judith sighed.

"Perhaps it is the case then, sir, that heaven's angels fancy *me,*" she said, returning his smirk and ignoring Judith's gasp. "Good night, then."

Liam chuckled, let go of her hand. "Good night, Miss Farnsworth. I anxiously await our next meeting."

Ellen stepped back beyond his reach and nodded demurely, wishing he would leave, just . . . *leave.* Leave her alone, leave her with her memories. That was the only way she knew how to live, wasn't it? Alone, with nothing but memories?

"Good night, and 'til the morrow," he said to them all, and as Filbert drew the massive doors open, Ellen peeked up through her lashes, watched him walk out into the night, and pushed down the little voice inside her that cried out for him to come back.

She took her leave of Judith and Richard immediately, citing a slight headache, to which Judith flashed her a knowing smile. "You get some rest, dearest, and we'll chat it all up on the morrow, shall we?" she said with a sly wink.

God save her. "Good night," she said, and quickly made her way upstairs to her dressing room, where she fell down on her knees, crawled under several gowns Judith had hung in the dressing room for her use, moved aside the hatboxes and pulled out the small portmanteau where she had put the beastie, wrapped tightly in Liam's plaid. She withdrew it, could tell by the weight of it that Liam had not somehow managed to steal it back, but she unwrapped it nevertheless.

It was still there, just as hideously ugly as it was the first time she had laid eyes on it. Ellen rocked back on her heels with a sigh of relief and stared down at the ugly little thing. What to do? There was no hope of keeping Liam from searching for it. If there was a way to gain entry to her suite, he would find it, if he hadn't already. And he wouldn't let it slip through his fingers again. She first thought to hide it someplace new, some-place he couldn't find in this massive house. But then she feared a servant would find it, or Judith and Richard. Even their children. There was Natalie's room—but if she found this thing, it would scare her half to death. No, better to leave it here. At least she could keep an eye on it.

The ugly thing winked up at her with its awful ruby eyes. Part of her wished he'd just go on and find it— *Ho, there!* A silly, ridiculous idea popped into her head. *Let him find it.* She thought about that, then laughed at her own foolishness. No, no, he'd never . . . *but wouldn't he?* Honestly, this was an idea that just might work. And really, what else could she do, given the circum-stance?

Ellen pushed herself to her feet, returned to the main room of her suite, and found the pair of shears Judith and her chambermaid had left when altering several hand-me-down gowns for her *(they are frightfully too small for me, Ellen)*. In the dressing room again, she grabbed a corner of Liam's kilt. Holding her breath, she made the first snip of the luxurious wool fabric. She could almost feel him out there somewhere, almost hear his roar of protest, and she quickly cut the plaid in half, releasing her breath when she had done it.

Ellen worked well into the night, even stealing out into the gardens on the east side of the house through an unused servant's entrance. When she had finished, she was certain it would never work. But she hid the beastie away nonetheless. And then she stepped into Natalie's room to have a look at her daughter.

In sleep, her young face was free of the lines of worry that Ellen so often noticed on her now. She tucked the coverlet more securely around Natalie, then quietly returned to her room and her bed, where she fell into a hard, fitful sleep, one peppered with dreams of Liam. Liam finding her, his eyes full of rage. Liam running from her, his eyes full of loathing . . . *Liam*.

She awoke before dawn, her head hurting from lack of sleep, and her sight blurred from the scars her dreams had left behind. After dressing, she checked one last time to make sure everything was in order. There was no longer any question—she had to leave Peasedown, and as soon as possible. How foolish she had been to have ever let down her guard. Now she would pay for her inattention and complacency.

Worse, there was no time to debate *where* she would go. So she decided she and Natalie would go to France. Richard had talked at length about it just two evenings past. He had said something she found quite interesting—that in the aftermath of war there was quite a lot of social and political reconstruction going on, and new faces, men and women alike, were gaining a foothold in popular politics and society. It had occurred to Ellen that a country recovering from war might be the very place for her and Natalie. They could, along with everyone else, start their lives over. Fresh. Anew.

When Natalie awoke, Ellen was sitting on the edge of her bed, gazing down at her with a soft smile.

"Mother?" she asked, yawning.

"Good morning, darling. I was waiting for you to wake." She leaned over, kissed Natalie's brow, then stood. "Let's get you dressed." Ellen walked to the small closet in Natalie's room, opened the door to remove the one frock she had not already packed away in anticipation of their escape.

"I had a funny dream last night," Natalie said, splashing water in the basin behind Ellen.

"Did you?"

"I dreamed that Captain Lockhart came and rescued us."

Ellen's blood ran cold. She turned slowly, glared at her daughter at the basin. "Is this another of your fantasies, Natalie?" she demanded. "If it is, it is hardly amusing."

Natalie turned a wide-eyed look of surprise to her. "No! Truly, I dreamed it!"

Ellen crossed the room in four strides and grabbed Natalie's upper arm. "Is that all there was to the dream? Did he say anything more?"

"N-no—"

"Where were you in this dream?"

"Here!" she cried, wincing at the force of Ellen's grip. "I only *dreamed* it! He's not come to my room—" The child gasped, slapped a hand over her mouth.

"What did you say?" Ellen demanded.

Natalie did not answer—she looked positively mortified. *Dear God.* Ellen's breath was coming fast and hard, and she swallowed, trying to see past Natalie's eyes, down into her very heart. Was it possible? "Have you seen him?" she asked, her voice barely above a whisper.

Tears began to stream down Natalie's face; she nodded uncertainly.

Ellen's heart sank. "What did he say?" she asked, trying desperately to remain calm.

"That he wanted to surprise you!"

"Is that all? Nothing more?"

"Just that we'd be rescued—"

"God in heaven, Natalie, this is not *Laria!*" Ellen cried with frustration.

"I didn't say that it was!" Natalie wailed, frightened now.

Ellen quickly grabbed her, held her close, and took several deep breaths in an attempt to calm her racing heart. "I'm sorry, darling. It's just that sometimes I don't know what is fantasy and what is real to you. Come on then, let's get you dressed," she said, and turned away so that Natalie could not see how truly distraught she was.

Twenty-five

❧

*J*udith was so pleased with Richard for having brought Captain Lockhart home that she showed her great appreciation for his thoughtfulness and match-making attempts by reviving their marital relations.

Which in turn meant that, in spite of the following day being a very dreary and wet one, Lord Peasedown was smiling brightly and walking with a spring in his step not witnessed by the house staff in several weeks. Although he was somewhat surprised to find Captain Lockhart already in the small drawing room off the back terrace, he assumed Filbert had shown him in, and left it at that happy thought, unwilling to think of anything but the image of a naked Judith perched pleasingly on his groin.

What he did not know was that Filbert had not let the captain in. It was a smiling parlor maid who, having seen the rough-hewn gentleman with the intriguing scar the day before in the company of her employers, had assumed it perfectly all right to show him through the house when he arrived that morning looking terribly confused about the various entrances and speaking with such a delightful accent. This much she had confessed (with pinkened cheeks and sparkling brown eyes) to Liam as she led him about the ground floor of the mansion.

The guided tour was appreciated, but it was not

exactly necessary, since Liam had roamed the house in the early morning hours (his skills at espionage quite intact, thank you) in an effort to determine the *exact* location of Ellen's suite of rooms. He knew the general area, of course, having hidden himself in the woods around the Peasedown mansion after leaving the drive the night before. From there he saw the light flooding the suite of rooms just above the ground floor shortly after his departure. He knew instinctively that it was *her* light, brought on by her nervous little scamper to check on that goddamned beastie.

But to make doubly sure of it, he had crept back into the house through a window he had noticed unlatched in the main drawing room. From the main drawing room, he had crept up the grand, curving staircase, past what he was certain was the master suite (judging by the sounds of lovemaking he heard coming from within), and down to the opposite end of the hall.

Unfortunately, his mission to exact his revenge was interrupted by the unexpected sound of a child's whimper. Standing there in the hall deciding just which door to try first, he had heard the child's sound, had known immediately who it was, and had crept to the door, pressed his ear against it, listening carefully. The instant he determined Natalie was crying, some strange and preternatural paternal instinct kicked him right in the arse; he had carelessly walked into the room without fear of discovery, only to stand there in shock, for he had not known that it was possible to sob so hard in one's sleep. When she opened her eyes and saw him hovering over her, so distraught was he by her unconscious sadness that he had not known what to do other than to promise her that he would indeed rescue her and her mother from this evil castle.

And then he silently cursed female tears to the blazing pits of hell.

So it was Nattie's unintentional doing that kept him from having his way with Ellie and retrieving the beastie.

Disturbed by it, Liam had returned to King's Lynn in the handy curricle and napped a few hours before returning to Peasedown Park, determined more than ever to have his beastie and be gone by the morrow. When the sun had finally crept in behind some ominous clouds, he was standing at the east entrance to the mansion feigning a look of confusion, claiming not to know which of the grand entrances was the grandest after all. It wouldn't hurt, he reckoned, to know more than one exit route, for there would be no more distractions. With renewed vigor, he *would* exact his revenge. Today.

The parlor maid had brightened like a morning flower when she found him, smiling broadly and leading him about the various rooms of the ground floor before finally depositing him in the small drawing room overlooking the back terrace. And had he not been so consumed with thoughts of the only woman he had ever loved, he might have taken the lass up on her offer to "help him in any way."

Unfortunately, *Ellie*, miserable creature that she was, was constantly in his thoughts. What a cruel thing for her to be the one woman in all of God's creation he should fall in love with. He despised her for it, deplored her betrayal, but he still, inexplicably, loved her, and seeing her yesterday had almost been his undoing. Never had he felt such mixed emotions—on the one hand, wanting to squeeze the life from her, and on the other, wanting to draw her into his arms and kiss the breath from her. There were moments he felt almost swept away by his grief. But then he'd recover with a feverish shiver and want to strangle her all over again.

It was a vicious little thing going on inside him, and it was, therefore, bittersweet news when Peasedown suggested that as the weather was "frightfully awful," they should postpone their shoot and indulge his wife and Miss Farnsworth by playing parlor games. "After luncheon, of course. Which naturally you'll take with me. Judith does not care for luncheon. But then we'll while away the afternoon by amusing the ladies. Until supper, of course, which naturally you will take with all of us."

Parlor games. Sounded perfectly tedious. Mared was terribly fond of them, but he and Grif preferred cards to the silly games women concocted. Nevertheless, this would afford him the opportunity to get his beastie and quit King's Lynn altogether. Before he did something remarkably stupid. Like kiss her and suffer another thousand consequences for it, bloody stupid fool that he was.

"Thank ye," Liam said. "I'm rather fond of shooting, I am, but in truth, I'm fonder of the company of ladies."

"*Ah,*" Peasedown said, chuckling. "As to that—" He paused, looked over his shoulder to make sure no one was listening in a room that was completely vacant, save the two of them, and said, "My lady wife is very much on your side in this matter." He inched closer to Liam. "I must warn you that she fancies herself a bit of a matchmaker, and can be rather zealous about it at times. Do you take my meaning?"

"Aye, I do," Liam said, trying hard not to smile. "And I'm no' above admitting I could use all help proffered," he added with a wink.

"*Splendid!*" Peasedown all but shouted, puffing up like a peacock. "*Well,* then! Shall we lunch, sir? A man can hardly match wits with a woman on an empty stomach, can he?"

Truer words, Liam thought, were never spoken.

* * *

While the two gentlemen finished up their luncheon and hied themselves to the green salon for parlor games, Ellen was suffering Judith's attentions, the intent of which was painfully obvious. One could not have known Judith for more than twenty-five years and not see the old girl was gleefully matchmaking, even with Judith vehemently denying it. "I couldn't possibly find time to concern myself with your lovers, Ellen . . . or lack of them."

It had started with a review of her wardrobe, Judith insisting that Ellen's "tiresome" and "dowdy" day gown was really not even suitable for the cold weather. Actually, her gown happened to have been one of last Season's most favored styles, and according to Eva (who had given it to her), it had received quite a lot of fine compliments the two times she had worn it. The fashionable gown, like most of Eva's castoffs, did not show Ellen's bosom to its greatest advantage. At least not like the overtight gown Judith made her don—the insufferably tight, ridiculously low-cut gown out of which she was practically falling. But Judith would not have it any other way—they argued a good quarter of an hour until Ellen finally gave in and threw up her hands. What did it matter? If she could survive one more day, she'd be gone.

They marched down to the green salon, Judith prattling on about how *charming* and *delightfully rustic* Liam was. Ellen said nothing, but pressed her lips firmly together to keep from groaning to Judith that her charming and delightfully rustic Scot would just as soon see her flayed open than alive, and if given the opportunity, would do the honors himself. But really, she did intend to be gone before *that* happy occurrence. If only she could have a moment of peace to *think*.

Naturally, therefore, it was to Ellen's great shock

and even greater chagrin to find Liam comfortably ensconced in an overstuffed armchair in the middle of the green salon. *Again.* With little Sarah and Charles and Natalie seated at his feet, making a pretty picture of country bliss. Ellen could not have been more perturbed if Liam had managed to steal the beastie from her.

She should have known from Judith's great grin as a footman opened the door to the salon, or suspected from Judith's early-morning call to her dressing room, that something unexpected might happen. And of course she should have suspected that there would be no shooting today, with rain coming down in buckets. But she had been too tired, too wrapped up in her own problems to think about that. Her inability to anticipate was, she thought irritably as she crossed the threshold, going to be her most spectacular downfall.

Liam grinned jovially as she entered the room.

"Mother!" Natalie cried, seeing her and rushing to Ellen's side. "I *told* you he had come to rescue us!"

"Oh my darling!" Judith laughed as she fondly ran a hand over Natalie's head. "How precious and *silly* you are!"

"Ah, what a lovely sight to behold on such a dreary morning," Liam said pleasantly as he came to his feet.

"Captain Lockhart," Ellen responded stiffly, and received a not-very-well-disguised elbow in the ribs from Judith.

"My *dear* Captain Lockhart, you are to be commended! For in spite of having all your plans dashed, you've agreed to spend the *entire* day with us! I assure you *our* day will be made infinitely brighter with your presence!" Judith sang as she took Ellen's elbow firmly in hand and marched her forward.

"Ah, but 'tis *I* who am pleased beyond comprehension," Liam spouted like a bloody dandy as Judith made Ellen extend her hand with another sharp jab to the side.

"Then I suspect your level of comprehension must be rather shallow, sir," Ellen said as she watched him bow over her hand, then lift his head with a smile and a sparkle in his eye that was just a little too gleeful to suit her, "for we are, as a whole, rather tedious and tiresome company."

"On the contrary, Miss Farnsworth, my comprehension is keener than ye understand. I could no' be more pleased if I were asked to dine with the king himself."

Ellen all but snorted and yanked her hand from his grasp. "What a pity that couldn't have been arranged."

"Dreadfully awful out," Richard was saying by way of explanation. "Couldn't shoot a thing even if we wanted, and I daresay we'd be swimming."

"Hmmm," said Ellen.

"Of course, you couldn't *possibly* go out in such horrid conditions!" Judith assured her husband. "I say a round of games is in order. Children! Come along, if you please! It's time you all adjourned to the nursery," Judith said as she sailed toward the bellpull.

The children dutifully came to their feet, but Natalie rushed to Ellen's side. "Mother, please let me stay!" she pleaded in a whisper, pulling on Ellen's skirts.

"I'm sorry, darling, but children belong in the—"

"But what if Captain Lockhart leaves without us?" she whispered desperately.

Inadvertently, Ellen looked up; Liam's eyes reflected her sadness for Natalie, and she felt as if a weight had been attached to her heart, pulling it down, sinking it into the mire that was suddenly her life. "He will certainly leave without us, Natalie. But I won't, I will never leave you. Now go on with you, off to the nursery."

"There's no need to send them off, Lady Peasedown,"

Liam tried. "I very much enjoy the company of children, I do."

"How *generous!*" Judith said happily, and shot Ellen what could only be termed a smirk. "But I rather think their governess has lots for them to accomplish today. We pay her handsomely enough for it, certainly. All right, then," she said, ushering Sarah and Charles toward the door, "Miss Peckinpaugh is waiting."

Natalie sighed and let go her grip of Ellen's skirt, looking terribly dejected. As the two Peasedown children left the room, she exchanged a glance with Liam, and Ellen saw something pass over his careful expression. *He cared about Natalie.* He truly cared about her strange little daughter.

Ellen's heart sank deeper into the mire as she kissed the top of Natalie's head and sent her to the nursery. How would she ever explain to her daughter that she couldn't have both Liam and her freedom? She watched Natalie walk out the door, lagging behind the other children. As the footman closed the door, Ellen turned listlessly, caught Liam looking at her, his expression a peculiar mix of anger and sympathy. This was too much—the sadness inside her was beginning to beat like a drum, and Ellen fell onto the nearest chair, staring morosely at one of the large, paned glass windows and the rivulets of water cascading down, forcing herself to think of her most immediate problem—what exactly was she to do *now*? With Liam underfoot, she'd never be able to slip away!

"It's rather cold in here, Richard," Judith was saying. "We should really bring someone round to stoke the fire a bit. I have a splendid idea," she continued cheerfully as Richard moved to stoke the fire, "Why don't we play a game? I haven't played charades in ever so long—"

"I despise charades, Judith, you know that," Richard said gruffly.

"I've a game, if ye donna mind the suggestion," Liam said. "One we particularly enjoy in Scotland. It's called Truth or Consequences. Do ye know it?"

That caught Ellen's attention.

"No!" Judith exclaimed, obviously delighted. Yes, well, neither did Ellen, but she did not like the name of the game at all. Nor did she particularly care for the diabolical little glint in Liam's eye.

"Simple, really. One player challenges another with the truth or a consequence. For example, I might challenge Miss Farnsworth. Truth or consequence, Miss Farnsworth?"

Oh, no, she really did *not* like the sound of this game. Ellen waved her hand flippantly at him and looked away. "It sounds to me a perfectly silly game, Captain Lockhart," she said coolly.

"Oh, come on, then, Ellen! It's all in fun! And what more do you have to do on such an appalling day?" Judith cried. "Truth or consequence?"

Dear God, *why* had she come to Peasedown at all? "Judith, I really prefer not—"

"Perhaps it would be best if I demonstrated with yer husband, Lady Peasedown," Liam said, shoving his hands in the pocket of his buckskins and walking casually to the hearth.

"Yes, yes, I'm rather keen to try," Richard said, putting the fire poker down and turning toward Liam. "How is it played?"

"If ye choose truth, I may ask ye whatever I like. If ye donna answer, or we catch ye in a lie, the person asking the question may choose yer consequence. If ye prefer not to risk the ugly truth," he said, smiling at Judith and Richard as if nothing could be more preposterous, "then I might name yer consequence."

"What jolly good fun!" Richard said, and eagerly assumed a seat, his hands braced against his knees.

"All right, then, I'll choose 'truth.' Certainly I've nothing to hide!" he said, laughing.

"May I go first?" Judith quickly interjected. "I've a question for my lord husband." Liam nodded; Judith eagerly sat up, her back ramrod straight. "Dearest, do you recall the afternoon you were late returning from your club?" she asked sweetly.

Richard immediately colored. "What afternoon?" he asked, laughing nervously and looking at Liam. "I go *every* afternoon, Judith, so I can't possibly guess which—"

"The afternoon of fourteen September."

The color drained from his face. "But . . . but that was so long ago, my love—"

"You arrived well past the dinner hour and you said that you had stopped off to have a word with Doctor Stafford. Do you recall now, dearest?" she asked sweetly.

Now white as a sheet, Richard looked desperately from Liam to Ellen, then to Judith again. "Why, this isn't very enjoyable at all! I prefer a consequence, actually," he said stiffly.

Judith smiled. "What a pity, that—for *you*, dear heart. For the inability to remember clearly your whereabouts on the afternoon of fourteen September, 1816, I decree that your consequence shall be the purchase of the divan I saw in York, which you refused me on the grounds I had overspent my allowance. And I think the consequence should be paid with presentation of a banknote at once to your *wife*, Richard." She smiled triumphantly.

Richard gaped at her. But a moment later, his shoulders sagged, and like a defeated man, he rose and stalked to the desk at the far end of the room, from which he withdrew a sheaf of papers and a pen, and hurriedly wrote something. Then he stalked to the sideboard, where he poured himself a generous serving of whiskey. "Go on with it, then!" he said irritably.

Judith beamed at Liam. "I think I should *like* this game!" she proclaimed. "You go next, Captain Lockhart. Who will you ask?"

"Why, Miss Farnsworth, naturally." He was leaning against the mantel, one leg crossed over the other, his arms folded at his chest and his smile terribly mischievous.

"I should like *not* to play," Ellen said instantly.

"Oh, don't be such a killjoy, Ellen!" Judith scolded her. "Say 'truth.' What would Captain Lockhart ask you that could possibly harm you in any way?"

Blast it all! Judging by Liam's deepening smile, she was in for a time of it. Ellen fussed about her skirt, tried to prepare herself. She would *not* accept his consequence, not being *quite* ready to die. But then again, she shuddered to think what he might ask her: *"Miss Farnsworth, did you break into the Lockhart mansion in Mayfair and steal a beastie that rightfully belonged to me? And did you run away from your father? And did you not betray me? Miss Farnsworth, are you in fact a liar and a thief?"*

"All right, then, if you want me to play so terribly much, I'll play. I'll choose 'truth,' Captain Lockhart."

"Ah," he said, nodding thoughtfully, and straightened, clasped his hands behind his back and strolled to stand in front of her. "Very well, then, 'truth.' " He paused; his eyes narrowed on her, as if he were considering his many choices. "Miss Farnsworth . . . have ye ever been in love?"

The question shocked her. "Wh-what? I beg your pardon?" she sputtered, flabbergasted.

"I asked, have ye ever been in love? A simple question really, Miss Farnsworth—an *aye* or a *nay* would suffice, then."

Judith and Richard had turned their full attention to her, delightedly watching her like some performing circus animal. Ellen looked at the three people staring at her and thought she had finally gone round the bend, had no idea which way was up or down any longer. Was she truly sitting in this room, with these people, playing some childish game with the man she had stolen from? And jilted? Had he honestly just asked her if she had *loved* him? The nerve! All right, he was aggrieved and all that, yes, of course. But this! *This* was plainly the most vulgar of manners! *"Yes!"* she said emphatically, to which Judith clapped her delight and Richard laughed.

Liam, however, did not laugh. He just looked at her with no expression at all, which left her even more bewildered.

" 'Tis yer turn, Miss Farnsworth," he said quietly.

"Marvelous! I choose you, Captain Lockhart. Truth or consequence?"

"Truth," he said without the slightest hesitation.

"Have *you* ever been in love?"

Liam chuckled low and shook his head. *"Never."*

Strangely, Ellen's heart plummeted; she felt very suddenly a fool, a reckless, silly fool.

"Until very recently," Liam added calmly, to which Judith did what was becoming an altogether too frequent little swoon, and Richard laughed nervously, as if he had sensed the game had moved beyond the absurd, and helped himself to more whiskey. But Liam made no expression at all—he simply kept a steady gaze on her until Ellen had to turn away.

The play went from her to Richard, who desperately wanted Judith to choose truth, and groused when she refused. "Very well, then, you leave me no choice. Your consequence is to hie yourself upstairs and bring me the pearl bracelet."

Judith gasped with outrage. "I'll do no such thing!"

"Madam, you agreed to the terms of this game, and as you refuse to give me the truth, I will have that damn bracelet as my consequence!"

Positively and obviously furious, Judith suddenly sprang to her feet and started marching for the door. "You'll have your bloody bracelet, all right!" she snapped.

"*Judith!*" Richard cried out, and was suddenly chasing after her. "I'll not stand for your impudence, madam!" he shouted after her, and Judith's reply to that was muffled by the great distance she had managed to already gain from her husband.

They were alone again. Ellen jerked her gaze to Liam; he was looking at her with a predatory expression. Instantly, she came to her feet, prepared to run if she must, but Liam chuckled low, obviously enjoying her discomfort. Ellen frowned as she backed away from him. "What a lovely little game you have brought us, sir."

"What is it, then, lass? Does it make ye feel a wee bit uncomfortable?"

"No!"

"I rather thought it seemed appropriate for the occasion. After all, it *is* the game we are playing—*have* been playing, eh? Truth or consequence? Granted, I have had yer consequence forced on me against me will, but I thought 'twas certainly appropriate all the same."

"Dear God, Liam, I *know* you are angry—"

"Ha!"

"—and if you want to embarrass me, if you want to expose me, then go ahead and do it. But why not leave the game playing to the children?"

"God blind me," he said, shaking his head. "How could ye forget so soon, Ellie? How could ye forget who started this awful game? No' me! *Ach*, no, I thought we were two people caught up in extraordinary circumstance, who had found each other in spite of it all, if only for a moment in time. I never thought it was a game, and I never thought we were anything but honest with one another. What a goddamn fool I was, eh? Aye, ye started this game, Ellie. But I intend to finish it." He lowered his head and took a step forward.

Fear and fatigue spiraled in her gut—Ellen started for the door, but Liam caught her easily, jerking her around and crushing her up against the wall with his body, looking down at her with a face twisted in anger and confusion. He grabbed her chin and held her head back so she was forced to look at him, to *see* the pain there. "How could ye?" he breathed as his eyes wildly roamed her face. "How could ye make me love ye, then betray me so?"

Tears welled in her eyes; she caught a sob in her throat and whispered hoarsely, *"I didn't want to do it!"*

"Bloody liar," he growled, and moved his hand slowly from her chin until his fingers were splayed against her neck, holding her captive against the wall. For a split moment, Ellen feared for her life as she watched a thousand emotions sweep across his dark green eyes. But then Liam shocked her by suddenly kissing her, his mouth indignantly devouring hers, his tongue thrusting deep into her mouth, searching for an answer, kissing her with all the angry emotion he felt. His knee pressed hard against her legs, forcing them open, so that he could hold her aloft with his leg. One hand went to her breast, caressing it roughly.

Ellen could feel his erection against her belly, hardening, and it was more than she could bear, more than she could endure. Helpless, *hopeless*, she responded to his primal call, her body lifting to his, pressing her breast into his palm, her hands running up and down his strong back while her body moved wantonly, riding his thigh. She wanted to memorize the feel of his body against her, every hard length of him, to hold him close one last time. All the emotions that had been boiling beneath the surface the last few days were suddenly bubbling out in that scorching kiss—all the overwhelming guilt, the gnawing hunger, the frightening uncertainty of what would happen to her now. To *them* now.

But her responsiveness seemed to dishearten him somehow; Liam suddenly let go of her, pushing away, pushing her out of his arms. He dragged the back of his hand across his mouth, wiping that dangerously passionate kiss from his lips as he considered her. "If I were a shrewd man, I'd go to me grave without asking ye. But I'm no' a shrewd man, I'm a simple man, one who had the bloody misfortune to fall in love with the likes of ye, Ellie. I canna help myself . . . I want to know, then, when ye said ye had ever been in love . . . did ye mean *me*? Or did ye mean Natalie's father?"

The need in his voice stabbed at her heart; she felt her knees begin to quake and pressed her hands to her breast, pushed her racing heart down as she cried out, "What *difference* does it make now?"

"It makes all the difference in the goddamn world to me! What did ye mean, then, Ellie? Me or him? Did ye ever love me, or did ye think to betray me from the beginning?"

That stung her badly. "*Liam!* You don't understand—"

"The hell I donna *understand,* Ellie! Ye left me bound up like a Christmas goose under the pretense of making love! Ye stole the one thing that can save me family! Ye know what it means to me just as well as ye know I'll take it back. Yer betrayal is done; I'll no' pursue it further, and we can go on with our lives. Just . . . answer me! Answer me *now,* or I will make ye answer me with yer friends present, I will *make* ye feel the humiliation ye put on me! I . . . I *must* know, Ellie."

Dear God, he *must* have truly loved her; and she had

hurt him deeply. She could see it in his eyes, the clench of his jaw, the fist at his side. That dreadful mix of hope and pain on his face. "I *meant* . . ." But Ellen choked on her own hope and pain, finding it impossible to speak, to say all the things out loud that were in her heart, the emotion inside her too thick. "I meant . . . *you*," she said softly, and let go the sob that had lodged in her throat.

It seemed almost as if her words hit him square in the jaw. Liam reeled backward, unable—or unwilling—to look at her. His hands went to his waist; his head dipped low.

Oh, God. *Oh God oh God.* "I meant *you*, Liam," she continued recklessly, desperate. "I love *you*—"

"Then . . . how *could* ye, Ellie?" he asked, his voice sadly distant.

"Dear God!" she cried to the ceiling. "How could I *not*? You saw what was happening to Natalie! Oh, how I wish it had never happened! I wish you had never come to my father's house, or come up those stairs! I wish you'd never told me—"

"Here we are, back again!"

Liam whirled toward the sound of Judith's voice just as quickly as Ellen turned away and walked unsteadily to the window, desperately trying to compose herself as Judith sailed through the door.

She stopped mid-stride, looked first at Ellen, then Liam, who had crossed his arms implacably across his chest, and smiled smugly. "I'm terribly sorry to interrupt you two!" she trilled. "But unfortunately, my lord husband could not find the bracelet in question, and I'm afraid he's putting on a bit of a sulk." She continued on to the sideboard and poured herself a small sip of wine. "Perhaps we might amuse ourselves with a game of loo until he feels up to joining us again?" she asked gaily, and swished toward the card table, expecting Ellen and Liam to join her.

* * *

Liam wasn't really very sure how he made it through the afternoon, seated across from the thieving vixen at the card table as he was. He could scarcely see the cards in front of him, could see nothing but her hair, made flaxen by the firelight, the curve of her slender neck, her pale blue eyes. And he could think of nothing but the feel of her in his arms, the taste of her mouth when he had kissed her. Supper was wearisomely protracted, with Lady Peasedown doing her best to match him with Ellie, and Lord Peasedown having lost his desire to participate after whatever it was that had gone on between him and his wife.

Truthfully, Liam had lost his taste for the fight. For some reason, to hear her say she loved him, to see the pain in her eyes when she had told him had been far more devastating than believing she had played him for a fool to betray him. It left him feeling terribly at sea, and silently, he debated what he should do. Did he give up the fight for the beastie, ask her to accompany him to God knew where? Not particularly his most brilliant thought, was it? How exactly would he provide for her and Natalie? In spite of her estrangement from her father, it was obvious she was accustomed to living at a high standard. How would she fare in small houses in cities, *countries* far from here and the comforts she had known all her life? How would Natalie? And could he really take her with him knowing that she had betrayed him? Could he ever trust her again? Or did he take what was rightfully his, leave with that and the ache in his heart, and hope that his military regiment would go somewhere so far away that his heart would eventually heal over and scar like an old battle wound?

Diah, his head hurt. Throbbed. And for the first time he could remember, he had no appetite.

But over the main course of supper, which he had difficulty eating, Lady Peasedown attempted almost frantically to engage him with tales of Ellen as a wee lass. Enchanting stories that painted a charming picture of a child living in luxury and privilege, accustomed to a certain way of life. And it was in that recitation that Liam finally understood there had never really been any question—he had to go home. He was all but out of funds, had nothing to offer her, and worse, had lost his trust in her. He would, he reckoned, have nothing of this extraordinary brush with love other than the memory of it . . . one he would carry in his heart for all eternity.

As supper drew to a close, and the port was served, Liam announced he was leaving on the morrow, and thanked the Peasedowns for their hospitality.

"I beg your pardon, you're to do *what?*" Lady Peasedown demanded, her voice full of the fatigue and bewilderment of matchmaking.

"I'm leaving on the morrow, Lady Peasedown. Our regiment will depart in a month or so, and there are matters that require me at home."

"But . . . but we had so hoped you'd *stay!*" she cried.

"Judith . . ." started Lord Peasedown, but wearily shook his head when Lady Peasedown began to protest.

"I'm certain you don't have to go *straight*away, Captain Lockhart!" Judith said, looking to Ellie for help.

But she'd get none there—Ellie bit her lower lip, looked at her china plate, and allowed Lady Peasedown to pout.

Liam declined the offer of a cheroot and begged their forgiveness as he stood to leave. "I must be up ere dawn," he lied.

The Peasedowns and Ellie accompanied him to the front hall, where he took his greatcoat, hat, and gloves from Filbert for the last time. Lord Peasedown shook his hand vigorously, declared he had had a splendid time of it, would send a man for the curricle on the morrow, then urged his wife to say good-bye. Lady Peasedown was not quite as endearing in her send-off, and Liam could see that she was hurt by his unwilling-ness to play at her game any longer. He thanked her profusely, and thought had it been any other circum-stance, he would have indulged her.

Lord Peasedown, openly embarrassed by his wife's sulk, forced her to accompany him to the salon, leaving Liam alone with Ellie.

Ellie stood with her arms crossed under her bosom, studying the pattern of the marble floor.

"Look at me, then," he softly commanded her as Filbert walked away to open the door.

She looked up; the tears shimmering in her eyes sur-prised him.

"I'll come back for it," he said, his voice wavering slightly. "Ye know I will."

She nodded; a tear slipped from the corner of her eye and spilled down her cheek. "You won't find it, Liam. I'm sorry, but I can't let you have it."

He smiled sadly. "I'll no' harm ye, Ellie. I could never." He drew a breath, put a finger under her chin, and lifted her face higher, so that he could see it one last time, take in every feature. Still and always an angel, wasn't she, a bloody angel who happened to be hurtling toward Earth. "I couldna harm ye in any way, for the truth is . . . *tha gràdh agam ort.*"

Another tear fell.

"That is to say, I love ye, above all else, and I always will."

More tears fell, streaming down her face, yet Ellie said nothing, just gazed at him, her thoughts hidden behind that shroud of tears. There was nothing left to say. He bent his head, kissed her softly on the lips, then stepped away and walked out the door, not daring to look back.

And in the dead of night, just before the sun would rise, he tiptoed from Ellie's dressing room into her bedroom, holding the plaid bundle under his arm. Natalie was sleeping soundly at her side, and Ellie was fully clothed. He knew she had waited for him, had tried to stay awake. And she had hidden the beastie well, but it had been exactly where Natalie had seen it last, and he had found it easily, wrapped in his kilt, the bulky shape and glint of a ruby where the plaid did not meet giving it away.

Liam leaned over, looked at Natalie. The lass was sleeping, her breath loud and deep, and he knew that disappointing her might possibly be the greatest regret of his life. *Someday yer prince will come, Nattie. Someday.*

He shifted his gaze to Ellie; saw the frown that creased her brow. How long he stood there he had no notion, but he finally turned and walked away, taking his beastie and the memory of his angel with him.

Twenty-six

It was no more than a pinprick of sound that woke Ellen that morning; a small and insignificant noise that wended its way down into her consciousness, penetrating her hated dreams. Whatever it was, her body remembered all at once that she was supposed to be awake, and she bolted upright, her heart pounding.

Everything looked the same.

Beside her, Natalie moaned in her sleep and rolled onto her side.

Ellen sat perfectly still, straining to hear whatever it was that had awakened her.

Nothing.

Complete silence—except for the cacophony of her tortured thoughts screaming in her head, of course, as they had done all night. Slowly, she put one leg over the side of the bed, then the other, and stood cautiously. Still nothing. Was it her imagination, nothing more? Another unfounded panic? She glanced at the clock on the mantel; it was four o'clock, and the embers still glowed warm in the hearth. She hadn't slept long then—an hour, maybe two.

Nevertheless, it was time to go. Everything was packed. The house was dead to the world and it wouldn't be long before the servants were stirring. With a little luck, she and Natalie would be on the six o'clock coach to Cambridge before anyone would notice them missing. Richard had asked her one interminable evening about her journey from London, then had explained the intricacies of the public coach system in King's Lynn. There were three in all, coming from and headed to three separate directions, all leaving promptly at six o'clock each morning, and returning at promptly six o'clock that very evening.

At the very least, she had come to the conclusion that with three coaches leaving at the same time and going in opposite directions from one another, it might add some necessary confusion to their flight. It was conceivable that no one would remember a woman with her young daughter at all, and if anyone did, perhaps would not remember with any clarity which coach they had boarded. That should at least give them time to reach Cambridge, where she thought she had the best chance of selling the damn beastie, before taking another public coach to the sea and sailing to France.

Her plan, hastily concocted, was undoubtedly full of holes, but was no longer open to internal debate, for if she and Natalie didn't start soon, there would be no hope of it.

Ellen collected herself and hurried to her dressing room to gather her things and wash before they fled. But as she entered the dressing room, she immediately noticed that an empty portmanteau had been moved slightly, if only a fraction of an inch. But there was no doubt in her mind—*it had been moved*. Her body reacted before her mind, flying to the case and shoving it aside, then the hatboxes—

It was gone.

Astounded, Ellen sat back on her heels, her mind racing as she gaped at the empty space where she had left the false beastie. Her mind raced along with her heart, unable to fathom how he had managed it, how he could have possibly come into this room, undetected, and taken the bundle she had left for him. Was that the sound that had awakened her? Was it possible he was still here? Had he discovered what she had done?

Panicking now, she jumped up, ran to her bedroom, and fell down on her knees before the bed, reaching under it. *It wasn't there!* She felt about wildly for it, grimacing at the dust balls, tears building in her eyes, thinking he had found them *both,* had left her here with no way to escape, no option but to return to her father—

There it was! Her hand closed around the foot of it; she dragged it out, the real beastie wrapped in part of his kilt. She tore the thing open to make sure he hadn't discovered her ruse and felt the tears stream down her face when she realized she had, by some miracle, managed to dupe him a second time.

Quickly, she wrapped the beastie again and held it close to her chest as she woke Natalie and whispered for her to get dressed.

Liam slept badly, tossing and turning on a horrid mattress, his dreams broken into images of Ellie and the beastie. He woke as the sun was turning the morning sky pink, his head still throbbing.

He rose, shoved into his buckskins, then yanked the frayed bellpull. When the chambermaid appeared, he ordered a bath, then wandered to the small little portal window of his room, braced his arms on either side of it, and stared out into the dirty courtyard. He wondered if she had awakened yet, if she had discovered that he had come while she was sleeping. What would she do now? Return to London and that bastard Farnsworth? Then what? And what of Natalie?

Natalie. His guilt was ripe on that one; for he had promised that child he would rescue her. Of course he had thought not a whit about her silly little game of princesses trapped in towers, at least not until he had found her sobbing in her sleep. And then, of course, he had seen the look of desperation in her blue eyes, had realized that for all her talk of Laria, it was not a game to Natalie. Her despair and her desire to be rescued were very real.

Mo creach, he could scarcely think of it without feeling ill. But he simply could not be her prince.

A knock on the door, and the chambermaid appeared carrying two pails of water, followed by a lad carrying three. They set the pails down and together dragged in a heavy hip bath. When they had departed, Liam shucked the buckskins, and grimacing, stepped into the ice-cold water. With the lye soap, he bathed quickly.

Now he was freezing, and he looked about for something suitable to cover him. *His kilt!* He immediately walked to the knapsack, which he had dropped the moment he entered the room this morning, and reached in, withdrawing the beastie. He noticed, as he untied the plaid that wrapped it, that the corner seemed frayed. That brought a frown to his face—she might have at least *cared* for it. He yanked at the plaid, saw the jagged corner was really a jagged edge, and clenched his jaw. What, was it not enough that she had to dupe him? She thought it necessary to go and ruin his kilt, too?

But then something else caught his eye and made him forget the kilt—the glint of ruby didn't seem quite as bright as it had last night, and he instantly knew, instantly felt the sick thud of his heart falling into the pit of his stomach. He feverishly unwrapped it, and his heart plunged even deeper, making it difficult to breathe. There was no shiny gold of the beastie; there was the dull gray of . . . *what?*

A rock. A bloody fucking *rock!*

His nakedness forgotten, his body warmed by the

rage boiling inside him, Liam angrily threw the plaid aside and stared at the large gray stone. This was *impossible*, inconceivable! She couldn't *possibly* have done it again, but bloody rotten hell, there it was, a big gray rock with a red glass bauble of some sort pasted to it . . . a bauble from the only necklace he had ever seen her wear. Her mother's necklace—she had told him so.

Liam let the thing crash to the floor; the red trinket went flying across the room. He stood, hands on hips, staring down at the rock, hopelessly incapable of understanding how this could have happened, how he could have been made such a monumental fool a second time. The rage burned through him, and he took several steps backward, recoiling from the rock and his carelessness, felt the frustration building in him, threatening to explode—

Into *laughter?*

By God, he'd lost his mind after all, but he was laughing, laughing like a madman as he stumbled toward the bed, shaking his head in bemusement as he donned his buckskin trousers.

Touché, *leannan.* Aye, but if she thought this war was won, she was sorely mistaken. She might have won the battle, but he had only begun to fight.

Twenty-seven

*I*n a small hotel room in Cambridge, near the university, Ellen peered into the small pouch where she kept her money. It was dreadfully close to empty—the coach fares, the cost of the hotel, all of it draining her meager resources to the point that she had just enough now to buy coach fare to reach a port city. Which meant the beastie had to be sold in Cambridge if she was to have enough to take her and Natalie across the sea to France.

She glanced at Natalie, seated at a small table and drawing on the newspaper a gentleman had given them on the coach ride to Cambridge. She had hardly spoken since their predawn departure; she had not complained about their quiet leaving of Peasedown, but had been rather disappointed that Ellen had no better plan in mind than to go to Cambridge.

"What of Captain Lockhart?" she had asked.

Ellen hadn't been able to look at her, had pretended to busy herself with their things. "The captain is not coming."

Natalie remained frostily silent the entire trip.

Ellen could only hope that she'd feel better once they reached France—actually, she could only hope that *she'd* feel better. It was the only thing she would allow herself to think, for she could not bear to think that Natalie might never be happy, might have fallen too far into the abyss of her little fantasies already. Dear God, what an ugly thought.

She immediately put it out of her mind, because frankly, at present, she had a more urgent matter to attend to—the selling of the beastie. The hotel clerk had been nice enough to point out where she might find a number of shops selling novelty items and antiquities, and she was anxious to get on with it, to see if she might interest a shopkeeper in acquiring the Scottish antique.

"I must go out and see if I might find a spot of supper for us, darling," she said to Natalie, putting her hand on the girl's shoulder.

Natalie shrugged it off, continuing to draw.

Ellen repressed a weary sigh. "Do not open the door to anyone, do you understand? Not to *anyone.*"

"Who should come *here?*" Natalie asked coldly, grimacing as she raised her head to glance at the tiny surroundings.

"You'll mind your tongue, young miss," Ellen said wearily. "It's the best I can do for you at present, but I intend to remedy that shortly. In the meantime, you will *not* open that door to *anyone.* Am I quite understood?"

"Quite," Natalie muttered, and dipped her head, focusing on her drawing. Ellen picked up her cloak, took one last look at Natalie and the drawing, and noticed that it was the same as all the others—a castle, a tower. And by the time she returned, the figure of a captive princess would have appeared.

With another heavy sigh, Ellen picked up the beastie and left.

She wandered through the market and onto Magdalene Street, but she met with precious little luck. Unfortunately, two shops had closed, and the one shopkeeper she spoke to recoiled at the sight of the beastie. "An unusual piece of art, madam," he said, his distaste clearly evident. "But I daresay most are looking for something a little less . . . *peacockish.*"

"But isn't there anyone who might want it? After all, it's made of gold, and the rubies certainly could be removed and used in a stunning piece of jewelry."

The man laid a finger next to his nose, grimacing at the thing. "I can think of no one."

A lump of tears burned in her throat.

"Unless . . . I hardly know what he's apt to buy, but there is a proprietor, Mr. Charles Stanley, who rather prides himself on unusual pieces. He's on High Street, just near the university," he said, smiling, apparently relieved for having thought of it.

Ellen hurried to High Street and the establishment of Stanley and Son.

The shop was small, darkly lit, and cluttered with a shocking variety of knickknacks, antiquities, and ornaments. A musty smell permeated everything and the little shop was so crowded, it was difficult to maneuver about the many tables and shelves. There was only one other customer that Ellen could see—a rather large, portly woman with a bonnet so ornate and so big that it defied logic by managing to skirt the cluttered contents of the shop without touching anything.

Ellen made her way to the back of the shop, where a tall, thin man, wearing shirtsleeves held up by arm garters in addition to his visor, was busily working on what looked like a music box. Ellen stood politely for a moment. But when he didn't raise his head, she carefully cleared her throat.

"Yes, yes, just give me a moment, will you?" he snapped, finished what he was doing, then looked up and peered at her closely, squinting. "*Yes?*"

"If you please, sir, I have an item I thought you might be interested in—"

"Not in the market," he said abruptly, and bent over his music box again.

That was it? Not in the market? He would not even do her the honor of *looking* at her item? Oh, no, no, no—he was in the market, all right, or she'd climb across the counter and shove the thing down his long skinny throat. "Pardon, sir, but if you would be so kind to indulge me but a moment—"

"Madam." He looked up and sighed at the ceiling before meeting her gaze. "I am well overstocked, if that is not painfully obvious to you. I've no *room* for your trinkets! I suggest you try Parker—"

"I have *been* to Parker, and he assures me that my object is so unusual and unique that it could only be of interest to *you*, sir."

That gained his attention; he looked at her with all due suspicion over the tops of his spectacles. "He did, did he? Well? What is it, then?"

"A beastie," she said eagerly, moving to unwrap it.

"A *beastie?* What nonsense is that?"

"It's really a rather remarkable story. It comes from Scotland, you see, commissioned by the lover of a doomed adulteress hundreds of years ago. It apparently meant something to the two of them, and he had it caste in gold and rubies. But then her adultery was discovered, and she was sentenced to death, and she gave the statue to her daughter. It has been passed . . . ah, passed to, um, *me* . . . through my, uh . . . Scottish cousin. However, I find it does not combine well with my decor, but as it is cast in gold, I thought perhaps that I might sell it—"

"In debt, are you?" he sneered, watching her unwrap the beastie. "That's a woman for you, no appreciation for even a farthing."

Ellen did not respond to that, just took the last fold of plaid from the beastie.

"Dear *God!*" the proprietor gasped, taking a small step backward. "What a hideously ugly piece!"

"Indeed it is. But as you can see, it is made of gold, and the eyes, they are rubies—"

"Rather ornate for such an ugly thing, isn't it? I couldn't sell that if my life depended on it. No, madam, you may take your hideous little beastie elsewhere."

"But . . . but can't you melt it down? Use the gold for something else?"

"If that is what you want, you should acquaint yourself with a goldsmith. *I* am not a goldsmith; I am a purveyor of fine goods." With that, he turned back to his music box.

The conversation apparently over, Ellen gaped at his back, paralyzed by a new wave of fear and indecision. "*I* think it is quite remarkable."

The woman's voice startled her; Ellen whirled about, saw the huge bonnet looking down at her, underneath which was a plump face with a kind smile.

"Lady Battenkirk," the woman said, inclining her head.

"Miss Farnsworth," Ellen muttered, her gaze falling to the bright red boa the woman was wearing with her walking gown.

"I'm rather a connoisseur of art, really. I take a keen interest in history, too. I find it all *so* engaging. Did I hear you say that this wonderful little thing is from Scotland?" she asked as her chubby fingers caressed the beastie.

"Ah . . . yes. Yes, from Scotland," Ellen said, trying to take in the celery green gown embroidered with yellow. Her bonnet, however, was black, adorned with blue and purple feathers. That, along with the red boa, made for quite a strange combination. But Lady Battenkirk didn't seem to notice her perusal, as she was far too interested in the god-awful beastie.

"It's *marvelous*," she said appreciatively. "Oh, I do so wish my friend Amelia was here!" She sighed, then looked at Ellen with a sly smile. "Amelia does not care for travel, says there is really little reason to leave London at all, and she thinks me gone quite round the bend for traipsing off to all the little villages."

"Oh?"

"She doesn't understand in the least, does she?" Lady Battenkirk exclaimed, waving a thick hand at her. "As it happens, I've been slowly working my way from the very northern tip of England all the way to the southern tip, and I'm determined to take in every little town I might. And do you see my reward? I'm destined to find such treasures as *this!*"

"This?" Ellen asked, confused, pointing at the beastie.

"Yes, *this!*" she said again, and clasping her chubby hands together, rested them atop her ample belly. "Did I hear you correctly, then, my dear? You are in the market to sell it?"

"Yes," Ellen said, far too quickly. "It . . . it hardly fits with my decor, for I am certain I have nothing quite as spectacular as the art *you've* managed to collect in your travels. But it's . . . it's all gold, and the eyes, they are rubies. The mouth, too. And the tail—"

"I should like to give it to Amelia, I think. I would offer you five hundred pounds cash!" Lady Battenkirk announced with cheerful amplification.

The proprietor looked up, shook his head, muttered under his breath.

"Five hundred?" Ellen said weakly. It was not, obviously, what Liam had thought it would bring. But at that moment it sounded like a veritable fortune and she feared if she didn't take it, she'd never find a buyer. "All right," she said weakly, feeling a little ill.

Lady Battenkirk beamed. "How *splendid!* Wait until Amelia sees what I have brought her from Cambridge!

I avow she'll be all atwitter to accompany me to York next month, then, won't she? And how fortuitous that I am to London today? I'll present it to her over supper, I think. Now, what of that lovely plaid?"

"The plaid?"

"Quite nice, that. Beautiful craftsmanship. How much would you like for it?" she asked, fingering Liam's kilt.

Not Liam's kilt. *Not* his kilt. *That* seemed to be even more egregious than selling the beastie. "But . . . but *that* has been cut, and it's really not so useful—"

"Nonsense! It will make for a *divine* collar," she said authoritatively. "I'll add twenty pounds for it."

"Done," Ellen said, and felt the last thread holding her heart aloft snap clean.

Twenty-eight

❧

*L*iam first went to Peasedown Park on the slim chance she had not yet left. But as he suspected, she was long gone, and Lady Peasedown was quite upset. She assumed, of course, that her friend had suffered some slight and had returned to London. He did not correct her.

Liam reached the public coach station well after the morning coaches had left. The clerk did not recall seeing a woman and a young girl in the morning rush. "Ye're certain of it, are ye?" Liam asked sternly, his fist on the counter, leaning across so that he could look directly in the man's eyes.

"Quite certain, sir!" he assured him, leaning back.

Liam pivoted sharply, stalked out of the station and stood on the porch, thinking. There were only three avenues out of King's Lynn: through Norwich, Peterborough, or Cambridge. Cambridge was south, which, he thought, would be too close to London to suit Ellie the Thief. Peterborough was inland, a crossroad to several different towns, but he thought those towns too industrial for such a delicate flower as Conniving Ellie. There was Norwich, then, which he knew the least about, other than it was in the direction of the sea. If she intended to make a quick escape, that seemed the likeliest destination. Then again, who could possibly guess what was going through the reprobate's little mind?

Nevertheless, he decided he had to at least take his chances. The fact of the matter was, his fury had subsided somewhat on the long walk out to Peasedown Park, and one thing had become unquestionably certain—he was more determined than ever to get that accursed beastie. But *this* time, he was doubly determined to retrieve Ellie first, the statue second. This woman, regardless of who she was, or where she belonged (or what she had *done,* damn her!), was, regrettably, perfect for the likes of him, for he was, fundamentally, a man who relished adventure and excitement, and with Ellie, he could rest assured that there would never be a dull moment. Not a single one. This particular cat-and-mouse game was outrageously exasperating, but his hat was off to her, for she played the game exceedingly well. He loved her. Truly, completely, and deeply. And he'd be damned for all eternity if he made the mistake of letting her go again.

Just one small change in his thinking was in order, apparently. He simply had to stop underestimating her!

Liam booked fare on the next public coach to Norwich, which would not, unfortunately, leave until the following morning. Which led Liam right back to the horrid little inn he had endured these few days, and to more ale than he had a right to buy, given his dwindling resources. But when he was well into his cups, he begged a piece of crude paper from the innkeeper and wrote his mother.

> *Greetings from bloody rotten England. Spot of trouble previously mentioned now a fat blot, and causes me to curse the fairer sex in all her many ~~froms~~ forms. How the good Lord above created such an indescribably treacherous creature, I shall undoubtedly still be wondering when they plant me in my grave. ~~Femles~~ Females should not be presented into society unless*

*accompanied by a stern warning for all men, to wit,
have a care, sir, for she will lie and cheat and steal your
bloody heart while she's about. And your kilt. Home
~~son.~~ soon. L.*

He managed to seal it, gave the innkeeper a half-shilling to post it, then fell into a dead sleep. His dreams, full of trolls and Ellie and Lord Peasedown who, by some troublesome transformation, had become Nigel, woke him shortly before dawn. His head throbbing, his belly roiling, Liam was the first passenger on the coach bound for Norwich.

With five hundred twenty-three pounds in her little pouch and safely put away in the pocket of her traveling gown, Ellen felt like a new person of sorts. The weight of worrying about where their next meal would come from had been lifted from her shoulders . . . to be replaced by the new, heavier weight of worrying how she might ever live with herself after what she had done. She did not *want* to be a thief, would have said three months ago it was entirely impossible for her to *be* a thief. It was, therefore, appalling to discover how astonishingly easily she had become a thief.

Ellen made the final preparations to leave Cambridge for France while a listless Natalie sat in the window seat staring morosely at the street below. There was nothing to be done for it, so Ellen went through their things. Having no conception of how long their journey might take, she decided that it would be wise to purchase some dry provisions to see them through. They had an hour before the scheduled departure of the public coach that would take them to Ipswich, where they would board the first vessel to take them south, where they would board a second vessel that would take them to France.

A cold north wind was blowing when Ellen stepped outside of the little hotel. No doubt from Scotland, she thought wryly, as she began walking at a brisk pace down the crowded thoroughfare to the small dry goods store she had seen on her earlier excursions. Her head down, her thoughts on Liam, it was a miracle that she heard anything at all, much less something as simple as a laugh, and an even greater miracle that she even recognized it after all these years. Yet somehow the familiar sound of that laugh pierced her thoughts; she jerked her head up, quickly scanned the crowd, and her heart climbed right into her throat and filled it, choking the air from her.

Daniel.

The sight of him was so shockingly unexpected, so incredibly unreal that she hadn't even realized she had stopped, mid-step, until a man gruffly reprimanded her for it as he was forced to step around to avoid colliding with her. But Ellen scarcely heard him; her mind and heart were spinning in savage turmoil. Her first pathetically deranged thought was that he had come for her. But she quickly realized that in addition to that being absolutely ludicrous, it couldn't possibly even be true, for how would he have known where to find her? Which meant, then, that this was nothing more than one of those strange little coincidences that rarely happened in a lifetime, something almost too odd to be true.

Yet there he was, flesh and blood. Ellen watched him walking with a woman. Two small boys trailed behind them, arguing and occasionally hitting one another. He was heavier than when she'd known him, his jowls fleshy like a soft-bellied country gent. With the woman on his arm, they strolled casually down the lane toward her, pausing to look in the different shop windows and seeming, Ellen thought angrily, perfectly at ease.

Seeming like a gentleman who had earned the right to be happy, one who had, presumably, lived an honorable life. He did *not* look like the dishonest bastard that he was.

How astounding it was to be looking at him now, she thought, as he casually moved closer. How astonishing, after all those years of pining for him, praying and hoping that he would come back, that she could be so frightfully happy that he hadn't. The blackguard had plunged her into hell, but Ellen was suddenly quite certain that it might have been far worse had he come back. He had never loved her, not like Liam. He had no honor in him at all, as did Liam. In fact, he was blatantly insignificant compared to Liam, reprehensible and pathetic.

The stabbing pain that rent her heart, then, was *not* for Daniel, it was for Liam, and she marveled at how much she missed him. More than all the days and weeks and months and years she had missed Daniel. Which only made her guilt soar to the point that she felt quite ill again.

Whatever possessed her to step in Daniel's path, she likely would never know, but there she was, suddenly darting around people just to stand in front of him, to see his expression. She was not to be disappointed; he recognized her almost immediately, and just as immediately tried to put a gap between him and the woman on his arm by dropping her elbow and stepping away from her.

"Daniel," she said, the name bitter on her tongue.

"My lucky stars, if it isn't Ellen Farnsworth! What a delight!" he said, and smiled that charming smile that had ensnared her as a girl. Except that now she didn't see it as charming in the least—she saw it for the oily, rapacious smile that it was. "Are you in Cambridge now?" he asked cheerfully, as if there were no history between them, as if there were no child between them, as if he had not forsaken her.

I'm nowhere now. I have no home. "London," she managed to choke out as she looked at the straining buttons of his waistcoat, the stained neckcloth. The trousers, threadbare at the pockets. Scuffed boots. He was paunchy, and his fleshy face showed none of the signs of beauty she had once seen in him. God in heaven, what had she ever loved about this man?

"I must say," he said, taking another step away from the woman and two boys, "that I'm rather surprised—"

"I'm quite sure that you are," she said acidly, and hearing her tone, the two boys stopped their fighting and looked at Ellen.

"Daniel?" the woman behind him mewled, and for the first time, Ellen looked at her. She was nondescript and rather plain in the face. Her figure was square, undoubtedly made so by the two little hellions now hanging on her skirts. Two ill-mannered urchins who could only be Natalie's brothers. *That* thought sent a cold shiver down her spine.

"Oh!" Daniel said, laughing, unable to distance himself from his wife. "Rather impolite of me. Darling, this is Miss . . . ?"

Ellen said nothing, just looked at him, let him guess.

"Ah . . . well, Miss Ellen Farnsworth. And this, of course, is my wife, Mrs. Goodman." He smiled thinly at his cow of a wife. "Miss Farnsworth and I were acquainted many years ago, one summer when I was in London."

"*Acquainted?*" Ellen echoed, incredulous. "I beg your pardon, but is that what you tell yourself so that you might sleep? That we were *acquainted*? Do you mean to say that you never pause to consider what a despicable rake you were, preying on a naïve debutante?"

"I beg your pardon, Miss Farnsworth!" Mrs. Goodman snapped indignantly, her back stiffening as she moved to stand next to her husband. One of the boys squeezed through the gap between his parents and stood directly in front of Ellen, looking up at her curiously, almost gleefully.

Daniel laughed nervously, pulled his son back and behind him, then tried again to step away from his plain wife. "It's a long story, dear," he said dismissively over his shoulder, then looked at Ellen again, his lecherous gaze wandering her body. "Are . . . are you in Cambridge long, Miss Farnsworth? Might we have a chance to renew our acquaintance?"

Ellen's shout of laughter startled several passersby. "You must be out of your *mind!* I shouldn't renew my acquaintance with *you,* sir, to save my very life! Haven't you *any* idea what you did—" She caught herself, stopped there, the image of Natalie suddenly looming in her mind.

"What I did?" he asked, laughing nervously, his eyes darting to everyone around them. "Why, I'm certain I've no idea what you mean! Your very own cousin Malcolm has never given me cause to believe that you were anything but perfectly well!"

He knew. The rotten bloody bounder *knew! No.* No, no, no, she would not sully Natalie's life any more than it had been with the likes of *him.* She could now readily accept what she had known all these years, in spite of the lies she had tried to tell herself. She had been used by this man. Terribly. Unconscionably. The attributes she had ascribed to his character had been hopelessly naïve and dead wrong. He had used her up and tossed her aside, and she would die before she would allow this . . . this *snake* to do the same to Natalie. As far as she was concerned, he had given up his right to Natalie when he abandoned her mother more than ten years ago.

"I beg your pardon, madam, but I cannot possibly

imagine what you think my husband has done to *you*," the woman chimed in.

"Mary, *hush*," Daniel snapped, then turned that oily, loathsome smile to Ellen again. "Clearly, there has been a terrible misunderstanding, Miss Farnsworth. Perhaps if you would consent to allow me to call on you on the morrow—"

"Shut up, Daniel," Ellen said easily, and turned her gaze to his wife, who looked at Ellen as if she were a madwoman. That was quite all right, really. She *was* a madwoman. Mad to have ever fallen in love with him. Mad to have ever pined for him. Her mother and father had been quite right. He was nowhere near good enough for her, not then, and certainly not now. "I'd be quite careful if I were you, Mary," she said calmly. "For if you sleep with snakes, you will most surely get bit." She turned away then, ignoring the woman's cry of outrage and Daniel's patronizing, *"My dear Miss Farnsworth, please don't dash off in such bad humor! You've clearly misunderstood!"*

Ellen kept walking, her head high, her indignation raging, oblivious to everything and everyone in her path. She should have felt liberated, freed at last from the heart sickening memories. She should have been relieved! At *peace*.

But she wasn't any of those things.

No, she was sick unto death, because she knew, with all certainty, that she was, in her own despicable way, just like Daniel. She had betrayed a man who loved her deeply, just as Daniel had betrayed her. She had left him without explanation, just as Daniel had left her. She was no better than the snake she had left slithering behind her, and she had never despised herself as much as she did at this moment.

Ellen continued on to the dry goods store, bought several provisions, then dragged herself back to the small hotel, her heart shattered, her mind blank.

Natalie was pacing the floor. "The coach leaves soon, Mother," she said anxiously as Ellen walked into the room and tossed aside her cloak.

"I know," she said softly, and continued to the bed, where she withdrew the money pouch from her pocket and dumped the contents on the coverlet. Staring down at the roll of bills, Ellen felt the nausea roil about in her belly, threatening to erupt. How was it she had ever managed to convince herself that she had reasonable cause to do what she did? Even if that money gave her the freedom she craved, even if it freed Natalie from a certain untenable future, it simply *did not belong to her.* It was Liam's money; Liam's hope. It belonged to him, and she had betrayed his trust . . . did she really think she could steal from him, too?

"Mother, what are you doing?" Natalie cried. "We'll miss the coach!"

Ellen sighed, sank onto the edge of the bed, and held out her hand for Natalie. Reluctantly, the girl put her small hand in her palm. "Do you want to go to France, Natalie?" she asked softly.

Natalie dropped her gaze, looked at her boots. She did not answer for a long moment, but finally said, "No," her voice barely above a whisper.

"Then we shan't go," Ellen said emphatically. "I've a better idea."

Natalie's head snapped up; she looked at her mother suspiciously. "May we go home? To London?"

Ellen shook her head and gave her daughter a smile that shone straight from her heart. "No, Natalie, not London. We are going to Laria."

Twenty-nine

❧

In Norwich, the clerk at the public coach station did not remember seeing a woman and young girl coming from King's Lynn. "The King's Lynn coach and one from Thetford come at about the same time every day," he said to Liam. "I can't rightly say if I would have noticed, what with all the hubbub."

Hubbub. Mary Queen of Scots, did *all* of life pass these clerks by? "Ye'd have noticed this one, ye would," Liam insisted. "Tall, quite bonny. The lass just like her mother."

"I'm sorry, I do not recall," he said, and started to turn away, but Liam put a hand on his arm.

"Think again," he said low.

The clerk looked at his hand, then at Liam, his eyes narrowing suspiciously. "I beg your pardon, sir, but does the lady know you are trying to reach her?"

His frustration was getting in the way of good soldiering, and Liam instantly retreated behind a forced smile. "Ah, I see ye've found me out, no?" He put a hand to his nape, rubbed it. "All right, then, here 'tis. The truth is that the lady and I, we've had a wee falling out. I've no' been as . . . er . . . *constant* as I should have been."

"*Ah,*" the clerk said, nodding, exchanging a purely male smile with Liam.

"She's, ah . . . a wee bit miffed with me, then," he said, looking sheepish.

"I completely understand, sir."

"What of the coaches bound for the sea?" Liam asked, before the clerk could understand anything more.

"The sea, you say?" he asked, fully in Liam's camp now, and wrinkled his brow as he looked at his log. "It really all depends, sir. Your, ah . . . *friend* might have taken a coach to Ipswich if she had in mind to cross the sea—" He paused, looked over Liam's shoulder and whispered conspiratorially, "Do you think it's as bad as that?"

Liam shrugged, feigned a helpless look. "I canna rightly say. The female brain is no' something I'm adept at understanding."

"No man is, sir," the clerk snorted. "Ipswich would be the logical direction if she thought to eventually *cross* the sea. But if not Ipswich, I'd suggest perhaps Yarbrough. But she'd not find more than a fishing boat there, so it's quite possible she might have journeyed to Cromer, or Sheringham, for a little sun by the seashore, although the cliffs—"

"The coach to Ipswich," Liam interrupted him, before the clerk gave him a discourse on the many coastal attractions. "When does it depart, then?"

"Twice daily, sir. At nine o'clock in the morning, and then again at three. Shall I reserve your fare?"

He almost agreed, but stopped himself. What, was he to chase her to Ipswich, now? On no more grounds than this man's guess? This *chase,* he was beginning to see, was more and more absurdly unreasonable—he couldn't be entirely certain she had even come this way at all, much less go traipsing after her to God knew where. For all he knew, she had gone to Peterborough, or Cambridge. It was possible she never even left King's Lynn, a bloody annoying thought that had occurred to him once he was miles from there.

"Sir?"

Liam looked up. "Suppose she had come to Norwich and simply asked after lodging—which inn would she have been directed to, then?"

"The Westwick Arms, just round the corner there and toward the center of town."

"Any other?"

"Not that *I* would recommend, no sir."

Liam straightened, dug in his pocket for one of his last crowns and tossed it on the counter. "Thank ye kindly . . . and if ye happen to remember aught else, ye can find me at the Westwick Arms."

"Good luck, sir," the clerk said, pocketing the crown.

Aye, good luck. He was fairly certain he'd spent all the good luck he was going to get. Liam tipped his hat, adjusted his knapsack, and walked out of the station in the direction the clerk had indicated. This was preposterous! He was down to his last few pounds, had nothing to show for it but a hole in the bottom of his boot. It was loathsome to even think of going home like this, empty-handed and having failed so miserably in his mission. But what else could he do? Spend his last few pounds in some mad dash across the English countryside after a woman? Particularly when he had no clue, no real intuition, no evidence of where she might have gone? She could be in Scotland for all he knew!

Face up to it, then, ye goddamn fool! Ye've been handed a good drubbing and ye've no one to blame but yerself for thinking with yer jock instead of yer soldier's mind, ye bloody imbecile!

Oh, *aye,* he had quite bungled this one, hadn't he? By the time he reached the Westwick Arms, Liam's already foul humor was worsening. He marched up to the desk clerk, dropped his knapsack, and put both hands flat on the counter before him.

The young man behind the counter seemed quite startled; he reared back, blinking big doelike brown eyes. "M-might I assist you, sir?" he asked, his wide-eyed gaze now traveling Liam's scar.

"*Aye,* ye might. A room, and be quick about it, then."

The man hastily pulled out a ledger, asked his name, and peeked up at him as if he expected him to come across the counter at any moment. He handed Liam the key and asked timidly, "Will that be all, sir?"

Liam took the key and leaned forward until he was just a few inches from the cowardly clerk. "No. I am looking for a woman in the company of a wee lass, about so tall," he said, indicating with his hand Natalie's height. "The woman, she is bonny, with lovely blond hair and a fair complexion. Has she sought lodging here?"

"I, ah . . . I'm not certain sir. I could, ah . . . I could check the names on our register."

"Farnsworth. Miss Ellen Farnsworth."

The man opened the ledger in which he had just registered Liam and ran his finger down a list of names. When his finger reached Liam's entry, he looked up, shook his head. "I'm sorry, sir, but I'm afraid we've no one by that name."

Ah . . . she hadn't used her own name, of course. *What name, then?* "Peasedown!" he snapped.

The man frowned, but ran his finger down the ledger all the same, squinting this time. "Umm . . . no Peasedown." He moved to shut the ledger, but Liam slapped his hand on it, forcing it open again.

"Look again! Fitzpatrick! Allen! Miller! I donna care what name, just *look* again!" he shouted, jabbing the ledger with his finger. "A bonny woman with a wee lass! Is that so hard to recall, then?"

The man gasped as he took a timid step backward. "I beg your pardon sir," he said weakly, his eyes now wide with terror. "But I do not believe we have an unescorted woman with a small child staying at this establishment."

Liam slapped the countertop, muttered a Gaelic curse beneath his breath that essentially condemned the young man to the life of a toad, and before the toad could hop off and summon help, he pivoted sharply and ascended the stairs to the room he had paid to let with what was almost his last pound.

Fortunately, Cambridge being the intellectual town that it was, there was quite a well-stocked lending library and there were two fine bookstores, which were all Ellen and Natalie needed to find Loch Chon. Poring over maps of Scotland, they finally found it and, their heads together, stared at the little blue mark northwest of Glasgow.

"Do you think it is very far away?" Natalie asked, tracing her finger to the edge of the map, which represented the very top of England.

"I do believe it is," Ellen said thoughtfully.

"Then shouldn't we set out soon?"

Ellen smiled at Natalie. "I think we should set out straightaway."

They departed Cambridge the very next morning.

It was, however, a long, arduous journey north, full of different sorts of people (and smells, Natalie helpfully pointed out), badly rutted roads, and stark, windswept landscapes. But by the time they reached Scotland, the barren landscape was giving way to gently rolling hills where sheep grazed and dark ponds glistened in the weak sun. The climate was colder, and the trees had turned brilliant shades of red, yellow, and purple. Ruined castle keeps dotted the landscape here and there, giving rise to Natalie's active imagination, and she regaled Ellen (as well as their fellow passengers) with tales of her princess, who, it seemed, led a rather extraordinary life, fighting off the English when she wasn't bearing children, withstanding capture several times over by fierce knights, and being forced against her will to marry (Ellen counted four such unfortunate events), then finally succumbing to true love and happiness with the last knight (who resembled Liam, Ellen couldn't help notice, what with the scar). Together, princess and warrior reclaimed the princess's castle, where she, her knight, and at least a dozen children resided happily ever after.

For once Ellen didn't mind Natalie's fantasy, for the girl was as happy as Ellen had seen her since leaving Cornwall more than two years ago. She stayed glued to the small coach window, studying every feature of the landscape, pointing out all sights of interest to her fellow passengers. They all looked when so prompted, and Ellen began to appreciate the stark beauty of Scotland. It was easy to see why Liam loved it. Easy to understand why he had found London so confining.

It was an awfully long trek, but they succeeded in reaching Glasgow in one piece. Ellen even managed to find suitable overnight lodgings for the two of them, complete with much needed hot baths.

It was the trek to Loch Chon that would, apparently, be an issue.

"Ye're to *where*, miss?" the man behind the little fare window asked her when she attempted to purchase passage.

"Loch Chon," she said, smiling.

That earned her a snort and a shake of his head. "Have ye the *slightest* notion where Loch Chon is, then?"

"Yes!" she said helpfully. "Just north, on the road to Loch Katrine and Ben Lommond—"

"*I* know where it is!" he snapped.

"Oh." She gripped her reticule tightly and cleared her throat. "Well, then . . . about the fare," she said, fearing suddenly that the maps in Cambridge might have been less than accurate.

He shook his head again, and looked as if he thought she was making some appalling mistake. "I can sell ye passage to Strathblane, no further. From there ye'll have to hire someone to carry ye to Killearn and Balfron. And then, if ye be lucky, ye might find a body to carry ye on as far as Aberfoyle. If the snows haven't come yet, that is."

"To Aber . . . ?"

"*Aberfoyle!*" he snapped. "*Ach* . . . and from Aberfoyle I canna help ye, lass. Ye'll have to make do from there."

There it was, that sick feeling in the pit of her stomach again, the one that warned her she had embarked on something terribly ill-advised. Nonetheless, she smiled brightly at the hateful man. "Well then! I should think I'll just inquire at the Aberfoyle coach house—"

His snort of laughter sounded more like a bark. "There's no *coach* house in Aberfoyle," he said, rolling his eyes. "Ye'll be lucky to find even a public house, ye will. Ah, but 'tis yer money, no' mine," he said as he wrote something down. He handed her two vouchers through the little window between them. "Two pounds per traveler. The coach to Strathblane leaves at eight o'clock on the morrow."

Ellen nodded and handed over the four pounds, which he quickly tucked away.

"Good day, then," he said, and pulled the window shade closed.

Ellen picked up the vouchers, stared at the closed window. "You've come too far, Ellen," she muttered low to herself. "Do not allow yourself to be undone by some batty old man—"

"I canna *see* ye, but I can certainly *hear* ye!" the batty old man snapped from behind the window, startling Ellen so badly that she quickly retreated outside, into the cold rain that had begun to fall. Not a good omen, that. But it was too late to turn back now, and even if she tried, she rather thought Natalie would have her head for it. If Aberfoyle had only a public house, so be it. She would think of something.

As it turned out, even Strathblane had little more than a public house. Natalie clung desperately to her skirts, her blue eyes wide as she took in the rough-looking patrons as Ellen spoke with the innkeeper, who, finally, over the din of several drinking men, shouted *"Seamus!"*

A man in dirty clothing and a soiled cap appeared from the crowd, eyeing Ellen as the innkeeper spoke to him in something sounding a bit like English and a bit like he was choking. Seamus, whoever he was, nodded as he listened, looking at Natalie.

"Aye," he said simply after the innkeeper had finished whatever it was he had said. "Ten pound."

"I beg your pardon?" Ellen asked politely.

"He'll take ten pound for the trouble of taking ye to Aberfoyle, then," the innkeeper repeated.

"B-but . . . it didn't cost me ten pounds to come all the way from England!" she stammered.

The innkeeper shrugged. "Seamus, he's all we 'ave to carry ye. If ye're desiring to reach Aberfoyle, I'd suggest ye agree to his price, miss."

Ellen looked at Seamus, then at the innkeeper. Both of them returned identical, stoic looks, and Ellen could see that they cared neither one way nor the other if she rode or walked or flew like a bird to Aberfoyle. "Very well," she said irritably, digging in her reticule. "But I'll expect to be put down there as soon as possible, sir." She held out the ten pounds to him.

Seamus casually took the money and shoved it into his pocket. "Aye," he said, and grinned. With all three of his yellowed teeth.

And Seamus meant to leave immediately, it seemed, in spite of the relentless rain and increasing fog. Ellen wouldn't have minded quite so much had Seamus had an actual carriage. But he had a wagon. A creaky old wagon pulled by a braying mule. And over the back of the wagon, he had strung a canvas tarpaulin, which was painted on one side with a foul-smelling oil to repel water.

"I beg your pardon sir, but it is *raining,*" Ellen said, gesturing to the sky as she and Natalie stood there, side by side, their bonnets getting heavier and drooping lower with the weight of the rain.

Seamus said nothing, just lifted the tarpaulin and gestured for them to crawl underneath. Ellen gaped at him in disbelief, then snorted. "You cannot be serious, sir! You expect us to put ourselves under that . . . that *thing?*"

"*Suithad,*" he said, gesturing again. "*A bheil thu a' dol?*"

"He wants us to climb aboard, Mother," Natalie said, as if Ellen hadn't figured that out quite yet.

"*Come!*" he said, only louder.

"I think we should do as he says," Natalie politely opined, and walked to the end of the wagon. The man leaned over, cupped his hands, said something in that strange language, and Natalie put her foot in his hand, as if she had understood every blasted word. He lifted her up; she landed with a bit of a thud on the back of the wagon, and crawled to the back. "There's hay, and it's quite dry!" she called to Ellen.

"Oh, for the love of God!" Ellen exclaimed angrily, and glared at Seamus. "You might have at least *mentioned* that for the princely sum of ten pounds there would *not* be a carriage!" He gestured at the wagon again. She stomped forward, and when Seamus leaned over, his hands cupped, she laughed derisively. "Oh, I think *not*, sir!" she said, and using both hands, her knee, and a lot of grunting, managed to climb onto the back of that atrocious wagon by herself. And she did not appreciate, not one tiny bit, the man's smile when she began to crawl to the back of the wagon on all fours.

The ride was excruciatingly uncomfortable, in spite of Natalie's attempts to assure Ellen that it was much more comfortable than a public coach, since they could stretch their legs all the way out. The girl did not seem to mind the definite smell of cow or horse that had last used this hay. And she pointed out that the canvas tarpaulin, oiled with whatever that foul-smelling scent was, did keep them quite dry. Ellen grudgingly admitted that it *was* a roomier mode of travel than the public coaches, and remarkably dry, given the almost wintry conditions, but the trails that passed for roads north of Strathblane were, to the average person, impassable. Not to Seamus and his erstwhile ass—they labored along until Ellen was aching in every joint of her body.

When the wagon did at last stop, she jerked the tarpaulin back—only to be hit square in the eye with a fat raindrop. "Are we in Aberfoyle?" she asked.

Soaked through, Seamus looked down at her as if she had lost her mind.

"Killearn," he said simply, and disappeared from her view by jumping off the rider's perch. A moment later, the tarpaulin was lifted from the back of the wagon, and Natalie scrambled forward. Ellen sighed, followed suit, exhausting herself with the struggle to keep her gown down around her ankles.

Killearn was little more than a few thatched houses and a mill of some sort, and she worried when Seamus motioned for them to follow him. The improbable but possible notion that Seamus was some sort of murderous criminal crossed Ellen's mind, but instead of taking them behind the mill and killing them, he took them into the house of one elderly lady. She regarded them curiously as Seamus spoke with her for a moment. She nodded; Seamus handed her a few coins and then left, purposefully ignoring Ellen's demands to know his exact whereabouts. The woman, sensing her distress, waved her hand toward a darkened room that seemed to be the only other room in the entire little house, and motioned her to follow. Ellen was having none of that, but Natalie, terrifically unafraid, followed the woman

After a moment, she called happily, "It's a chamber-pot, Mother!"

All right. Ellen had to admit that was indeed a rather happy bit of information.

When they finally emerged from the adjoining room, the woman motioned to a long crude table on which sat two steaming bowls. She smiled a toothless smile and motioned for them to sit.

"I wonder if our *driver* is coming back," Ellen remarked in a whisper as she and Natalie sat themselves.

"Of course he is," Natalie said authoritatively, and picked up a wooden spoon. She took a careful bite, wrinkled her nose a bit, and looked at Ellen. "It's a bit odd-tasting. But I like it!"

Ellen looked at her bowl. It *looked* like stew, but it had a rather peculiar smell to it. Not wanting to offend the woman, she took a bite. Actually, it *was* rather tasty! Having eaten nothing but dry goods provisions for several days now, she and Natalie devoured the hot stew. In the end, Ellen smiled at the woman, made a gesture against her belly to indicate she was quite sated. "What is it?" she asked, pointing at the bowl.

"*Haggis*," the woman said.

"We must remember that, mustn't we, Natalie?" she remarked, to which the girl nodded her head enthusiastically.

As it turned out, Seamus had not left them there, just as Natalie said he wouldn't, but returned an hour later, wearing dry clothes and a wide-brimmed hat. He spoke to the woman, then gestured for Ellen and Natalie to follow. Into the tarpaulin-covered wagon they went, and notably, without argument. Ellen hadn't realized quite how exhausted she was, and in spite of the rough go, she and Natalie drifted off to sleep, snuggled down into the hay with Ellen's cloak to keep them warm.

It was Seamus who woke them, lifting the canvas. A bright beam of sunlight struck Ellen's face, and she came up with a start, sputtering. Seamus laughed. They had slept long enough for the rain to stop and the night to pass, and had awakened to a morning that was clear and cold. Moreover, they were in another small village of sorts. As Natalie scampered down, Ellen tried to make something of her hair.

"Aberfoyle," said Seamus proudly.

Aberfoyle? Lord in heaven, the clerk at the coach station had been right. Ellen glanced around, grimacing inwardly, for there was hardly anything of Aberfoyle save a few shops. They disembarked from the odd wagon (causing quite a stir among the few inhabitants of Aberfoyle), and tried to straighten themselves as best they could as Seamus delivered their bags to Ellen's feet, then proceeded to turn his wagon about. With a wave to the few onlookers, he started back the way they had come.

Ellen and Natalie picked up their portmanteaux, and walked into the first shop they saw, which, oddly enough, given that they were in the middle of absolutely nowhere, was a confectioner. The elderly proprietor confirmed what Ellen already knew—there was no ride to be hired from Aberfoyle to Loch Chon. But the confectioner took pity on Natalie (gave her sweetmeats), and suggested they could walk to Loch Ard, which was just south of Loch Chon. "No' that ye'll find anything there, mistress," he said in heavily accented English. "Naugh' there but a bunch of coos."

"Oh," Ellen said, uncertain what a "coo" was. "Actually, I'm bound for a place called Talla Dileas. Do you know it?"

The shopkeeper blinked. "Talla Dileas?" he repeated, disbelieving.

"Yes," she said emphatically, nodding. "Do you know it?"

"Aye, everyone knows it. Do they no' send a carriage for ye, then?"

"Oh . . . I, ah . . . Well, no. No, they haven't. Perhaps because they aren't expecting me, exactly. You see, I've something for him—er, *them,* that I'd like to deliver. Is it possible to get there from here?"

"*Ach,* what is wrong with ye, then, ye'd come all this way unannounced? Come on, gather yer things," he said gruffly, and motioned them to follow. "I'll no' send a bairn to walking eight miles in high country, I won't. I'll take ye as far as Loch Ard, and ye can walk from there, God willin'. But ye shouldna come so far without making arrangements, lass, for 'tis wild country here."

"I won't do it again," she quickly assured him.

But the shopkeeper continued to berate her for what he termed her foolhardiness all the way to Loch Ard. Ellen could hardly argue that, and she and Natalie nodded politely to his ranting, half in English and half in the language they had heard Liam speak. Really, they scarcely heard him at all; they were overwhelmed by the pristine beauty of the countryside. It was just as Liam had said—hills of purple rolling into streams and rivers and lakes so deep and dark and clear one could not see the bottom. Trees rose majestically to the sky, forming canopies of red and gold and yellow, absorbing so much sunlight that only the strongest rays made it down to the forest floor, giving it a sort of dreamlike look. Fallen leaves and pine needles formed a carpet throughout the forest on either side of the rugged path, and nothing could be heard for miles but the creak of the wagon, the occasional chirp of birds, and the rustling of the trees in the late autumn wind.

Natalie seemed just as enthralled; when the confectioner pulled aside and pointed to a path leading north, she eagerly jumped down. "Dileas, she's up there, she is," he said.

Ellen followed the point of his finger, saw a narrow path disappearing into the wood. "Up *where?*"

"There," he said, jabbing a crooked finger at a mountain. The shopkeeper helped them unload their bags, warned them of the dangers of straying off the path, then ended with a cheery, "Kindest regards to the Lockharts, if ye please!" With that, he turned his wagon about and headed back down to Aberfoyle, whistling cheerfully.

Ellen and Natalie looked up the path he had indicated and exchanged a wary look. "Well. We've come *this* far," Ellen said carefully.

"Yes," Natalie agreed.

"We might as well go on with it and find Laria, don't you think?"

"I *think,*" Natalie said, less certainly, but hauled up her bag nonetheless, and they set out for "up there."

They walked blindly uphill, for the uneven, rocky path wound around, and the trees were so thick that they obscured any view of what lay ahead. Dragging their bags soon became something of an ordeal, and they began to walk a ways, then rest, then walk again for what seemed like an eternity. When Natalie began to tire, Ellen had no notion of how much farther they might have to walk. Feeling a little desperate, she made a game. They took turns naming all the rooms Talla Dileas had, both of them picturing a castle to rival any of the king's.

They could not possibly have imagined the horrible monstrosity that awaited them as they rounded the last bend of the path, but there it was, suddenly looming before them in a large clearing, so horrible that Ellen came to a dead stop, gaping in disbelief. It was not at all what she had imagined, but a huge, monolith of a house, a hodgepodge of various styles and architectures, as if over the centuries different houses had been piled on top and beside one another. Part of it was castle—dark stone, turrets, and slivers of windows. Yet other parts looked almost Georgian, with pinkish new stone. Windows of various shapes and sizes glinted the sun back to them.

"There are sixteen chimneys, Mother," Natalie said, her voice full of awe.

"And two battlements," Ellen added, curious about that.

"It *is* Laria!" Natalie exclaimed happily. Ellen jerked her gaze to her daughter. How she could see something so foreboding and think it a kingdom of dreams . . . But never mind that, for Natalie was running toward the mansion.

Thirty

❧

*M*ared found their only producing bull tied to a tree on Din Footh.

Seething, she stood there, debating whether or not to walk on to the Douglas's house and surprise him with a fist to the nose or to untie the poor thing (actually, he didn't seem to be in *too* dire of straits, since he was munching quite contentedly on a patch of clover), walk home, and write another scathing letter to the Traitor to all Highlanders, Payton Douglas.

While she much preferred the former, she chose the latter, since the last time he had pulled such a prank she *had* gone to his door, only to find him entertaining Miss Hermione Lewis, who had just returned from Edinburgh and obviously thought herself rather grand. It had irritated Mared so very much that she had gone off in a wee bit of a pique and, in doing so, had stomped right into a rabbit hole and twisted her ankle. Letter writing seemed to be safer, really, and she could put an awful lot on paper that she couldn't seem to remember when she was glaring at those gray eyes of his, and all in all, she'd just as soon *not* know who the Douglas was entertaining.

So there she was, in the old great hall, starting on her fourth attempt:

To the Odiously Objectionable, Highly Offensive,
Overbearingly Arrogant Laird Douglas

amid the clutter of the first three attempts, when Dudley walked in and cleared his throat.

"Yes, Dudley?" she asked, sighing testily, upset that she *still* could not seem to find the right words to convey her feelings.

"A strange thing, miss, and as the laird is nowhere to be found, nor her ladyship . . . a woman and wee lass at the door, desiring to speak with Captain Lockhart."

Mared looked up from her letter. "To *whom?*"

"The captain, miss."

Payton, that bloody scoundrel! He was up to something, she was certain of it, and was instantly on her feet. *Ah, but wait . . .* Payton knew full well that Liam was in England, as he was forever asking after him. Not Payton, then. Mared sat again. "What woman would come for Liam?" she thought aloud.

"Beggin' yer pardon, miss, but she's . . . *Sassenach.*"

Mared gasped.

Dudley nodded feverishly; his nose wrinkled with his distaste, and whispered, "*English!* And high born, by the sound of it."

"Dear God!" Mared exclaimed. This could not be good—Liam's letters home had been . . . well, in a word, *odd.* They all suspected something was dreadfully amiss—a *spot of trouble* for Liam (such as he had written in the last letter they received) *usually* meant a matter rather stupendous in consequence for mere mortals. No, this was not good, not good at all, and Mared stood again and marched for the door.

"I'll see to it," she said with great authority, and sailed down the long, narrow corridor to the front door, which was, in actuality, an old fortress entrance, which meant that it was extremely narrow, so no more than one attacker could enter at a time. Highlanders were really so very clever.

She opened the thick wood-planked door, stepped

through the narrow entrance, and caught a breath in her throat. It was a woman all right, a bonny one. Tall and willowy, blond (she was missing a bonnet, actually), and fair complexioned (which made Mared instantly aware of how starkly different she was, with her own thick black hair and rather pink complexion, what with all the walking around Loch Chon). Even more startling was that the woman looked very refined, as if she'd never seen a day of the bloody sun. Which would not have surprised her, as she was English, and Mared had the distinct impression that English ladies sat about all day fanning themselves.

But *this* one surprised her because, first, she was calling on Liam, *not* Griffin, and second, her hair and clothing were in disarray. She looked, quite literally, as if she had been dragged to Loch Chon. Even more astounding, there were *two* of them, for standing beside her was a smaller version of the woman, just as mussed.

"Ah . . . how do you do? Might I introduce myself?" the woman asked in clipped, proper English.

"Aye," Mared said, peering cautiously at her. She had lovely blue eyes, didn't she? Not the green moldy color that she and her brothers were cursed with.

"*Ahem.*" The woman smiled, nervously tried to smooth her horribly ratted hair. "I'm afraid I look a dreadful fright. I had no idea how . . . *arduous* it would be to come here."

And why wouldn't she know *that?* Mared instantly wondered.

"Um . . . I am Miss Ellen Farnsworth. And this is my daughter, Natalie." She paused and looked at the girl, who was staring at Mared as if she were seeing a ghost. "Say 'Good day,' Natalie."

"Good day."

Mared nodded at her and was a little unnerved by

the way the girl stared at her, as if she were in some kind of shock.

"You . . . you must be Mared—er, *Miss* Lockhart—"

Mared jerked her gaze back to the woman so quickly that it startled her. But not nearly as much as she startled Mared. How could she possibly know who she was?

"I . . . well, I know you have no idea who *I* am, and why should you?" She nervously cleared her throat again. "But, you see, it happens that I am acquainted with Captain Lockhart, and he described you perfectly. And it happens that I . . . I have something I should like to give him." She paused, shook her head as she thought about what she'd said. "I don't mean I have a *gift*, but rather something that belongs to him."

Instantly, Mared suspected a trick. She could hardly be the younger sister of Liam Lockhart without learning a thing or two about intrigue and sneaking about and all that. And Liam's letters *had* been very enigmatic. What could a woman like this possibly have of Liam's? Reinforcements, that's what Liam would say. If one is on sinking ground, one should seek reinforcements.

Mared instantly stepped back into the narrow door passage. "Beg yer pardon, Miss Farnsworth, but I . . ." But she *what*—needed to get reinforcements? "Ah . . . a moment, please," she said, and hastily shut the door in front of her, even debated locking it, lest this Farnsworth lady thought to come in.

" 'Tis *odd*, eh?" Dudley whispered.

At the very least! Mared whirled about, grabbed Dudley by the sleeve, and raced for the study where she knew Griffin to be, going over the estate accounts. Not bothering to knock, she burst through the door, startling him.

"Mary Queen of Scots, Mared, can ye at least *attempt* to enter a room like a lady, then?" he said irritably.

"There's an Englishwoman at the door who has

come for Liam. She claims to have something belonging to him, she does."

"What?" Griffin said, looking equally alarmed, and coming to his feet.

"A *bonny* Englishwoman!" Mared added excitedly. "With a *lass!*"

Griffin did not need to hear more. He strode past Mared and Dudley, down the narrow corridor. When he swung the front door open, with Mared practically glued to his back, the woman was still standing there, but the girl had seated herself on the stone steps, and quickly clambered to her feet.

"Oh!" Miss Farnsworth said brightly when she saw Griffin. "My, you look something alike, don't you? There's a resemblance, certainly."

Mared and Griffin exchanged a wary look.

"Oh, no, I see what you think of that. I didn't mean the two of *you,* although there is certainly a resemblance there, too. I meant that *you,* sir, look a bit like Captain Lockhart."

The girl nodded in agreement, then resumed her ogling of Mared.

"Then . . . then ye've seen our brother, eh?" Griffin asked carefully.

Miss Farnsworth broke into a wreath of smiles. "Many times! We were, ah . . . acquainted in London. I am Miss Ellen Farnsworth, and this is my daughter, Natalie."

The girl dipped into an instant curtsy and bounced back up again, her eyes still on Mared.

Again Mared and Griffin exchanged a look, and Mared could see her brother was wondering (just as she was) what in God's name Liam had gotten himself into *this* time.

"Might I at least speak with him? I've something that belongs to him," Miss Farnsworth added.

"He's no' here presently," Griffin said.

"Not here?" she asked, her eyes widening with surprise.

"Aye. He's away just now."

"Away?" she said, her voice going higher. "As in away for the day? Or could you possibly mean . . . could you *possibly* mean that he hasn't yet returned?"

"Maybe he's still in King's Lynn," the girl calmly suggested, still looking at Mared.

What was King's Lynn? Mared wondered, frowning at the girl. There was something very wrong about this, and Griffin obviously agreed, for he said, "Perhaps ye could leave yer card then, Miss Farnsworth. But he's no' here and he's no' expected for some time yet. We'll pass it along to him, we will."

"But . . . *but* . . ." Her voice trailed off, and honestly, she looked to be in a bit of shock for a moment before looking down and covering her eyes with one hand.

Griffin turned, looked at Mared over his shoulder, and made a bobbing motion with his head toward the woman in a silent question as to what she was doing.

Mared shrugged, just as confused.

But then she made a sound, and startled, Mared and Griffin jerked their gaze to her again. The woman was *crying*.

"I beg your pardon," she said, sniffing, and swiping at the tears with her dirty gloves. "I'm *appalled* that I should present myself on your doorstep in such horrible attire and . . . and *weep*. But it's just that . . . that we've come so *far*, and we've no place to *go*, and we just wanted to give it *back*—"

"Give *what* back?" Griffin asked.

"Oh, dear, I'm afraid I can't *tell you!*" she sobbed.

"It's all right, Mother," the lass said, and wrapped her arms around her mother's waist and began to cry, too.

* * *

There were four of them, standing at one end of the impossibly long dining table, underneath an elaborate and obviously old coat of arms of some sort, flanked by swords and sabers of varying design. All of them were silent for the most part, staring curiously at Ellen and Natalie, who were seated at the opposite end of the table, and whispering in Liam's language to one another from time to time. At least, Ellen thought, wryly, she didn't have to worry about Natalie, for she seemed right at home. She was sitting in a huge oak chair, looking around the room with great interest, her feet swinging beneath the table.

Finally, the elder Lockhart cleared his voice, looked at his wife (this Ellen knew because they had at last introduced themselves to her after a long and whispered consultation). "Ah . . . Miss Farnsworth, is it?"

She nodded.

"Aye. Well, then. We find ourselves in a wee spot of . . . of . . ."

"It's rather unusual," Lady Lockhart interjected helpfully.

"Aye," the old man agreed. "Ah . . . ye see, Miss Farnsworth, our son, he went to London on . . . on, er . . ."

"A family matter," Mared offered.

"Aye. That," the old man agreed again. "And . . . he did no' mention in his letters that we were to expect a caller—"

"Oh, no, of course not, my lord, for he didn't know I would be calling, you see," Ellen tried. But her several attempts at explanation—without just admitting, out and out, that she had stolen the blasted beastie—seemed almost ludicrous. To suggest that she knew their son well enough to travel all the way to Scotland to call on him was absurd, particularly when he had never mentioned her. Particularly when she could not admit *why* she had come, other than to say she had something that belonged to their son. If the shoe were on the other foot, it would seem to her to be rather ominous, too. *Rather brilliant plan, Ellen. Not quite the conniver you determined yourself to be, are you?*

"Aye, aye," the man said carefully. "But ye see, can ye now, what a perplexing situation we find ourselves in?"

"Yes, but I—"

"If ye might just tell us what it is ye have for him, so that we might clear it all up," Griffin kindly suggested.

Beside her, Natalie sneezed.

"Bless ye," they all murmured in unison.

Ellen absently patted Natalie's hand. "I beg you to trust me, sir. I know you've no reason to do so, and this is all quite unusual, but I assure you, your son is on his way home, and what I have of his I could not possibly trust with another person. It's something I must give him personally, and—"

Natalie sneezed again; Ellen stopped her plea and looked down at her daughter. Natalie smiled up at her mother with bright eyes, and Ellen instantly put her hand on Natalie's forehead, felt the warmth of fever there. "Dear God," she said, and looked at the four Lockharts. "I shan't ask any longer, I shall beg and plead for you to see your way to giving us shelter, if just for the night. I thought Captain Lockhart was *here*, for at least that is what he said, and as it happens, I have not a farthing to my name, and unfortunately, I fear my daughter is ill."

The four of them exchanged suspicious looks with one another.

That was it, then.

Too weary to beg, it seemed as if her extraordinary journey had finally caught up to her, and Ellen felt all the will bleed right out of her. She hardly cared what they did to her any longer; she just wanted it all to end. She just wanted a bed for herself and Natalie, just the chance to sleep, and suddenly, without thought or care, she folded her arms on the table, put her forehead on them, and began to sob like a newborn baby, unable to stop.

And it was in that haze of frightful, gut-wrenching sobs that she felt the hand on her forehead and heard the kind Lady Lockhart say, "Carson, she's burning with fever."

"What a sweet lass ye are," Ellen heard through the haze of sleep. "But I'm no' a princess. Would that I were, for I'd make some changes around here, I would, beginning with the immediate removal of a certain Douglas from the— Oh, look now, she's awake!"

Ellen blinked at the sight of Mared, seated at the end of a massive four-poster bed with Natalie, who was wearing a clean and pressed frock. How had *that* happened? She didn't remember much of anything after Lady Lockhart had made her sit up and wiped her tears with the hem of her shawl, and had only a vague recollection of being forced upstairs, Grif (they called him) on one side, Lady Lockhart on the other, insisting that she lie down for a time. She came up on her elbows and felt a dizziness in her head. "How long have I been asleep?"

"*Mo creach!* Ye sleep like the dead, ye do. All through the night and here it is, twelve o'clock," Mared said, coming to her feet. She walked to the side of the bed and casually peered down at Ellen, her arms folded across her middle. "Still a wee peaked, I'd wager. What do ye make of it, Nattie?"

Nattie. That's what Liam had called her.

"Aye, she looks rather pale, doesn't she?" Natalie answered.

"I thought so from the start," Mared said, nodding. A long tail of braided black hair fell over her shoulder. "How are ye feeling, then, Miss Farnsworth?"

"Exhausted," Ellen answered truthfully, and looked at Natalie. "But what of you Natalie? Do you still have a fever?"

Natalie shook her head. "Mared gave me some tea this morning and said I was quite all right."

"Miss Lockhart, darling," Ellen muttered weakly.

Mared laughed. "We donna stand on much ceremony here, Miss Farnsworth. Ye might as well call me by me Christian name, for it looks as if ye'll stay a while yet."

"It does?" she asked, lifting a hand to her forehead.

"Aye. The post came early this morning, and there was a letter from Liam. I wasna privy to what it said, exactly, but Mother said that ye'd stay until he came home, for she thought he wanted it back, whatever it is ye have."

"*Ooh,*" Ellen said, wincing a little.

That caused Mared to laugh—she smiled broadly, her smile as warm and inviting as Liam's. "And she said ye're to stay abed until ye're better. In the meantime, if ye donna mind it, I'll take Nattie for a tour of a *real* castle."

Ellen smiled at Natalie, but her daughter hardly noticed, for she was looking up at Mared with great awe. "That would be lovely, Mared. You've no idea how lovely. And please, call me Ellie."

"The lass will be quite all right while ye rest, Ellie," she said, and held out her hand for Natalie. Ellen sank back against the goose-down pillows, glad for once someone had ordered her to bed. "Thank you," she murmured, and as her eyelids were sliding shut, she saw Mared and Natalie walk away, hand in hand, and she thought how lovely it was in Laria.

* * *

Liam left for Edinburgh with his pockets near to empty and his heart overwhelmingly heavy, detouring from his course only once, to speak with the Peasedowns.

No, they had not heard from Ellie. But a letter had arrived from her father, telling her to come home at once or risk complete estrangement. Lady Peasedown was distraught, sobbing quite vociferously, now blaming herself for Ellie's running away. There was nothing Liam could say to appease her, so he promised, should he cross Miss Farnsworth's path again, that he himself would write and let them know of her welfare. Lady Peasedown promised to do the same, and very carefully took down the direction of Talla Dileas.

Liam never expected to hear from the Peasedowns again, actually. He never expected to see Ellie again, a notion that left him feeling empty and old. Fate was cruel, he thought, to give a man like him a taste of a woman like that and then take her away. He had all but forgotten what she had done, and thought he'd trade a thousand beasties just to look at her lovely face one more time.

But he would not, and there was not a happier man in all of England when, in Kingston-upon-Hull, Liam talked his way onto a packet ship bound for Edinburgh. Fortunately, the week it took to reach Edinburgh went by quickly, in spite of the one incident with a sailor who attempted to take the dirty, crumpled kerchief that had belonged to Ellie. It was the only thing that Liam had to keep close to his heart, and the attempted theft proved to be all he could endure for one long journey to England. It was as if all his frustrations (and *Diah*, there were a frightening lot of frustrations of late) came bubbling up all at once.

The poor, unsuspecting shipmate never knew what hit him. Liam sent him flying across the deck, and before anyone could react to what he'd done, he chased after the man, took the kerchief from his grimy hand, and managed to slide it into his pocket before the sailor's chums fell on him. Liam emerged from the brawl with a sizable black eye, a broken finger, and what felt like a broken knee. But he had the kerchief.

When they at last docked in Edinburgh, Liam was the first off the ship, and immediately set out for Loch Chon, where he expected nothing when he arrived but to hear his father's roar over his bungling of the beastie. He just hoped he hadn't missed the deployment of his new regiment, for the farther away from this mess he could take himself, the better he'd be.

Ellen improved rapidly, thanks foremost to a concoction of medicinal herbs Lady Lockhart gave her twice daily. In a few days, she was walking the grounds of Talla Dileas with Mared, awed by the wild beauty of it, even beneath a light dusting of snow.

Mared was quite colorful, she thought, seemingly without inhibition and free to do as she pleased. Ellen admired Mared for it. The only thing that seemed to annoy Mared was their neighbor, "the Douglas," as she called him, and she spoke frequently of how vexing the man was. He sounded like a dreadful ogre, really. But beyond that, Mared was enormously entertaining and seemed happy for the company. How wonderful, Ellen thought, that women enjoyed such social freedom here. How stifled she had felt in London. And the more she was in and around Talla Dileas, the more she could see why Liam was so attached to it. This *was* Laria.

Certainly she had never seen Natalie happier. The girl's fever had come and gone quickly, and she blossomed in a few short days, always laughing, always eager to help one of the Lockharts. Mared took quite a liking to her, and so did Griffin, although Ellen sensed his patience for young children was more closely aligned with Liam's. The Laird and Lady Lockhart were very kind, but were quite curious about what had gone on in England. Lady Lockhart in particular asked several times if she had met the English Lockharts, or if Liam had mentioned them. Each time the subject came up, Ellen was as vague as she could be, but felt herself color with shame all the same, feeling more and more horridly guilty for what she'd done, particularly seeing with her own eyes what the beastie might have done for them.

Life was idyllic, but she couldn't help noticing the signs of deterioration. Even in the spacious, ornate room they had put her in, where the furnishings were of the finest quality, she noticed cracks in the walls and shutters that weren't properly mended. A brazier was used in that room as opposed to the fireplace, because, the laird explained, they hadn't had the chimney properly cleaned in some time.

The food was rather nondescript, and she noticed that potatoes were often the focal point of the evening meal. More than once, Ellen thought to give them the five hundred pounds and confess what she had done. But inevitably, she would wonder how she and Natalie would fare when they tossed her out on her ear for it. It was best to wait for Liam, she convinced herself. At least if he were to toss her out, he'd think twice before doing so to Natalie.

And as to that, where *was* Liam? Ellen often lay in bed at night wondering if he was still looking for her or had decided to go on to his regiment. The Lockharts openly looked for a letter from him every day, and Mared often walked across the hills to the neighboring estate to see if the post had come. If he didn't come soon, she'd have to think of something, for she couldn't impose on the Lockharts more than she already had.

And in fact, she thought Griffin was beginning to wonder if she was telling them the truth—she even heard him say to his father one day that they really had no proof that she'd ever met Liam.

Which was why, then, that Ellen began to sing for her supper, so to speak, by regaling them with tales of Liam in London each night at supper. Of Liam in Hyde Park. Liam dancing. Of how he and Natalie met (Natalie helping with that one). Liam and the mouse, Liam and the partridges. Liam's unusual method of laundering his clothes (Griffin seemed particularly perturbed by that story). The tales of Liam were all true, and they made the Lockharts laugh. Above all else, those tales allowed Ellen and Natalie to remain in good graces at Talla Dileas.

She just hoped that she would not use them all up before he returned.

Where was he?

He was, as it happened, in Aberfoyle.

He'd had a bit of luck in getting from Edinburgh to Stirling, but from there he had walked, camping for a few hours when he thought he couldn't take another step, living off berries (far too many for good digestion), a fish or a grouse here and there, and at long last, he had reached Aberfoyle. That was quite a milestone, he thought, having been quite dejected by the latest turn of events. In reaching Aberfoyle he determined that he might still make a decent soldier. With considerable remediation, of course.

It was late; most of the shopkeepers had closed their doors, but he saw, much to his great relief, Payton Douglas's wagon just outside the confectioner's. When Payton emerged, Liam was so glad to see him that he almost kissed the man.

Payton reared back as Liam threw his arms around

his shoulders, laughing hysterically. He put out his hand, both to protect himself from Liam's strange elation and to welcome him home. "Lockhart! And I thought ye'd no' come back, I did," he said grinning. "Did they kick ye out of England, then? What happened to ye, lad?" Payton asked, wrinkling his nose at the foul odor as he looked at the yellow and green skin around Liam's eye, the scratches on his hands and face, and the buckskins that could, were he to remove them, stand alone.

Liam laughed. "*Ach*, the English! Barmy, the lot of them! I'll be happy to tell ye all over a pint one day, but at the moment I'm rather anxious to be home, I am, if ye'd do me that favor."

"Aye, certainly," Payton said, clapping him on the back. "At the very least, yer mother would want to see that ugly face, I'd wager. Climb on, then."

They shared a sweetmeat, which, for some strange reason, reminded Payton to complain mightily of Mared. "She's no' right, that one," he said, munching the last confection. "A more willful or stubborn lass ye'll never know, I'd swear by it. She penned me sheep!" he complained loudly, then frowned at Liam's burst of laughter. While *he* might have undergone an enormous change while he was gone, it was comforting to know that at least in Scotland, some things remained the same. He was, he realized, rather relieved to know it.

"And Grif? He's no' run off to Edinburra to seek his fortune, has he, then?"

Payton shrugged as he drew the team to a halt in front of the long path up to the Lockhart estate. "In truth, I've no' seen yer family for more than a week now." He grinned sheepishly. "I had a wee encounter with one of yer bulls, and yer sister, well . . . she's bloody angry just now, so I thought it best to stay away for a time."

Liam grinned, grabbed his knapsack, and leapt to the ground. "Ye might as well admit it, Douglas. Ye love her, ye do," he said, and laughed at Payton's animated claims to the contrary. They parted with a wave and a promise to have that ale soon; Payton drove on and Liam turned, looked up the winding path, and drew a long breath.

He couldn't avoid it any longer. He just prayed, when he told them how he'd lost the damn beastie, that they'd show him a wee bit of mercy, for he was so grateful to be at home at last.

As he walked up the steep, curving path, the sun sank behind Din Footh, and the air grew still. It smelled of pine, fresh and clean, not full of soot and animals like London had smelled. It brought a lump to Liam's throat, for he couldn't imagine home being anywhere but here, and he realized they'd have to fight to keep it. When he turned the bend and saw the house, both repugnant and stately all at once, he wondered what would become of the Lockharts without Talla Dileas as the foundation beneath them, without centuries from which to build their lives.

He paused and looked at the structure he called home. It was dark on one side—to save costs, he gathered—but there was light in the dining room. They'd be gathering just about now, he thought, and walked on, through the huge stone gates. But instead of going inside, he walked around the edge of the lawn until he reached the dining room, and stood back, looking up so he might see them all.

Ah, there they were, coming in now. Mother and Father—he was glad to see them looking well. Grif, who'd kill him for what he'd done to his clothing. Mared, sweet Mared, and—

Liam's heart stopped; for a moment he thought he was seeing a ghost. How could Nattie be there? *Nattie!*

No, no, it was impossible. His fatigue—he closed his eyes, shook his head, and opened them again, but there she was, a little blond head following Mared. *How? How could—*

Diah! There she was—the single, burning ache in his heart, that vision that kept him awake at night and dogged his every waking step. The heavy knapsack slid from his shoulder and fell to the ground beside him. Unable to comprehend, to believe, he stood gaping, pounding his thigh with his fist to make certain he wasn't dreaming, that he hadn't at last lost his mind. But it *was* her, his angel, the one woman he had ever, *would* ever love, and Liam, in a spasm of relief or hope or fear, fell to his knees and looked heavenward. After all he'd been through, all he'd learned, after the two accursed tears he had shed one night aboard ship, he was to be given this dream?

"*Thank ye,*" he whispered hoarsely. "Thank ye. I'll no' let ye down." And he thought, looking up at the half-moon over Talla Dileas, that he'd cherish this moment and this woman forever, that God had given him this second chance at love, something he had never realized how deeply he needed . . . until the flash of a fallen star streaked the sky, startling him, jolting him back to the reality of an angel flying low.

Thirty-one

❧

The wine they had at supper had left Ellen feeling drowsy, for which she was grateful, for she had not, in the ten days or so she had been at Talla Dileas, recovered fully from her fever. The heat had left her, but the burn in her heart was ever present, burning the hole in her heart from missing him so.

She saw Natalie to bed, deflecting the questions that were coming with more regularity: *Might we stay here forever? Mared is not a real princess, but she'll be a lady someday, which is really almost the same. Do you think the laird likes us very much? I think he does, and I think he should like us to stay forever. Will Captain Lockhart ever come home? Perhaps Griffin will go and look for him, because he doesn't seem very happy here. He said it was far away from the rest of the world. If Griffin goes to look for him, may we stay here in his place?*

When she was at last certain that Natalie had fallen into a deep slumber, Ellen walked through the door adjoining their rooms and quietly closed it behind her, so she could pace in peace. That had become her ritual, pacing in front of the cold hearth, her hands clasped behind her back, *thinking, thinking*, trying to come up with a new strategy, a reasonable course for her and Natalie. The only problem was, she couldn't seem to come up with a bloody thing. It was almost as if reaching Talla Dileas had taken everything from her. But she had to think what to do if Liam did not come home straightaway—she'd been here more than a week since his last letter had come, and still there was nothing. She could not continue to exist off the kindness of the Lockharts any longer, and in truth, she and Natalie had already overstayed their welcome—it was clear the Lockharts were struggling, too.

That was all well and good, but she had managed to get herself here without any hope of leaving. Without any income whatsoever, she had no hope of getting past Aberfoyle. *Aberfoyle!* If she could only think of a way to return to Glasgow without incurring the outrageous cost of ten pounds for the privilege. But if she *reached* Glasgow, perhaps she could find employment. . . .

"Of course you won't find employment, you ninny!" she angrily chided herself. Who would want you? And for what? Do you think you might pass yourself off as a governess? You have no references! A housekeeper, then? As if you know the first thing about managing a large household!

Which left her, of course, with absolutely nowhere to go. Her only option—and it was scarcely an option—was to write her father. Or Eva. Or Judith.

Oh *God.*

Ellen paused in her pacing to laugh derisively at the ceiling. Oh, yes, her father would send for her, wouldn't he? Never, not in her lifetime, not in a million years. And Eva? Eva might send her a few pounds, but she'd never defy their father by taking her in. Then there was Judith, dear Judith, the only true friend she had ever had. But needless to say, she had irreparably harmed *that* friendship. She was certain neither Judith nor Richard would be terribly eager to aid her now.

Her pacing ended as it always did—with no solutions, no answers, nothing but more anxiety to strangle her sleep. And as she lay in the massive four-poster bed, those troubling thoughts chased about her mind. The last thing she remembered before drifting off completely was Liam. It was *always* Liam.

She dreamed of him again, the same dream, Liam running from her, putting distance between them as she called out to him and begged him to come back. But he disappeared into blackness, and Ellen was once again in her father's house, in her old room, in an old, lumpy bed. Then the bed changed into the large four-poster bed at Talla Dileas, and Liam was standing at the foot of it, his arms folded across his chest, calmly observing her at her toilette. In her dream Ellen was brushing her hair, one long stroke after the other, slowly, languidly, as Liam watched her. Then he moved toward her, silently and cautiously, reaching for the brush. With a smile, Ellen handed it to him, and he began to brush her hair, but then the brush disappeared, and his hand was on her neck, his fingers resting lightly on her pulse. He leaned down, touched her ear with his lip, and then, *and then . . .*

His hand drifted across her mouth, and he pressed down, silencing her. *Silencing her.*

A shudder of fear awakened her; Ellen screamed against his hand, but Liam smiled down at her as he grabbed her flailing arm, twisted it behind her back, and forced her onto her side by pressing his weight against her, holding her down so that she could not move. His mouth drifted across her ear, breathing into her, its warmth frightening. "Ah, Ellie," he whispered. "What a wicked lass ye are."

Shivering with fright, Ellen could only nod her complete agreement.

"*Ach,*" he breathed, the tip of his tongue dipping furtively into her ear. "Then ye'll *admit* ye are a wicked one."

Ellen nodded again; she could smell him, could

smell the road he'd traveled, the hell he had gone through to come here.

"I donna know what to do with ye, Ellie, on me word. Shall I kill ye? Bind ye and punish ye, slowly and surely? Or leave ye unbound and begging for me mercy?"

Kill me. Punish me. Let me beg for mercy. All of it. Ellen closed her eyes and felt a tear slide from the corner onto the goose-down pillow. She was frightened of him, frightened of his anger. Yet at the same time she relished the familiar feel of his callused hand against her lips, her face.

The sound of his quiet laugh was ominous, though, and sent another raw shiver down her spine. His mouth grazed her temple, her ear, her jaw. "No, I donna think I would kill ye, no' yet," he murmured as he kissed her cheek, then the corner of her eye. "What will it be, then? Unbound?" He kissed her neck, then abruptly shoved her onto her back, straddling her. She could barely see him by the glow of the brazier, but she could see his eyes, dark green and ablaze with fury, roaming her face. His hair was wildly mussed, his shirt stained dark from perspiration. He looked as if he had just crawled out of the woods. And he was grinning, a wild, mad grin that sharpened her fear. "Unbound? No. I rather like this, I do."

Ellie tried to speak, tried to tell him that he could do whatever he pleased to her and it still would not be enough, but he just chuckled and shook his head. *"Hush . . .* be still and let me have a look at ye, then. Ah, what a beauty ye are, Ellie. 'Tis the only thing that remains constant about ye, eh?" Her sight was blurring with the tears of her fright and regret; Liam leaned over, whispered in her ear, "When I remove me hand from yer mouth, ye willna cry out, and ye willna speak, will ye now?"

She shook her head.

"Do ye think I might trust yer promise at least on this?" he asked, smiling menacingly at his own jest. Slowly, Ellen nodded. His hand slid from her mouth, and still straddling her, he leaned back, his powerful thighs pinning her still beneath him. Ellen opened her mouth to speak, to explain, but he quickly shook his head, and frowning darkly, pressed a finger to her lips. "*No!*"

She obeyed him.

He smiled that dark, unnatural smile again, and reached for her hand. He held it in his own, caressed her fingers, threaded them through his, then lowered her hand and pushed it between his thigh and her body so that she could not move it. Then he took the other arm, caressed her wrist, kissed the soft inside of her elbow, and slowly raised her arm up and away from her body. With the other hand, he reached behind his back, took something from his belt, and before she realized what was happening, he began to tie her to the bedpost.

"*Liam—*"

"*Ach,* but I told ye no' to speak, did I no'?" he asked patiently, as if chastising a child. From his pocket, he withdrew what looked like a kerchief. "Lift yer head, then," he said amicably as he wound a dirty kerchief into a long strip. When Ellen did not move to do so, he lifted it for her, forced the kerchief between her teeth, and tied it loosely at the back of her head, enough to keep her from speaking. Carefully, he lowered her head, reached around his back, and took another strip of cloth or rope, and taking the hand he held captive, raised it, too.

Ellen attempted to pull free, but he was much stronger, and moreover, she had lost the will to fight. Let him do to her what he would—she deserved it and more. He bound her other arm by the wrist to the opposite bedpost so that she was stretched across the bed, unable to move, gagged so that she could not speak.

Liam smiled as his gaze wandered over her body. "Have ye any idea how long I've wanted ye like this? Trussed up so that ye couldna move and at me complete mercy?"

Oh, yes, she knew. She knew almost to the moment, and locking her gaze with his, nodded solemnly.

Liam cocked a brow. "Do ye, indeed? Then ye must also know all the things I thought to do to ye, eh?" he asked, his brows dipping into a vee.

Do anything. Hurt me. Make the guilt go away.

"Aye," he said, as if responding to her thoughts, "I've dreamed of it all. Every wee thing a man could do to a woman, I've thought of it. But those dreams, they always come back to the same place."

Ellen cringed, not wanting to hear that place voiced aloud. But Liam laughed low, and with his finger, traced a line from the top of her forehead, between her eyes, and down to the tip of her nose. "I want ye to know the frustration, Ellie. I want to push ye headlong into that state of being unfulfilled, to know what it means to have life breathed into ye, golden and fresh, then have it knocked clean from yer lungs with one blow."

Ah, God, dear God, how he must despise her! She loved him—loved him so completely that she finally understood what endless love meant. It did not mean pining, did not mean aching, it meant no beginning and no end, and in her heart, there was only Liam. *Liam.* The man she had betrayed. Another tear slipped from the corner of her eye, and she expected the worst for her crime, tried to prepare herself for it, but Liam just sat there, straddled across her, looking down at her,

half in awe, half in triumph. And then he hooked one finger in the tie of her sleeping gown and pulled it free.

She felt the garment slide open; Liam casually pushed the rest of it aside, baring her shoulder. He touched it. Gingerly, reverently. Then a caress, his rough hand moving like silk over her skin, the inconsonant sensation of it bringing a rush of tortured memories to her. She whimpered with regret and longing against the gag, but Liam ignored her, just gathered the hem of her sleeping gown and pushed it up, exposing her. There was a rush of cold air on her skin; her nipples tautening. Liam came off her then and stood by the side of the bed, gazing down at her naked torso. The look in his eye was mad, she thought, but he suddenly turned away, walked across the darkened room, rummaged about her dressing table. After a moment, he turned, holding one of her stockings. "I want ye to feel what ye did to me, every moment of it," he said, and leaned over her, draping the stocking across her eye.

He meant to blindfold her. *Blind her,* so that she could not see the revenge he exacted. Instinctively, she strained against the bindings, heard Liam's low laugh. Blindfolded, bound, and gagged, she lay naked before him, her gown bunched at her throat, and could feel her chest rising and falling with every tortured breath. His hand on her abdomen made her start; his low chuckle next to her ear was another surprise. And then his lips, *so soft,* on her shoulder, trailing down her side, his hand skimming her breast, kneading, rolling the stiffened tip between his fingers.

A warmth filled her, spreading between her legs, flooding her body. Ellen moved in response to his touch, but then suddenly, he was gone again. She froze, waiting—but there was no sound, no movement, and her first thought was that he had left her, left her bound to be discovered just as she had done to him. The very

thought of being discovered like this was horrifying;
she was suddenly straining against the bindings, turning her head, trying to see beneath the blindfold.

And then, just as suddenly, his hand was on her
ankle, softly caressing, lightly trailing a path up to her
thigh, brushing carelessly against the apex. Ellie shifted
unthinkingly, closer or further away from him, she
couldn't tell. His mouth was suddenly on her stomach,
and she unthinkingly arched into it, heard the low
moan as his lips left her skin again. "No, ye'll no' have
it as easy as this, Ellie," he said, and without warning,
he yanked the gag free of her mouth. Before she could
take a breath, his lips were on hers, his tongue sweeping boldly into the recesses of her mouth, his teeth nipping at her lips, suckling them, kissing her with the
passion she had felt at Peasedown Park, the crushing,
bruising passion that was banging about her chest now.
She wanted her arms free, wanted to hold him, and
turned her head, breaking the kiss.

"*Untie me,*" she whispered, but Liam just laughed
against her throat, and was suddenly gone again. She
waited for what seemed like an eternity before she felt
his hand on her knee, pushing her leg aside, then the
other, spreading her open. Ellen's body was on fire,
every inch of her screaming with desire. She had
expected to be punished, had expected to feel his
wrath, but this . . . *this* was *exquisite* torture.

Something brushed against her sex, something light,
something soft. *There it is again.* A feather. He was teas-
ing her with a feather! Ellen strained with her body to
find him, to touch him, but he had stepped away again.
Panting, she waited.

"Ye want me, lass," she heard him say from somewhere on her right, near the windows. "I can see that
ye do." *His hand, between her legs.* "How does it feel,
then?" he asked, this time from somewhere on the left

of her, near the door. "How does it feel to want some-one so completely, so thoroughly, and have that desire, that *love* so cruelly torn from yer breast?"

"*Don't leave,*" she whispered hoarsely, panicking now.

"Ah, *leannan,* ye'll no' leave me sight again."

She felt her legs being pushed aside, his fingers on her thigh, and then—*oh!*—his mouth on her sex, lap-ping her up, devouring her, taking every part of her into his mouth, and what he could not have in him, fill-ing with his tongue. Ellen writhed beneath him—this dark assault on her senses was overwhelming, and she felt it building between her thighs as he buried his face there. Her body began to respond with need, bucking and arching up to meet him . . .

And then he was gone.

She released her frustration with a cry in the dark; a hand immediately clapped over her mouth. "*Be still* . . . be still," he whispered, soothing her, caressing her neck and her cheek, leaving the scent of her own body behind.

"Liam, I love you," she moaned.

"Ye love me hands, me mouth," he whispered, seem-ingly from somewhere above her, and shoved his hand roughly between her legs again.

Ellen closed her thighs, holding him there. "You won't believe me, I know, and you have every right. But I was wrong, Liam, I was so *wrong* to have betrayed you! I came here to tell you so, I came here to beg you to forgive me!"

"Beg, then," he said coldly, jerking his hand from her thighs and moving again. "What a fool I've been, Ellie, for I thought ye couldna possibly love me and betray me as ye did."

"No, no," she moaned, shaking her head dumbly. His hand fell to her breast; she caught her breath and held it for a moment as he caressed it. "No," she sighed again. "I love you. I loved you from the beginning. I just . . . I thought it would never last, and I thought I had no choice, that Natalie would die in that place if I didn't do something—"

His hand drifting down her belly, to her sex.

She swallowed a long sigh, forced herself to keep talking. "I thought I could do it, I thought I could just walk away and know in my heart that I had done the right thing for my daughter. But then . . ." She gasped as his fingers slipped between her wet folds. "But then, you came to . . . to Peasedown, and I—"

"Ye what?" he breathed, massaging her now. "Ye *what?* Say it or I'll stop, I swear I will."

"I . . ." She tried to catch her breath, tried not to sink into the furious blaze of desire he had rekindled. "*I wanted you,*" she breathed. "I wanted you so, wanted you just like this, your hands on me, your mouth on me. I wanted to show you that I thought only of you, dreamed only of you, that I loved only you. *I wanted you, Liam*—"

She caught a sob in her throat as he increased the pressure, pressing her home, to a naked release. And as she felt herself falling away, falling hard, he said, "Did ye want me like *this*, Ellie?"

"*Yes!*"

"And like this?" he said roughly, mounting her now, his body stretching the length of hers, sliding into her wet sheath until she shuddered with the emotion of it.

"I never wanted anything else," she whimpered into his ear as he began to stroke, long and smooth, gathering her tightly in his arms as he moved. "I wanted to crawl inside of you and stay there, I wanted to hold you in my arms and kiss you, I wanted to *feel* you, hard and hot inside me."

Liam moaned; his stroke lengthened, and he held

her more tightly, his arms surrounding her. Ellen lifted her hips, let her head fall back with the glorious feel of him. His mouth fell to her throat, and she could scarcely talk, scarcely breathe, so divine was their joining. "I love you," she gasped, trying to catch her breath. "I shall *always* love you. With my last breath I shall love you," she moaned, feeling the pressure building again, building fast, in tune with Liam's frantic strokes. "So take *all* of me," she said, gulping, "take every inch of me, take me deep, take me hard and fast, I pray you, for I cannot endure a life without you, Liam, I cannot."

His cry of release, in time with hers, was muffled against her throat; he clung to her, his breathing ragged, until his body spasmed once more. And then they lay, panting, their bodies wet with the exertion of his revenge.

Liam had no idea how long they lay there, but when he at last lifted his head, he saw Ellie, her head lolling back, blindfolded. Her body completely still, partially beneath him, the only evidence of life her heart pounding wildly against her chest. Slowly, he pushed himself up. He untied one of her arms, which fell limply to her side. He untied the other, watched it fall, too. Still she did not move, just lay there, as if all the life had bled out of her with that last, terrific climax. With his finger, he pushed her head to the side, removed the loosely tied blindfold, then slipped two fingers beneath her chin and turned her face so that he could look at her.

There were tears glistening in her eyes, tears that burned him; he thought that he had hurt her somehow, and that had not been his intent. But then Ellie smiled up at him, that charming, glorious smile of hers that he had kept in his heart, and she whispered, exhausted, "I *do* love you, Liam."

Mo creach, he loved her, too. More than he could have

even realized. But gazing on her now, he still didn't know if he could trust her, or how he might keep her. The only thing he knew with certainty was that he couldn't be without her. Ever. Not for a moment, a single moment. It left him feeling as if there were several pieces of himself that didn't quite fit together.

That raw need, so strange, so unusual, flustered him, and he stood, walked around the bed to where he had tossed his clothing, and picked up the soiled buckskins. "I donna know if that is good enough, Ellie," he said gruffly. "In London I would have sworn on me mother's heart that ye loved me."

"I *did!*" she insisted, pushing up on her elbows, watching him. "I love you, Liam. I don't know what else to say except that I am *sorry,* so terribly sorry, and I beg your forgiveness for what I did."

"Aye, but should I give it to ye?" he asked the wall, pausing to rub his chin. "If ye love me, ye'll return the goddamn beastie—"

"Yes, well. As to that . . ." she said, looking away.

Liam stopped what he was doing and stared down at her. "As to *that?*"

"All right, then, will you please listen to me?" she asked frantically, and turned abruptly, clasping her hands together to plead with him. "I was so torn! I didn't know *what* to do, but then I came to my senses at last, and I realized that the statue did not belong to *me,* it belonged to *you,* and there is nothing I can say or think to justify taking it, *nothing!* And now, if you toss me out on my ear, or take me to the authorities, then so be it, I would not blame you, not at all!"

"Well, then? Where is it?" he asked sternly, his hands on his naked waist.

She winced. "I thought all these things, truly I did, and I felt them rather strongly . . . but I suppose I thought them a moment too late—"

"Too *late?*"

Cringing, Ellie drew her knees to her chest, hugged them tightly to her. "I had already sold it."

"Ye did *what?*" he asked weakly, disbelieving.

"But that is why I am here!" she said, brightening. "I brought the money to you. Every last farthing—well, except for your kilt—"

"Aye, ye butchered me kilt!"

"I sold it, too," she said, wincing again.

Would the cruel indignities ever cease? Liam groaned, covered his face with his hands.

"And used the proceeds to come here, to give you the money I got for the beastie. Don't you see? I am trying to make amends."

The loss of his kilt momentarily forgotten, Liam peeked up at her. All right, he had to figure out a way to see this as *good* news, didn't he? And in truth, he supposed that was exactly what his family had intended to do. Ellie had simply done that for them! *Ah-ha!* He grinned at her proudly. "Ellie, what a clever lass ye are! Did ye give it to me father, then?"

"Um . . . no."

"No?"

She shook her head and bit her lower lip.

Liam felt his heart sink a little. "Why?"

"Well, I wanted to give it to *you*, of course, so that you would know how sorry I am," she said, clasping her hands to her naked breast, and to which Liam nodded impatiently. "But . . . but it didn't bring quite what you had hoped, I think."

Mary Queen of Scots, was *that* all? He smiled with relief. "Lass, a few hundred pounds one way or the other—"

"Five hundred?"

"Aye, five hundred pounds less than what we hoped, 'tis still a pretty sum."

"No—I mean, five hundred pounds for the beastie. In total, that is."

Liam blinked. Was certain he had misunderstood. "Ye mean five hundred *less*," he tried to help her.

Ellie dipped her gaze away from him. "I was desperate, Liam." Liam gasped with shock and was instantly beside her, holding her hand, beseeching her. "No, no, Ellie, say ye are jesting with me! Do no' say ye sold the beastie for a mere five hundred pounds!"

"All right, I won't say it," she said weakly, and he knew a glimmer of hope in that moment . . . until she added softly, "But it's true."

"*Ah, Christ,*" he said, and slapping his forehead, he turned and slid to the floor, leaning against the bed on his haunches, covering his face with his hands. "Have ye any idea what ye've done, Ellie?" he cried angrily.

"Yes, I know," she said quickly. "Believe me, I know very well what I've done—"

"No, ye canna possibly understand. Ye've given away our one chance to keep Talla Dileas, the one bloody thing we had in hand!" he exclaimed, shaking his empty palm to the ceiling.

"I know," she said softly, and slid off the bed to sit next to him on the floor. "I know better than perhaps you how much this place means to all the Lockharts. I know how your mother walks the halls every morning, looking for things she might sell to put food on the table," she whispered, drawing her knees up to her chin. "I know how your father goes to Aberfoyle every other day and says he's gone calling on friends, when really, I suspect, he's gone to look for work. I know how Griffin wants to be free, to go and live the life of a gentleman, but how his conscience won't let him leave the family he loves so dearly. And I know how Mared walks to the top of Din Footh and looks over this valley and dreams of the day when her children will run on the grassy lawns and fish in the loch like you and she and Griffin did when you were children."

Liam looked at her then, saw the tears shimmering. "Ah, Ellie . . ."

"I know what I've done, Liam. I know very well and I beg God every day to forgive me."

He shook his head, felt the anger ebbing away.

"I'll do anything to make up for it," she said, putting a hand on his arm. "I'll do *anything*. I'll clean, I'll dig trenches, I'll learn how to hunt for food . . ."

Dig trenches, indeed. Liam sighed, looked heavenward, and smiled. He had known it, hadn't he, that he'd never know a moment's peace? He lowered his gaze, took her hand, and kissed her palm. "It must be true what they say about the beastie, eh? That it's English and will slip through the fingers of the Scot who tries to possess it."

"Liam . . . *please* forgive me," she asked earnestly.

" 'Twill no' be so easy, lass," he said solemnly, and lifted his gaze to hers. "Ye'll pay for it all right, with yer very life, *mo ghraid*, for now ye must consent to marry me. I canna let ye out of me sight, clearly. And I canna live a moment with ye, so there ye have it. I've gone and fallen in love with a conniving little thief, the bonniest woman in all of Britain."

"*Liam!*" she cried, throwing her arms around his neck. "Do you mean it? You'll not toss me out? You truly love me still, even after all I've done to you?"

"Aye," he said, his voice filled with bewilderment. "I donna understand it in the least, I swear it, and it will take the rest of yer days to repay the price of the beastie, I'd wager, though I'm bloody certain I'll be the one to pay for it many times over. But the truth is, I love ye, Ellie. Deeply and completely, I do. I'll forgive ye being English, and stealing from me—*twice*—and selling the beastie, if ye'll just say that ye and Natalie will be mine."

"Oh, *Liam*," she sighed into his neck, and lifted her head as her hands slid from his neck to his chest. "How I *love* you! You've made me so happy," she exclaimed, her eyes shimmering with happiness now. "I promise not to disappoint you, I *promise*," she said, and put her arms around him, kissing him madly, passionately. Then abruptly, she stopped, her angel eyes still gleaming. "Let's go wake Natalie and tell her that her prince has come at last!"

Aye, and the princess was rescued from her tower and lived happily ever after.

Liam helped her up; they dressed quickly, and hand in hand, walked across the room to the adjoining door, where Ellie paused and peeked up at him. "Ah . . . Liam, pardon, but I didn't actually hear you say that you forgave me the kilt—"

"Now *that*," he said, "a man canna forgive. It will cost ye dearly, it will," and he gathered her in his arms, crushing her to him as he kissed her with all the promise of a happy life ever after.

Except that she would *never* so much as *touch* his kilt again. *Never.*

Thirty-two

❧

$\mathcal{T}$he Lockharts were, of course, ecstatically happy that Liam was home, safe and sound. They gathered in the main salon, anxious to hear the entire tale. They listened with great interest, all on the edge of their seats. But as the tale went on, they fell back, one by one, in shocked disbelief.

They were not, needless to say, terribly enthusiastic about the prospect of Liam's nuptials with the woman who had sold their beastie for a pittance, and while not one of them would ever be impolite to Miss Farnsworth, they exchanged glances with one another, fidgeted with their clothing or whatever they could lay a hand on to avoid Liam's happy smile.

It wasn't that they didn't care for Ellie—they all thought her quite pleasing and agreeable, and it was a fact that the laird had grown quite attached to the child, since his bairns had all grown up and were no longer as awed by his presence as they once had been. And privately, Mared liked having Ellie about, as she had never had much in the way of female companionship. But the family was, to a person, quite perturbed that she had both stolen the beastie (Liam, mercifully had been rather sketchy in the details of that fiasco) and had sold the beastie for a mere five hundred pounds. *That* seemed an inexcusable offense no matter how desperate she thought her situation to be.

But nevertheless, their mother, Aila, pointed out she had never seen her eldest son look quite so happy or besotted, and in truth, Ellie looked rather happy herself, to which both parties readily agreed, smiling so foolishly at one another that both Mared and Griffin moaned.

"Aye, then we'll see them married straightaway, for I willna have the entire glen speaking ill of us," Carson had said gruffly, to which Liam had snorted, but Mared and his mother had squealed with delight at the mere mention of a wedding.

It was Griffin who remained rather perturbed, for he had seen the beastie as their one path out of what had become a huge financial mess. "We should no' have sent a soldier to do a gentleman's job," he complained loudly.

"And just what do ye mean by that?" Liam demanded.

Griffin rolled his eyes. "Just as I said, Liam. Ye never saw this as anything but another military mission! Ye went storming into London with the intent of taking prisoners and overthrowing the whole *ton*. A mission like *this* requires delicate handling, a little finesse, if ye will. *No'* running roughshod over the whole populace."

"Well, Griffin, if ye're so knowledgeable about it, then, why do ye stand here? Go to London and retrieve the bloody beastie yerself!" Liam had said irritably, and moved to turn away, but froze, a light dawning on his face. In fact, a light dawned on *everyone's* face, and they looked at one another questioningly.

A smile slowly spread across Griffin's lips.

"We've no money," Aila quickly warned him.

"I'll take a loan from the Douglas. He'll no' mind it if Mared asks him."

"*Aiee*, I'll do no such thing!" Mared cried, horrified.

"Aye, ye *will*," said Carson sternly, and held up his hand to her before her rant could begin.

"But how will ye find the beastie? At least when Liam went, we *knew* who had it. Now all we have is a name, naugh' more," said Aila, unconvinced.

"*Ach*, Mother, how difficult could it be to find one Lady Battenkirk?" Griffin asked.

"As if ye've ever been to London," Mared scoffed. "There could very well be a thousand Battenkirks if there's one! What, will ye hunt down each of them, then?"

"Ah . . . I beg your pardon, but if I might," Ellie politely interjected. Still in high dudgeon over her crime, all five Lockhart heads whipped around at once in her direction, frowning. Ellie took a small step back in surprise. "*Ahem*. Um . . . I just thought . . . I mean to say that I *did* live most of my life in London, and while I am not *personally* acquainted with Lady Battenkirk, I know her sort of lady, and I have several ideas as to where one might locate her."

"Mother knows where all the shops and markets and parks are, too," Natalie casually reported from her perch near the window.

They peered imperiously at Ellie, then curiously at Natalie. Ellie gulped at their intense gazes and said anxiously, "I, ah . . . I think I can help you find it."

It took a moment or two, but Griffin was the first to break into a warm smile. "Ah, Liam, ye couldna have chosen better had *I* chosen her for ye, which, of course, I was determined to do if we were to ever see ye married," he said, walking toward Ellie with open arms.

"Do ye see, then?" Mared demanded to no one in particular. "I was right about her, but ye will no' listen to me, no!" she insisted, following Griffin.

"I never doubted it, lass, no' for a moment," said Carson, standing and holding out his arm to Aila.

"Well, *I* certainly never doubted she was perfect for our family," Aila said, sniffing indignantly. "Did I no' say that the lass was quite a bright spot at Talla Dileas?"

And as they took their turns, welcoming Ellie and Nattie into the family, Liam watched, feeling positively barmy with all the love burgeoning in his heart for the people in this room. When his father asked Ellie had she *really* stolen the beastie from him, she instantly answered that it was true, but that since the beastie was English, it had slipped through her fingers.

Liam glanced heavenward with a smile and winked. "Aye, sir, ye have me word. I'll no' let her out of me sight. Or me heart."

The Lockharts eagerly turned their attention to crafting yet another plot to kidnap the beastie, quickly becoming engrossed in their arguing (as they were wont to do) about how exactly to go about it. When the question arose how one might find Lady Battenkirk in all of London, they turned expectantly to Ellie. Only Ellie wasn't there. Neither was Nattie. Or Liam, for that matter.

On a hunch, Mared walked to the windows and looked out; she laughed at what she saw and gestured for her mother to join her. Griffin, Aila, and Carson came to the window overlooking what had once been a bailey, but was now a sweeping lawn between crumbling stone walls. And in that old bailey walked Liam and Ellie, hand in hand with Nattie between them. They strolled leisurely toward the loch, their smiling gazes intent on one another, while Nattie alternately skipped and swung from their hands, her golden hair shining in the afternoon sun, her small cloak dragging the grass behind her.

The lass looked, Mared remarked, just like a princess.